I0665940

The Woman Who Wanted the Moon

A novel by
Joanna van der Gracht de Rosado

HAMACA
PRESS

ISBN: 978-0-9884337-7-9

Book design by Lee Steele
Portrait photography by Colleen Casey

Published by Hamaca Press
www.hamacapress.com

This is a work of fiction. Names, characters,
places, and incidents either are products of the
author's imagination or are used fictitiously. Any
resemblance to actual events or locales or persons,
living or dead, is entirely coincidental.

～

"As raindrops accumulate to breach a levee, growing government oppression erupted with flood force ten days before Mexico City hosted the 1968 Olympics, leaving hundreds dead, thousands disappeared, and millions shunted down tortuous paths. *The Woman Who Wanted the Moon* chronicles the altered lives of one extended family after the Tlatelolco massacre, personalizing this watershed event in Mexico's history with intimate detail and unforgettable prose."

—MARIANNE KEHOE
Poet and author of *Sidewalk Symphony*

～

"With *The Woman Who Wanted the Moon*, Joanna van der Gracht de Rosado has created a novel whose protagonist is at times an astonished eyewitness to Mexico's tumultuous twentieth century. By interweaving historical events—in particular the fierce repression of Mexican students in 1968 by the Mexican government—the author creates a poignant allegory of revolution and repression, life and death, love and freedom."

—MICHAEL K. SCHUESSLER
Author of *Peregrina: Love and Death in Mexico*

～

"*The Woman Who Wanted the Moon* embodies the colors and flavors, as well as the sociopolitical climate of Mexico during the 1960s through to the '80s. The author has crafted a fast-paced novel with unforgettable authentic characters, especially Amalia, whose life experiences parallel those of her country."

—SUSAN PAGE
Author of *Why Talking Is Not Enough*
and Director of the annual San Miguel Writers' Conference

Dedicated to Jorge,
"mi amor, mi cómplice en todo"

backstory

During the summer of 1968, university students took to the streets of Mexico City. Waving placards and banners, they called for change. They wanted their voices to be heard. Poised to host the XIX Summer Olympics, the autocratic government leadership found themselves under global scrutiny, and they set out to definitively end the public disobedience.

On October 2, ten days before the Games were to begin, the army received orders to open fire on a crowd of 10,000 gathered in the Plaza of Three Cultures at Tlatelolco, a residential development near the main square. The death and destruction shocked the nation. The press was censored—any unauthorized reporting about the massacre meant immediate incarceration.

And to the present day, an accurate accounting for the violence and an admission of responsibility has never been made public.

one

"Amalia! I know you can hear me. Now open the door!"

Three thousand nights ago, Alejandro Mendez locked me out of his life, and I mean completely out. I never heard from him again. So, after all this time, why was he in my hallway begging to be let inside? If he had to ask *me* for help, he probably didn't have a single friend left in this world.

Squinting through the peephole, I could see he looked frantic. His voice kept getting louder, and soon the neighbors would be poking their heads out of their apartments, expecting me to explain the appearance of this strange man.

The only way to stop the noise would be to give him what he wanted. I wiped the perspiration off my hands and then fumbled with the lock until the tumblers clunked into place. I took a step back as the door opened, and no way did he miss his chance. He pitched forward, landing squarely at my feet. I felt my eyes widen, and my throat went dry. Stretched out on the floor, he looked nothing like the man I used to know. I waited for him to get up, but obviously he didn't have enough strength to do anything but lie there.

He smelled of mud and burnt metal, and I sensed fear swirling all around. I dreaded getting closer, but I needed to take a better look—and that's when I saw the blood.

It snaked from a deep gash behind his left ear and ran onto his torn shirt. There were other wounds too and his dark hair was as matted as the fur on a stray dog's back.

"Alejandro, what happened to you?"

"Amalia, just shut the damned door!"

I didn't want to do that because once it closed, the portal to our past would swing wide open.

He needed help getting up. I bent down and hauled him to his feet, but he fell right back onto the floor and rolled into a ball. He covered his head with his arms and started shaking. I did too—what had I gotten myself into?

"You're scaring me, Alejandro."

He kept his face hidden and slowly shifted his weight. I could tell he was in pain. He dragged himself over to a chair, pulled up, and leaned against the wall. His eyes then scanned the room.

"If they come here looking for me, where can I hide?" he asked.

Danger had drained away the bravado I remembered. I had to find out what the hell was going on and who 'they' were. I forced my voice to sound steady.

"In there," I said, pointing to the open door of the closet in my bedroom. But he shook his head.

"There's no room, Amalia! You've got too many clothes and shoes in there."

I ignored his implied disapproval. "At the back. There's a cubbyhole with a grid."

He limped over, shoved my hanging dresses to the side, and spied the recessed compartment.

"It's actually part of the ventilation system, but if you had to, you could squeeze yourself in there," I said.

"I guess I could and with all this stuff stacked in front of the opening, it might be okay."

His face looked less tense. Maybe now I'd learn what brought him here.

"I have to lie down," he said as he stumbled toward the bed

and collapsed on top of the coverlet. He drew his long legs up to his chest—grimy shoes and all. Countless times I'd pictured him there, but not like this.

I felt like I needed to rescue him, but from what, I had no idea. He groaned and when I moved closer, I saw that his eyes had rolled back.

"You can't breathe! I have to loosen your clothes!"

I didn't wait for permission. I got him flipped onto his back and ripped open his shirt. I unhitched his belt and pried loose the first stud of his button-down Levi's. He coughed and the sound reminded me of storm shutters rattling. Then he passed out. I stared at him, completely at a loss as to what to do next.

The whorls of hair on his chest glistened damp with sweat, and his eyes twitched underneath closed lids. I had no medical experience, no training at all. I took a face cloth from the linen closet and carefully dabbed at his wounds. What a mess!

Heavy traffic, car horns, sirens, and—I think—machine-gun fire screamed from somewhere. My head swung toward the angry sounds. Cool autumn air blew through the lace curtains and a whiff of sulfurous smoke burned my eyes. I shot up and slammed the sash all the way down.

My watch read 8:25. In less than thirty minutes, Alejandro had managed to raze most of my carefully constructed defenses. How could I keep the rest of them in place?

Should I be trying to keep him awake? What would I do if he went into convulsions, or even a coma? If I had to call for an ambulance, how would I explain his presence in my bed?

I listened hard and decided that his breathing now sounded normal. I struggled to keep mine even, too—no matter what, I absolutely had to stay calm. I placed my dressing table's stool just centimeters away from him, sat down, and waited.

~

An hour and a half elapsed before Alejandro shifted his weight, tried to raise his head, and then fell back onto the oversized pillows. Not completely awake, he blinked at me.

"Amalia? Where are we?"

"In my bedroom. Don't you remember? Do you want me to call anyone?" I asked.

"No! No one can know where I am. Amalia, just tell me about the massacre."

"What are you talking about? A while ago I thought I heard machine-gun fire outside and maybe tear gas stung my eyes. But that's all I can tell you. I don't know anything about a massacre."

When he realized that I had no more information, a groan rumbled in his throat and he looked at me incredulously.

"You haven't heard about what's going down at the Plaza of the Three Cultures tonight?"

I knew he meant the main square in Tlatelolco, a huge public housing complex of yellow concrete apartment buildings, not far from downtown Mexico City. More people lived in those bunker-like flats than in my hometown of Merida.

"No, I don't have a clue what's 'going down,' but from the looks of you, there has been trouble—serious trouble."

His face flushed with rage. He wanted me on his side, but I felt terrified of getting more involved. He gripped my arms and glared into my eyes.

"Don't you get it Amalia? Because of the 'serious trouble' tonight, your life will change. Mine, too. Everything will change. Nothing will ever be the same after this."

I couldn't understand. I hadn't been there. I hadn't seen anything. My mistrust of his radical politics had broken us up years ago, and I still did not want to be involved in any mayhem. I could tell he felt disappointed because I refused to act like a "comrade." Well that was just tough!

"So why are you here then instead of over at Tlatelolco helping your students deal with all this huge 'change' you're going on about?"

He inhaled and closed his eyes.

"Amalia, I *was* there. Don't you see what the government's doing? They want to contain the protests at any price." His mouth sneered.

"*¡Coño!* They call us dangerous, but they're the criminals. At the plaza, thousands gathered and the army went berserk. They opened fire on the crowd."

No! I couldn't believe that. I tried to leave the room and see what information I could find on the television. But before I could get out of range, his hands caught my wrists, and he looked frantically toward the window.

"Can anyone see us from the street? Please, Amalia, stay right here with me."

Looking at his pleading face, I knew that his need for me had begun to thaw out the ice I'd piled up in my heart.

"Don't worry, Alejandro, we're completely hidden," I said with all the conviction I could muster. Sitting back down beside him, I tried to get his mind focused on something else. But he began jerking and flailing about, and his eyes filled with tears. I pushed a pillow at him. "Grip this," I commanded.

He took the soft cushion, clutched it to his midsection and rocked back and forth. He closed his eyes tightly.

"Amalia," he said, "it looked like Armageddon. The residents couldn't believe what was happening right outside their homes. All of them were trapped and us too—protestors, city cops, old people, mothers with their children, school kids, little dogs. Everyone pushed and screamed—trying to get away—but they couldn't. The army had blocked all the main exits. I wanted to keep my group together, but when we heard the shots and saw bodies falling, the kids panicked and stampeded toward the buildings. I ran after them, but a tank blocked my path."

A tank? In a public square? No, that had to be a fabrication and I told him so. His grip on my arm began hurting.

"Amalia, are you listening at all?" he snapped. "Do you think the army would come on bicycles to stifle what they're calling 'a full-scale, goddamn student rebellion?'"

I wrestled myself loose and turned away from his cold stare. This was too much. How did he imagine that he could just show up—like some phantom from the past—and expect me to join his struggle?

When we first met, he used to send me love notes, and he gave me a gold locket on Valentine's Day. He listened to my dreams and encouraged me to become an architect.

"You aren't like the other girls, Amalia. You have originality, energy, curiosity, and passion," he'd said. He admired my ideas, and over coffee one summer afternoon he took my hands and kissed them. "We'll get married and when I've graduated, I'll find a job, and pay for you to go to the University of Mexico for your degree."

I'd fallen in love with *that* Alejandro. And he with me, until Susana came along and convinced him I would be a drag on his ambitions. Listening now, I realized that she had been at least partly right. I'd never exactly felt an obsession to help the oppressed. And that's what fueled Alejandro's commitment and made him choose Susana over me.

His parting words still stung. "Amalia, you are just too young, too self-absorbed, and unconcerned with the needs of people. I don't think you're the woman I need."

I'd stopped replaying the past when he started raving again.

"So many people were bleeding. I saw a school girl—maybe twelve years old—she was crying and pulling on the arm of a soldier who held a semi-conscious kid—probably her brother—by the collar. The *cabrón* just laughed and shot her point blank in the face. Just like that. I saw the blood come out through her mouth and knew she was beyond help. He realized that I'd witnessed his crime, and he raised his gun again. I wanted to strike back for the girl, for her brother—for myself—so I flew at him and with a sickening thud, his head smashed onto the unyielding ground. When he didn't get up, I tore off."

Had Alejandro killed him? I felt bile rising up into my throat. I couldn't listen anymore. I'd gotten so out of my depth already.

"Why don't you let me clean up those cuts?" I asked.

He didn't even hear me. His mind was stuck on the battleground.

"I tried to help the people who had fallen. But another couple of those bastards caught me and slammed me with their clubs. Harder and harder. I knew they wanted to kill me, but an explosion distracted them for a split second. They lost their grip, and I ran like a madman. I goddamn flew until I'd put six blocks between me and everything back there. I sank down and crawled out of sight."

Alejandro sounded defeated, but I had no way of judging how much of what he'd said might be true. His story sounded so terrible.

"What I want to know is why you think the government is behind all this?"

He looked at me as though I were a three-year-old.

"Amalia, how can you ask that? Everyone knows that the president desperately wants to shut us up. Over the past several years it has taken billions of pesos to get ready for the Mexico City Olympics. The politicians are not about to let the so-called 'whiny students' or anyone else derail their carefully orchestrated plans. They want the world to see our country as the most developed nation in Latin America. That goal trumps every other consideration, and if they have to mow us down, well, so be it. They're like animals."

After that he sat up, ripped off the soiled shirt that clung to his back, and flung it across the room.

"I thought my lungs would burst," he said. "I flagged a taxi, but the son of a bitch wouldn't stop, so I crawled toward a bank of pay phones. I figured if I could call Susana, she'd come and get me. I fished in my pocket for some change, but I felt no wallet, handkerchief, or coins—everything had fallen out."

If he noticed me flush at the mention of his wife or his lack of cash, he ignored it. I squared my shoulders. I'd figured out what he would say next.

"If the army had my ID, I knew they'd be looking for me. I couldn't risk going home. But I remembered that you live close by."

The easy way that he let that slip out abruptly tempered any enthusiasm I felt about seeing him again. I lowered my voice and made my eyes as sharp as skewers. I looked at him straight on.

"Ten years with zero contact between us and you choose precisely this moment to drop in? I bet you've scoped this building out, haven't you? My apartment is on the third floor and the street is hidden away. I bet that you've had me in mind for a long time. What do you think this is? Your personal safe house? Who gave you that right?"

He had no answer. I needed a drink. I marched out of the bedroom and into the kitchen, grabbed the open bottle of tequila off the sideboard, poured a full glass, and carried it back to my bedroom. I took a big gulp. This was no night for sipping. I bent down and placed the rim between Alejandro's lips. He gagged and the clear fire spewed onto his chest and into his open wounds. He yelped at the sting.

I didn't mean to do that—I needed a first aid kit, gauze, and something to wipe up the mess. Maybe if I tidied him up and gave him some money, he would leave and let me try to reconstruct the life I'd had up until two hours ago. I stalked out of the room again—with new purpose this time—but when I returned, it was as if someone had changed the channel and I no longer found myself watching a horror film.

"I'm sorry, Amalia," Alejandro said softly. "I shouldn't have yelled at you. I'm grateful to be here, safe in your place. But I'll leave whenever you say."

He looked absolutely sincere.

His gentleness was harder to deal with than the aggressive attitude and verbal abuse he'd been flinging at me. The man I once knew had returned, and he looked at me just as I remembered. The clock on the wall read 11:10. I couldn't turn him out.

"Let's see how you are in the morning. Now stay as still as possible and I'll clean you up," I said.

I stuffed old towels underneath his back to sop up the muddy, bloody bedding. I swabbed his broad chest with astringent and carefully patted iodine into the jagged cuts on his face, the face that had stirred up too many old feelings.

I caught him sizing me up, too. I had stayed in pretty good shape. My job as a folk art buyer involved some office work and lots of rigorous travel to remote places. My tanned legs and arms were strong, and my auburn hair still waved way down my back. I remembered how he used to like twisting it into a curl at my waist.

I felt sure he noticed the way my hazel eyes looked at him with more directness and confidence. I was no longer the needy, greedy girl that I'd been when we met.

In those days, my parents kept me in their sights as much as they could. When I turned fifteen—in part to get me away from him—our family moved 1,600 kilometers from Yucatan to Mexico City. With me in the country's capital, and Alejandro finishing his last year of high school at home, we endured a year of forced separation. But he followed me to La Capital and enrolled in social sciences at La Universidad de Mexico.

Try as she did, some days not even my mother could resist his bad-boy charm. On one of the many occasions when she refused to allow me to go out, he smiled and conceded to her wishes. Mamá looked triumphant—I felt cheated—but when he winked at me and squeezed my hand, I should have known he had a plan. He walked out the door, but soon returned with a bunch of ripe red bananas, my mother's favorite fruit.

"Ten of these beauties for ten minutes with your daughter?" he asked as he waved them in front of her. She laughed and relented. We ran for the door. I loved how he could turn any situation around.

Alejandro and I wanted to be together all the time. My friends thought that we had a perfectly inappropriate relationship, but his quirky personality was as compelling as his body.

Mamá said his family was too political. I can still see her with one hand on her hip wagging a finger back and forth.

"You'll be setting yourself up for disaster if you get any more involved with him," she had said.

She did have a point. During those years, anyone who opposed the ruling regime could expect rough reprisals, and it seemed as though the situation had changed little since. If my parents had been less judgmental, I would have been less stubborn, and I might have realized that Alejandro would bring me no happiness. I'd have eventually left him. But Mamá's refusal to even try and understand how I felt made my adoration of him all the stronger.

At the time, teenage girls traveled with chaperones. I would have none of that. I openly flaunted my relationship with Alejandro. We were young; we thrived on the excitement of being seen as rebels and were besotted by passion and promises. It was hardly the stuff that builds a lasting union. I loved him deeply—I did—but I despised his politics.

"Someone has to defend the underclass," he had said over and over.

"Petitioning and marching are a waste of time," I finally said. I should have taken his stricken look seriously, yet I was vain enough to think my body and my pretty face would be enough to keep him.

But when he met Susana Lara, a smoky, sexy sculptress who shared his leftist views, she became his new love. She understood how to handle Alejandro. More experienced and at an advantage under the covers, she forced him to choose between the two of us. When I learned what she'd done, I should have been just as daring, but I didn't know how. Of course, he chose her. Destroyed and humiliated, I lied to save face.

"Alejandro was a rite of passage and now I need to move on," I told my parents.

They had told me time and again that when he had played with me for long enough, he'd toss me aside. Mamá loved to be right, especially about Alejandro. But she knew all too well the power he had over me. To put some distance between us, she suggested I visit my brother Toño, who lived in the United States with his friend Paul. I couldn't stand one more day of her self-satisfied smirking and gladly went.

I hoped Alejandro would come for me, but a month later, I learned that he and Susana had married. I held back my tears and told myself that I didn't care. I deflected my sadness with my studies and became a top assistant at Toño's company. That worked well for years; then I returned to Mexico City and saw him and Susana together.

I'd gone to a lecture by the artist Carlos Merida, who was working with the most renowned architects. His murals decorated a score of La Capital's contemporary façades. Of course, his name attracted me because it was the same as my hometown. I had just settled into a chair not far from the front when I heard Alejandro and Susana's voices. Alejandro didn't see me, but Susana raised her eyebrows then turned away with dismissive shrug.

I lurched out of that auditorium as fast as I could. Somehow I made my way home, threw on warm pajamas, and opened a liter of strawberry sherbet. With my "Bésame Mucho" 45 on repeat, I stretched out on the couch, salving my wounds.

All that happened a long time ago, but even then, I knew that when it comes to Alejandro, I have no backbone. Since breaking up with him, all my relationships with men have lasted about as long as hard rolls from the bakery. After a short time, they'd seem ordinary and dry, and I'd lose all interest.

I never stopped believing that Alejandro rightfully belonged to me. But up until tonight, I didn't dare dream that he would land back in my bed.

His tapered hands clutched at mine, and one of them briefly grazed against my left breast. A deep moan threatened to escape through my parted lips, but I choked it back before he could hear. I'd made sure that all his wounds were clean and no bones appeared broken. A few of the cuts looked deep and painful, but most proved to be superficial. Thank God he had escaped without more serious injuries. The worst damage seemed to be psychological. He started shaking again.

"Amalia. Hold me!"

"*Please* calm down, Alejandro. If the neighbors hear you, they'll call the cops."

His arms caught around my waist, he buried his face into my chest, and I felt him tremble from something I suspected had nothing to do with his fear. My body reacted to his embrace like a mango ripening in the sun.

I forced myself to push backwards, and his late-night café eyes surveyed the two meters of physical space that I had created. Memories of the past swirled between us and our passion lay as close to the surface as our panic.

two

"Come over here with me."

We both knew that under ordinary circumstances what we were poised to do would be absolutely wrong, but looking back, I think that night was many things—impetuous, ill-timed, and fateful—but not wrong.

I leaned forward again, stretched out my arms, and let a knee rest on the edge of the mattress. I lowered my hands, fanned them, and paused. How would I handle the complications of giving myself to the man lying in my bed?

"You know what will happen if I move one centimeter closer, don't you?" I asked.

He held out his arms, and I let myself fall. For me, this would not be a random fling. I saw he wore a smile of anticipation. He'd always been like that—ready for me whenever I came near him—and his need was contagious.

His cracked lips brushed mine. I returned a real kiss, deep and full. The salty taste of blood and tears and of his raw-edged fear yanked at my heart. His breath came hard; his brown eyes looked wild. He ran a hand under my caftan, felt between my legs, and I completely succumbed to the desire I'd bottled up for ten long years.

From the moment I first saw him in the hallway, I'd tried to deny that this was inevitable. My arms and legs entwined around him. I moved again, carefully. My eyes lowered and fixed on the swell inside his already loosened Levi's. I raised my head, my gaze met his, and my hand slipped into the open fly of those well-worn jeans.

His torment subsided. His mouth locked on mine and I heard him breathe in my scent. Gripping the hem, he raised my caftan, but I felt it catch under my arms. I smiled at him, took the fabric in hand, pulled it over my head, and flung it into the air. We laughed as it fell to the floor in a blue cascade.

Diffused light from the bedroom window softly illuminated the shadows and he said my naked body seemed surrounded by an aura. He inched both his hands up the full length of me and then between my legs again.

An excruciating crescendo built like loud hard rock. Hendrix, Clapton, and Morrison wailed inside my brain. Oblivious to pain, Alejandro took me again and again, and a spark kindled deep inside. I wanted the night to last forever. Overwhelmed by nostalgia and need, I refused to hear—much less heed—the alarm bells competing with the music in my mind.

Slowly emerging from the bliss, I felt exhausted and wouldn't speculate past that. Alejandro seemed dazed but tranquil. He wanted a shower. We entered together. I lathered him all over, and he did the same for me—like a ritual cleansing.

Looking around for something to put on, Alejandro's eyes landed on the stretched-out sweat suit that always hangs from a hook in my bathroom. It fit him far too snugly, but as I rummaged around for something else, he stopped me.

"Amalia, this is perfect. It hugs me and it smells like you."

I remembered him stringing words together like that—like pearls on a linen thread. If any other man had told me such things, they would have sounded silly. But coming from Alejandro, the endearments felt like intimate verbal caresses. I recalled that even in the midst of one of our fiery debates, or when we'd visit an art gallery—wherever, whenever—he'd let me know with a word, a gesture, or a touch that I was always on his mind. I loved that.

We didn't talk about anything meaningful. I fed him cold meats, cheeses, fresh fruit, and toast. He couldn't eat much, but what he managed to swallow seemed to calm his agitation. Then he needed to lie back down. Seeing the bed in such a mess, he turned toward my living room and stretched out on one of the overstuffed couches, just as though he owned the place. I stacked Bob Dylan's *Blonde on Blonde* album on the turntable and his eyes closed to the strains of "Just Like a Woman."

When I removed the LP, Alejandro stirred but didn't wake. I brought blankets, covered him with one, and arranged the other on the companion couch. I lay down there, right across from him. I wanted to wake him and ask if he felt like I did. Had this night brought back good memories that helped to ease the pain he carried into my home from Tlatelolco? I watched the way his chest rose high and fell low and remembered how I used to place my hand there and run my fingers across his skin. In his sleep, he would always move closer to me.

He looked as though he belonged on that couch. The room, the lighting, and the peacefulness started fooling with my mind. My eyes refused to close, and I began to wonder if this might be a new beginning for us. What raised my hopes most was that in his sleep, he called *my* name, not hers. After this empty decade, more than anything, I wanted to believe that something besides the riot had brought him back to me.

When I'd met Alejandro at my *quinceñera*—my fifteenth birthday party—I felt sure that I would break the family curse. My mother did not have a loving marriage, nor had my grandmother been happy with her husband. My father and grandfather were impatient and condescending toward women. In those days

Alejandro acted gallant, solicitous, and determined to sweep me off my feet. I thought of him as my Prince Charming. And after tonight, I knew that he could still kiss the life back into my sleeping soul. If only I had a magic wand to make Susana vanish for good.

His condition had improved slightly during the night, but he looked lost. It wounded me to realize that lovemaking wasn't his main focus that morning.

"Amalia, can I stay here a while longer? Three nights at the most. I know I'm a burden, but I don't know what else to do."

I knew he needed to bide time, just enough for him to make a safe escape.

"Well, you're here now," I said as I turned my face away. "As long as there's no possibility of the police finding you, I guess it will be all right. You didn't tell anyone you'd be coming here, did you?"

Alejandro assured me that no one knew he'd fled to my home. Yet, even as he spoke I wondered if I'd made another bad decision. In just ten hours, he had thrown my orderly world into a completely new orbit. I tried to stop myself from hoping that three more days in my home would increase the chances that he'd stay longer still.

Languidly, my thoughts returned to last night, but I needed to push all that away. If I was to psychologically survive the next seventy-two hours, I had to keep my wits about me.

After drinking a cup of steaming coffee, Alejandro began a tour of my home. I hoped the cut flowers and plants wouldn't bring on an allergic reaction. Mamá—who never missed the chance for a dig—said my apartment smelled like the florist's stall in the market. She rarely visited me, but when she did, she wheezed the whole time.

I didn't hear him sniffing or sneezing, and it pleased me when he nodded appreciatively at my art. I could see he looked particularly impressed by the small canvas of bright red watermelons.

"Is this a Tamayo?" he asked.

"Yes, it is," I answered. "The painting cost me six months' salary, but I couldn't resist the opportunity to own it." He seemed to be enjoying himself.

"Your home is just like you—full of color and fragrance," said Alejandro. "I've always admired how you make your world so beautiful. You taught me to understand art, listen to music, and even to like poetry."

I wanted him to keep talking just like that. But he stopped short, startled by the sight of one of Susana's sculptures prominently displayed in the foyer. She had hewn the strong upright back and shoulders of a male figure from light-colored cantera stone. The imposing torso sat atop an unpolished black onyx cube. From the moment I first laid eyes on it, although no facial features were depicted, I knew the model could have been no one but Alejandro.

"Where did you get that?" he asked.

I looked straight at him and slid my hand down the sculpture's smooth surface.

"I bought it in a private sale when your wife had just begun her career."

He looked upset with me and brought his hands to his hips. Certainly his blank expression was meant to be noncommittal, but the way he chewed on his lower lip gave him away. He didn't appreciate seeing his likeness in my home.

"Susana and I always wondered who had purchased that particular piece. Her agent would only tell us that an anonymous buyer had paid in cash. I never imagined that it could have been you. . . . Let me buy it back."

"Alejandro, I have nothing else to remind me of the time when we meant so much to one another and, perverse as it sounds, I like having this memento."

He lowered his arms and turned away from the statue and from me. I guess the sincerity of my reply stopped him from asking more questions. A frown like a funerary mask settled on his face, and he returned to rest on his couch.

When it seemed he'd gotten past his annoyance about the sculpture in the hallway, I sat down next to him and asked why seeing it had bothered him so much. His back stiffened and I decided I'd drop the whole issue. But when I got up my robe parted.

He moved quickly for a man who had been beaten just a day ago. He caught my hands before I could do up the sash and pulled the sides further open. My naked body clearly turned him on. He suggested that I remove the silk, and I let it drop to the floor.

Later that day, he called one of his colleagues at the university.

"No, I can't tell you where I am," I heard him say.

That relieved me. But during the conversation, he turned back into the ranting revolutionary from the night before. He slammed the phone down and shouted.

"On top of all that's happened, the government has begun a cover-up. They will not allow anyone to speak openly about what happened in Tlatelolco," Alejandro said

"What do you mean?" I asked. I didn't care if I sounded ignorant of the facts and I appreciated that he treated my question respectfully.

"Censorship in the media has escalated and spreading information about the extent of the killings means immediate arrest," he explained.

The next three nights he spent at my place, he slept fitfully and woke frequently, not able to separate truth from reality. I awoke once to find him clenching his fists as he looked out the window.

"What's keeping you up? I asked as gently as I could, and he told me about his latest nightmare.

"I had walked back to the Plaza de las Tres Culturas hoping to find my wallet," he began. "I kept behind rubble piles and other debris—to hide from the soldiers. I found nothing and had turned to leave when I came upon Rolando, one of my graduate students. I saw that he had my black money-pouch clutched in his bloodied hand. I smiled, but when I tried to take it from him, I couldn't because rigor mortis had set in. I realized then that he had died— propped on the side of the square. His death grimace forever frozen in terror."

He looked into my eyes and I wished I could say something that would comfort him.

"Why did mindless violence need to be the final scene of this brilliant boy's life?" Alejandro asked me. "And what if it wasn't a dream?"

He ran his hands through his hair and pushed his head down until his chin rested on the windowsill. The cool air seeping through a small opening seemed to soothe him.

At some stage in my childhood I had learned about the parallel spiritual realm from my nanny, Hortensia Gómez. Nana claimed that in times of extreme stress, our souls could space-time travel and sometimes true events would be revealed. Perhaps that had happened to Alejandro? I didn't possess paranormal gifts like she did, but I'd learned to trust my feelings. I did not discount the idea that Alejandro had visited the place where his student died.

The next day Alejandro looked jumpy.

"Will you go out and buy a copy of every newspaper on the stand? Maybe there will be something about Tlatelolco in one of them."

I agreed to go, but I didn't want to be out in the streets for long.

Down on the sidewalk, it still seemed abnormally quiet. Don Tacho, my regular vendor, brightened when I stopped by.

"I haven't seen you for a couple of days. I'm glad you're safe, but please, stay in your apartment till the end of the week," he said.

I looked around the empty street. "Is it really that bad?"

"I've sold papers on this corner for twenty-five years and I've never seen so many uniforms." He drew a finger over his closed mouth, clasped my arm, and leaned in toward me. "No one knows what's going on, and I don't ask questions." Sidling his big frame still closer and in a whisper that I could barely hear, he continued. "I'm always here before dawn, waiting for the papers to be delivered. I slink down and pretend not to see a thing. But yesterday they hauled body bags right past here."

This man knew the street. If he thought I should be inside, I would take him seriously. All I wanted to do now was get what I came for and go back home to hide behind a locked door. Danger paralyzed me to the point that I couldn't do anything useful. Alejandro never understood that about me.

As soon as I gave him the papers, he spread the pile out on my dining room table. He threw back the pages, swearing more loudly with each turn.

"This is it? Amalia, were there no pamphlets or handouts from the student union?"

"I couldn't find anything else. You're right about the absolute control that the government is using," I admitted.

Alejandro nodded. "So now you believe what I said about the main periodicals printing misleading accounts."

"Yes, and even at that, there are only a few articles about the aftermath," I added.

"Like here. Look at this!" he said, jabbing his finger at the front page of *El Sol de Mexico* as he read aloud.

"*Foreign interlopers are attempting to damage Mexico's national image. The objective: Preventing the nineteenth Olympic Games from being held . . . Sharpshooters fire on army troops in Tlatelolco: One general and eleven soldiers wounded; two soldiers and more than twenty civilians killed in a terrible gun battle . . . The sharpshooters were all government assassins.*" Alejandro shook his head and pointed to additional evidence that the press was in league with the authorities. *Excelsior* printed this headline: *Serious fighting as army breaks up meeting of strikers: Twenty dead, seventy-five wounded, 400 jailed.*

"I can't believe it, Amalia! One paper says four hundred have been jailed and the next one claims a thousand. Can you simply round off casualties to the nearest six hundred? *¡Coño!* Listen to this one!"

" *. . . Tlatelolco was a battlefield. There was serious fighting for hours between terrorists and soldiers. Twenty-nine dead and more than eighty wounded; casualties on both sides; one thousand arrested.*"

Alejandro threw down all the newspapers onto the table again. When I gathered them up, he told me to put the papers in the garbage can.

"It's not worth keeping such drivel," he said.

I felt terrible for him. His life's work centered on students' rights. Though I'd sometimes thought he was posturing more than protesting, I could see how deeply the Tlatelolco massacre had cut into him.

I did what I could to divert his thoughts. I prepared the old familiar Yucatecan treats for him—*papádzules, panuchos, salbutes, codzitos*—all with different toppings and sauces. I tried talking about Merida, the city where we grew up. I felt such yearning when I remembered our youthful infatuation.

But his mind incessantly returned to the awful events of October 2. "Amalia, I know you're trying to help, and I am truly grateful. You were always there for me, and I realize that I made so many mistakes with you."

I waited for him to say more, but instead he pulled me into his arms and searched my eyes. Over the past three days, I'd lost count of how many times he had turned to me like this.

Later, while lying together on my thick hand-hooked rug, he traced a finger over my hipbones.

"I have never met another woman like you," he said. "I'm never happier than when we're together like this."

"It could last forever you know," I said without thinking.

He stopped stroking me and moved away.

"You know this can't go anywhere. I am married and my future depends on Susana's connections."

I knew he felt guilty, and I had no business further involving myself, either. But stopping would come soon enough. I regretted my words, but the subject was now in the open. He got up, sat on the bed, and wrapped himself with the sheet.

Still lying on the rug where he'd left me, I thought about Susana. The truth is, I'd always figured that she stole Alejandro from me. She used to seek him out while I was at my office. As a draftsperson I had to put in long hours. I hoped that my boss would value my work and sponsor my studies because that would be the only way I could go to university. I sure didn't have the funds.

Susana made me feel like an ingénue. The contrast between her sexy look and my teenybopper appearance flattered her; I knew that she teased Alejandro and asked why he bothered with a baby like me. So even if it seemed I should feel shame for going to bed with a man who didn't belong to me, I also felt justified in getting a little of my own back.

He tried to make me believe that he stayed with her because she furthered his career. Didn't he realize that his soul, his passion, would wither away with her? I knew how much he needed both emotional and physical fire; after the past three days, could he live without me in his life?

"How can you be so callous, Alejandro? Marriage should not be a question of convenience." I couldn't stop goading him.

"With Susana and me it is," he replied. "We've had a pact for years, and we've done a lot for one another. Her father is a political lobbyist and he arranged for my tenure at the university. He made it clear that marrying Susana would bring many advantages my way. You know what they say, 'In Mexico you do what you have to, and that isn't always what you want.'"

He looked and sounded as calculating and cold as Mamá and Hortensia always claimed he was. Nonetheless, I convinced myself that his cruel words were nothing more than a rationale for his decision to reject me for her. He tried to fill the silence with more talk about the student movement, but that made me feel even more uncomfortable.

For ten years I'd wanted to forget him, but it seemed that all my intellectual, creative, emotional, and sexual appetites were stimulated by him, and if Alejandro left me now, I doubted I would ever again feel as alive as I had during these past three days.

Get a grip, I told myself. I needed to remember how easily he had tossed me aside when a person more advantageous to his goals presented herself and I had to accept that he would surely do it again.

"Amalia, I will always be grateful to you for showing me that there are beautiful experiences to be shared, even in tragedy."

Was that melodramatic monologue the best goodbye he could muster? Dried blood and bruises were the only remaining evidence of Tlatelolco. Three nights ago, when he had fallen through my doorway, I'd known with total certainty that my life path would be changed. But at that point I couldn't imagine how much it would hurt.

Nonetheless, I couldn't regret that Alejandro had involved me in the events of October 2, 1968. Like almost everyone else, I'd watched the university students protesting for months, but with detachment. Now, I was wide awake. I'd seen the greatest tragedy of Mexico's contemporary history through the eyes of a man who understood our country for what it truly is. The Tlatelolco massacre made all Mexicans—including me—feel both weary and leery. The age of innocence had passed.

Alejandro hit the table with his fists. "¡Chinga! It's worse than I imagined. My comrades say the plaza is empty now, but the army and police are withholding medical care, even for the most critically wounded. Many will die from their injuries and infections, and the survivors will be gathered up and taken away to be interrogated."

According to him, hundreds of protestors, maybe thousands, were lying dead or injured. Most of them were inexperienced kids who found themselves in the middle of a power struggle they were not fully aware of.

"No one who has shown any support for the movement is safe," he said. "But you don't have to worry. I have not told a living soul about you. You'll be safe from any reprisals. I promise you that."

And what about you, Alejandro? I wanted to ask, but didn't. I feared that a dismissive response from him would make me lose the small bit of composure I still managed to hang onto. I would not let him see me cry.

On October 6, when he exited my apartment, I didn't even get a proper goodbye. He had turned on the afternoon TV news program, and after seeing no reports on Tlatelolco, he turned to face me.

"You know that I need to go now."

He had nothing to gather up. I gave him a wool sweater that Toño had left at my place during one of his visits. It hugged Alejandro's torso and looked good with the Levi's and his high-top Converse sneakers. I had scrubbed those runners until not a trace of Tlatelolco remained. I hoped he'd stay out of danger, but I doubted he would.

"Amalia, I've told you I will never forget these past four days. I came because I knew I could trust you. I asked too much, I know. But you didn't let me down. I really don't know what else to say except, thank you."

Those were his parting words to me—more melodrama. There were lots of things I wished he would have said instead, the top of the list being, *I love you and I'm going to leave Susana.* Even a simple, *I'll call you and we can have lunch* might have made me feel a bit better. I barely managed to keep from weeping as we shared a last kiss, and then he turned and thumped down the same three flights he'd dragged himself up four nights ago.

I watched from the window. When he burst through the building's front door, he turned and looked up—searching for my window—but he was looking in the wrong direction. He shrugged and turned around again, then marched down the street. He strode away like a man who knows his purpose in the world.

three

I shook my head at the way most of my friends had let the Olympic Games and government propaganda blot out their tragic memories. Before the Tlatelolco massacre, was I as naïve and disconnected as them?

I read more skeptically now. I no longer swallowed everything printed in the newspapers, and I asked a lot more questions. I didn't want to be perceived as an empty person. If I saw Alejandro again, would he notice the difference in me? Probably not. I think it suited his vanity to see me as a perpetually young and naïve girl.

Keeping active seemed imperative. If I let myself get pensive, I'd start reliving my time with him. I didn't know what to think or what to do, but he and I needed to speak soon.

On the first Saturday in December, I went to a craft exhibition in San Angel. I made only one purchase—a box of Christmas cards decorated with pink tin hearts, ruby poinsettias, and silver stars.

"My clients will love these. Do you have any more?" I asked the vendor.

"That's all I have of those. How about these?" she said, as she held out a different box.

The second set was embellished with Disney decals that depressed me. Sorry, but knockoffs had no place on my shopping list.

"I'll just take the one box," I said as I turned to leave.

My feet, legs, and back ached after spending the whole day walking aimlessly through rows and rows of poorly stocked booths. The sun hung low in the sky and the early winter wind whirled under my skirt. My bare legs felt chilled. I craved a cup of hot chocolate, but saw no place to buy one. Daunted by the prospect of a crowded bus trip back to my apartment, I decided to take a cab. But none was available.

Reluctantly, I joined the long line for the bus and I wondered if we would all fit into the next one to come along. To keep myself from thinking about the cold, I started counting people in line. When my eyes landed on the back of a well-built man wearing a pearl gray trench coat, my heart beat harder. "Alejandro!" I called out.

He turned and forced his mouth into a surprised smile. He hurried over to where I stood. The way his torso angled forward, I knew he wanted to embrace me, but he held back.

"How are you, Amalia?"

"I've been okay."

He squirmed and did not even allude to the four days after the massacre. Instead, he offered excuses.

"I wanted to call, but it's been hectic these past few weeks. Susana had a show at a Polanco gallery. Actually, she sold well."

Her success held little interest for me, but I couldn't make that too obvious.

"How nice for both of you," I said politely.

Something else occupied my mind. I really needed to talk to Alejandro, but I felt so unprepared. I looked down and fidgeted with my beads. What could I say here and now? The cold seemed to intensify and my body shook even harder. I needed to get out of this wind and prayed the bus would arrive soon.

"You're shivering!" He craned his neck to see where we might go and pointed to a small restaurant on the other side of the busy thoroughfare.

"Let's go over there and get some warmth into you."

I didn't protest when he took my arm and skillfully steered me through the traffic.

He held the door, and we stepped into a garishly lit room. The smell of over-used frying oil assailed my nose and a scratchy recording of love-gone-wrong ranchera music grated in my ears. Yet the steamy warmth emanating from dozens of bodies in close proximity redeemed all these shortcomings.

Alejandro found a corner table and I sank into the cracked leather upholstery of the chair. I hadn't planned on this setting, but it would have to do. He asked what I wanted to drink. I'd lost my earlier craving for hot cocoa.

"Whatever you choose will be fine," I said as I rubbed my arms.

He signaled the waiter. "What's good?" I heard him ask. While the two spoke, I tried to think of how I'd open the conversation, but I couldn't come up with anything that would make what I had to say any easier.

He looked at me in expectation. "Amalia, you look like you have something that you want to tell me."

"It is amazing that for years we never ran into one another, and yet this is the second time in as many months," I replied.

I knew I sounded like an idiot.

"Actually, I've seen you from a distance dozens of times," he volleyed back, "but I never approached you. I worried about how you'd react. I didn't want a confrontation. When we broke up all those years ago, you were so angry. Susana believed that given the chance, you'd attack one of us."

I hated thinking that he'd discussed me with her and that she'd judged me capable of violence.

"Is that so? Well, in October, you certainly overcame the fear of approaching me."

"Amalia, please don't start," he said. "I wish it could be different between us, but I've explained the thing with Susana."

The thing with Susana. How could he use such a phrase to describe his marriage?

He touched my hand and again asked me what I wanted to talk about. I pulled away; finding the right words seemed impossible. Then it came to me. I sat up straight and looked right into his eyes.

"Why don't we talk about coffee?"

He looked puzzled. But quite frankly, I enjoyed seeing him at a loss for words.

"Coffee? You want to talk about coffee?"

I dug my trembling hands into my lap. He looked at me so intensely, and I knew I'd need to help him along.

"Alejandro, remember how I used to love coffee?"

He smiled and relaxed a bit. He thought we'd hit on a safe topic.

"That was years ago. You loved going to El Café de La Opera. It is still one of my favorite bistros. I remember that you could drink the dark brew all night. Do you want a cup now? What they have here smells good. I could change your order."

"No," I said. "I haven't been able to stand coffee since early October."

I watched his face. Did he catch my cryptic message? Whether he did or not, I saw that he now realized coffee was not a safe topic after all. His eyes swung toward the exit sign and I worried that he'd bolt for the door. Inhaling deeply, he narrowed his eyes and braced himself.

"Spell it out, Amalia."

"I'm telling you that I'm pregnant," I said. "And you are definitely the father."

He lunged across the table and put his face right up in front of mine.

"You and I were together for four days! What kind of cosmic joke is this?"

"You think I'm joking? I had my suspicions by the end of October. Through November, I noticed changes in my body and Hortensia, of course, picked up on them. She urged me to have the lab test done. It was positive. Her spirit guides tell us that this child is a girl."

His breathing sounded jagged. I could see that he would have preferred to face just about anything else. He threw his arms into the air and raised his voice to the ceiling.

"I can't take this! Amalia, why weren't you more careful?"

My voice stayed level. "Why weren't you?"

I stroked my still-flat stomach, worried that the baby could somehow sense his anger, and yes, mine too. I wanted to choke him! Together we created this new life; both of us should be taking responsibility. I realized it would be up to me to move this discussion forward.

"Damn you, Alejandro, maybe you 'can't take this,' but you can't choose to do nothing. Who should I turn to other than you? Hortensia will probably agree to do what she can, but she's no longer a young woman. How will the two of us be able to look after the baby and provide her with all she needs?"

He grabbed my upper arms. He must have known his grip hurt, but he pressed his fingers in harder. I felt relieved that we had a crowd around us. If he got more violent, I'd have people to help me. How did I ever imagine he might have acted differently?

"I don't give a shit how things are with Hortensia. I can't do anything for you. Susana and I are married!"

The waiter returned with our order. He looked poised to intervene. Alejandro let go of my arms, and I pushed my chair further back. I nodded to my champion, and his expression told me that he'd continue to watch this table. I turned my attention back to Alejandro.

"Do you think I don't know that you and Susana are married? You've told me all about your convenient relationship. But you can't tell me this is enough for you. If it was, how could we have made love at my apartment—for four days straight?"

The color drained from his face and he screwed his mouth into a sneer.

"Amalia, we did not make love. We fucked. We fucked like crazy! That's all it was!"

four

Thunderstruck, and so sorry for myself and for the child, I burrowed down to heal and work out a plan of just how I would manage.

For a week, I didn't go out at all. I didn't answer the telephone. I didn't feel like bathing or eating, but I knew the importance of nourishing the life inside me. My baby needed me to do the best I could for her. My resolve to do just that kept me focused and moving through the pain.

Over and over, I replayed the two-month-old scene of Alejandro's arrival back into my life. At the time, I had allowed myself to think that my patience had paid off. That he'd returned to me. That he loved me after all. But he'd only been looking for the comfort of my body and temporary refuge in my home. He didn't care about commitment or love. He had used me.

I'd assumed that he and Susana enjoyed a good life, but no, I could see he doesn't care about her either. He married her because she satisfies his every whim. She calms him down. She carries the load. She takes all the flack. Ten years ago, he did not choose me. I made too many demands. Why didn't I see that he's like spun sugar floss; he's got no substance when the heat is on.

On the third day of my self-imposed withdrawal from the world, I shampooed my hair at the kitchen sink. As I watched the sudsy water flow down the drain, I wished that all my memories of Alejandro would slosh away like that. He had not only rejected me, but he had denied the existence of his own child. What kind of man does such a thing? How had I let myself imagine that I was still in love with him?

The parallels between my personal story and that of post-Tlate-lolco Mexico struck me as profound. When the government troops mowed down the students, all trust shattered. Citizens had no idea how they would be able to come to terms with the tyranny. When Alejandro threw me over and refused to help support our baby, he destroyed my hope. I did not know where to turn for help.

I couldn't tell Mamá and Papá. Long ago they recognized the pitiless places in Alejandro's personality and they loathed him. Eventually, I would tell my brother Toño and dearest Paul. But for now, secrecy seemed the best way to protect my baby from more negativity. I knew that I'd have to leave Mexico City, and luckily, I had a place to go.

From the recessed place in my bedroom closet, I brought out the deed to a property I owned. Three years previously, I gave my parents part of the money they needed to build a new house in La Capital. In return they had presented me with the title to our old family home in Merida.

"We can't accept any charity. This is a business transaction. We won't ever move back to Yucatan," my father had insisted. "But you're young. Your future could take you anywhere."

I protested at the time; I didn't want to accept anything from them, but as it turned out, the hundred-year-old house would be my lifeline. Big and sprawling, and far from Mexico City, it would be the best place to raise my daughter. The more I thought about it, the more I liked the idea of giving birth in the place where I'd come into the world.

By the end of the week, I knew the time had come to let Hortensia know about my plan to move away. We often shared meals at my apartment, but she knew that unusual circumstances motivated this invitation. As she stepped through my doorway, her burnt-almond eyes told me that she knew something momentous would happen at this luncheon.

~

"Amalia, you're like a racehorse. You gallop way out in front of everyone else, swinging your long, red mane," she said as she caressed my shoulder. "But today I sense that you need someone to soothe and quiet you."

I didn't quite know how I felt about being compared to an animal, even an attractive one, but I played along.

"Well, Nana, come on into my corral and we'll have some hay and oats."

She laughed at my bad joke and gave me a hug to bolster my spirits.

Short, sturdy, dark-skinned, and wrinkled, Hortensia, as always, wore the Maya *huipil*—a white cotton shift with bands of bright embroidery around the neck and hem. In the Yucatecan village where she grew up, all the women wear this garment; she wouldn't feel comfortable in anything else. A gold chain and medallion, dangling filigree earrings, flat sandals, and a silken shawl completed her outfit.

Given Hortensia's physical appearance, people expected to hear a peasant woman's voice and attitudes. But five minutes in her company changed that first impression. Even my parents' friends, from the elite circles of entertainment and haute couture, recognized her as a gifted homeopathic healer. Her small stature belied great physical strength, and her confident voice held barely a trace of the place that she'd come from. My nana was a powerhouse and, at the same time, the most caring and perceptive person I knew.

"You've set out your best china and I smell my favorite foods:

mole, saffron rice, fresh hot tortillas. You must be ready to hand me very important information. Is that so, Amalia?"

"Why don't we enjoy the meal," I suggested. "A full stomach helps to ease a heavy heart."

She looked at me with many unasked questions but she had learned all about patience during her life of service to others. She shrugged and sat down to eat.

Although she no longer worked as a servant for our family, she still lived with my mother and father. Her sunny room overlooked the garden she had coaxed from a plot of dry dirt. Beds of roses and kitchen herbs—basil, rosemary, and cilantro—overran one another. She had medicinal roots, bark, berries, and white ginger for an upset stomach, and flowers such as red bougainvillea to cure a persistent cough. She offered relief from whatever problem a person might have—physical, emotional, or spiritual.

"But I am just a facilitator," I often heard her say. "People do their own soul work. They heal themselves."

My job as head buyer for my brother's company paid well, and I made commissions, too. I could afford to provide Nana a monthly pension. I didn't have to do this, and by rights it should have been my parents' responsibility to take care of her financially. But it pleased me to offer her some independence and that was part of the reason why this afternoon would be so hard for me. I had given her something that I'd now take away.

I sat up straight when Hortensia cleared her throat. She'd obviously grown tired of waiting for me to get our discussion underway. I considered her my other mother and a trusted confidante. I knew that I would be telling her little that she didn't already know, but still, saying everything out loud felt like coughing up dust.

"Last week, in a queue for the bus, I ran into Alejandro," I told her. "We spoke, and to make a long, painful story short, he wants nothing to do with me or our child."

Hortensia raised an eyebrow and shifted in her seat. Hearing that Alejandro had refused to help me at all made her look as angry as the wasps I used to catch in glass jars when I was a girl.

"I didn't expect much from him, but I had hoped for more than I got," I said.

Tears threatened, but I took a few deep breaths and managed to settle down.

"Nana, I feel so alone, and I get panicky just thinking about how my baby will be ridiculed for not having a daddy."

Hortensia held her palms wide open and stated the obvious.

"Amalia, you have no husband and your daughter will not have a father. Yes, people have a closed attitude when it comes to single motherhood. The sooner you accept what's in store for you, the better off you'll be. But I have to ask—you know about using birth control—how did you allow this to happen?"

I looked down at my shaking hands and locked them together in an attempt to regain some self-control.

"Of course I know about preventing pregnancy. You told me all I needed to know. But I had nothing on hand and Alejandro didn't either." Hortensia shifted in her chair.

I knew that the explanation I gave her sounded empty and my nana deserved the truth. I shrugged my shoulders and reached to take her hands in mine.

"Nana—really—I didn't care. I thought only of the moment. I wanted Alejandro so much that I lost my fear of the possible consequences."

Hortensia's withdrew her hands from mine. "And no doubt he eagerly took what you offered him because he assumed he'd not have to pay anything in return"

She turned to look out the window so I couldn't read her face. She remained still as I told her about my final humiliating exchange with Alejandro, ending with that cruel words statement about how we had merely "fucked"—not made love.

～

My nana whipped her head around. She seemed discouraged with me, but she looked as though she would have enjoyed torturing Alejandro until he screamed for mercy.

"He's a complete coward. You're right, he doesn't love Susana and he certainly doesn't love you. But Amalia, there's nothing to be gained by trying to change him. He is as selfish as he is detached—he loves no one but himself—you need to put him back into your past."

She stood up, offered me her hand, and I allowed her to lead me into the living room. We sat down on the couch that faced the window. I slid over closer and hugged her.

"You have cared for me and supported me much more than Mamá ever did. I love you Nana. I'm going to miss you so much when I go to Merida."

"What are you telling me?" she asked.

"Well, as you said, I need to make some practical plans, and I figure the only way to give my daughter a chance for a normal life is to move back where we used to live. The neighbors will remember our family. However, they won't be aware of how we've lived for the past sixteen years. If I'm asked, I'll say that I married, but my husband disappeared after Tlatelolco. Actually, that's the truth in a way, and it's all I'll tell anyone. In our old house I'll be able to remain almost cloistered while I wait for the birth."

Hortensia clucked and fussed with me, trying to get me to change my mind.

"But why do you want to invent stories and stay hidden away? Even under these circumstances, having a child should be a joy to share."

I looked at my feet and traced them along the design of the throw rug. The rings of yarn went round and round, just like my thoughts.

"I am willing to live a lie—a big one—so my daughter will not have to suffer taunting in the future. People can be so quick to judge. If no one sees me while I'm pregnant, the sudden appearance of my child will cause excitement, but I bet the rumblings won't be nasty."

Hortensia's voice sounded as though it came from far away.

"Will you be able to continue your job with Toño and Paul? Otherwise, what kind of work will you look for?"

Tears threatened to take the place of my words. My brother Toño had given me my start in life and I loved my job with his company. I tried to get up, but Nana urged me to stay sitting beside her.

"I sure can't keep my old position," I told her. "Traveling would be too hard with a baby. I'm trusting that something will present itself once I'm in Merida."

Hortensia held my face in her two warm hands, paused, and then made the sign of the cross over my heart. She usually came to decisions after much cautious thought, but that afternoon, she did not deliberate at all. She let go of me, sat up as tall as she could, and taking a deep breath, she commenced to save my life.

"I have often dreamed about returning to Yucatan," she said, "but I never mentioned it to anyone in the family because you all seemed happy here in La Capital. But I could go with you, Amalia, and take care of the baby when she comes. It's been a long time since I've had a little girl to care for. It would feel like a new start."

I wanted to collapse with relief, but I felt like a total hypocrite.

"As soon as I decided to go to Merida, I wanted to ask you to come with me, but I don't know how I can do that. It's not fair for me to uproot you. I have always criticized my mother for making you come along when we moved here."

Yet, how I needed her to come with me to Merida. The two of us had shared all the major events of my life since my birth thirty-one years ago.

"I know you need me. You'll feel more confident and better able to handle everything," said Hortensia. "Take me with you, Amalia."

My gratitude washed over me like a huge warm wave. I let the tears come. I pulled Hortensia's hands to my lips and kissed them.

She bowed and took my face in her hands. "You are *Mi' ja*—my daughter. We have lots to sort out. Maybe I'll stay here tonight."

She had made up her mind. And though I knew I was being selfish, I needed her so much. I swore that somehow I would make it up to her.

Hortensia asked how I planned to dispose of my apartment and my Mexico City life. I held up my arms. I had been so focused on my baby that I hadn't given much thought to the dozens of practical details.

Both of us well remembered the old house in Merida and we discussed what furniture, linens, china, and art we should carry with us. We made lists, so many lists. By seven o'clock we both needed quiet time and we kissed one another good night.

I knew that as soon as she closed her door, she would light candles and burn copal incense at the small altar she had set up in the spare bedroom. She would surely speak with her spirit guides about the momentous decisions we'd made this afternoon. Their opinion would cement her decision or bring up new questions.

While my nana slept, I had a vivid dream.

I found myself in a meadow, between two rolling Chiapas hillsides. I could feel the bracing, high-altitude air, and smell the pine and eucalyptus forests. Maybe I'd been there before and yet, a creek I'd never seen ran down the grassy slope. On the edge sat a young girl. She grimaced as she pulled an ivory comb through the tangles in her dark curls.

"Can I help you fix your hair?" I asked her.

"It's really messy," she warned.

And in truth, knots were spread all through. But I started at the back, along the nape of her neck and worked my way to the crown. When I had finished, I dipped my hands in the water and ran the cool liquid over her bare arms and legs.

"I want to jump in. Will you come with me?" she asked.

"No," I said, "but I'll wait here and watch you."

The girl could swim like an otter. After ten minutes, she threw herself back on to the bank. When she turned I knew I was looking at my daughter—the open grin was just like Alejandro's.

five

At eight the following morning, as I nibbled on a saltine, Hortensia came into my room trailing the long extension cord from the hallway phone.

"It's Toño. He says he wants you to go on an extra pre-Christmas buying trip," she said.

I hoped the crackers had settled my stomach and that I'd be able to talk. I knew the pregnancy couldn't be all that was causing my nausea. I felt selfish and guilty. Hortensia had offered to leave the world she'd created for herself in Mexico City and come with me to Merida. Even though my parents knew nothing about my situation, her leaving would disrupt their lives. I would upset my brother right now, and soon, my sister too. We weren't a strong family; the complications I'd set in motion would be like rocks thrown into the revolving wheels of a bicycle.

"Hi there, Toño."

"To you, too, but what's going on? Hortensia says you can't go on another shopping excursion. The wall hangings you sent last month—the ones with embroidered birds—are all gone. We need more," he said.

"I can't travel right now, and really, I won't be able to make any more trips for quite some time. In fact, I've written you a resignation letter."

I could picture Toño staring at the phone's receiver. I had never turned him down before, not once. When he found his voice, my brother sounded wounded, or irritated. I never could be sure with him.

"This must be serious. Why won't you talk to me about whatever is bothering you? Paul and I have always been here for you."

"You'll just have to trust me on this. I have my reasons and as soon as I know what I'm doing, I'll tell you and Paul the whole story."

He hung up abruptly and I looked at Hortensia.

"Oh, Nana, I'm asking too much!"

"Amalia, what else can you do? Bringing your baby into the world is more important than anything else. But there are two things you must do before we talk anymore—eat something and drink this tea I've prepared."

Holding up a full mug, she told me it would be good for both the baby and me. I gagged just thinking about how vile it probably tasted.

"What's in it?"

"All manner of magic and merriment . . . vitamins and vitality . . . promises and prophesies. Believe me, Amalia."

Hortensia gave everything a mystical explanation. My gut heaved again and she brought me an ice cube in a napkin.

"Lick on this for a little while and then drink your tea."

The coolness on my lips brought some relief. I raised my head to look at my nana.

"How do you keep yourself so together when everything around you is falling apart?" I asked.

"Amalia, you'll feel better after eating a little. I'll toast some biscuits and brew some more tea for you."

I didn't protest. I knew it would be hopeless to try and sway her. She pulled out a chair for me at the kitchen table. The smell of warm pastry stuffed with a mild melted cheese and smoked ham threatened to send me stumbling to the bathroom again, but once I actually got the first bites down, I realized how famished I was. I nibbled away until I'd eaten everything Hortensia had put in front of me.

The morning's rough start seemed to be over. I showered, braided my hair, and got dressed. Like Hortensia, I wore a loose *huipil,* but mine came from Oaxaca. The color suited my complexion and it matched the jade beads looped around my neck. There, presentable but comfortable, I padded out of my room to join my nana.

I found her in the living room looking over the flat rooftops of the neighboring buildings. I could smell traces of last night's copal incense and a cold draft blew into the apartment through the two-centimeter gap between the windowpane and the casing. She had her eyes closed and she didn't hear me walk into the room. She was chanting in a low voice and I knew by the cadence that she had entered into communication with the spirit world. Witnessing this always unnerved me, but I paid attention, hoping to pick up clues as to how she might really be feeling about the move.

"Away from the ghosts of my past, I have made a good life," she said. "When I get back to Yucatan, will I be seen again as just the humble village girl?"

After saying that, Hortensia must have sensed my presence; she stopped, turned, and gave me a big smile.

"Oh, Amalia! I didn't realize you were there! Does it bother you when I invoke the guides?"

"It doesn't bother me, but it does strike me as strange when you talk to them as though they were in the room."

"But they are in the room, and the goddesses answer me. They are in favor of our move, Amalia."

Like many women of the Latina culture, Hortensia has an unshakable faith in La Virgen de Guadalupe. My nana believes that she can speak directly with La Virgen, with Ixel, the Mayan fertility goddess, and with Tonánzin, the Aztec mother of us all. She recognizes the three as representations of the same Divine Mother. However, she treats them as separate entities, like a female Holy Trinity. Her faith is at the heart of who she is; it sustains her every day.

"Is that why you left your village and came to live in Merida? Did the goddesses say you should?"

She laughed and gathered up her ceremonial paraphernalia.

"At the time I didn't even realize that the voices came through the goddesses. Let's sit down like we did yesterday and I'll tell you how it all happened. My childhood home was a plain town with a pretty name: La Villa de Santa Cecilia."

Hortensia had already told me that. Except for the centuries-old Catholic church, there were no large buildings in Santa Cecilia. I closed my eyes as she described the six oldest women of the village painfully climbing up the broad steps to mop the limestone floor. Their arthritic hands would scrape the black candle soot off the walls, and they'd set out bouquets of wild margaritas in front of the statues of the saints. Sometimes, before feast days, one of their grandsons would slap a fresh coat of whitewash over the most crumbling places in the plaster. Nothing more was ever done to enhance the village. No one kept a flower garden and no one worried about repairing the worn *chozas*—the one-room, thatch-roofed huts that everyone lived in.

Since girlhood, Hortensia had received visions, but of course she didn't call them that at first. She said she never found it strange that she could *see* who would be bitten by a snake before it happened, and she thought everyone had the ability to *know* when a lie was being told to them.

At first her mother thought that an overactive imagination must be making Hortensia say the things she did. But after the ten-year-old foretold a hurricane, she began to tiptoe around her daughter.

"Never tell anyone about these 'visions.' They are the work of the Devil!"

"I'm trying to block them out," Nana had told her mamá. "But I have little control. They come or they don't." She said it deeply saddened her when her mother turned her back in rejection.

In Santa Cecilia, the homes were grouped together in family compounds with several generations living together. The women cared for the children, the livestock, and kitchen gardens; they cooked, sewed and did housework. Their husbands cultivated the communal land. Such proximity gave everyone a sense of security. But it also created inflexible attitudes; Hortensia said the villagers argued about who worked the hardest and who deserved additional rewards.

The main crop was a type of agave called *sisal*. Three or four times a year, a buyer arrived to purchase the long fibers that the men pounded out by hand from the mature spiky leaves of the plants. These strong strands were packed into tight bales and pulled by mules along a Decoville rail network that connected Yucatan's largest haciendas.

The people of Santa Cecilia needed money to buy the things they were unable to grow or make. Sadly, from the *sisal* they received too few pesos to pay for even their most basic needs.

In the Haciendas' steam-powered manufacturing plants, rope and other items were fashioned from the sinuous fiber. These products were in high demand from the agricultural and shipping industries, so the hacienda owners made handsome profits. No wonder they had their own name for *sisal*. They called it—*oro verde*—green gold.

Every spring, Hortensia joined the rest of the villagers in praying for the end of the yearly drought. Unless something unexpected happened, they had nothing to do but sit around waiting for dark clouds to roll across the sky. My nana hated the boredom, but one blustery March morning, La Madrina—The Godmother—arrived on the weekly bus from Merida. The inhabitants of Santa Cecilia feared the faraway, unfathomable capital city; only a handful of them had ever been there.

When La Madrina climbed down off the bus, the west wind got under her full-skirted dress and it billowed out like the sail of a boat. She strode through the streets like a sea commander. The children followed behind chanting, "*Buenos días,* Madrina."

The villagers called her a *dzul*—a non-Maya. Her husband's family had owned the nearby hacienda for generations, and having lived in Santa Cecilia for so many years, she spoke Yucatec Mayan. Because she alone had extra funds for baptisms, funerals, or weddings, she had become La Madrina to all.

The little ones kissed her cheek and stroked her hand. They hoped for some *dulces* or a few *centavos*, and La Madrina didn't disappoint them. When she arrived at my nana's family compound, she handed out sweet, chewy marzipans, and small coins. Off the children ran with their treats. Hortensia's mother showed the godmother into their home and sat her in the place of honor. As is the pueblo custom, La Madrina was served alone at the table and ate first. She quickly gobbled up half the stewed hen that Hortensia's mother had prepared.

For hours the family had looked forward to that meal. There had been no meat in their bowls for several weeks. And once again, it looked as though they'd have precious little to share.

La Madrina stopped chewing and dabbed her lips with a monogrammed Irish linen handkerchief. She seemed to be full and all eyes hungrily watched the five pieces of chicken still floating in the sauce. But when she harshly called for Hortensia, the rest forgot about the food and waited to see what would happen next.

"You ungrateful girl. Let me look at you," the godmother said. Hortensia jumped at her words. What had she done?

Her hands trembled as she stood in front of the overbearing, overweight guest. Those who had gathered around pointed and laughed. She bowed her head to hide her anger and made fists to stop her hands from shaking. She didn't look at La Madrina. She'd learned that passive conduct usually saved her from the worst punishments.

La Madrina raised her arms high in the air and pointed a finger at Hortensia. "Girl, your mother asked me to find work for you, away from here. Everyone will be better off. You are unmarried, yet you're determined to dismiss your local suitor. It's clear you'll be an old maid. You're an embarrassment and a burden your family can't endure. I've made arrangements to take you away from here. As of tomorrow, you'll be employed as a servant in the home of Don Antonio Vásquez and his wife Doña Teresa in Merida."

Her parents had arranged a marriage for her, they sure had. But she would never consider that man. He was much older and his first wife had died from an untreated infection. He had grown angry and mean. Hortensia's father wanted her married because he desperately needed the economic boost of another man who could bring in money. Hortensia refused to cooperate and that's how she came to live in Merida.

This was not her choice. Yet she understood the rules. Everyone expected girls like her to do as they were told. Hortensia wanted to cry, but she would not give the bullies any more enjoyment. She felt relieved when they went back to what they were doing. For them, the fun was over.

Hortensia said that she took a long, hard look at the tired scene: mangy dogs sniffing through the garbage and a handful of children playing with *kinbombas*—homemade toys— in front of the house. The men stretched out in their hammocks while the women continued with their never-ending chores: splitting and chopping dry wood, scrubbing and hanging clothes, getting pots of meager food ready for the smoky cooking fires. She asked herself, *What will there be to miss? Maybe leaving Santa Cecilia would be a good thing.*

~~~

Half a year later, Doña Teresa summoned the young maid to her parlor. She must have wondered what she'd done—yet again—to anger her mistress. Hortensia entered the room, hugging the wall, with her head lowered.

"Hortensia, you have a visitor."

And there sat La Madrina. She looked closely at Hortensia and stretched out a hand to touch her arm.

"I'll give you two some privacy," Mamá said as she left the two alone.

Hortensia looked for an escape. She had no idea what would happen next.

"Don't be scared. Doña Teresa says you are doing an excellent job and she plans to give you new responsibilities. She will soon have another child and you will become the nana."

Hortensia didn't believe her, but her ears strained to hear every word.

"I have come to tell you that you should not be afraid," La Madrina said. "Now, tell me about the visions."

Hortensia said she looked again for a way out of the parlor. The older woman put a hand on her arm to reassure her.

"On the day I brought you to Merida, I suspected you had *the gift*. Premonition is a blessing. You will likely channel more abilities as you age. I'm wondering—would you like to meet others who are like you?"

Young Hortensia's legs still twitched with the urge to run; she suspected that Madrina was playing a trick or testing her in some way. However, her need to know was a tiny bit stronger than her fear—to meet others like herself was a constant yearning. She knew they were nearby because she could sense them. Sometimes she'd be in a room, or walking to the market, and her ears would start to ring, the temperature lowered, and the light would turn misty. Shapes would swirl around, but she could never actually understand what caused the strange perception. Her eyes widened—she felt a bit like that around La Madrina.

"Yes, I have abilities like yours Hortensia. I know why your mother felt frightened of you."

"I thought she was angry with me. She told me to end the visions."

"No, Hortensia, your mother couldn't understand you. She felt afraid. Did you obey her?"

For the first time, Hortensia found herself speaking with someone who could answer the questions that had tormented her for years.

"If I never asked for the visions, why do I get them and how can I stop them?"

"With time, you'll learn the answers to those questions. I hope you'll let me help you, and I trust you understand why I had to get you away from that ignorant village. I was afraid they would decide you were a witch and they'd hurt you—it has happened before, you know."

My nana could not be angry at La Madrina for the charade. She had done her a favor by getting her out of that place.

From then on, the two saw each other every Sunday afternoon. Doña Teresa gave her maid permission to go with La Madrina to the church of San José de la Montaña. My nana got to know other girls there and learned that La Madrina had also saved them. Much of what Hortensia knows about using her spiritual powers comes from the congregation at San José.

La Madrina died eleven years after bringing the scared village girl to our house. In Merida, La Madrina was known as Doña Jacinta O'Horan, my mother's aunt. On Sundays, she often came home with Hortensia after church. She'd have dinner and play with my brother, my sister, and me. I remember how much we liked her jokes, little games, and the marzipans she always carried in her pockets.

Actually, my mother had received the house as part of her dowry from my grandmother—Doña Julia O'Horan—La Madrina's sister. The uncommon red hair and light-colored eyes that all we children have also came from our Irish grandmother.

Hortensia and I loved each other. But when I started school, I felt betrayed because she would not help me with my lessons. Nana made all kinds of excuses. But I soon saw through her. She had never learned to read or write and for some pitiful reason, this made her feel ashamed. I started to share what my teacher showed me each day, and it didn't take long for Nana to figure out the initially confusing letters. She began writing stories about her life in the village, about her beliefs, and about our family. She also recorded traditional remedies for a wide range of ailments.

Our day-long conversation came to an end when Nana said, "Let's get something to eat. I see there's still some cooked chicken. I'll add it to some rice and make a green salad."

I slept soundly that night and awoke to the smell of coffee brewing. Maybe I'd get up and try a little. I found Hortensia dressed, waiting for me in the living room. After a loving hug, she gave me a good look over and must have been satisfied.

"Amalia, if you're feeling well, I'm going home. We both have lots to do. I'll be back on the night of the 19th and I'll help you prepare for your Christmas party."

"That's right!" I said. "I still need to buy everything. Nana, I don't know how to thank you."

"Don't worry about that. Call me if you need anything at all."

six

I placed Beethoven's "Ode to Joy" on the stereo and felt myself soar with the crescendo.

Like a chess player plotting strategy, I had to carefully plan each day prior to my departure for Merida. The Christmas party would give me the opportunity to tell friends and family that I'd be leaving Mexico City. And thanks to Hortensia, I would not be leaving alone. But the jarring telephone spoiled my mood and when I picked up the receiver, I feared I'd be ill. The caller got right to the point.

"Hello, Amalia. There have been new developments and I need to talk to you about the baby."

My heart stopped. Had Alejandro change his mind? Did he want the child to bring us together after all? No, his tone sounded too abrupt, and remembering his behavior the last time I saw him, he couldn't possibly imagine that I would want that. Although I felt uneasy about facing him again, I didn't want the scene at the café to be the one that would repeat in my mind forever. I agreed to meet him at my home that night.

When I opened the door, he flashed a smile that a few weeks ago would have made me run into his arms. Dressed in a business suit, his sharp ensemble contrasted starkly with my jeans and sweater. He brought flowers that gave off a heady sweet aroma.

"Come inside," I said. "We'll sit in the living room."

He placed the bouquet in my hands and headed immediately for "his" couch. I left him and turned toward the kitchen to put the blooms in water and to bolster my resolve. *Breathe deeply!* I coached myself. Pasting on a smile, I strode in carrying a vase of fragrant white lilies. I centered them on the coffee table. "They are lovely—thank you." I didn't offer him anything to eat or drink.

It seemed odd to see him in business clothes. The Alejandro I knew wore jeans and raggedy shirts that hugged his torso.

"I've just come from a meeting. After Tlatelolco, the administration promoted those of us who had given our all in the students' cause. I am now next in line to be the chair of the Political Science Department. Once a month we meet with the university president. They expect us to wear suits. Looks pretty good, don't you think?"

I couldn't believe what I was hearing and seeing. Alejandro still had his long dark ponytail, but his sideburns were shaped. He said that the most politically active academics had been rewarded by the very establishment they had fought. Lies! Alejandro and his colleagues had been bought off. Didn't he understand that?

A shadow passed across his face. He knew by my shocked expression that I wanted to question him further and he distracted me by placing a silver-wrapped box down on the table.

"I—*uh*—brought a little gift. Why don't you open it?"

He kept a formal distance. Rather than seducing me, I realized that he wanted something else this evening. I looked at him suspiciously as I picked up the shiny package. Inside several layers of crisp tissue paper, I found a circular white porcelain plaque with a plump Raphaelite cherub embossed on the front; the name of a well-known seventeenth-century Italian ceramist had been inscribed on the back. The exquisite plate was a peace offering. Did he think I could be bribed too?

"I found it in an antique shop in La Laguilla, and I thought of the baby. I know you collect this sort of ornaments. Do you like it?" A smile started to turn up his lips and he moved closer.

I closed up the box again, pushed it back toward him and looked at the floor. "I have already given you all I have to give—you didn't want to keep it. I can't accept this."

I couldn't see his face, but I knew my words had made him wince.

"Amalia, you have no idea how much I regret what I said to you at the café. I have no excuse, except that your news came as such a shock. Nonetheless, as unfairly as I've acted toward you, now that I've had a chance to think it through, I feel incredibly happy about the baby."

I tried to keep my features passive, but I couldn't stop my eyebrows from shooting up.

"How has this change come about, Alejandro? When we last saw each other, you were absolutely negative about her."

True to form, Alejandro had an agenda. He ignored my question, and I quickly understood why he'd come here tonight.

"You know I can't leave Susana, especially now when she's having a difficult time. But Amalia, the fact that you and I can't live together doesn't mean we can't still be a part of one another's lives. I want to contribute to my daughter's care. I want the chance to know her and to see you often."

I threw my arms into the air. "You want to set me up as a mistress?"

He looked on the verge of an icy retort, but I fended him off with one very obvious question.

"Why don't you and Susana have your own babies?"

He stammered trying to get out his next sentence. "I told you that Susana is in poor shape. She cannot have children. Her inverted uterus keeps her from conceiving."

"When did you discover this?"

He absentmindedly caressed the silver box.

"We tried to start a family with no luck and finally we saw a specialist. The diagnosis was confirmed to us a year ago. Susana fell into a deep depression and now with your news, she has taken another turn for the worse."

"So she knows you that you are the father of my baby?"

"Yes. I knew she'd be devastated, but I figured she had to hear it from me. She fell to the floor when I told her. I feel awful for what I've done to her and to you, but as I said, I am thrilled about the baby."

He gently set the silver box in front of me again and looked expectantly into my eyes.

"How can you sit there and tell me that Susana is 'devastated' but you are 'thrilled' about the baby? You are so out of touch with her feelings. How can you be so careless with her?"

"Well, I hope that Susana will feel better when she has the chance to at least be a step mom. She and I can offer the baby many advantages, Amalia. Have you thought about joint custody?"

I wanted to slap his arrogant face. "And what gives you that right? All we did was 'fuck,' isn't that what you said? Now you want to stake claim on this baby, the only biological child you're likely to have. After all that's happened, how can you think for one second that I would be willing to share *my baby* with you and Susana? Get out of here!"

Alejandro didn't move. He plied me with every argument he could think of.

"The past is the past. We want to be part of the baby's life. My wife, who is so good to me, deserves to share in the experience. We'll provide financial support. The baby will have a better future with our involvement," he droned on and on.

I would have none of it. When he let me walk out of that café alone, he abdicated all rights to this baby. She would be my daughter, mine alone. I would raise her—and I would not let Susana see her, let alone regard herself as stepmother.

I stood up, crossed back to the apartment's entrance, and held the door open. As he reluctantly came forward, I couldn't help thinking that this was the same spot where he'd re-entered my life on October 2. In just ten weeks our relationship had taken every turn possible. All my emotional reserves had been used up. "You have to go now."

He tried one more ploy. "I'm sorry if what I've proposed has come as a shock, but think, Amalia, think about my offer. We have to consider our little one first and do what's best for her."

Why had I let him come here? I should have known he would try to get something from me. He'd called her "our little one." He had it all wrong. She belonged to me.

I thought of my child as a delicate morning glory climbing up along a hidden wall. She needed love and nurturing and I provided that. But I also recognized the truth: Her little tendrils would keep Alejandro and I bound to one another.

I didn't go to the window and watch him leave. I felt emptied out, but not despondent as I had at other times during the past ten weeks. I had a plan; Hortensia would help. I accepted that Alejandro and I would have a long, complicated relationship, but for now at least, I felt as though I had staved him off. I caressed my child through my skin and thought about sitting back down in the living room. But the scene with Alejandro had worn me out. The best thing would be for me to go to bed.

～

I woke up feeling as though I'd run a marathon the night before. There was no winning or losing when it came to Alejandro, but at least I didn't let him leave me in a fit of tears. Keeping him out of my mind was the best I could hope for.

I'd bought all the food we'd need. It looked to be an unbelievable amount. Hortensia arrived, ready to bake cookies, roll out pies, stuff birds, chop fruit, and peel vegetables.

"Are you well today?" she asked.

I forced my voice to sound emotionally strong and I hugged her. I didn't want her probing for any details about last night.

"I will miss my life here. I have my apartment, I make good money, and have lots of friends. I doubt our adjustment will be hassle free in Merida. Let's enjoy these last weeks we have."

"Start with the heat!" she reminded me. "Except from November through March, the temperatures are high every single day. In that kind of climate, the mid-day hours are a write-off. The best thing you can do is take a siesta."

"Maybe we should practice that right now," I teased.

She gave me a wink and told me to get back to work.

"We have a lot of hungry people to feed and entertain in a day and-a-half's time," she said.

My nana fluttered around my kitchen happily preparing a feast we would remember for a long time: an American-style stuffed turkey and a Yucatecan *lechón*—suckling pig—four salads, including the traditional *Ensalada de Noche Buena* made with fruit, and others made from fresh greens, plus her rice pilaf and scalloped potatoes. Breads, both savory and sweet, and desserts from crème caramel to *torta del cielo*.

I concentrated on trimming the tree, setting the tables, and wrapping gifts. Maybe in a few years, I'd host a Yuletide dinner in Merida. Who could know? Of the thirty people who'd be coming, family made up half of that number. A few of our best clients and six of my favorite friends completed the list.

At my annual Christmas dinner, Hortensia and I always wore special outfits; she had a *huipil* embroidered with poinsettias and I had my red velvet dress. Did I imagine it fit a little tighter?

Company began arriving at five on the dot. The decorated evergreen lit up the room with a soft multi-colored glow. My collection of handcrafted ornaments hung from the branches. After some hesitation, I added the little plaque that Alejandro had left behind, but I placed it well to the back. I didn't want Hortensia to ask where it came from.

Smells of candied pears and apples, rich meats, and scrumptious accompaniments wafted from the kitchen. Armando Manzanero and Angelica María's new album was playing on the stereo, but the music could barely be heard above all the excited voices. My father kept happily occupied at the bar making *ronpope*—eggnog—for everyone except Tio Manuel, who would only drink double whiskeys, and my mother, who would drink no alcohol.

"*¡Feliz Navidad!*" I called out. Expecting my usual words about the significance of the holiday season, everyone grew quiet and listened attentively.

"This Christmas dinner is special for me. It's the last one I'll be celebrating in this apartment."

The surprised voices asked if I would be moving into a house.

"Indeed, I will be, but not one near here. I'm going back to Merida and Hortensia's coming with me. We'll be leaving soon—next month in fact. The old family home needs a lot of work and I want to supervise the repairs myself."

Only my parents saw this coming because a few days ago, at my request, Hortensia told them about our plans. I got bombarded with questions, and I did my best to dodge and deflect the pointed ones.

"You'll be living in the Santiago house?" my cousin Luisa asked. "I remember visiting there one summer. We went to the beach, too. I hope you'll invite me to come see you."

I hugged her close. "You'll always be welcome."

"What kind of work will you do there?" she wanted to know.

"I am going to start a new life. Maybe I'll go back to school. You know that I have always wanted to study architecture."

When Hortensia came from the kitchen, she was swarmed by the guests and I got a break from the Inquisition.

"You can't be going, too. I'll miss you so much," one of my sister's sons told Nana.

She stroked his handsome face with her gentle hands. "I know, Pépe. I'll miss you too," she said, "but one day you'll visit us and then you'll understand why your Auntie Amalia and I are going back. Merida is a wonderful place." After giving him a quick kiss, she announced: "Come on everyone—dinner is served!"

The guests rushed toward the table and took their fill of the holiday spread. I could see Mamá and Papá sitting quietly to one side and I went over to them. My father knew a firm decision when faced with one. He said simply and formally, "I am proud of how you came up with the idea of moving back to Yucatan. I wish you every success in Merida."

My mother looked as though she would choke if she articulated her feelings on the subject. I could also tell by the way her eyes appraised me that she suspected there might be more to my decision than I let on. But rather than dwelling on that thorny possibility, she moved her head up and down in agreement with Papá.

When they got up to take their turn at the buffet, she turned and tightly held me. "I will miss you, Amalia. Is there nothing I can say to make you change your mind?"

I couldn't believe it. For so many years, my mother had been unaffectionate. Since my early teens, when I refused to have anything to do with her dressmaking business, she disapproved of everything I did. For a few seconds, I toyed with the idea of changing my mind and staying in Mexico City. Could Mamá and I arrive at a peaceful compromise? Would she accept my daughter and allow us all to live as we choose? What a shame I'd never be able to answer that question. For my baby's sake, there would be no better option than going to Merida.

The only vocal opposition came from an unexpected source. My sister Manuela's eyes flashed blue darts at me as she threw back her shoulders and pushed her auburn bangs out of her eyes.

"So there goes the last of my siblings. I am now the only one of us still in Mexico City—looking after Mamá and Papá as they age will fall to me—and you're taking Hortensia with you to boot. What a wonderful Christmas present."

Her comment cut deep because, in many ways, I saw my older sister as an example to follow. She had seen Mamá's *salón* as her career opportunity. Manuela eagerly learned everything our mother could teach her, and then she developed her own unique style. Now she was indisputably the maven of trendy couture in Mexico City. Before leaving, I wished I could confide in her and tell her the full reason for my move. Motherhood had been her justification for staying in her loveless marriage. If she'd known I planned to return to Merida so that my child would stand a chance of growing up in a nurturing environment, maybe she'd not have been so harsh.

seven

My body felt as plump as a peach, yet the reflection in the mirror was not anything close to that of a pregnant woman.

Last spring when I had visited London's Carnaby Street, I couldn't resist the pencil-straight, electric-blue mini dress. Accessorized with a silver chain belt, fishnet tights, spike-heeled boots, and a black suede jacket—maybe it was a bit much for a trip to the airport—but I planned on going for a late lunch. So what the hell.

An alert driver watched from behind the wheel of one of the plentiful lime-green VW taxis lining the curb just down the street from my building. I climbed in. "Mexicana Airlines arrivals terminal please."

Settling back as best I could in the back seat, I dug out Toño's letter from my oversized purse. On the first read, I didn't think it sounded critical, but since my sister had been so upset about my plans to move, I wanted to read Toño's letter over again before I saw him—to make sure I hadn't missed anything:

> Dearest Amalia,
>
> I received your notice of resignation and I am worried. What's this about leaving Mexico City and returning to live in Merida? A sudden decision is not your usual behavior, and I can't help but think you have some kind of serious problem. I will not give you a chance to dissuade my visit. Paul and I will arrive on New Year's Eve on our usual flight at 2:10 p.m.

The jerky movements of the cab didn't allow me to keep the page still, so I stuffed it back into my bag. The cabbie careened through the traffic like a maniac. I leaned forward and touched his shoulder, "Take it easy!" Was he deaf? He didn't slow down at all. My left hand clutched the back of the front bucket seat in a hopeless attempt at keeping myself upright. I hardly breathed until we arrived at our destination. Once he'd screeched to a halt in front of the terminal, he turned around and faced me with a demonic grin.

"Under twenty minutes! A record!" he said.

Exiting quickly in such a short skirt involved some minor gymnastics. Several men standing nearby openly enjoyed viewing the back of my legs and my tucked rump. I shook my head, exhaled my relief, and pressed my clothes into place. "*Buenas tardes,*" I said stiffly. They laughed like teenagers with a girlie magazine.

To compose myself, I plunked down on a metal mesh bench just outside the entrance. I watched a quick-moving teenager hawk commemorative Olympics souvenirs. While the luggage emerged from the shuttle bus, he sold ten flags to a group of tourists. He had to jump out of the way when three private radio limos—filled with presumptuous businessmen and self-aggrandizing politicians—roared up to the curb.

I wondered how young people like him felt. He probably had friends who had been hurt—maybe even killed—at Tlatelolco. And less than three months later, the directors of the massacre lived their lives as though nothing had happened. Their power remained intact, but beneath the outward façade, a truce had been breached, and I doubted it would ever heal.

I had wanted to speak with Manuela before this last day of the year, but she seemed to be avoiding my calls. I felt miserable being on the outs with her. Maybe Toño would think of a way for me to make peace, short of telling her about the baby, of course. Mamá always knew when her eldest daughter had a secret, and she'd wheedle it out of her in less time than it took her to hem a skirt.

I thought about how strong my sister had been all through her own pregnancy. Mamá, Papá, Hortensia, and I had arrived on her doorstep after we left Merida. Pushing me forward, Mamá had told Manuela, "We had to leave in such a hurry. We had to get Amalia off her reckless path. We had no time to make housing arrangements."

I held back my temper. Before leaving Merida, Hortensia had confided, "Your father has debts and we have to leave Yucatan for a while. Please don't cause your mother to suffer more. Let her use you as the excuse for our flight." Only because Hortensia had asked, I accepted the ruse.

Despite her expanding abdomen, Manuela had welcomed us into her cramped home and she deflected her husband's anger. She also agreed to help Mamá with her fledgling dressmaking business. Bent over the old Singer, often well into the night, she seemed to be in communion with that perfectly adjusted and oiled sewing machine. It sang like a Stradivarius. One day Manuela felt inspired to paint a band of red dots around the neckline of a soft gray silk dress she'd just sewn. Then she took some leftover crimson satin and made a matching shawl. Her client danced around the room, delighted with how those simple touches had turned a plain shift into an ensemble. This detailing would become Manuela's signature.

One afternoon, a minor actress named Dolores took one look at Manuela's work and said, "I want you to create a dress that will convey my deep passion for life." Wow!

Manuela's swollen midriff grazed the floor as she threw swirls of vibrant oranges, pinks, and reds onto frothy chiffon. Once the paint had dried, she cut and sewed the fabric into what could not really be called a dress. It was like wearable art. When tall, voluptuous Dolores tried on the gown, she stood speechless. Later that month, she wore Manuela's original creation to a big film gala, and after that event, Dolores won more important roles, and orders poured into the Salón. My sister felt like she'd won the lottery.

Mamá and Manuela would discuss the new styles and were not shy about telling their customers what would, and what would not, suit their different figure types. Five months after opening, they employed an additional two seamstresses.

Angel Gustavo—Manuela's husband—pretty much stayed out of the way. He had his work at the hospital and his "other life" in after-hours cocktail lounges. When he found himself at home, he did not upset his wife. He was a doctor after all, and he knew she needed to keep calm. He wanted her healthy and for the pregnancy to be problem free.

In La Capital, Papá had also fulfilled a lifelong dream; he became a professional musician. He felt happy dressed in his white *guayabera* with a guitar under his arms. He had joined Las Aguilas, a Yucatecan-style trio that played for parties and at small night clubs. They were managed by El Grande, a fat, balding obnoxious man who had connections in the entertainment industry. My father played almost every night of the week. El Grande kept forty percent of the earnings and split the remaining sixty among the members of the group.

Mamá's *Salón* flourished and she taunted my father nonstop. "You don't earn enough to buy the beans for this family!" she'd say.

"It won't always be like this," he promised, holding his own. He would not give up his musical career even though Mamá wanted him to get a job at one of the nearby factories. During the business day, she banished him from her workplace. Even as young as I was, I could see that my parents' relationship got worse every week. Mamá resented Papá, but her partnership with Manuela—and their combined dressmaking genius—made her glad to be in La Capital.

Manuela worked right up to the evening before she delivered. The next morning, I knew something shocking had happened when I saw Hortensia rushing up the street. I'd not even realized that my sister had started labor in the night and that Angel Gustavo had taken her, Mamá, and Hortensia to the hospital.

My father looked alarmed. "I don't think I've ever seen Nana hurry like that."

Hortensia dropped into the chair I held out for her and managed to say, "Two, two . . . there are two!"

"Two . . . what are you talking about?" my father asked her.

"Two babies, Manuela had twins."

My sister had a big tummy, but what pregnant woman doesn't? She'd had pre-natal care and her husband is a doctor. How could this have been missed?

Hortensia rolled her eyes. "It happens," she said.

Papá and I rushed away to see for ourselves.

I remember their wrinkly red faces, tightly-closed eyes, tiny noses and O-shaped mouths. They both had caps of silky light brown hair.

"They are not identical, but they strongly resemble one another," said Manuela.

Yet from their first hours of life, we could tell them apart. Once home, they slept together in the same crib. Although they'd be laid down quite a distance apart, Max would squirm his way over to Pépe and practically squish him. Pépe would try to ease himself away, but as soon as he'd put a little space between the two, Max would inch closer and closer until poor Pépe was jammed right up against the bars of the crib. There he'd stay, resigned to his brother's needy presence.

Even though Mamá had resolved to stay aloof, when Manuela's twins came into the world, she let those two tiny boys into her heart and they chipped away at the bitterness she wore like a cloak. Life became more pleasant for us all—especially for my father.

~~~

I looked at my watch: two o'clock. I figured I'd better get into the main terminal. Since my brother had gone to live in Texas I'd held this waiting room vigil at least fifty times.

At seventeen, in January 1947, he simply stepped across the border near Juarez and once there, he told everyone that he had just turned twenty. His presence in the border town never raised suspicion; the Americans assumed that he'd be joining up.

"Welcome to America, son. The recruitment station is right over there," said a middle-aged man leaning against the café wall. "I wish they'd take *me*, but I'm a little long in the tooth."

Toño had told me that he didn't understand what the idiom meant, but he smiled as though he did. Even though World War II had finished, conflict loomed in Korea and fresh foot soldiers were needed. The US gladly enlisted Mexican boys in need of a job.

But Toño did not have any intension of joining the American army.

"I'm going to find a job that will make me lots of money," he told us all. Nobody in the family wanted him to leave Mexico, but at the time, none of us knew his secret.

He found a room in a boarding house owned by a couple from Campeche. Señora Catalina smiled proudly as she gave him the key to her best room. Toño tried to look grateful, but he later said that the crocheted patchwork afghan and hanging velvet art pictures of the Sacred Heart of Jesus and Our Lady of Sorrows gave him nightmares.

Toño got to know a neighbor, Paul Sutton. Paul taught Toño to speak better English and showed him how to get along in the gringo world. Their company, El Sol Imports, started with Mexican tile and pottery—flower pots, tableware, and decorative items. Partly because of Toño's ability to speak Spanish and bargain with the suppliers, the business did well from the start. Toño selected the best, most durable pieces and got them through customs. Paul's role involved selling the shipments. Within five years, their company had a well-established reputation and both earned a good income.

During one of his visits to Merida, Toño had told Hortensia, "Paul is as dark as I am fair but, otherwise, we quite resemble one another."

She thought it seemed odd that he talked so much about his new buddy. But she figured it all out when Toño and Paul bought a house together in Austin. Hortensia kept silent, though, and for many years, my parents went on thinking that Toño lived in the US for purely economic reasons.

After Alejandro and I broke up, my brother offered to pay my tuition at the University of Texas, and I felt like a greyhound released into the chute. Even though I would have preferred to study architecture, if Toño thought I should earn my degree in fine arts, fine arts it would be. We agreed that I'd work part time for his company.

One evening, after all the visa requirements and paperwork had been processed, Toño asked me to sit with him and Paul. Plans for my enrollment at the university needed final confirmation. I overflowed with enthusiasm, but my brother knew I was naïve. I wondered why he had moved closer to his friend and wrapped an arm around his waist.

"Before you make the commitment to stay here," he said, "I want you to be sure of what you're getting into. Do you understand what Paul and I mean to each other?"

I had no idea and waited expectantly for further explanation. When it came, I felt bewildered. I saw my brother's nervous, anxious smile and observed the way Paul avoided my quizzical gaze. They thought that I didn't like them anymore. I admitted to being confused, but my blond, green-eyed brother seemed so comfortable with this black-haired, mocha-skinned gringo. What a peculiar but perfect pair. I had to find a way to make them see I would be fine with whatever they meant to each other.

I spread my arms open trying to get both of them into one hug and said, "I'll be the daughter you thought you'd never have."

They laughed and held me tight.

I got teary remembering their tenderness and the Texas home they shared with me. In many ways I played the role of Toño and Paul's little girl. In return, they assumed the role my parents should have taken, and after I graduated we became business partners. I worked as head buyer and traveled throughout Mexico looking for unique handcrafts. I felt overwhelmed with sadness when I thought about losing that adventurous lifestyle and no longer seeing the friends I'd made in the indigenous communities.

And now, after more than a decade of living out of a suitcase, bumping along in rickety buses, and sleeping in huts, I'd be moving on to a new life in Merida. Toño and Paul's investment in me had been enormous, and my carefully cultivated clientele would probably not respond as well to an unfamiliar buyer. Yet I'd given El Sol Imports ten years of loyal service. Wasn't that enough?

~~~

"Amalia!" There they stood, distressed to find me obviously upset.

"You're here!" I stood up and wiped my eyes. An indirect approach wouldn't be appropriate right now. "Before we go to my place, I want to tell you exactly what's going on," I said. "But not here. I think we should go to a restaurant and have lunch."

That caught their interest and they quickly hailed a cab. Relieved to see a white Ford and not the kamikaze green VW, I slid into the back seat and held their hands.

"Let's splurge and go to El Café de Paris," I suggested. "They have private booths and we'll be able to talk. Hortensia will meet us there."

From the moment we entered the restaurant, Toño and Paul were captivated by the French culinary bouquet—sautéed garlic, freshly baked baguette, and succulent stewing meats. The sight of bottle after bottle of excellent Burgundy, Bordeaux, and Cabernet had them salivating. Authentically Gaelic in ambiance and cuisine, this restaurant had a well-deserved reputation among the city's Francophiles. I saw Hortensia and waved. The three of us hustled to where she waited and arranged ourselves along the curved brown leather-covered bench.

"Don't you adore Édith Piaf?" Paul moved his torso in time to her classic "La Vie en Rose," and the maître'd presented us with the impressive menu.

"Let's make up our minds and order right away," I advised. "Sometimes the wait here can stretch out to more than an hour." Something cool to drink would divert my attention from my growling stomach. I felt constantly hungry.

"You're not having a real drink?" Toño asked me.

I lifted my water glass and joked with him.

"No, someone has to keep a clear head."

Although it took quite an effort to keep Toño and Paul away

from heavy topics, I managed to steer the conversation lightly throughout the waiting period. I felt relieved that even the small talk ceased when the foie gras, duck confit, and other classic French dishes arrived. Patting his mouth with a gravy-spotted linen napkin, Paul gushed to the waiter about the superb quality of the meal we'd completely cleaned from our plates.

Dessert ushered in another hush that was as immediate as a change in the weather. But our appetites had been placated and even Paul only picked at his chocolate éclair. Toño seized the opportunity to move things along.

"Amalia, it's time to tell us about your decision. Why are you going to leave the company and move to Merida?"

Prior to coming here, Hortensia and I had decided that Toño and Paul needed the full truth. I pushed away my half-eaten apple tarte.

"Get ready for a shock because my life has taken an unexpected turn over the past two months," I said.

Our late lunch at this French bistro in Mexico City could have inspired a Dalí painting: Me, explaining my pregnancy and the fact that the father, Alejandro, is married to another woman to a gay couple from Austin with our Mayan nanny watching over us all. I spared no details, and when I'd finished, I leaned against Hortensia, panting like a winded runner who had barely managed to make it to the finish line.

Paul looked and acted the part of a knight ready to defend my honor. "Amalia, how can I help?" he asked. "What do you need?"

But Toño's face had turned stop-sign red. He slammed a flattened palm down on the table. "How could this have happened? How are you going to manage financially? And the baby? I don't see how you're going to be able to do this."

The ins and outs of the move and the financial insecurity did scare me, and Toño's reaction sent my stress level soaring still higher.

"I'm frightened," I admitted, "but what do you propose I do?"

Toño stared at me. "Haven't you considered getting rid of it?"

Paul's voice shook. "What are you saying?" He regarded Toño as though seeing him for the first time. "Your sister needs our support. Obviously, she has thought of that option, and if she had wanted to end the pregnancy, she would have done so quietly and we would not be having this conversation. But, Amalia, maybe Toño needs to hear this from you. Do you want to keep your child?"

I looked directly at Toño. "I feel that if she has begun her life, it isn't up to me to end it." I hoped my brother wouldn't blow up further. "I hate the way Alejandro has treated me, but I am carrying his child. I have the best part of him and I am determined to be the best mother I can be."

Toño's shoulders stiffened. "Are you sure Alejandro's the father?"

I could see that this bothered him most of all. His eyes flashed with such anger; he'd have preferred to think I'd conceived this child with anyone else.

"Amalia, how could you have done this? All those years that Paul and I helped you get him out of your head were a waste of time. I can't take this. I have to be alone. The three of you need to go now, but I'm staying. I need some time alone to sort this out."

Paul pulled me to my feet. "Leave him to fight with his demons," he said.

We piled into yet another uncomfortable cab and drove through horrendous holiday traffic to my apartment. As soon as we got inside, Paul collapsed onto the sofa. He said he'd never seen Toño act so coldly, and his imagination put a series of dark scenarios in place. Hortensia sat in the chair facing him. I went to the kitchen, wrapped some ice cubes in a soft face cloth, then sat down by Paul and held the cool compress on his forehead.

"I can't understand," Paul moaned. "Oh God, I wonder where he is?"

I worried that he'd soon be crying. He had worked himself into such a state. Hortensia watched—still as a sphinx—until she finally broke her silence.

"Ten years ago, Toño was so angry at the way Alejandro threw Amalia aside for that arty Susana," she said. "He is her big brother, and he can't bear the idea that someone she can't help loving has broken her heart for the second time."

Paul blew his nose and tried for some composure. "Bringing up money is his way of showing how scared he is for you," Paul said, looking at me. "To be without money is his greatest fear. I should know—he does the same thing with me all the time."

Hortensia still looked disturbed. "But to suggest abortion—this doesn't jibe with the kind of man Toño is," she said.

Paul looked at me and took my hand in his. "Thanks to you, Amalia, we have made buckets of money and we've saved a good deal of it. Having a grandniece can only make us much richer. But Toño isn't seeing that yet."

He looked over at Hortensia and asked her to join the two of us on the couch. She stood and came to sit on my right.

Paul hugged us both. "I'm going to tell you something," he began. "Before we received your letter of resignation, we had started to wonder if maybe it might be time for us to semi-retire."

"You're both too young to retire," Hortensia said. "You have at least 20 more years before you can do that."

"But I'm tired of all the hassle," Paul said. "When I told Toño how I felt, he hinted that he would not mind taking some time off and maybe later get into a different line of work. We fantasized about selling El Sol and then Toño said the wildest thing. "What would you think about moving to Mexico?"

Once Paul started, the confidences kept flowing.

"Toño and I talked a few more times and he got more and more serious about the idea. I knew he'd made up his mind when he told me, 'Get out your decorating books and start planning.' "

"Are you telling me that when my letter arrived, you had already discussed a possible move yourselves?"

"Yes, we had. Toño is like all Yucatecans—he has often regretted leaving his home. He couldn't handle his sexuality, and now he wants to quash those demons and enjoy the opportunities for the sumptuous, civilized living that Merida offers. He's been talking about retiring in Merida since we celebrated our tenth anniversary together. Now that fantasy can even include a little girl to dote on."

I felt my hands start to shake and I sat on them before Paul noticed. "But who knows what will happen now? I am so afraid of Toño's hostile side. What do you think we should do?" I asked.

"I can't think of anything right now. All I know is that if you want to keep your baby, with or without Toño, I will be here for you."

He did not miss the misery and confusion in my eyes, and he took a deep breath. "You are keeping her, there's no question of that, is there?" Paul sounded more plaintive than positive.

"Absolutely, I hope that once we all settle down my baby will bring us together, closer than ever."

Hortensia had a far off look in her eyes. She blinked, stood up, and leaned over the two of us. "She will Amalia. The ways of the goddess are weird, but wise and wonderful."

~~~

I wished I could put my troubles in the hands of an ethereal being like she did, but I worried that Hortensia's conviction might be more wishful thinking than certainty.

Toño didn't come to my apartment that night. When he showed up at ten the next morning he looked ready to fall apart, but Paul had beaten him to it. He'd not slept since leaving my brother at the restaurant.

When Toño saw how drawn and broken his longtime companion looked, he simply said, "I have your suitcase."

Looking at the tattered but intact leather case that we had forgotten to bring with us when we hurried away last night, I wondered where it and my brother had been. I wished that Toño and Paul would fall into one another's arms, but I knew it would take time.

"Don't talk about this now," I counseled them.

But Toño could not stop himself. "I hate Alejandro. I have always hated him. When you told us you'd been with him again, and then—even worse—you are carrying his child, I felt angrier than I have ever felt in my life."

"Why didn't you come here last night?" Paul asked quietly.

Toño lowered himself onto the sofa.

"You wouldn't want me to tell you. But know this: I can't live without you. And, Amalia, no matter how I feel about that *cabrón*, I am sorry for what I said about the baby."

Toño would have gone even crazier if I'd pointed out that Alejandro and he had reacted the same way to the news of my little morning glory. They were both too quick to blurt out hurtful things.

Paul must have felt even more desperate than I had realized because he resorted to a moralizing tone with his partner. "I'm glad you've come back. I'm glad you're safe. But you will never do this to me again—understood? As well, you'd better be prepared to respect your sister and to accept her child." Paul crossed his arms and stuck out his chin; it quivered with emotion.

Whatever had happened to Toño while he'd been on his own, Paul's theatrics seemed to completely chastise him. "Forgive me, Amalia," he said. "I'll do what I can to make it up to you."

"Maybe the four of us should go to Merida and see what presents itself," I suggested.

"No, Hortensia and I will stay in Mexico City and begin packing," said Paul. "You two need some brother-sister time."

The very next afternoon, comfortable and quick, I flew with Toño to the Yucatecan capital—both of us full of expectations.

eight

Toño and I stood speechless before the once-familiar façade on Calle 57. We had not come a day too soon.

The hundred-year-old structure looked sound, but the plaster had crumbled, the paint had peeled, and rust flaked off the iron grillwork. Thick, dry bougainvillea limbs spilled over onto the sidewalk. Yet, surprisingly, amid this neglect, I saw laundry hanging on a makeshift line and someone coming toward me. A squatter?

A once-attractive woman glared at me through the gate. "What do you want?" she asked in a tone that reminded me of a hawker from the market.

"*Buenos días*," I replied as cheerfully as I could. I knew if I revealed any outrage, I wouldn't find out why a stranger was here on my property.

"This is a lovely old place. I heard it is for sale or have you purchased it?" I asked.

She straightened her back. "This dump—no way. A lawyer moved me in here."

Her explanation seemed pretty flimsy, so I left without telling her that she had ensconced herself in my home without my knowledge, let alone consent.

As soon as we got out of earshot, Toño turned to me. "We'd better go to your real estate office pronto," he said. "Perhaps we can find out how the monthly maintenance money you send has been used? This smells like fish that have lain out too long in the sun."

Inversiones Prediales had the best reputation in Merida that's why I had contracted them. If they acted this shoddily, I'd not want to see how the lesser competition did business. From the agency's poster board of houses for sale, I could see that most were located in the new subdivisions that had sprung up in former sisal fields around town. But a selection of downtown homes also graced the roster, my old mansion among them. I had wanted to sell the place, but there had been no takers. Good thing.

Toño looked disgusted with the disheveled atmosphere, and the agent, Rodrigo Jiménez, didn't impress either of us. Loose-limbed and sweaty, he fawned over us as only a commission-motivated man could. Wiping the dust off two chairs with his handkerchief he urged us to seat ourselves. "Welcome. How can I help you?"

Until that moment I'd never seen a more perfect example of the verb *to grovel*. I needed to be careful. In Yucatan—and in fact all over the country—laws favor the renter, even when the "tenant" is illegally occupying someone else's home. If the shady salesman got upset he could make things difficult.

"I live in Mexico City," I began, "but also own a house here—on Calle 57. I went by with the intention of going in to look around, but someone seems to be living there." I waited for Señor Jiménez to explain.

He straightened the pencils and pens on his desk, then looked at me as though I were a child having a tantrum. "Yes, I wrote to you about this. When Sra. Flores took up residence in your house, I attempted to get her to leave. But when she told me that she would open up the place to keep it from sliding into worse shape, I figured that you would be pleased. As you know, unoccupied buildings deteriorate quickly," he said. "And, after all, you were not even living in the city."

He tried not to sound like a boldfaced liar, but his over-wide smile would not have fooled a three-year-old.

"Oh, I'm sorry. I don't remember receiving any correspondence from you. Do you have copies?" I asked him.

He moved the pens some more. "Of course, Señorita. Excuse me while I check the file." He slithered away—undoubtedly to call the woman I saw at my house.

Toño couldn't keep quiet. He squinted in Señor Jimenez' direction and said, "What a swindler! Thank God Mamá and Papá will never see the mess our poor home has fallen into. Imagine what it looks like inside. Did you catch the smell?" he added. "For sure there are bats, mice, and probably every insect endemic to the Yucatan. I bet there's a veritable ecosystem inside the gates."

I shivered and hushed my brother. I thought we'd be wise to save the commentary until after we left the office. But he could not let it go. "Remember the courtyard, Amalia? The trellised roses and the night-blooming jasmine?"

Lost in our remembrances of the house's former beauty, we had to haul ourselves back into the present when Señor Jiménez returned. Without any shame—and oblivious of his promise to produce a copy of the alleged letter—he arranged himself back down behind the desk.

"I am so very sorry, Señorita Vásquez. Señora Flores insists that it is her right to remain in the house as long as she wants. She seems to consider herself a tenant and knows that the law will support her. I'm sad to be the bearer of bad news, but I would advise you to pay her off. It's the only recourse unless you're willing to wait for several years while the wheels of justice turn at a snail's pace."

I knew it would do no good to mention that he should have forced her to leave my property. She wanted money and no doubt he'd get a cut. I'd been taken advantage of and had no alternative but to cave and pay what they demanded. Two thousand pesos—a lot of money in those days.

Once I agreed to cough up the cash, the agent said he'd get the woman out of my home. I wanted to wipe the slick grin off his face, and I could see that Toño wished he could do even more damage. That would get us nowhere, though. Worse yet, I knew I'd have to offer a little "incentive" to enhance his resolve still further.

"When I return on February 1, I want to contract repairs. If Sra. Flores is gone, could you help me to arrange that?" With an innocent smile and all the enthusiasm I could fake, I added, "You seem to know how to get things done around here."

"It's my pleasure to humbly serve my clients in any way possible," he assured me.

My brother took my arm and hustled us out of there. As soon as the door shut, he raged, "How did you keep yourself from losing your temper?"

"You know, Toño, working for El Sol Imports all those years, I learned that it's best to adapt and be flexible. On my travels into the countryside, I encountered so many different ways of doing business that I developed a practical policy: adjust to the other person's tactics. I knew that only a payoff would work with Jiménez, so why fool around?"

We started walking to my next destination, the Convent of the Sacred Heart.

"Tell me again why you want to go see a bunch of nuns," Toño said.

"Hortensia's friend Sandra Hollis is a midwife and she lives at the convent. It's not far. We'll be there in fifteen minutes."

"You know what Amalia? Maybe you should make this call on your own. I'm feeling hot and frustrated. I want to have a swim.

Let's meet back at the hotel at one."

I agreed. He might get all upset again if he met the midwife who would deliver my child. I navigated Merida's streets easily. The even-numbered ones run north to south and the odd-numbered ones travel from east to west. I knew the street where I thought the convent would be located and I knew the cross streets, so I simply followed the grid, and there it stood—right in front of me.

I rang the doorbell and soon an ancient Mayan woman opened the small window set into the massive wooden door. "*¿En que le puedo servir?*" she asked.

"I am looking for Sandra Hollis," I explained. I hoped that Sandra would remember our family.

The older woman's tone and demeanor turned grave. She seemed even more bent over and shrunken. "It will be best for you to come inside," she said. I wondered what I'd said to cause such a strong reaction. She ushered me into the convent sitting room. "Mother Superior will be with you soon," she told me and turned away.

The parlor smelled of furniture polish. On three walls hung pictures of the Virgin Mary, a likeness of the Pope, and a framed prayer—La Desiderata. I tried to find a comfortable position on one of the straight-backed vintage chairs and observed the copy of the thirteenth-century Cimabue cross placed over the doorway. Every convent reception area that I'd ever been in radiated the same ultra-orderly aura.

I'd been waiting for five minutes when a middle-aged nun in street clothing came into the room. She looked at me and poked her pale hands self-consciously through her short straight hair. She had a kindly, bemused face, but when she spoke, her surprisingly firm voice filled the small room. I could easily picture what she had looked like back in the days when all sisters wore a floor-length black habit, a white wimple, a crucifix dangling over the starched bib, and rosary beads hanging from a cord at the waist.

"I am Sister Belén. I'm told you are looking for Sandra. May I ask why?"

"Good morning, Mother Superior," I replied. "Sandra's a friend of my nana, Hortensia Gómez. We've lived in La Capital for many years, but now we plan to return to live here, at least for a while."

Sister Belén bowed her head, "Sandra is no longer with us. She was killed in … an … an accident three months ago. She spent more than thirty years here and we all miss her terribly."

I felt the grief cut into my own heart. I'd been hoping Sandra would deliver my baby. What would I do now? Then it hit me. "Was Sandra at Tlatelolco?"

"Ay-ay-ay. That she was. She always stepped up for others. She had a passing friendship with some of the student leaders and so, off she went." Madre Belén put her face in her hands. "We never saw her again, not even her dear corpse. We'd given up hope of ever knowing the details until someone mailed us her medallion with a note that said Sandra had returned to the Lord. No explanation, no signature."

I touched her hand, and asked to see Sandra's medallion. Somehow I knew she wanted me to. Pulling the well-worn gold disc from under her habit, she kissed it before holding it out in front of herself. I bit my lower lip, bowed, and backed away. "I am sorry for upsetting you," I murmured and saw myself out the door.

Dazed and disoriented, I passed alongside an imposing Colonial church and its plaza. Constructed in the seventeenth century, the Franciscan façade still looked rock solid. Under Spanish rule, the followers of Saint Francis had been the prominent religious order in Yucatan. Their style seemed austere when compared to the richly ornamented Dominican religious buildings of central Mexico. All the same, the simple architectural lines seen in Merida's edifices seemed harmonious with the climate. I thought about going inside to offer a prayer for the midwife I'd never know, but with no Mass in progress, the great wooden doors were sealed shut. I quietly crossed myself—that would have to do.

The market on the western side of the plaza buzzed with matrons rushing to finish their daily shopping. *¡Ah su mecha!* I could well recall the delicious aromas that wafted from the neighborhood kitchens of my childhood. The mothers and their cooks vied to see who could produce the most fragrant welcome for husbands and children who'd spent their mornings away at school or work or wherever.

Several blocks further east, I found myself walking past a small clinic, El Central Pediátrica. It looked new. I stood in the entrance way and saw what I imagined were doctors' offices, a delivery room, and dispensary. Everything seemed clean and professional. With Sandra gone, I knew I'd have to find a physician and, impulsively, I stepped inside. When I inquired about gynecologists, the receptionist pointed to a door second down on the left. "Doctor Montañez would be available to see you," she said.

Before I lost my nerve, I walked toward his office.

I needed to be completely up front. If he acted disapproving or unsympathetic, I'd find someone else.

On the wall behind his desk, I noticed his diploma in a new frame. A recently graduated M.D. from the University of Yucatan, he appeared to be younger than I. Alert eyes behind wireless John Lennon glasses regarded me with openness. His mop of longish hair reinforced my impression that he looked more like a pop singer than a physician.

"How can I help you?" he asked.

I told my story straight—from start to finish.

"You're brave. Not many women are able to face motherhood on their own as well as you seem to be doing." He asked a few more questions regarding my lifestyle.

No, I'd never used drugs . . . No, I didn't smoke . . . Yes, I sometimes drank wine . . . No, not to excess . . . No, I hadn't seen a doctor up until now, but . . . Yes, I did have the pregnancy test done at a lab and the results were positive. I agreed to a prenatal exam.

He showed me where to change and pointed to an intimidating examination table that he'd covered with a blue sheet. I removed my clothing and put on one of the neatly folded blue gowns that I found in the cubicle. Blue seemed to be the preferred color around here.

Dr. Montañez gave me a thorough examination. He said nothing as he performed the procedure.

With my legs spread apart and my feet inserted into high metal stirrups, I felt exposed and embarrassed. I bet I wouldn't have needed to do this for Sandra Hollis. Finally, the doctor lowered the metal frame and helped me to sit up again.

"There—that's over with. I know it can't be pleasant. Please get dressed and come back into my office when you're ready."

Wanting to feel in control again, I quickly got into my clothes and returned to the chair in front of the doctor's desk.

"Everything seems fine. You are healthy and still in your first trimester." He explained the different stages of gestation and asked me to get some blood work done. I told him I'd return to see him soon after February 1. It seemed as though he could read my thoughts. "You will only be four months along and no one will suspect a thing," he said as he gave me a prescription for vitamins.

As an afterthought, I asked, "Would it be possible to have a home birth?"

"Let's see how the pregnancy progresses. If there are no complications, I might consider it."

Feeling well cared for, I smiled at my new doctor. I'd arrived at a turning point. I rested my hand on my abdomen and thought of the life growing there. I loved this baby—my little morning glory. But a constant question loomed over me like a black cloud: *How will I manage?* No comforting person came forward to tell me it would all work out, so I straightened my shoulders and walked directly back to the hotel. I just couldn't afford to let my fears get the better of me. I felt a rush of gratitude for my three allies—Hortensia, Toño, and Paul. I'd try not to be too demanding.

~~~

Toño waited for me in the lobby. "You'll never believe who I ran into." He didn't wait for me to guess. "Your old friend Layla Thompson. She lives here, and we've been chatting for the past half hour. She's in the bathroom right now, but I invited her to have lunch with us."

Layla! What a funny girl she had been. When we were in our teens, her father was the American consul for southeastern Mexico. For five years, she and I had been best friends, but when the family moved away, we'd lost touch. I couldn't believe all the shocks this day had delivered—one after the other.

She and I took one look at each other, and it seemed clear that time had not diminished our feelings. Rocking back and forth in each other's arms, I felt like I'd found a long lost sister. She loved to talk and launched right into abridged chapters of the past decade and a half.

"My life has taken so many twists. I fell in love and out of love many times and eventually I married James. Never get involved with a gambler! When he lost his job, he began playing cards with his unemployed buddies, 'Just to pass the time,' he said. A couple of them were into numbers, too, and that's how it all got going. He would steal from me, from his mother, from anyone. Soon he'd pawned everything of any value from our apartment. He resorted to petty robbery and it escalated even more. He owed a lot of money and couldn't pay it back."

What a story. I wondered what she was doing back in Merida?

"James did a fine job of covering his tracks until one day a collector who couldn't get a hold of him came and beat me up. He left me in a bruised heap on the floor, saying, 'This will show your low-life husband that I'll get satisfaction one way or another!' Though I was barely conscious when Hubby came home, he decided I didn't need to go to the hospital. He hoisted me into bed and then left to join a game. When I heard him slam the front door, I let myself fall to the floor, crawled to the phone in the kitchen, and called my brother. He took me into his home that very night and the next day I filed for divorce."

I couldn't believe that Layla had opened up like this in front of me and Toño. We hadn't seen each other for at least fifteen years, yet she didn't hold back any of the dramatic details of her past. Was she aware that other people had turned to get a closer look at this woman with the shocking stories?

"But James wouldn't sign. He needed a meal ticket, you see. It took three years to get the final papers, and to celebrate, I took a holiday in Cozumel. There my life morphed into a wild thing! Swaying palms, turquoise sea—talk about living in 'Divorcee Dreamland.' So many willing hands—and other body parts—and so little time. Oh yeah, I went crazy. But the craziness saved me. It truly did. During the days, I hung out half—sometimes fully—naked on the sunny beach."

Layla placed one hand over her fabulous breasts, illustrating still further her lusty tale. Both Toño and I let out an audible gasp, but Layla kept going.

"And I drank wonky margaritas every single evening. As my tan deepened and my liver atrophied, I had enough sense to recognize that even though I was living dangerously, I was in fact, interviewing. And did I ever collect some out-of-sight stories.

"People wanted to tell me everything about themselves. After six months I had enough material to write what I knew would be a sensational book. I moved to Merida where I could detox from my indulgence in all those eager beach boys and cheap booze. I got serious and worked steadily for another half year. I started looking for a publisher who could appreciate my humor. I found one here in Merida and he signed me up right away. That was his lucky day and mine. My book is called ¡Buenísima! and it's in its third printing. I have freelance work, too. I absolutely love my life! But enough about me. Tell me what are you and Toño doing in Merida? Did you get frightened away by what happened at Tlatelolco?"

"Tlatelolco is one of the reasons that I want to leave Mexico City. Just the other day, as I was walking close to my home in Colonia Santa María La Ribera, a terrified teenager came up behind me, begging me to help him because the police were gathering up students. 'I'm so afraid,' he said. 'Take my arm and if they come, tell them I'm your brother and we are out shopping.' I don't want to live with that kind of fear all around me."

I did not tell Layla my most pressing reason for moving to Merida. I figured I would do so once Hortensia and I had settled in.

Maybe sensing that she would not be gathering any more gossip, Layla announced that she had to go. But our parting was filled with anticipation for a renewed friendship.

"I cannot think of a single person I'd have rather seen today," I said as I hugged her. "Being with you makes me feel like a young girl again. I'll call once I'm actually living in Merida."

"You are a young girl, Amalia. I will be leaving for New York in a week's time. I need to spend time promoting *¡Buenísima!* and some other projects. But as soon as I get back, you've got a date."

"And will I be able to buy a signed copy of your book?"

"Of course. I'll bring you one. But I am giving you fair warning, it is pretty steamy."

I didn't mention to her that I would like that. I doubted I'd be getting any action of my own for a long time to come.

Toño could see I had exhausted myself and suggested we go back to our rooms, but I wanted to return to Mexico City that afternoon. I felt that I'd done all I could on this trip. At the hotel's travel agency, we found out that no seats were available until the next day. I took in a big breath of air and reminded myself that I could not become distraught when details didn't pan out a hundred percent. Much still hung in the air, but I could see that I'd be happy returning here to live and raise my child.

Toño kissed my cheek. "Enjoy your siesta," he said as we toddled off to our cool darkened rooms.

After a two-hour afternoon nap, I awoke to the sound of the bedside telephone ringing. "It has finally cooled off. Let's take a stroll," Toño suggested.

We headed for the stately Paseo de Montejo, a wide boulevard that runs through the city from north to south. Late nineteenth- and early twentieth-century mansions, outdoor cafés and tourist boutiques lined the leafy sidewalk. The moon tipped at a precarious angle amid a muddle of stars and fallen *flamboyan* blossoms carpeted the ground, reminding me of saffron. Although the night was but an hour old, dew already shone on the surface of the wrought-iron benches. Toño wiped one off, and we sat down to people watch.

The city seemed as sultry as I remembered. So many memories. I smiled at the chaperones keeping a constant lookout for impropriety. The young people paraded up and down, boys sauntering in one direction and girls in the other. Some kept their shy eyes downcast, and some flirted openly—just the way it had been during my own promenades here. Alejandro and I had first noticed one another at my *Quince Años* party, but because we hadn't been formally introduced, he couldn't address me in public. But he did manage to pass a note to Hortensia, which she'd been reluctant to give me. Prying it from her hand, my heart had raced when I read:

> *Will you be at Luisa Orozco's party next Saturday? I long to see you again!*

Once it had been deemed proper for us to speak to one another, no one could make us stop. He'd been so interested in everything about me.

"The other girls only aspire to marriage and to having babies. But you want to be an architect. How did you decide on that?" he asked. He listened intently to my reply, and he encouraged me to not let go of my dreams.

"Maybe you'll build me a house one day," he said.

Maybe I'll build "us" a house one day, I secretly hoped.

Toño pulled my mind away from my reminiscing. "Do you think Hortensia will be happy here in Merida?" he asked.

"I know she'll be upset to learn about Sandra. She had looked forward to seeing her again. And she's worried about being dragged back into old patterns."

Toño looked puzzled. "What do you mean when you say 'old patterns?'"

"Provincial attitudes. In La Capital, Hortensia has status. She's known as *la Curandera Maya*—the Mayan Healer. She likes the respect that comes with her title. But in Merida she's afraid that people will only see *la India*—the peasant—and not even bother with her. I'll wait until the weekend to speak with her about all of her concerns. As much as I need her, if she's going to be unhappy, I don't want her to come here."

"I don't like to even contemplate that, Amalia. Paul and I will be heading back to Austin on Friday. We need time to reshuffle our deck and come to some decisions."

The weight of all the sudden changes made Toño look ten years older than he did when he and Paul arrived in Mexico City. In less than a week, so much had happened.

～

On Saturday, I put off more packing to spend a leisurely morning with Hortensia and I told her about Sandra.

"I thought that might be the case," she said. "I have felt her presence at odd times and this doesn't happen with the living." Tears glistened in her dark eyes.

"And I wonder if you are having some doubts . . ."

"I know it will take me awhile to adjust," she said after a pause, "but soon the Merida house will feel like home again. I know you and I will find satisfying new paths in Merida."

Her assurance bolstered my lagging resolve.

On January 31, a Muebles y Mudanzas moving van took away my household items—the art, a few special pieces of furniture, clothing, and other assorted goods. Forty-seven boxes' worth.

I spent the final night of my Mexico City life alone in my apartment. For what seemed the millionth time, I wondered if I was taking the right path. Magenta, turquoise, and lime fireworks from a religious celebration lit the sky and magical Mariachi music danced downwind from the plaza. Rising from my chair, I moved inside and slid the thick glass door closed behind me. The thought of no longer being able to enjoy the El Capital's nightscape was too much to bear.

But the next day, February 1, 1969, Hortensia and I boarded the plane to Merida. I pulled the black nylon strap of the seat belt snugly over my child, buckling us both in safely, and never looked back.

~~~

It took just two days for my shipment to arrive. The pair of sweaty long-distance truckers sat back and rested while the ten construction laborers I'd just hired stored my forty-seven boxes and locked them into one of the rooms of the main house. Hortensia and I would be comfortable enough in the guest suite during the renovations. I made lemonade with lemons from my own garden, and we settled into our new rockers under the spreading branches of a twisted mango tree. I didn't recognize the strange sensation in my abdomen; it felt as though a feather was tickling me from inside. When I described the feeling to Hortensia, she looked surprised.

"It's early for the baby to move, but that's what's happening"

"She must like it here," I said and closed my eyes, very satisfied with all we'd done since our arrival in Merida. We planned to live on site and would have the advantage of being able to supervise the reconstruction.

I knew the crew worried that we'd get in the way. "My guys make a lot of noise. There will be loud banging and dust all over everything. You'll live to regret moving in now," said Luis, the project supervisor. But I figured not too much could go wrong with us watching the contractor's every move.

Hortensia could understand that I didn't want to use up all my money paying rent for a quieter apartment. I hoped to be able to go back to school. She was all for my plan. "Once the baby is born, you can look into what's available at the University of Yucatan and also the work possibilities." She never laughed at me or tried to talk me out of my ideas the way Mamá always did.

"Can't you just picture Mamá listening to my plans to raise a baby and go to school at the same time?" I said to Hortensia. "She'd be red as a beet, with one hand on her hip and the other wagging a finger in my face." We both laughed.

"And to put me in my place, she might call on La Madrina to take me back to La Villa de Santa Cecilia," Hortensia joked. But then she turned serious. "You will soon be a mother yourself, and I bet that when that happens, you'll have a new appreciation for your own mamá."

I couldn't imagine that, but I couldn't rule it out. I had begun to suspect that the goddess had mapped out a life for me that I could not have dreamed.

nine

I stood in the backyard talking with Don Luis' sixteen-year-old son Lalo—my new gardener. The kid knew little about lawns, flowers, or shrubbery and needed a lot of direction.

But I didn't mind teaching him—not that I knew much either. He had an intelligent face, calm disposition, and delicate hands. Those hands could be trained for surgery or they could master the piano. I'd be pleased to schedule his work so that he could finish high school and maybe go beyond. I wanted to ask him if he'd like that, but the insistent buzz of the doorbell forced me to leave Lalo and run to the front entrance. My hurrying increased the pressure on my cervix—so uncomfortable! I planned to give hell to whoever I'd find on my stoop as I yanked back the door.

"Got room in this big ol' house for some kin?" Paul asked.

Toño gave me a wide grin and playfully poked his friend in the ribs. "I told you we'd be back," he said, "We're renting a small apartment nearby while we search for a place of our own. Don't pay any attention to Paul."

They both looked flushed and excited.

"Hortensia! Come look who's here. Toño and Paul."

They burst out laughing when Hortensia peeked around my shoulders and let out a delighted whoop.

"Don't get too excited. We come bearing no gifts," my brother teased. "Can we come in anyway?"

"¡Sí, sí, sí! Come in, come in!" Hortensia said, pulling them inside. She removed her kitchen apron.

"You must have been ready to give up your business. You managed to tie everything up so quickly," she said.

Toño lowered himself into one of the wicker rockers on the porch. "You bet we were ready. With Amalia's withdrawal from the company, hiring a new buyer and restructuring seemed like way more than we wanted to deal with. And when our major competitor offered to buy us out, it seemed like the green light to move on."

"We both love the beach," said Paul, draping his tall frame over the rocker next to Toño's, "and here we figure we'll spend lots of time exploring along the Gulf of Mexico and the Caribbean. You look wonderful, Amalia."

"Oh Paul, I bet you say that to all us pregnant girls." I felt delighted with the idea that this man would be a doting uncle to my daughter. "Why didn't you tell me you'd be coming? We would have prepared a feast."

"We know you have plenty to take care of without us under foot. Our rental place is nearby, but it doesn't have a pool, so you'll probably see more of us than you want to," Paul teased. "It is damn hot here."

I wanted them here in the house with Nana and me, but I knew it wouldn't be a good idea to pressure Toño. I watched him bantering back and forth with Hortensia and I sensed underlying tension. Even if moving to Mexico had been my brother's idea, the change would be harder for him than for Paul.

I told them that they could hang out here and use the pool whenever they wanted, but today I'd need to leave the house for a couple of hours.

"Hortensia and I have an appointment to see my doctor at noon, but we won't be gone long. Help yourself to anything in the fridge—there's a nice fruit plate in there right now."

"Do you think you'll be back by two o'clock? Toño has told me all about the Hotel Panamericana, and I'd love it if the two of you could share our first lunch in Merida," Paul said.

Hortensia looked more than ready. Paul perked her up as much as he did me, and she'd always had a soft spot in her heart for Toño.

"You've got a date," I assured them. "We'll meet you there, at the poolside restaurant at two o'clock."

~

While my nana sat in the reception area waiting for me to finish in the examination room, she noticed a country couple fidgeting and whispering. Without warning she received a strong premonition. She saw that they already had a ten-year-old daughter they called Perla. They longed for more children. Hortensia foresaw that the woman would learn today that she's expecting. She'd have another daughter and two years from now, she would give her husband the son he longed for. He would adore his daughters and proudly provide for them. When his son came along, he would love him neither more nor less than his two precious girls.

Hortensia further saw that she would meet the eldest child later on in her life, and with that, her vision ended. It frustrated her how she only learned partial future-life stories.

With no self-consciousness, she stood up and got closer. She asked the woman her name.

At first Hortensia's new acquaintance seemed puzzled that a stranger wanted to know, but she didn't mind telling her. "Inés Martínez de Suaste," she answered.

Nana told me that she wrote that name down in her notebook. She wanted to have it when she meets Perla sometime in the future. She moved closer still to the worried-looking couple. She smiled and closed her eyes. Then she shared her happy secret.

"You'll be blessed with a loving family. One of your children, the eldest daughter, will become quite famous." Hortensia knew that even though they didn't understand why, the couple believed what the spirit guides had revealed.

Yet there was no chance to speak further; the doctor asked Hortensia to join me in the consultation room.

"Dr. Montañez has agreed to a home birth!" I told my nana.

Hortensia looked concerned, but she'd grown tired of arguing. I had nothing against hospitals, but I could just imagine some gossipy admissions nurse telling the whole city that I'd come in "alone" to give birth. "*Noooo,* no husband's name went on the record . . ." she'd say. And that would be enough to get the rumor mill rolling. Having a home birth would shield me from all that and protect my child. Besides, delivering my baby in a more natural setting just felt right to me.

"Don't be nervous," I told my nana. "The doctor says everything is perfect. My little morning glory is facing the light, and if she stays this way, the labor will be easy."

Hortensia shook her head and gave one more half-hearted try. "Dr. Montañez shouldn't tell you such a thing, he's showing his maleness. No birth is easy, Amalia," she said.

She did not sway me even a little bit. And there was one important thing I didn't want to mention. Once the baby had been born, I wanted to be where I could look closely at her and see the small signs of Alejandro. Hortensia was the one who told me that my daughter would resemble him. Besides, the doctor lived a five-minute car ride away from our house. What could go wrong?

～～

Hortensia and I arrived at the Hotel Panamericana to find Paul and my brother holding half-empty blue-rimmed cocktail glasses.

"Toño was right. I love the margaritas here. We've had one each, but I think we need another round, don't you?"

The frothy iced drinks did look inviting. I sighed. "I can't wait for the day when I can join you!"

When we returned home after lunch, I rolled into the hammock strung on the cool back terrace. I fell deeply asleep and awoke to the sight of Paul and Toño emerging from the pool area.

Paul whistled happily. "This is fantastic," he said.

"You're sure you don't mind that we use your pool until we have our own?" Toño asked.

"You both look so fit and handsome in your swimsuits, I'll be pleased for you to come over any time to swim. I love seeing you so relaxed and happy. Keep it up."

Paul pointed his right index finger at Toño, and in his slow Southern drawl he said, "And your spirits aren't all you'll need to keep up."

～～

Watching the masons and tradesmen, I'd received an education. Mostly Mayan, their strong, compact bodies could carry a surprising amount of weight. To them, the scorching sun seemed nothing more than a mild irritant. Day after day, they had chipped away at what needed to be torn down and skillfully raised the new additions. Arches soared where plain trestles once stood and delicate detailing replaced purely functional surfaces. Light poured into the once-dingy rooms and every night when there was a moon, I watched it reflect off the pool, casting a serene blue glow through the back garden. It made me think I could see *los aluxes*—the Mayan elves. When I mentioned this to the work crew, they took my words seriously.

"We are from the countryside. Our home is Tahmec, a place of old traditions," said Don Chepo, the eldest of the group, a wrinkled sixty-three-year-old who could out lift and outlast all the young workers. "We have spoken about the *aluxes* here. The work goes well, and we know they are watching over us and keeping the bad winds from sweeping down."

Hortensia listened with respect. She nodded her agreement and smiled at Don Chepo. This unplanned exchange made me realize that I would have opportunities in Merida to learn much more than I had anticipated.

I didn't know many people in town and this is how I wanted it for the duration of the pregnancy. Hortensia enjoyed doing the daily grocery shopping at the nearby Santiago market and if she couldn't find all that she needed, Toño and Paul were available to run errands. The few times I'd left the house, I wore an oversized *huipil* that hid my ever-thickening torso. On a couple of occasions I ran into a former acquaintance or two, but no one suspected a thing. I knew they didn't because I watched their faces for the signs.

My room calmed me like the inner sanctuary of an oasis. Although not the largest bedroom in the house, the dimensions suited my needs. I decorated the smooth white-stucco walls with several groups of small oils and watercolors that came from my Mexico City apartment. The Tamayo still life and the Frida Kahlo colored pencil sketch of an old woman with a *rebozo* covering her head would become quite valuable in time. Not that I was interested in selling them; I loved looking at them.

Though I treasured exquisite things, I threw away the crocheted coverlet that had been permanently stained on the night of Tlatelolco. Ironically, as my pregnancy advanced, I started to understand the many layers of what had occurred; I now called that night *la noche de la decepción*—the night of deception. I'd bought a sunshine-yellow satin spread to drape my bed. To me the color represented hope and my optimism that meaningful change would one day come into my life and to our country.

Hortensia's refuge had enough space for her altar. We used the office for whatever else wouldn't fit into our private quarters, keeping clutter to a minimum. The room between us would be for the baby. In the storage area, we found the bassinet that had cuddled three generations of babies in our family. My child would be the fourth. Don Luis painstakingly repaired and painted the broken strands of wicker and Hortensia sewed lacy frills and a mosquito net. Together they transformed the dusty old relic into a secure little nest for a brand-new life.

On the TV one early June morning, I saw Alejandro on a talk show. It hurt to see how attractive he looked in his corduroy pants and checkered shirt. As usual, his hair was pulled back in a ponytail and when he turned to answer questions, I could see a faint white scar behind his left ear. He spoke about what happened to him on the night of the Tlatelolco massacre. He's a mesmerizing speaker and the way he looked right into the cameras made me feel as though he could see me.

"How did you escape from the Plaza of Three Cultures? Did you hide in the streets?" the interviewer asked.

I held my breath.

"No, if I'd stayed in the area I would have been arrested. I went to the home of an old friend who protected me."

I knew it wouldn't be good for me to watch any more of this, but I couldn't make myself turn the set off. The program continued and I noticed that Alejandro had the skill to manipulate the answers to his advantage—like a symphony conductor does with his musicians. But then the show's host threw out a rogue inquiry.

"Can you tell us who your old friend is—the one who hid you?"

He wouldn't reveal my name—I felt sure he wouldn't—but still, in case he did, I tried to think of somewhere I could hide.

Alejandro's eyes grew dark as a pit, but he got himself under control and his voice softened. "You know I cannot," he said. He seemed to look even more intensely into the camera lens and added, "But I think of that angel every day."

Why did he say things like that? It was easier for me when I focused on his negative qualities. But Alejandro was not always unkind; he could still string those pearls on a linen thread and make me long to wear the necklace. I didn't miss him when he acted distant. *What if? What if? What if?* I couldn't keep the agonizing litany out of my mind.

ten

I felt hot, heavy, and short-tempered with everyone. My due date, July 2, came and went and my baby showed no signs of leaving her sheltered place.

Two afternoons later, I sat on the stone steps of the pool soaking my swollen feet in the cool water. I felt calm and detached until the ever-present, low-level discomfort morphed into a sharp pain that stabbed through my lower back. I wanted to stand, but my feet seemed waterlogged and I couldn't find my footing. I turned around to call my brother.

"Help me! Get me up!" The cramping steadily worsened, but once Paul and Toño hauled me up, it diminished and I could walk around. "Something's happening," I said, "and I don't think it's indigestion."

The guys looked at one another. "We'll find Hortensia," they said in unison. The time had arrived. My daughter would finally make her entrance. I grabbed Toño's arm and searched his face; we hadn't ever spoken again about the night at El Café de Paris.

"Are you sure you're up to this?" I asked.

"Haven't I shown you how I feel? Paul is over-the-top excited about becoming an uncle and I can't tell you how sorry I am for making that awful scene at the restaurant." He looked so remorseful and so anxious, I knew we'd never have to bring this up again.

"I'm going to my room," I told them. "Come running if you hear me scream." Ten minutes passed with no further action and I started to wonder if indeed labor had begun. Thirty seconds later another strong spasm surged through my spine, grew to a crescendo, then eased. Hortensia found me doubled over my bed.

"Tell me what you need, Amalia, I'll help you."

But no one could help me. What lay ahead tonight would be hard and the most difficult part would follow. It seemed likely that this baby would be the only one I'd ever have. The birth would be soon, and I had to admit that despite all that had happened between Alejandro and me, more than anything, I wished I could raise my daughter with him. I wondered what kind of parents we'd be.

Years ago, I had been too proud. I should have fought harder to keep him. He wanted me to understand his cause. He gave me books to read: Lenin, Marx, Che Guevara, and Fidel Castro—all the revolutionaries. Sometimes I'd play along, but mostly I acted sullen at the political rallies. Had I made more of an effort and gone with him, he wouldn't have met Susana and maybe we would have stayed lovers. Maybe we'd have married? But enough endless wondering— I didn't need to make this any harder.

I could not find any position that eased the pain. Another jarring spasm tore through me and I felt a wet, gushing stickiness—my water had broken. I was definitely in labor. Hortensia helped me into the shower, dried me, and put a white linen nightdress over my shuddering body.

"I've never seen this gown before. Where did it come from?" I asked.

"Your mother wore it the night you were born. It is from Ireland, the land of her forefathers. Her spirit was strong. This will help you tonight. Valor is woven into the fabric."

It pleased me that Hortensia had kept the birthing garment for all these years. I felt more ready to be a mother when she slipped it on me. Then she called the doctor, who arrived promptly, examined me, and pronounced that everything seemed to be as it should be.

"You have dilated just three centimeters, but you're progressing well," he confirmed.

What did he mean? *Progressing well.* I felt a relentless tearing down my middle. I tried to convince him that something must be terribly wrong. Hortensia and Dr. Montañez looked sympathetic but also calm and unworried. At ten p.m., I'd been in established labor for five hours and the contractions were five minutes apart. I felt weary beyond belief.

"It has not been nearly long enough," Hortensia said, not unkindly.

"I know that," I snapped. "This will probably continue for the whole night." I wanted it to be over. I concentrated as hard as possible and followed every suggestion from Hortensia. All the books I'd read led me to believe I would experience a contraction. It would reach a peak, and the pain would be gone until the next surge crested. But *no-o-o-o-o!* The ripping inside never quit. *Didn't some women die in childbirth?* I wondered how Alejandro would feel if he could see what I was going through. *Damn it. He should be here.*

Hortensia urged me to concentrate on my breathing—in and out—in and out, and when the pain reached a peak—*puff, puff, puff.* She stepped out of the room for a few minutes, and a gut-contorting, flesh-ripping, agonizing contraction hit—the worst so far. I screamed every obscenity I could think of. The dreadful transitional labor had begun.

She came back into the room and congratulated me for holding my own. Although I had yelled, I had not panicked. If I could handle the intensity of giving birth, maybe afterwards I'd do better with managing my life than I'd done up until now.

And so it went throughout the night. At some point, rain

started falling. I fixated on the rhythm and matched my breathing to the even thumping of the deluge on the veranda. I had always loved the sound of tropical storms and the sweet heady odor they bring forth from the earth.

Stay focused, Amalia . . .

～

When Hortensia called Dr. Montañez at 4:20 a.m., we knew the delivery would happen in next to no time. But even sooner than that, my baby decided that the time had come. The doctor had not yet shown up. This is what Hortensia had feared, but she didn't remind me of that fact and, *gracias a Dios*, she knew what had to be done.

She pushed up her sleeves and said to me, "It will just be the two of us, Amalia. Will you be all right?"

I trusted no one more. "I will do exactly as you say, but . . . *plea-ea-ea-se* . . . make this end!" Fatigue had gained ground. For hours I had been pacing the room or sitting in a towel-cushioned rocker and now the time had come for me to lie down on the oilcloth-covered bed.

"Grip the headboard and raise your knees. Pull hard with your hands. Push your pelvis downward." Hortensia wiped my forehead and massaged my shoulders. Then she positioned herself to receive the baby.

"The head has crowned and I see a cap of dark hair. When you feel the urge, push, Amalia, push hard!"

I tried. I tried many times—with all my might, but nothing moved.

"With the next contraction, inhale deeply and let the air out of your lungs in one long breath," Hortensia said. "The baby will follow."

I gripped the wrought iron even more tightly and concentrated on the even rhythm of the rain. I let the pain swell, took in air, and expelled it all at once.

"She's coming," my nana said. "The head is coming out—I see an eye! Once more now, Amalia."

I pushed a final time and brought my daughter into the light at 4:40 on the morning of July 5, 1969. Toño and Paul heard her cry and began cheering from their places right outside my room. Hortensia and I looked at each other and I felt my tears coming as hard as the rain.

My baby's face looked like the center of an exquisite flower. Her flailing arms and legs waved like petals in a breeze and the umbilical cord held fast to me like a stem imbedded in the earth. Within the first seconds of her new life, she began rooting for my breast. Through my misty eyes, I could see a pink glow in the east. The rain still fell, but softer, and the aroma of the rich, replenished red earth mingled with the intimate scent of childbirth.

The moist morning tasted of prophesy and I knew the name this baby should carry. I would call her Aurora—the Latin name for dawn, the time of day that she came into the world and the beginning of our life together.

I asked her, "Is this what you want? Shall I name you Aurora?" The wee eyes seemed to agree with my choice. How immediately she filled up my heart . . . a heart that didn't even realize just how much it needed to be filled.

Hortensia needed my attention. "Amalia, is it time to cut the cord and clamp it off?" I nodded. I could find no words to let her know how grateful I felt. "Nana, I could not have done this . . ."

She hushed me. "It's fine, *Mi'ja*. You are safe and so is your beautiful child."

The procedure took but a minute. I turned my head to the opposite side of the bed. Paul entered the room and came closer. Tears clogged my voice as I handed Aurora to him. "Here is your uncle. He's been waiting for you for so long."

How had this happened? I'd been so scared when the doctor failed to arrive, but now it seemed right that only Toño, Paul, and Hortensia had been with Aurora and me. I had not only birthed my baby, tonight we had forged a family—we would never be a very conventional one perhaps, but the love we have would take on everything in our path.

Paul, always tender and caring, caressed the baby's sweet face and looked toward the door. Toño came inside and warily joined his partner by my bed. He couldn't take his eyes off our lovely Aurora.

"*Bienvenida al mundo,* Aurora." Paul passed the baby back to Hortensia, who said she hoped the doctor would arrive soon.

~

Soaked to the bone, he showed up five minutes later. The rain had poured down so heavily that he'd been unable to navigate the flooded streets and so, abandoning his car three blocks away, he came to the house on foot carrying his heavy bag. Seeing the baby, apparently safe, relieved him, but he still needed to examine me and thoroughly check the newborn.

He asked to wash up. He joked that I looked like a wrung-out floor mop, but otherwise seemed to be in good shape. Wiping his eyes on his sleeve, he said, "You did well, Amalia. The baby is as lovely as I've ever seen. Three kilos, 250 grams, fifty-two centimeters long. What a hardy little morning glory. And Hortensia . . . you are full of surprises."

Then he added that he'd not met a midwife, or a doctor for that matter, who would have been more professional than Hortensia. Dr.

Montañez closed his bag and Paul offered to help him walk back to the car with the all his equipment that even included a baby scale. He accepted, but before he left, he asked me to come to his office with Aurora as soon as I felt up to leaving the house.

"We'll do up the birth certificate and so on," he said.

In the emotional moments following Aurora's birth, I swore I'd be a perfect mother, and I thought she would be a perfect daughter, but that didn't happen. Neither of us proved to be anything of the sort, but I've learned since that love never hinges on perfection . . . not real love.

Toño and Paul had moved into the guesthouse three weeks previously so they'd be close by in case they were needed. Thank God for that. Now that the big event had taken place, everyone was trying to get some much-needed sleep—except for Toño. He paced outside my room like a faithful golden retriever. I longed for a hug from my brother and called him inside.

He sat down and cradled my hand on his lap, then he leaned over to stroke my hair. "You did an incredible job, but now you need to sleep. We'll talk another time," he said and moved to leave.

"Wait, Toño. Stay with me a few more minutes." I could see that he had something on his mind, and I wanted to give him a chance to get it into the open.

Toño shifted his position on the edge of my bed. "You know, Amalia, we men are too proud and too preoccupied. Too much gloriousness goes right past us, but tonight Paul and I got to share this with you. Alejandro's failings now include missing out on the birth of his daughter. His loss—our joy. He provided an opportunity for Paul and me that we never thought would come to us. Aurora's arrival into the world is the most thrilling thing that has ever happened. We both feel that way, Amalia. We will be her daddies. We are here for the two of you."

This morning had been extraordinary in so many ways. Once Toño left me, I found myself alone with my thoughts for the first time since Aurora's birth. Through the frothy folds of netting, I watched her sleep. Maybe her second name should be *Milagros*—Miracles? No, that would be taking it too far. All the same, that's how I saw her: a little miracle.

She resembled Alejandro. She had curls spread tightly across her hairline. She had long arms and legs—those sloe café eyes—would she too be a heartbreaker?

Toño bringing up Alejandro's absence had not upset me. He would either come around or he wouldn't. Whatever he did, Aurora and I would be fine. I decided that later on today I would call him . . . he must be thinking that the baby had been born by now.

I didn't have to make the call because at eleven in the morning, he rang me. Our conversation went tersely. I let him have the facts and evaded the emotional parts. He didn't ask any questions, but just before hanging up, he said, "Amalia, I'm so sorry."

"What are you sorry about, Alejandro?" I was losing patience with him and wanted to cut this call short.

His voice caught. "Not really 'about' Amalia, sorry *for*. Sorry for myself. I'll miss out on so much."

Did he want me to beg him, to cajole him, or appease him? That would be his style. He hadn't been here and so he couldn't imagine the wonder of it. I needed to be careful—I couldn't trust him even if I wished that I could. No matter, my self-confidence had evolved. I aimed to discover where I could go from here. "Goodbye, Alejandro," I said, and clicked the receiver down.

Layla had returned to Merida shortly after Aurora's birth. She arrived at my house unannounced, and Hortensia led her out onto the shady patio where I lay in a hammock nursing Aurora. She'd not known about my pregnancy, so the tableau made her stare as though another woman occupied my body.

"I must still be drunk from last week's wrap-up party in LA!" she said. Then she turned serious. She waved her arm in a broad circle. "Amalia, tell me about *this*—I have to know everything."

"It's the oldest story in the world," I told her.

"Yeah, probably, but I want to hear your version," my friend said. She sat down across from me. "What's the baby's name?"

"Aurora. And I know you're going to ask about the father. He's Alejandro Méndez."

"*Whoa* . . . back up! Didn't he turn into old news a decade ago?"

I sighed, took a deep breath, and related the convoluted sequence of events that had led up to this moment by the pool.

"Until my daughter was born, I could never have imagined that I'd find myself actually grateful to be in this position. But Aurora is the best, and holding her in my arms I feel so blessed. Alejandro has been cruel in untold ways, but he gave me my daughter. And whether he realizes this or not, she has bound us together forever."

"Well, Amalia, I think I understand your feelings for Alejandro. After all, I saw you two the day you met. All the other boys had buzz cuts that showed their funny-shaped heads and their big ears stuck out like road signs. Alejandro had loose black curls that brushed onto his beautiful arched brows. And his eyes glowed like amber when he looked at you. . . . Watching the two of you was my first view of what is politely called chemistry. I call it lust, and I envied you for it. Nothing can compare to knowing that you are so hot for one another that complete surrender is inevitable. You've never lost that, have you?"

Aurora had finished nursing . . . for now. I knew she'd soon want more and so I didn't put her into her bed. She slept happily propped on my shoulder while I patted her tiny back and gave my attention once again to Layla, who would not drop her probing about my conflicting emotions.

Layla gave a sly smile. "I can't believe it, Amalia. You fell right back under his spell after Tlatelolco, didn't you, girl?"

I shook my head and looked at Layla. "I suspect you'd be able to get a juicy confession from a nun."

Aurora had started to whimper again. Yes, she knew when my mind had wandered and all my focus didn't center on her.

"Let me hold her," said Layla. "You continue with your story."

I passed my daughter into Layla's arms and wondered if Alejandro would find me as glamorous a mother as Layla looked at this moment. I had to get off this topic; it aroused a longing that I wanted to put behind me. I had just one more bit to add.

"Layla, this might sound like wishful thinking, but I believe Alejandro came to me after Tlatelolco because he felt desperate and knew that no one else would be able to soothe him. Not that he'd admit that. He is still too caught up in his own concerns, his career, and his image. He takes me for granted—and he still doesn't realize that worldly success pales next to love."

Layla's curious expression made me realize that I should not have mentioned that; it only made her dig deeper into my guarded feelings.

"But he's married to Susana and not you. Doesn't that make you furious?"

"Yes, of course it does. Nonetheless, I suspect he will come around, and when he does, I'll be waiting for him—with our daughter. It's hard to explain. Because of Aurora, he'll always be bound to me, but I know that one day he'll realize that he has missed out—big time—by turning away from me and the love I have for him."

I could tell that Layla was on my side—not making judgments—not criticizing me for loving Alejandro in my weird way. She knew he and I should be together, but not at any price.

I knew she would always remind me to keep sight of that. Always.

Layla got the last word in.

"Well, join the millions who belong to the Undervalued Women of the World Club. I have done well and James is jealous of my success. You're going places, girl, and you're right—one day Alejandro will regret that he's not by your side. You are a very complex person, Amalia. I wish you were a character in one of my books."

eleven

I added a bit more liquid and whirred the Osterizer again to blend the boiled carrots and potatoes into smooth baby food like Hortensia makes. The mess sprayed up all over me, onto the counter, and down on the floor . . . *¡Mierda!*

The perfect moment for the phone to ring. The weather had been stormy and the telephone crackled with static. I had no trouble recognizing Alejandro's voice, but I couldn't believe what he told me.

"They know about Aurora," he said right off the bat.

My legs felt wobbly and I had to sit down. Even though I'd guessed the answer, I asked, "Who do you mean when you say 'they'?"

"Your parents."

"You told them?"

"I'd have liked to give them the good tidings," he said, "but actually, they already knew. A few weeks ago, an acquaintance of theirs had been in Merida and saw you walking downtown with an infant. They asked your mother when the baby had been born."

It was my turn to be the one who couldn't "take it" and I hung up. The phone shrilled out several times during the next hour, but I ignored it. I couldn't speak with Alejandro now—maybe I'd never be able to speak to him again. His conceit, his disregard for my wishes, and the disrespectful way he played with my parents' feelings made me feel so angry with him. I slid down onto the cool tiles and hung my head between my knees.

Thank God Hortensia had taken Aurora out today. I'd have to call my parents and I could think of nothing I dreaded more. But it wouldn't get any easier, no matter how long I waited, so better to get it done. I dialed the Mexico City operator. Absurdly, I worried about the bill—daytime rates, the most expensive.

As soon as Mamá picked up the phone she started in on me. "What a disaster! Amalia, you have never done one single thing we've counseled and look where your stubbornness has landed you. From the start I knew Alejandro would break your heart."

"You are absolutely one hundred percent right. Alejandro has broken my heart Mamá, but he also has given me my daughter. When I became pregnant, I thought I needed to conceal her, but now I'm glad you know." I wanted to be a good daughter, but Mamá was pushing all my anger buttons. "Aurora is not 'a disaster.' She's the best thing in my life."

Mamá couldn't stop berating me. She didn't once ask me who Aurora looked like . . . how the birth went . . . nothing that had anything to do with *family*. As I had seen throughout my entire life, the only thing she knew how to do was to criticize.

She ended her tirade by asking, "And when will we get to see this child of yours?"

I couldn't tell if she was being edgy or plaintive. She had always been too proud to relax any of her rules, but it did sound like she wanted to meet her granddaughter.

"Not just now," I said. I had enough to deal with at this point. I lowered my voice a little. "Goodbye, Mamá, I'll call you another day."

She had been right about one thing: I'd been a fool to think I could raise a baby on my own. I needed greater financial independence. After Alejandro's latest stunt, I could not allow him to have control over me with support checks. I knew that I needed to have my own income and my mind kept returning to the idea that struck me during the renovation of my home.

Looking around my neighborhood, I could see that El Centro no longer held sway as a fashionable area to live; real estate in the downtown area had depreciated. The local middle-class families all seemed to be moving into the suburbs. Yet the international community had discovered Merida. Three retired American couples now lived on my street. More would surely follow—just as it had happened in other Mexican cities like Cuernavaca, Lake Chapala, and San Miguel de Allende. I needed some figures and statistics, and as much as I loathed going near our real estate agent, I decided I'd have to pay a visit to Señor Jiménez.

When I opened the door to his cigarette smoke-filled office, he must have seen me coming because he slithered into his swivel chair and tried to look important. When I told him that I needed some information, he puffed up like the expert he considered himself to be.

"For less than $20,000, you could buy a grand house, albeit in poor repair," he said.

I couldn't wait to share my news with Toño and Paul. I had already broached my idea of starting a renovation business with Paul.

"The sooner the better," he said. "Toño is climbing the walls. He watches our bank balance go down and refuses to believe we have enough money to last forever. If he doesn't start working again, he'll drive us both crazy."

"Don't worry, Paul, you and I will find a way to lighten Toño up." We hugged and I knew we understood one another perfectly.

That very afternoon, I asked Hortensia to take Aurora out to the park. She agreed immediately—she loved pushing my daughter in the stroller and chatting with everyone who stopped to admire our dark-haired darling.

I invited Paul and Toño to come over while it was quiet. And once they arrived, we settled into the living room wing chairs. Paul knew what we'd be talking about, but Toño squirmed; he'd guessed that the formal setting presaged an important topic. I picked up my fact sheet and photos off the coffee table—best not to waste anyone's time. I learned forward and stared into Toño's eyes.

"Do you want to hear my idea for a business we could start?"

Toño's face looked impassive and Paul had to help me out.

"Okay, even if Toño doesn't, I'm interested," he said.

"You know the house at the end of our block?" I asked.

"Sure," said Paul. "It's got a wraparound porch."

"Well, it's for sale. And so is the two-story red one on the plaza—both are priced at 20,000 US dollars."

"I know that's what they cost," my brother cut in. Obviously feeling a bit trapped, he wanted to play the part of Mr. Know-It-All, and I thought it best to let him.

I had collected the kind of information I knew he'd want. I spread open the folder and revealed the rest of my idea. "Look at this," I said as I handed the presentation to Paul.

He and Toño put their heads together and inspected the contents. "I've done some other pricing as well, and my estimate runs about $30,000 for the addition of top quality, state-of-the-art plumbing and lighting, restoring of *pasta* tiles, incorporating arches, digging a natural stone pool, and surrounding it with lush gardens. We could detail in the Old World Mexican style that foreigners find so romantic. I bet we could resell for at least $100,000—that's a one-hundred-percent profit."

Knowing Paul would be interested in the aesthetic aspects, I showed him another folder I'd compiled. "I've done some drawings. Why don't you have a look at them?"

The two studied at the series of color sketches and I could see that Paul loved the concept, but Toño questioned the need for such elaborate decoration.

"What if people don't want all that thematic fluff—talavera-tiled fountains, niches with urns and sculpted door frames? It's so much money to risk. What if we can't sell? Amalia, just because you succeeded with your own house, doesn't mean you've learned the business."

"No, but I've figured out what people are attracted to. For a long time you have been looking for a house to buy. I doubt that many would have so much patience. Most new arrivals in Merida would love to hire people like us—hip, Spanish-speaking local residents."

Toño looked as though he might be coming around and I knew Paul had already set up his tent in my camp, so I plunged forward. "There's more good news—tacked onto the outer wall of a dilapidated manor near the Park of the Americas is a faded *for sale* sign. It could be *the perfect property* for you. And I think it could also be the cornerstone of our business. I know I could convert that house into a showplace."

I stood up, fished in my skirt pocket, and pulled out an old key ring that Señor Jimenez had given me. "Want to have a look?" I felt victorious when I caught the eager glance that passed between them.

~

I knew we'd have to bushwhack our way into the grounds and I came prepared. I pulled two machetes out of the trunk of my brand-new cherry red Volkswagen and gave one to both Toño and Paul. They looked like a couple of little boys as they swung the blades back and forth.

In the afternoon sunlight, the house shimmered like a miniature chateau. Toño was all smiles. "After seeing so many awful dumps, this property looks ideal—not that it isn't a dump, too."

Once inside, Paul paced his way through the rooms. "Do you

know anything about the owners?" he asked.

"The elderly couple who built the place fifty years ago died recently, and the heirs can barely contain their excitement at the prospect of unloading the old homestead. Señor Jiménez seems eager to close the deal and get his cut. If we move fast, I bet we can get it for $18,000."

"Now tell me how our homes will be the 'cornerstone' of the new business," my brother wanted to know.

"Open your mind up, Toño, I think Amalia is onto something," said Paul, "Am I right, Amalia?"

"I paid careful attention during the restoration of my house. I took detailed notes, made drawings and kept receipts. I have at least a hundred photographs. After we've finished fixing your house, we'll all know a lot about the details and techniques, and we can use your place as well as mine to show future clients what they too could own."

Anticipating Toño's objections, Paul interjected, "Even if we don't get anyone interested, we won't have lost anything. As Amalia pointed out, we have to live somewhere."

I felt that Toño wouldn't need much time to mull over my ideas. If he thought they might be viable, he'd join in my enthusiasm and we'd soon be earning money—I felt sure we'd make a success of this, and I couldn't wait for my future partners to feel as confident as I did.

And Paul was good at making Toño get past his inflated anxieties.

Two days later, Paul called me to announce: "Toño has seen the light. When do we start, boss?"

"Be careful, Paul. We'd better use the term *partner.*"

"Good idea," he agreed. Toño had a talent for business, but he could get thorny if he didn't feel in control.

We began the renovation project with a huge clean up. Vandals had thrown rocks through several windows—even the colored-glass one. Debris from used-up lives littered the rooms. We piled up grimy shreds of old clothing, great stacks of yellowing newspapers, hundreds of empty glass jars and bottles, a stained mattress, and a tarnished brass headboard. We'd need to take many truck loads to the municipal dump.

Paul considered the ornate headboard again, thought better of throwing it away, and dragged it back inside. Toño frowned and his friend shrugged. "This could polish up nicely—maybe."

"I'd say it's beyond help. And this whole project is just as nuts!"

Paul had taken enough. "That's it, Toño. If you can't enjoy seeing this restoration process from beginning to end, go find something else to do. Read the classified ads and see what you can find at this price. Amalia and I seem to recognize a diamond in the rough when we see one, whereas you refuse to open your short-sighted eyes!"

We'd had tussles like this all the time at El Sol Imports, and I didn't like the idea of that behavior making the move to Merida.

Toño looked as mottled as the old brass headboard. But he knew that Paul had reached his limit. "I'm really sorry," my brother said. He grabbed his friend and me into a big bear hug. "I'm nervous about this and I'm taking it out on the two of you."

"So we noticed, Toño," I said. "Let's leave here for today and have a nice lunch."

"We're not dressed to go out," said the always dapper Paul.

"Don't worry, I know just the place," I reassured him.

La Ruina, a one-room, dingy working-class bar was fairly close by. "It doesn't look like much," I said, "but they serve ice cold beer and abundant food." We gorged on greasy pork rinds, squash seed dip, refried beans, and guacamole with tostadas. After the fourth round of Coronas, our waiter brought tacos and *empanadas*.

"I don't know why they call this place The Ruin," said Paul, "it's great!"

"I think it's probably a reference to what coming here does to the diet," I said.

"Or to one's reputation, " said Toño, pointing at an obviously secretive couple at the bar.

With our full stomachs and beer-besotted brains, we didn't feel much like going back to work. I laid down in my hammock for a siesta, but Hortensia had other plans.

"Amalia, Aurora is sleeping for once. We rarely get a chance to talk on our own, and I want to discuss something with you. Do you have time right now?"

What could I say? "Of course, Hortensia, come into the hammock with me."

With our heads at opposite ends of my soft cotton sling, and our bodies nestled against one another, I felt a closeness we'd both missed. "What's up?" I asked.

She looked as though starting this conversation would be difficult, and I quickly deduced it would have to do with Mamá.

"Amalia, your mother has called me a couple of times."

"What do you think I should do?"

"Phoning would be a good start. You can't leave her hanging much longer."

"Then let's call now," I said. Once my nana broached the subject, I knew she would not let it go, so why drag things out? We both straightened up and went inside to the kitchen.

When Mamá realized she had me on the line, she exhaled long and loud. "Amalia, it's about time you got off that high horse . . . you've got some explaining to do. We have a right to know how all this came about and why you've been so secretive about it."

I imitated her long sigh . . . now she wanted details. I spoke in a calm voice and gave her the bare bones. I wanted to ring off as quickly as I could, and neither did she seem to want to stay on the phone.

When I said goodbye, she let out another little moan and made a terse attempt at solidarity.

"Amalia, I am here if you need me," she said.

Mamá and I had many past hurts that needed to heal, but at least we had broken the ice.

"You made a start," said Hortensia. "I know it must have been hard. I am proud of you."

She hugged me and I felt her warm body soaking up my troubles.

~~~

Once the clutter had been cleared out of Paul and Toño's house, Hortensia found a team of people from the market who scoured the place from top to bottom. They pulled stubborn weeds and burned them with the fallen leaves and limbs from the gnarly old avocado and mango trees. The light company re-connected the power and we placed mega-watt bulbs in the sockets. Under the glare of the bright lamps, we could at last get a good look at the colorful patterns of the pasta tile floors and the lacy ceiling moldings The more we unveiled, the more we realized the house's elegant potential.

At one time, the García Ginerés neighborhood had been the exclusive precinct of Merida's wealthiest families. Grand mansions lined the main boulevards: Avenida Colón and Avenida Cupules. The gardens surrounding the estates—called *quintas*—featured tall royal palms, wide-limbed *acacias*, and towering tamarinds. Peacocks strutted across the manicured lawns. The residents rather resembled the trees—they looked firmly rooted in a time of former glory. Their social circle was not open to "strangers." And yet Paul's open heart—and his delicious jam cookies—were making inroads. The refined dowagers had progressed to giving him half smiles and regal waves.

"No problem with these ladies," said my confident friend *sotto voce*. Soon they'll be inviting me for tea and Canasta."

Toño, Paul, and I worked with Benito Carranza, the same architect who had renovated my home. We needed him to draw up the blueprints and get building permits from City Hall. He'd also be the one to determine the condition of the *mamposteria*—the rock and stucco walls—the state of the wiring and plumbing, and the permeability of the roof. As we expected, much had deteriorated beyond repair. Paul and Toño were looking at extensive renovations.

We wanted the house to be attractive to foreign buyers, so Benito suggested knocking out a few walls to create larger, spacious rooms and a more contemporary floor plan; there would also be a pool. He encouraged us to think creatively about the changes we had in mind.

The three of us discussed this in detail and I sketched the entire layout. Benito seemed surprised and definitely a bit protective of his turf.

"You have ability, Amalia," he said, "but you would need to take formal training. You have ideas, but you are lacking perspective."

"Well, you're right, I have never studied architecture, but ever since I was a small girl, I've enjoyed looking at a room and thinking how I could make it beautiful—also more practical—so that people would love being in the space. After high school, I worked as a draftsperson for a few months."

"You should think about going to architectural college. Have you ever considered that? There are several excellent ones in Mexico City."

"My new baby makes relocating impossible. When I was younger, I had no money and my parents didn't either. They sent me to the US where Toño and Paul lived. My brother provided me with funds to attend the university in Austin, so I followed his proposal and studied fine arts.

"*¡Ay, Amalia!* By the time your baby is old enough to be weaned, there will be a program opening at the University of Yucatan. You should look into it."

I liked Benito's suggestion of going to the University of Yucatan to see what they might be offering in the near future.

Eight months and many pesos later, Paul and Toño had completed what they called "Our Fantasy." On moving day, they ceremoniously opened the ornate front gate. We walked slowly across the lawn and formal garden, climbed five wide steps up to a covered portico, and passed through the delicate wrought-iron-and-glass door.

Aurora squirmed out of my arms and took a few steps into the room. She raised her head and looked up. We cheered her on, but she must have felt intimidated by the deep blue ceiling that peered down like a mile-high night sky. She shook her curly head, dropped to all fours, and quickly crawled back to me.

The front foyer opened fully onto the elegant living room, complete with an ebony Steinway. I could envision how perfect the house would be for entertaining. The dining room featured replicas of eighteenth-century Spanish baroque furniture, including a massive mahogany table that could extend to seat sixteen guests. Paul said he couldn't wait to host their first dinner party.

I knew he would be anxious to widen their social circle, and a party would fit in well with what I knew we needed to do. To me it seemed imperative that we cultivate a professional reputation in the community.

twelve

Paul kept asking when we'd host a dinner party, and I knew Layla would be the perfect cultural attaché.

"Sure, many people are curious to meet you. I could fill this place twice over," Layla said. "What kind of party do you want to have? What sort of guests?"

Buoyed by her enthusiasm, Paul couldn't wait to start planning. At first we talked about a formal sit-down affair for sixteen, but he thought something outdoors for a larger, more casual crowd might work better.

"We aren't going to click with everyone at the party, so the more who come, the more new friends we'll make."

Thirty seemed to be the magic number—just like my Yuletide dinners in Mexico City. In fact, the party would be held in mid-December and I wondered if it might not be the start of a new tradition.

Paul got us into high gear. We rented long tables, white table cloths, and tents. Toño hung delicate tissue-paper poinsettias and blinking white lights. Hortensia, who professed no interest in decorating, got out the boxes of tree ornaments from the storage room and festooned a potted Norfolk pine. The garden had been transformed. "But what about the food?" I asked Paul. I saw no evidence of his usual pre-party culinary flurry.

"Don't worry," he said as he showed me the door. "Come back at nine tonight."

Hortensia and I put on the same seasonal finery we'd worn at my Christmas dinners in Mexico City, and in her white lace dress, Aurora looked like a Christmas angel. Seeing my one-and-a-half year-old daughter brought tears to the eyes of Dr. Montañez and his petite wife Mayté .

Hortensia smiled. "I think you two should think about having one these!" she said, patting Mayté's arm.

A quick smile passed between the couple and my nana knew that seven months later they would have their first son, Sebastian.

A cracked, old-fashioned terra cotta bread oven had been one of the features that my brother and Paul loved best about the garden. During the renovation, the contractor had been poised to demolish it and cart away the shards, but both owners had insisted that it be restored. Usually the oven served a strictly ornamental purpose, but tonight Paul had decided to make pizza—such a common cuisine in the Texas neighborhood where he grew up, but Merida did not have even one Italian restaurant. He figured our guests would enthusiastically embrace the ethnic change.

Understatement! The baker Paul hired to help out for the evening worked double time to keep up with the demand for more pizza and garlic bread. Waiting around the oven for "just one more piece," our guests' conversations flowed as easily as the robust red wine Paul had selected. Fresh green salad completed the main course and Hortensia's top desserts ended the meal.

Our new friends looked impressed with the improvements we'd made to Toño and Paul's early twentieth-century home. In fact, several of them told us about houses they had for sale. Eventually, we would settle on two properties we liked a lot. Worlds apart with regards to location, price and size, we felt they'd appeal to very different sets of clients. The first—a hacienda—lay fourteen kilometers east of Merida. Toño surprised us when he insisted we put a bid on it; he felt sure it would be perfectly suited to a couple he and Paul knew from Wilmington, Indiana—Catherine and Van Raymond.

"What's the difference between a hacienda and a ranch?" Paul asked.

I'd picked up this information from my reading. "Most haciendas are abandoned now, but in their day, a country estate could only be called a hacienda if it had a commercial crop, a manufacturing center, workers' accommodations, a fine manor house, and a consecrated chapel."

The agricultural fields of the hacienda had been sold off years ago, but five hectares remained attached to the house. This land would be a source of great pleasure to the two gardening enthusiasts Toño had in mind. Additionally, the distance from the city would fulfill their need for seclusion, and we could easily revamp the main house to provide what Van and Catherine would need to release their creative energies.

The other building we set our hopes on was on Calle 66. Toño and Paul knew ideal buyers for this place, too. Maura Sánchez lived in Austin, but was born in Cuba. For many years she'd dreamed of moving to a Latin country with her aging mother, Jimena, who had never adapted well to life in the US. Maura thought she'd like to own and operate a bed and breakfast. She felt sure that Mexico would be the best country for her and her mamá. Merida appealed to her because the city has always enjoyed traditional ties to Cuba. Much of Yucatan's food, music, building style, and everyday idioms come from the Latin-Caribbean country. By her own description, Maura would never be a beach person, but she liked to be close to the ocean.

"The Gulf of Mexico is only thirty kilometers north," I told her.

She took her mother's hand and squeezed it. "¡Perfecto! I get the urge to dip my feet in salt water about twice a year, and Mamá would feel great peace knowing that her homeland, La Isla, lies not too far away."

"The Calle 66 building was made for you," Toño told Maura. "It used to be a clinic, and so there are already many individual rooms—sixteen, in fact. The large front ones would make lovely reception and common areas. The former operating theater could become a dining room. The patients' rooms could be converted into the guest suites."

We decided it would be best to have Catherine and Van and Maura and Jimena come for a week-long visit. We planned the itinerary with as much care as a protocol committee would execute a State visit. In mid-January, the weather would be at its best in Yucatan and its worst up north; it would be the ideal time to put our plan into effect.

On January 18, Toño and I met the two couples at the airport, and when we arrived at Paul and Toño's García Ginerés house, we had margaritas and Yucatecan snacks by the pool—tiny *salbutes* and *panuchos*, an eggplant dip with pita chips, tightly wrapped *tamalitos*, a fresh fruit-and-vegetable tray, and toasted nuts. The visitors quickly tucked away most of the food.

"I wonder what the weather is like in Wilmington?" Van cut in.

We all laughed—everyone seemed delighted so far. But then Van said, "I'll want a pair of *cholos* to give me my money's worth for a ten-hour day. I don't plan on doing much heavy yard work, but I'll want my place to look like I do."

I looked toward Toño for some help. With characteristic directness, he set the demanding Northerner straight. "Van, you'll meet lots of hard-working people, but in this climate, no one can work ten consecutive hours."

That point made, I suggested we be on our way to have a look at the two properties. As we passed Hortensia on our way out, everyone thanked her for the snacks—except Van.

On the drive I asked Catherine what qualities would be important to her. I tried to get a dialogue going by listing some of the features I myself find essential, like large rooms with cross ventilation.

She listened politely while Van leaned his head back and closed his eyes. Taking his hand she told me, "Van is a successful writer and I'm an illustrator. I design all his covers and draw whatever else he needs. And I work for other authors and publishers as well. We both need separate areas to work."

Thanks to his wife, Van had re-established his place as the center of attention. He came wide awake and resumed his self-important monologue.

"Damn right I do. As I write, I rant and rave like my characters do. She says that distracts her."

I couldn't imagine why.

Later, out at the hacienda, the couple did not say much to the rest of us, but they whispered back and forth with one another, and I knew that the house and grounds suited them.

"This very week, I could complete sketches of some renovation ideas," I said. "You'll be able to return with them to Wilmington, and then, let us know how you want to proceed."

"Oh, I can tell you right now, we like this place," said Van. "The question is—will your outfit be right for us? I deal only with people who pay attention to me and get me what I want."

Catherine looked ready to follow along with his decisions, and I suspected our business relationship had died. Finally, Van let out a huge guffaw. Everyone else managed relief-edged giggles because they wanted to think he was only joking around. But he didn't fool me for a second—the guy could not be trusted.

Maura and her mother were absolutely different. They had done the math and debated hotly—the daughter in English and her mamá in Spanish—as to whether or not they could afford the house on Calle 66. With the renovations, it would cost more than they'd planned on spending.

"It reminds me of our home in Cuba," Jimena said as she touched her daughter's cheek

. "I want it more than anything, and I have my jewelry, you know. We could sell some of the bigger stones and manage easily."

Maura didn't want to think about selling the diamonds. Jimena had traveled to America with forty carats of gem stones hidden in her braids and curls. This nest egg was to be used for a dire emergency, not for buying a house in Mexico. If her father had still been alive, he would have been horrified.

"How much longer am I going to live?" asked Jimena. "I want to enjoy the time I have left. If there's an emergency, we'll manage somehow." She wandered away to look at the bedroom to her left.

"If selling some of the stones would provide her with the environment she wants to re-create, maybe I should consider that," Maura said. She and Paul watched as the elderly woman peered happily through the louvered panes.

Her face took on a far-away look. "I had a window like this in Havana, and it looked out onto a busy street just as this one does."

The longing in her mother's voice cinched Maura's decision. She walked over to Jimena, put her arms around the older woman's shoulders and said, "Get used to that view, Mamá, you'll be looking at it for the rest of your days."

After a week of pampering, our four clients returned to their respective homes in the US. If they decided to buy, money could be transferred to cover the cost of our finder's fee and the purchase of the properties. When the deeds were in their hands, they would need to deposit funds for the renovations. This part worried me because once they had the final papers and the bank trusts had been established, either client could hire another contractor.

We took the gamble and as I suspected, Maura came through but not the Raymonds. They didn't contact us again, not even a thank-you note. Paul and Toño felt disappointed, but not me. I didn't want to work with Van and Catherine.

Hortensia echoed my sentiments. "Their attitude felt wrong. Such people drain away energy."

~~~

A year after Catherine and Van backed out of the sale, our option to buy the hacienda expired and we faced a dilemma. We had to either purchase it outright or miss the opportunity.

"I don't want to risk the capital we have," said Toño. "I've tried to interest other clients, but the necessary renovations are too extensive. We'll have to let this one go and lose the $10,000 deposit."

I could tell he was set to get really angry and, of course, take it out on Paul and me.

"We've overextended ourselves, and I can't have that," he said.

Hortensia walked into the room and gently put her hand on my brother's back. "Toño, I think you've forgotten that you wanted to buy the hacienda. You are the one who tried to interest Van and Catherine. You can't lay the blame on Amalia and Paul."

His nostrils flared—but he knew she had him beat, and reluctantly, we said goodbye to our money. It hurt to lose that much-needed cash but again, we'd faced an obstacle and had made it over to the other side. I knew it would be like this—forever. Paul and I would need to keep Toño appeased, but in a way, this worked out for the best.

I laughed, clapping Paul and Hortensia on the back. "You know what, partners, if we didn't have Toño to keep our feet on the ground, it would be pretty easy to go completely overboard, wouldn't it?"

"You bet it would," said Paul. "And speaking of 'overboard,' you know the chandelier at Alberto's Continental Patio?"

I nodded. I had long coveted that glittery crystal fixture and thought how it would look over my glass-topped table.

"Well, happy birthday, darlin'!"

I hurried into the dining room and saw it burning brightly. As bright as Paul's smile . . .

~~~

Another of our greatest challenges was to keep the workers motivated. Accustomed to largely absent employers, they complained that we were always underfoot. The truth of the matter was that with us around, they were unable to siphon off anything. We called this stealing, but feeling underpaid, the crew saw it as an accepted practice for adding to their income.

I knew we couldn't go against tradition. Our workers, and in fact the entire population of the Yucatan Peninsula, were mired in that ethic. "If we don't give them what they think is fair, we are going to lose every crew we put together," I finally said.

Predictably, Toño got furious. He paced around the office like a caged tiger. But I insisted, "This culture won't change because certain aspects don't suit us. We just have to learn to deal with it."

Back-and-forth debate finally produced a solution that seemed to be well received. "You'll get a ten percent bonus," I told Don Luis, "if, and only if, the projects come in on time and on budget." Under this arrangement, they labored like Trojans. Even in the heat of the dry season, they arrived on time, ready for a full day's work.

Every evening at six, I'd join Toño and Paul for a meeting at the current work site. We'd put our feet up, sometimes share a bottle of wine or a pot of coffee, depending how much we needed to review the day's progress or how complicated it might be to map out the next day's strategy. Usually finished by seven-thirty, I'd drive back to my house, with the feeling of satisfaction that good work brings.

~

When I arrived home, Hortensia would often go out to meet with one of her groups. She belonged to a spiritual circle, she mentored a recovering addicts' group, and she loved her gardening club. These evening hours allowed me to have special time with Aurora. Curled up together in one of the big wicker rockers, I'd read to her. Or when my daughter was too excited or felt too hot for sleep, we'd go for a swim before bed. Because I'd had her in the pool since infancy, she seemed to be half fish.

And we were safe. When Toño told me about the latest violence in Mexico City, I felt relieved that it couldn't touch me or my child.

Everyone in the country knew that our current president was the government henchman who gave the order to slaughter the students on October 2, 1968. He professed to be a staunch leftist and yet he tolerated no opinion contrary to his own.

On June 10, 1971, students in La Capital held a rally in support of their colleagues in the northern city of Monterrey. And once again the young people were faced with the full force of the Establishment. A special brigade known as *Los Halcones*—The Hawks—were deployed against those who had assembled in Tacuba, a Mexico City subway station. Again, many young people died pointlessly and more were beaten and held without medical attention.

I often reflected that when I first learned of my pregnancy, I'd thought that by moving to Merida, life as I knew it would be ending. I didn't realize that on the day Hortensia and I left Mexico City, a better life would begin for us. As I helped Aurora get ready for bed and combed her curly hair, I reflected that sooner or later I would have to take her to La Capital—she and Mamá needed to meet.

And Alejandro called often. Last year it had finally sunk in that his demands and intimidation didn't work with me. I thought back to the day he'd called me and asked for a truce.

"I'm by myself this weekend, Amalia. Susana has gone to an art show in Puebla, and I am thinking how wonderful it would be to see you and meet our daughter."

"That is not going to happen until I say it does," I'd fired back.

"Okay, Amalia, okay. I understand how wrong I've been to try and pressure you. My work is a constant battle and I'm used to shouting and bullying to get my way," he said, "but it isn't healthy for any of us. Can't we start again?"

I looked at Aurora and saw her make the same grin as her father's. Heredity is unbelievable—she's never laid eyes on him but that gesture is unique.

"She has your smile," I offered, "and your dark curls."

"Do you think you could send me a more recent photograph? The one I have is from last Christmas."

I looked at the framed studio portrait of Aurora that I had placed on the sideboard. I had four more; I could spare one of them.

"I'll send it tomorrow, and I'll also send you a drawing she did."

I heard his intake of air. "Thank you, Amalia, I can't wait until the package arrives."

But much had to be taken care of before I could think about going to Mexico City. I had to wait until I could take time off from work.

thirteen

Keeping our fledgling business going shortchanged many other areas of my life. Aurora's third birthday was coming up and I didn't even have time to plan a party.

I rationalized to Hortensia that there would be time for that when she got older. Arriving home a little later than usual, I dropped my briefcase and purse onto a wicker chair and Aurora came running.

"*¡Mamá, Mamá!*" she called, all out of breath. My nana's brown-and-gold gaze warned me that my guilty conscience was about to get another jolt.

"Come here to your mommy," I said, holding out my arms. She lowered her head and tackled me to the floor. We fell into a heap, laughing. I nuzzled my face into her tummy and blew kisses on her belly button.

She squealed, squirmed away, and with a sly smile she asked, "Do you have a present for me?"

"*Ah*," I said, "First tell me, were you a good girl for Hortensia?"

"Always! And for *Tio* Toño and Uncle Paul . . ."

Just like her father, there was no holding back when Aurora wanted something. Caution and deliberation were not part of her nature. She'd had more than her share of tumbles, scrapes, and even a broken collarbone last spring. Miss Aili, her guide at the Montessori school, reported that the minute they let Aurora out of their sight, my daughter would be into mischief. Once she pulled the poster paints down, opened them up, and dug both hands into

the canary yellow and rooster red. She swirled the color on herself
and was poised to begin decorating the wall when she got busted.
Maybe there's a little bit of my sister's creative genius in her, too.

Many well-meaning, but absolutely mistaken mothers scolded
me for not controlling her more. But from my own experience, I
knew that my little one would need her full-size personality. I did
not intend to do any taming.

Nonetheless, I had to admit that I couldn't keep up with her.
Paul suggested that we employ a high school student to come to the
house for a couple of hours every day. A girl from the neighborhood answered the ad we placed in the newspaper. Maribel seemed
perfect. Athletic and energetic, some days she ran Aurora until she
nearly collapsed. But Maribel also liked to bake and paint and sew
and make piñatas; she had a willing partner in Aurora.

"Nana, how does she know this is her birthday?"

"Maribel told her, I guess." Nana sounded livid.

I hugged her and opened my bag. I drew out a doll—not just any
doll, but the one Aurora had begged me for. I'd been dead set against
buying a Barbie, but I knew nothing would please her more. I worried that she would cut her fingers on the ragged edge of the hard
cardboard box as she tried to rip the doll loose. Barbie had curly
blonde hair and bright blue eyes and her dress sparkled. Aurora's
eyes danced when I showed her the extra outfits I had splurged on.
Little boots, high heels, a fur coat, a ballet costume . . . that Barbie
was one lucky piece of plastic!

After tucking Aurora and Barbie into bed, I found Hortensia
in a stew that was ready to boil over.

"I knew you'd be cross about Aurora knowing that today is her
birthday. I told Maribel not to tell her. But she doesn't listen to me.
I want you to get rid of her, or do you think I'm getting too old to

look after your daughter? Maybe I should stick to the cooking and supervising the cleaning people? You could hire Maribel full time to look after Aurora."

My head snapped up in surprise.

"What's happened? I thought you liked having her here and that she seemed happy with her after-school job."

Again I urged Nana to sit by me, but she wanted to stand. And from the set of her jaw, I knew she would not be easily appeased.

"I can't concentrate with you marching all over the kitchen," I said as I held out a chair for the third time.

Hortensia settled down with a thud. "The girl excites Aurora to the point of frenzy," Hortensia told me while keeping her eyes averted from mine.

I kept my voice level. "But Aurora needs to get rid of her excess energy," I reminded Hortensia.

"Yes, she does. But Maribel lets Aurora run around like a monkey and doesn't even keep her clean. She allows her to shout and sing at the top of her lungs."

What had gotten into Hortensia? She sounded just like the mothers who wanted Aurora to be more sedate. The more Nana talked, the more I realized it wasn't Maribel's exuberance she wanted to rein in. Hortensia was jealous. I could understand how she might feel displaced by Aurora's obvious affection for Maribel, and I wondered if the physical stress had tired Nana. I needed to say something that would restore her confidence.

"Neither of us can keep up with a whirlwind like my daughter. We need Maribel for that. Perhaps when Maribel and Aurora are too loud and rambunctious, you could spend that time at the clinic to help the Sisters of Charity."

My attempt at tact backfired badly.

"Amalia!" Her eyes flew at me like two pointed darts toward the bull's eye. "How many times have you told me that you always trust my advice? That you respect my wisdom? Now it seems all that has changed. I certainly don't need to spend more time with the nuns. They have learned very well how to run the center without me. If you want Maribel to stay, I am going back to Mexico City. I think your mother will let me have my old room."

I knew Hortensia wasn't giving me the whole story. She liked spending as much time as possible with Sister Belén and the others. I couldn't let her leave over a trifle like this. I'd have to be blunt.

"What does Maribel have to do with your not wanting to spend time at the center?"

Hortensia's face turned to stone. I tried again. "What did Maribel do that has upset you so much? You have to tell me!"

Finally my nana confessed. "She brought them to see me."

Her resistance was breaking down, so I moved toward her but she stood up again and backed away.

"Amalia, I never imagined this could happen. Before today, I didn't know that Maribel and I are related. Her mother is my second cousin, and when Maribel blabbed about me, three of them came. These are people from Santa Cecilia, my village!"

Before my eyes, Hortensia seemed to shrink into the inexperienced girl she described herself as being when she first came to Merida. She clenched and unclenched her hands and compulsively smoothed the front of her *huipil*.

"What can be so bad about meeting your cousins?" I asked. Now that she had started her tale, I sensed she needed to tell me everything.

"I told you that my parents tried to arrange a horrible marriage for me with our village's co-op leader. He was old, he had bad teeth, and he turned violent when I wouldn't allow him to have relations with me." Hortensia put her face in her hands, then she squared herself once more. "I got so angry that I did the unpardonable. I didn't ask the guides to help me forgive him. I conjured up evil and asked for vengeance. I had never before misused my abilities—I didn't even know I had the power to do so. But I sure did that one time."

No wonder Hortensia had gotten so distraught; these memories were the most traumatic of her life.

"Over the next few days the man aged. He seemed to shrink. I made it happen—the negative force in me felt so omnipotent. My mother didn't know what I had done, but she was furious that I had dismissed the only suitor I'd ever had. A girl as graceless as me should be grateful, she said. The man developed a rash and a lethargy that never left him. No one could reverse the malady. The shamans suspected that I had tapped the power of *Ah Puch*—God of Death—and one of them whispered, 'I will see you banished for this.'"

Hortensia finished by telling me, "Two weeks later, La Madrina arrived to announce that I was being sent to work for your parents. I think that shaman planted the idea of sending me away into my mother's head."

Confiding in me had released some of her fear, but she kept herself away. I took a firm hold of her right hand anyway, figuring that she needed at least some physical reassurance.

"Hortensia," I said calmly, "you tell me that sometimes you sense impending disaster and sometimes not. Are you ever wrong?"

"Sometimes it can be unclear and I need to interpret the signs as best I can. I'm not always right. What are you getting at, Amalia?"

I let her hand go, smiled, and broadsided her with the truth.

"Hortensia, you're making me realize how important it is for all of us to make peace with our families. There is nothing to be gained by prolonging the pain. I need to make a trip to Mexico City and let my family meet Aurora. Will you come with me?"

She looked as unmovable as a Mayan pyramid. But finally she closed her eyes and conceded, "You're right, Amalia. I have also let this pain swell between my family and me for too long. But my solution is not as easy as yours. I'll need some time."

Hortensia's equanimity did not return immediately, but she agreed to go to La Capital with Aurora and me. The only thing that worried me nonstop was the thought of an encounter with Alejandro. I told myself that I didn't want to see him, and yet I had to admit he did deserve to meet his daughter. I decided that I'd call Mamá in the morning.

Paul, Toño, and I restored another three homes that year. Our workdays often stretched longer than I liked and stressful situations came up when we least expected them, but we'd made a pact that one of us would always be available to the workers.

Layla and I had planned on dinner and the movies. We hadn't been out together for months and I looked forward to this respite from work and parenting. My partners were away in Cozumel. I had agreed to be on call for three weekends before the Mexico City trip and just as I finished putting on my lipstick, the foreman called.

"The water has stopped. We're dry in the middle of a cement pour," he said.

"What does he think you can do about that?" asked Layla.

"I don't know, but I need to go and see."

"I'll come along," she offered hoisting herself up into the cab of the truck. She settled her stiletto heels on either side of two paint cans and smiled at me.

"Amalia, you really know how to show a girl a good time!"

She laughed as I pressed my foot down hard on the clutch, got into gear, and drove off. At the site we found that the workmen had rigged a suction hose into the well and were able to bring water up.

"There, you see it all worked out," I said smiling and handing Don Luis a few rolled bills. "Get some tacos for the crew once you're done here."

"We have to keep the workers happy," I explained to Layla as I drove to the restaurant. "They found their own solution, but they like to know we're there for them if they need anything. Sometimes we all wish we had more time for ourselves, but this work exhilarates us."

"Whatever you're doing, you're doing it right!" said Layla. I noticed her looking at my new emerald. "That's quite a beautiful ring. Have you got a sugar daddy you're keeping a secret?"

"I have a sugar *self*. Just because there's no man around to give me nice things, I am not prepared to do without."

My best friend nodded her pretty head. "You're growing up, girl!"

It was too late for a movie, but we ate a magnificent three-course meal at El Pórtico del Peregrino. The two bottles of wine we drank were way more than I'm used to. Layla had insisted on the second because she said she needed some inner fortitude if I wanted her to tell me about her vacation at Secretos—the new resort on a remote beach at her much-missed Cozumel. She ended her racy account by saying, "Let's just say it's one of those places where less is more."

I felt ready to head for home, but when Layla asked, "Do you want to go to El Aloha?" I could tell her question was actually a command, and if she could handle a place like Secretos, I figured she could certainly get me in and out safely from the local club. I left the truck parked near the restaurant. I'd pick it up in the morning. Layla and I tumbled into a cab.

The popular night spot was decorated with tall artificial palm trees and a canoe hanging from the ceiling. The waiters wore formal dress, but the women working there were nearly naked. The chorus line and even the chanteuse stripped down to pasties and a G-string. Couples danced close.

Two guys with mutton-chop sideburns and satin shirts opened to the waist noticed us and stumbled over to our table. One of them wore several gold chains that had tangled-up in his blond chest hair while the other wobbled unsteadily in his platform boots. There didn't seem to be any way to politely avoid dancing with the pair. "We work for Braniff Airlines and we're in town on a two-day lay-over," said one of them as he moved in to kiss Layla.

"Well laying-over me isn't gonna happen," she declared as she pushed herself away from him. "Amalia, unless you're interested in a romp with one of these disco dudes, I suggest we leave." I called for our check and we were quickly on our way.

During the drive back home, I told her about my mother wanting to meet Aurora.

"Yeah, it's time Amalia . . . you and your mamá have to get on better terms and she needs to meet her granddaughter."

~~~

The November 20 long weekend would be as good a date as any. Hortensia got excited about the trip, as I knew she would.

She even suggested we pay Maribel for the days we'd be gone. "I know her family depends on the income," she explained.

Hortensia wanted to stay at Mamá's house, but I did not. For a first visit, it would be enough for Aurora to see my parents for a little while on each of the four days we would spend in La Capital. I also wanted to have time alone with her.

During our first afternoon, my father looked proud to see that Aurora could readily play back the simple tunes he picked out on the piano. He said she had natural musical talent. But when she got into Mamá's sewing room, her eyes grew twice their size. She couldn't resist touching the fabrics, even smelling them. She sat down with a big fashion magazine and looked at every page. Mamá showed her a picture of a singing star and asked Aurora what colors she would use for the woman's stage dress. Without hesitation, Aurora pointed at the teal blue silk trimmed with ivory.

Mamá looked at me with an air of victory and said, "I guess that in some families, genius skips a generation." I laughed, pleased that my daughter had given my parents such joy.

I had reserved a room at the Hotel Bamer right downtown so that I could take Aurora to all my special places. Her favorite seemed to be Sunday at the Chapultepec Zoo. Seeing all the families sparked an impulsive decision.

"Let's find a pay phone," I said to Aurora. I dialed a number that had burned itself into my memory. If *she* answered, I'd just hang up. But Alejandro picked up the receiver on the second ring. He sounded shocked to hear my voice. "I am at Chapultepec with Aurora. Do you want to join us?"

"Amalia! I'd love that. I'll be there in half an hour."

"What about Susana?" I asked.

"She's at a show in Acapulco this week."

As Hortensia would say, it looked as though the goddess wanted this to happen. When Alejandro arrived, my heart turned over. He wore crisply ironed denim jeans and a snug white polo shirt. His dark curls were still damp from the shower. As he walked toward me, his eyes were fixed on his little double standing at my side.

Aurora had an eager expression in her eyes. "Is that my daddy?" she asked.

I trembled so hard I could hardly reply. "Yes, that's him."

They didn't embrace, not in the first ten minutes, but after that, it was as though they'd been glued to one another. I had dreaded this encounter—wondered what it would be like—worried about my reaction, but the dynamic between the three of us seemed natural and relaxed. The rift in my defenses now gaped as wide as the seismic fault under Mexico City.

Since we'd be flying home early in the morning, we needed to get back to the hotel before dark. Hortensia would be waiting for us in the lobby and planned to stay in our room that night. Alejandro drove us to the entrance and said he would be there the next day to take us to the airport.

I told him I didn't think he'd better do that. "This has been a perfect day. Let's not spoil it with a melodramatic goodbye."

He finally agreed and hugged us both until we lost our breath.

"Daddy, you're squeezing too hard!"

I watched Aurora for signs of confusion, but her happy smile told me that acting on my instincts had been the right thing. I would need to be careful and not get my hopes up nor did I want Aurora to start counting on her father for anything. It was one thing for him to disappoint me, but if he hurt my daughter, I would have to contend with thoughts of murder.

At the hotel entrance Alejandro picked Aurora up and gave her another big hug.

His eyes smiled at me. "I want to see both of you again soon," he said.

I couldn't help myself—I felt frightened—but I also knew it was too late to second guess my moves. I looked at "our" daughter, so content in her daddy's arms and knew without a doubt that I had opened Pandora's Box.

fourteen

Layla and I sat on the patio watching Aurora and her friends playing hide-and-seek—running first one way, then the next. "Do you remember how we used to go flat out like that, and don't you wish we still could?" I asked Layla.

The girls screamed at the top of their lungs and then fell into a heap on the floor. They looked like a litter of kittens. Paul and Toño agreed with me—what a release it would be to let go like that. But, of course, we did nothing of the sort. We were waiting.

I looked at the sparkly lights and loopy garlands strung above me. Aurora and Maribel had put them up. Balloons of every color floated in the pool and the pink-and-purple crepe paper piñata that they bought at the market hung from a rope—ready to be burst open. Over the past six months, Hortensia and Maribel had put aside their differences and between the two of them, my daughter got all the thoughtful nurturing and stimulating attention she needed. I smiled at Layla.

"This is going to be an exciting fall," I said. "The architectural college will open in two months, and I've been accepted. I feel like all my dreams are on the verge of coming true."

Layla arched her perfectly plucked eyebrows. "Better not get too excited until you find out how tough the government opposition is going to be. My sources tell me that the moratorium on new schools is still very much in effect. The politicians don't want more university students because they're still nervous about rebellion."

I knew what she meant. The university board of directors had tired of being put on hold and the governor did not look as though he would capitulate, even a little bit. He created roadblock after roadblock, hoping that the professors and potential students would give up. The opening of the architectural college was at a standstill.

Layla gave me a sisterly pat on the arm. "If the others are anything like you, I doubt that the governor stands a chance," she said.

"I wish I had half the strength you give me credit for," I said, swallowing a long drink of water. "What will happen in just a few minutes has me petrified. If I can get through today, school start-up will be as easy as spending money in a shoe store."

Before Layla could laugh at my joke, the doorbell rang. Alejandro had arrived.

This first visit to Merida had involved months of negotiation. After our rendezvous in Chapultapec Park, he thought the door stood open wide. He wanted me to allow Aurora to travel to Mexico City and spend time with him and Susana. Once he figured out that he couldn't bend me to his will, he decided he would be satisfied, for now, with a solo trip to see her in Merida. He and I finally agreed that our daughter's fourth birthday would be the ideal date. I can only imagine how angry that made Susana.

I squared my shoulders, took a deep breath, and walked to the massive door. When Toño saw me hesitate, he held up his hands and moved forward to open it.

"Alejandro, how are you?" he asked with all the enthusiasm he could force into his voice.

"I'm fine Toño," Alejandro replied, nodding curtly. Then he turned his eyes toward me and said, "Amalia, it's amazing seeing you here . . . after all these years."

My heart beat as hard as it had when I was fourteen. He moved to kiss me, but spotted Aurora watching us. "And there's the birthday girl!" he cried out. After a quick peck on the cheek, he left me gasping and hurried to catch his daughter who ran right into his arms. She had only seen him the one time, eight months ago, and yet their bond had already grown strong.

Uncharacteristically silent, Aurora lay in his embrace for what seemed to me a long time. Her friends watched—transfixed by the sight of the tall stranger. And he came prepared to win them all over.

From two large Palacio de Hierro shopping bags, he pulled out a huge pink-wrapped present that he gave to Aurora. Then he handed each of her friends a smaller package. There was also one for me, Layla, Paul and Toño, Hortensia, and Maribel.

"You don't have a present, Daddy," Aurora said, her eyes wide with wonderment for all the bounty he had produced.

"Yes, I do and mine is the best one in the world—I am here with you on your birthday," he said.

I had to admire his style—he'd sure managed to get things off to a promising start.

We all opened our gifts at the same time. Aurora's friends each received a plush panda—just like the one at the Chapultepec Park Zoo—books about remodeling Colonial homes for Paul and Toño, and fuzzy cardigans for Hortensia and Maribel. Layla and I got a faux pearl bracelet each, and Aurora, the birthday girl, received the largest gift—a playhouse for Barbie. I felt quite surprised that Alejandro had done so well. I couldn't resist being catty and whispered to Layla, "I am sure that he didn't ask Susana to choose these!"

My best friend put on her best mock-serious face. "Behave!" she hissed, and then put up her hand so as to hide her smirk. I blessed her for standing beside me on this awkward afternoon.

Aurora delighted in having her father at the house. She showed him her special treasures: her favorite watering can, her shell collection, and the trees where the warbler nests hung. He paid absolute attention to every word she uttered.

When it came time to hoist the piñata up and down, serve the cake, and play the games, he joined in full-heartedly. Aurora had eyes for only him. I felt left out of her favor as I'm sure Layla, Hortensia, and Maribel did, but I felt sorriest for Toño and Paul who did not get so much as a nod from their niece.

It had turned dark by the time the other children's mothers came to collect them. Usually they did not act overly friendly. They'd mumble their thanks, take the little girls' hands and be off. But they too had lots of interest in handsome Alejandro and lingered in the doorway longer than they had to. Their curious faces held so many questions. I had no idea how to logically explain his appearance, so I opted to convey that this situation was perfectly comfortable for me. The ladies remained quiet, but I wondered how long their silence would last.

They left reluctantly, yet Alejandro showed no sign of doing likewise. I wanted Layla to stay on, but she gave me a teasing wink and whispered, "I can't stay, girl . . . but I'm sure you'll find a way to deal with whatever comes up . . ."

I smacked her hip and tried to act offended, but her humor always got the better of me. Maribel caught a ride with her, and Toño and Paul also made their excuses. I felt embarrassed by my daughter's behavior and started apologizing to them.

Paul touched my hand on his way out the door. "Don't worry about us, Amalia . . . Aurora is a little young to be the perfect hostess," he whispered. "We'll be back to normal soon enough. Right?"

Hortensia told me that she would be going to her room. "If you and Alejandro decide to go out, let me know and I'll listen for Aurora—though I'm sure she'll sleep soundly after all the excitement today." She pretended to be preoccupied with getting things straightened up and walked away.

At eight o'clock, just Alejandro and Aurora remained in the garden. They seemed so at ease with one another, but I saw she had started yawning and rubbing her eyes. Alejandro had checked into a nearby hotel, but obviously he didn't want to be going over there so early.

He suddenly let out a booming laugh. I walked over to find out what he'd found so funny and when he saw me he asked, "Does Miss Aili really have eyes in the back of her head?"

"Ah, her teacher! That's what she says," I confirmed. "She has a pair of sunglasses she likes to prop on the back of her pageboy and she tells Aurora that the second set of peepers lies underneath. She's a clever woman that Miss Aili."

He laughed again and I told Aurora she had to come and get ready for bed. As I knew she would, my daughter protested wildly.

But Alejandro said, "Come on, do as Mommy says. The sooner you have your sleep, the sooner it will be morning and we'll have another whole day together." She didn't utter another word. She kissed him and followed me to her bedroom.

After a quick bath, she climbed into her frilly bed and asked, "Won't Daddy come and say good night?" How could I refuse?

Alejandro still sat where I left him. He'd undone a couple of buttons on his shirt and fanned himself with a shopping bag he had accordion-folded. "She wants you to say good night in her room. It's the second door on the right." He hurried off and half an hour passed before he rejoined me in the garden.

I'd undone a couple of buttons as well, and as I watched him leave the house and return to the garden, I wondered if I'd revealed too much cleavage.

"Your fan works great," I said. The heat of the day had not yet been vanquished by the night breezes. With no rain all week, the high humidity felt oppressive. But it didn't seem to bother him; he called it sultry.

"You have done such a good job with Aurora. She's such a smart little girl. She got out her books and read to me. At first I thought she was showing me a story she'd memorized, but no, she can read. It feels so good to see her and get to know her. I ache to be part of her life. How can we manage this, Amalia?"

I had no answer because as long as he remained married to Susana, I could not agree to my daughter visiting his house. I shook my head. "I cannot understand the way you and your wife live."

He looked at me with complete candor. "Susana keeps the machine running. She makes sure we get invited to all the right parties. Her dad always puts in a good word for me at UNAM trustee meetings. He's on the advisory board, you know. Susana is a fine hostess—our dinner parties are sought-after invitations."

"Do you have sex with her?"

His eyes flashed, and then softened again. I guess he figured I deserved to know how things really are between him and his wife. After all, his intent gaze made it all too clear where he was trying to lead me.

"I guess that's a fair question for you to ask. Yes, we do. But I hope you don't want details."

"No, of course I don't . . ." *Well, maybe I did, but I wouldn't be able to bear it if he said she made him happy.*

He moved closer. "I can't remember much of what happened the night we conceived Aurora. You were like a safe haven. You were my refuge. When you told me about the pregnancy, I behaved so badly. I can't defend myself."

If he wanted to get me between the sheets, he should be whispering sweet nothings, not bringing up all that. But what he said next surprised me.

"We have to be honest with each other from now on. You know what I want. Tell me what your thoughts are."

The moment had come for me to fully speak my mind. "Okay, the bottom line? I can't go to bed with you knowing that you'll never leave Susana. I know that as much as you 'love me,' you will never give up that woman and come here to live with Aurora and me." I straightened my back and waited to hear him start finessing some more, but instead he stiffened and asked hard questions that I couldn't answer.

"Would you leave Merida to be with me? Could you uproot Hortensia again and stick Paul and Toño with the business? Would you give up your chance to go back to university? Do you want to raise Aurora in La Capital? Would you trust me enough to do all that?"

I couldn't deny his logic. "No, Alejandro, I couldn't do that to the people who have made my life as full as it is. And I know you're not completely happy with Susana, but you do owe her. I have to accept that. What's more, I don't think I could ever come to terms with your politics. You put yourself at risk every day with the things you say and do. I've seen you on TV—you push the public to action. People have been thrown in prison for less. I couldn't stand waiting for you to come home each night, picturing you in some awful jail. I know you'll never change!"

"Amalia, you haven't changed either. You didn't understand me all those years ago, and I wish more than anything that you could understand me now. I can't renege on my commitment. If I back down, others will too. When I go to the district headquarters of the Student Action League, I know how to get people motivated."

He looked searchingly into my eyes and grabbed my hands. "But that's a separate issue. What I want you to see is that despite all that keeps us apart, I am willing to make the best of what we do have. I want to be with you whenever I can. I want the two of us to spend time together as lovers, and with Aurora—I want to feel like we're a family. I've said it before, nothing about us will ever be conventional, but we can enjoy the good parts and not just endure the difficulties." His hands moved to the small of my back, and he pulled me closer to him.

I had nothing to challenge that twisted argument—I knew by now that love wasn't enough to dislodge Alejandro from his political path. Would it be right to drop my defenses tonight?

Like the last number of a safe's combination clicking into place, I fell for the "logical" conclusion that something *is* better than nothing. Besides, I was sick and tired of denying myself—and yes—I felt very turned on by him.

"It's so hot tonight. Let's cool off." Before I could change my mind, I stood and walked over to the pool. I shed my summer shift and underwear and dove into the water. I rose up again, allowing my breasts to peak through the surface. Alejandro heard the splash, stripped off quickly and dove in beside me. He kissed me and rubbed hard against my naked body.

But we both worried that Aurora or Hortensia would discover us. From behind, he grasped my breasts and said, "Let's go to your bed."

I had taken a long time ditching my defenses. Maybe I should have hung onto to them—and my clothes—but I could hardly wait to make love with Alejandro. I couldn't say no. We wrapped ourselves in a couple of the large towels that are always folded by the pool, gathered our clothes together, and ran on tiptoes to my room.

As soon as we got through the door, he backed me onto my bed.

No one else could make me feel like this. His tongue flicked at my lids and licked my lips. The room swirled.

"You are the only woman I love," he said.

I reached my hands behind his neck and loosened the elastic band that held his dark curls. They spread across his broad tanned shoulders, and I saw that his hair was almost as long as mine. I ran my fingers through the shiny strands. "I've wanted to do this ever since I first saw you this afternoon," I told him.

He found my right hand and moved it down his body. Needing no encouragement, I stroked him while his fingers caressed and probed me. His eyes stayed fixed on mine until finally he bent my knees, moved over me, and thrust deeply.

Ah-h-h-h . . . we still fit perfectly and we couldn't get enough of each other. A tear trickled down from his left eye. I licked it up, then my tongue traveled further. Our lovemaking stretched long into the night.

Lying in Alejandro's arms, I couldn't stop myself from making comparisons between now and the last time we'd been with one another. Four years ago I had been swept up by all the turmoil and felt furtive. Now our passion seemed true. And if I was deluding myself, I couldn't have cared less. I had Alejandro in my bed and nothing would keep me from savoring every second with him.

One of his hands slipped between my legs again. His moves were those of an artist and his fingers felt like sable paintbrushes tracing circles on my skin. I pulled him inside me. I sailed so far off the edge I wondered if I'd ever return.

From the mauve glow in the sky, I knew we'd been in my bed for many hours. Against our will, real life had begun intruding on this sensual enjoyment. He didn't argue when I said it was time for him to go.

He held me tenderly and kissed my nose, my ears, my forehead, and finally my lips. "It will be all right, Amalia. In time we'll find a way to be open about this part of our relationship, but the time is not now."

For many good reasons, I agreed, but I wondered if that time would ever come. I wrapped a towel around myself and walked quietly with him to the door. Watching how he sauntered down my street, I thought once again that he looked like a man who knew his place in the world. . . and I knew his place in my heart. Returning to my bed and breathing in the scent of him, sleep came like a warm cloud of musk, memories, and magic.

fifteen

Layla and I arranged cheese and crackers on a plate, a good choice for dinner on this hot, stuffy night. She had not been at all surprised when I called and asked her to come over so I could tell her all about my first day at architectural school.

Hortensia joined us and delivered the best news I'd heard all day: "Aurora is fast asleep!" I placed my palms together and bowed in her direction.

"You look like a Buddhist nun," Layla said laughing.

After my first day at the University of Yucatan, dealing with my daughter's nightly tantrum over bedtime seemed like more than I could manage. I wiped the perspiration from my upper lip and grabbed Layla's hand. "Come on, let's go sit by the pool."

The sun had set and barely visible from our comfy chairs, a sliver of moon rose behind the gazebo. I wondered if the next new moon would see our school still open; today certainly could not be called an auspicious start.

"Good idea. I'll bring you some lemonade," Hortensia added.

My best friend frowned. "On this day of all days, Hortensia, I think we need something stronger. It looks as though Amalia has had a rough time."

"Ah, Layla, you're right about that. There's a nice bottle of Chianti I could open," my nana suggested.

I gave her a hug and then headed across the lawn, once again wondering what I would do without the love and support of these two women.

Hortensia brought out the wine but she didn't join Layla and me. "Amalia, I have to turn in. I have a busy day tomorrow, but you've got a lot to tell Layla—don't forget the part about that awful building!"

"I won't leave out one gory detail," I promised, and Hortensia retreated to her private sanctuary. I turned in Layla's direction and saw she was ready to listen and—no doubt—would have a strong opinion about everything I'd be telling her.

"For starters, Layla, of the forty-three students, only eight of us are women, and I'm at least ten or fifteen years older than everyone else."

Layla frowned again. "I'm sure the age difference couldn't have been your major concern this morning. I've heard that the state authorities are completely behind the federal government's policy of no university expansion. Rumor has it that the governor might approve a few design courses into engineering's curriculum, but a separate school? He said never!"

"We have a benefactor," I said, "and although he's not offering financial support for supplies or equipment, he has provided a building that we will use as our classroom. It's an unused warehouse he owns, behind the old state prison."

Layla didn't say anything. She always waited for full disclosure before offering an opinion. But I couldn't miss the big gulp of wine she took. I took one too.

"We had to tromp through overgrown weeds and drag back a rusty gate to get into the barn-like room that was furnished with just a few flimsy tables and a scarred old blackboard. We have no books, no electricity, no running water, and no bathroom. Later we learned that we'll have to bring our own desks or continue to sit on the floor and take notes in copybooks balanced on our knees."

"It sounds like the governor is hoping this whole initiative will just fade away from sheer disgust," said Layla.

I nodded. "You're right about that. But I'm with a pretty determined group of people. At nine o'clock sharp, Professor Arcel Espadas-Carrillo, the self-appointed director of our program, strode in, followed by his plump assistant carrying two folding chairs and a portfolio. The professor looked uneasy as his companion set up. He laid some papers and his books on the table. Then they both lowered onto the rickety wooden seats and motioned for us to settle down on the floor and listen up."

Layla asked if I had met anyone interesting, which made me laugh.

"I told you. I'm practically as old as their mothers. They wear *huaraches* on bare feet, have shag haircuts, and dress in the universal student uniform—tight jeans and baggy T-shirts. My floral miniskirt and vest were totally out of place. Only one other woman wore a dress, and she looked as nervous as me. When I moved to sit down, she offered her hand and introduced herself, saying 'Hi, I'm Evangelina, and I have no idea what I'm doing here.' And as we helped one another into position, she added, 'If I come here tomorrow, I'll wear jeans like everyone else.'" Layla urged me to continue.

~~~

Once we seemed ready, the professor looked at us and smiled apologetically.

"Pretty primitive, isn't it? I'm afraid the message is loud and clear. The authorities do not want this school to open, but they are tolerating us today because they think we'll give up before we've even begun. I have met with your professors and they are prepared to endure whatever it takes. But you need to have the same commitment. The first lesson will be at ten a.m.'"

He then stood up, left his books on the table, and went outside. A few of the students moved closer to have a look.

The other woman in a skirt gave me a hapless smile. "Amalia, let's find a neighbor who will lend us a bathroom when we need it."

No easy task; our warehouse/classroom was in a working-class area where latrines were far more common than proper bathrooms. When we spotted a freshly painted house with riotous spears of hot pink bougainvillea growing along the front wall, we knew that we'd found our best chance.

Doña Landy Eugenia answered our knock, and like a generous *abuela,* she chuckled with understanding. "*Mi casa es tu casa*—my bathroom too!" She pulled on my arm, doubled over, pressed a hand on her abdomen, and pantomimed cramps and discomfort. She was an odd woman, but willing to help—and we couldn't afford to be choosy.

We returned and told the others that we'd found a WC nearby. The rest of the girls looked relieved.

Two of the boys had dragged in some cement blocks they found piled up in the yard. They covered them with dusty cardboard and invited us to sit.

Professor Espadas-Carrillo's voice went solemn. "Let's start— today is September 17, 1973. It is ten a.m., and you have the dubious honor of being the pioneer class of the new School of Architecture and Urban Planning of the Southeast—I.A.U.S. The two courses I will teach are Architectural History and Investigative Methodology. Shall we begin?"

~~~

"This whole idea of opening the architectural school without the governor's approval is crazy," Layla said. "Why do you insist on complicating your life?"

"I have wanted to study architecture for as long as I can remember," I said. "As a teenager I would sneak away to hear lectures by Luis Barragán, Juan O'Gorman, and other famous Mexico City architects. I loved wandering through La Capital, overwhelmed by the beauty of the contrasting styles—pre-Columbian, Colonial, Porfiriano, Contemporary. I have lived my life on the fringe of professionalism. I have done the work, but never earned the accolades."

"And are you so hungry for accreditation that you're willing to put up with all you've just described to me?" Layla asked.

"You bet I am! Alejandro once told me, 'A degree does the talking.' And I want mine to speak loud and clear."

sixteen

On Valentine's Day, I arrived at school with heart-shaped, pink-iced cookies that Aurora and I had made. But before I could greet anyone, I saw Evangelina crying in a corner.

A young woman shouldn't be crying on this day. Had someone broken her heart? Before I could approach, a couple of the boys took me aside.

"What's wrong with Evangelina?" I asked.

"Did you hear about what they've done to El Charras?"

The entire university community only numbered about six thousand, and we all knew of Efrain Calderón Lara—El Charras—a law student with a passion for the labor movement. The sweets I'd brought for my classmates were immediately forgotten.

"El Charras' body was found on the road to Chetumal in a remote part of Quintana Roo," Miguel explained. "It seems the perpetrators hoped that if the body were found outside Yucatan, the blame would fall elsewhere. Just how stupid do they think we are?"

El Charras had organized a textile workers union made up mostly of women who worked under deplorable conditions for low wages. Law professors and students supported his efforts, but not certain sweatshop owners and merchants. When he'd disappeared, everyone feared the worst. And on this day of love and friendship, we learned that El Charras had been dead for a week. The state authorities had fully aligned themselves with the federal government, and everyone knows that puppets react when their strings are pulled.

Outrage boiled up and an angry crowd thundered over to the

main university building. I went along, but when shots were fired into the walls, I felt terrified. Months ago I had told my classmates about the horrors of the Tlatelolco massacre. They urged me to go home. I thought of Professor Espadas-Carrillo's trust in all of us, and knew I had to stay—we had to stand up to the institutional bullying. And for the first time I gleaned an understanding of why Alejandro felt compelled to risk his life for his causes. I realized that sometimes moral outrage is so overwhelming that we cannot keep quiet.

The architectural students joined the law faculty vigil until the police brought out tear gas. Then we huddled in nearby parks and plazas to talk until we could safely walk home. Our group had gathered at the Café Express, just a block down Calle 60 from the university.

The police began to taunt us, daring some of the boys to step outside. Hearing the provocation, a group of older men, who meet there every afternoon for coffee and gossip, stood up *en masse*. They gently moved us toward the back of the restaurant and sat down at the front tables. "*Buenas tardes, oficiales,*" one of them said. The message was clear. In Merida, there would be no hauling away of young people like in Mexico City.

Within a few weeks, the discontent seemed placated. A federal investigative team came to Yucatan. Arrests were made, a few of the minor anti-labor agitators were incarcerated, and one of them who talked too much about his own duplicity on behalf of the government "committed suicide." The governor's ability to keep the peace had been contested, but the system backed him up.

~~

Throughout the rest of that year, we tolerated the wretched conditions for the sake of the education we knew to be our right. We did not protest, make demands, or do anything at all to call attention to ourselves; we hoped that the government would just forget what we were up to and let us quietly work away. The kindness of our neighbors helped us carry on. Doña Landy teased us daily when we used her bathroom, and Doña Mercy, a plump young mother with four children and no apparent husband, fed us. She appreciated the little income we students provided.

At ten, when we had our morning break, she would arrive at the gate carrying a huge basket of *tortas*—toasted buns stuffed with savory fillings. Two, sometimes three of her children lugged an enamel bucket containing *aguas de fruta*—lemonade, watermelon, pineapple, or, best of all, mango. She charged just five pesos for the *torta y agua,* but most of us gave her a little more. When she tried to return the change, we'd say, "Buy a treat for the little guys."

Several of the other female students, like Margarita, had quit; Maria Eugenia and Nirsa had transferred to Engineering and some others had moved to different cities. The thirty-one of us who remained wondered if we were struggling in vain.

Just as our morale hit rock bottom, there was a turn of events. A large house in the affluent neighborhood of Itzimná had been designated as our new quarters. We would have electricity, running water, and bathrooms. Parents and friends made donations and we held raffles to raise funds for desks, blackboards, and books. We felt like birds let out of a cage.

In these new surroundings, our work flourished. We missed Doña Mercy's *tortas*, though, and none of us would ever forget Doña Landy's good spirits and bad jokes. "Hurry up, I don't want my floor to get wet."

We told each other we'd go to visit and we did a few times. But in reality, things were not the same. Since we no longer studied in their midst, our former neighbors didn't feel so comfortable with us.

They began to assume that we saw ourselves as better than them. I hoped that one day our group would be able to re-establish rapport with these kind people because without their help, we'd never have made it through those first months.

We no longer worked on abstract theoretical problems. We actually undertook projects that would be developed. Héctor, Evangelina, me, and a few others began measuring and mapping the downtown core with the hope it would lead to a grand-scale urbanization project. Merida was founded in 1542 atop the remains of a Mayan city called T'ho. Since that time, there had been countless renovations. The Colonials had laid their new city out on a grid using a cord as the measuring tool and the axis was the main square, *La Plaza Grande*.

Our talk of change seemed threatening to El Centro's merchants and homeowners, who said that they feared their buildings would be expropriated to make way for roads and sidewalks.

They were mistaken. We wanted to preserve the older structures, but we wanted traffic to flow better and the rain to drain back into the water table while safeguarding the Colonial ambiance.

Once again, the authorities attempted to stop us, but we found another way—we worked at night. A few pesos into the hands of the watchmen allowed us after-hours entrance into all the historic buildings. But those late nights took their toll. My over-stressed schedule could not make room for one more activity.

Every weekday, I got up at seven to have breakfast and spend a little time with Aurora. At eight, I dropped her off at playschool, and then drove my red VW to Itzimná, where I attended classes until three in the afternoon. Sometimes those hours would be interrupted for a quick business lunch with Toño and Paul, or for a site inspection. From four to six o'clock, the three of us would meet in the little office at their García Ginerés house. There we made decisions, divided duties, and tracked expenses. I'd get back home for dinner at seven, enjoy an hour of play and bath time with Aurora, do two more hours of studying or surveying after she went to sleep.

Aurora left babyhood behind and turned into a talkative, bright, and curious almost-six-year-old. I chose to spend my few free hours with her. I could still see the infant I'd held in my arms, and I saw hints of the proud woman she'd soon be. Her untamed black curls and chocolate-brown eyes constantly reminded me of her father. People often remarked that her fair skin and curious expression were exactly like mine.

She skipped all the way to the local school house on the day she began first grade and in dancing class, she excelled at pirouettes. At weekly art classes, she got to use all the paint she wanted and brought me brightly colored suns that warmed my heart. She continued to swim nearly every day and now begged me to teach her to dive. "When you are nine," I said. I worried that if she once started jumping off high platforms, she'd get hurt. Like her father, she knew no fear.

I found myself constantly regretting that I couldn't have more time with her. Of course, she picked up on my guilt and played it to her advantage. When she wanted something, she prefaced her request with "If you aren't too busy . . ."

And as if I didn't have enough to worry about, I'd received a summons for a custody hearing. Susana had decided that Alejandro's paternal rights should enable them to take Aurora to live with them in Mexico City.

I fired off a call to Alejandro at his office. "I thought you said I could trust you. You said that Susana would not ever be a part of 'us.' You've come to see Aurora and me every six months and shared my bed. Why are you no longer willing to live up to the arrangements we agreed to abide by?"

"I know, Amalia, but Susana won't give up. She knows she can't take Aurora away, but her lawyer told her that she needs to establish the fact that she wants to have a relationship with my daughter. She can't possibly win custody, but petitioning for it would make her intention legally clear."

"You're letting her call the shots here? No, that's not how you told me your marriage works. I know Susana doesn't care about Aurora. She is doing this to get back at me. She knows you have been with me in Merida, doesn't she?"

"You know that she and I are open with each other, Amalia. Up until now she accepted your terms in order to make me happy, but it's hard for her to be so completely cut out of the most important aspect of my life."

The more he tried to placate me, the more angry I got. And if Aurora and I were such "important aspects," how could he even contemplate upsetting us like this. Had Susana's father maybe stepped up the pressure? I got the impression that Alejandro had to keep "Daddy" happy.

"Susana and I want to be able to see Aurora, but you won't agree to that. She's my wife, and your refusal to let her and Aurora meet is the source of constant fighting between us. Amalia, please be reasonable and let Susana get to know my daughter. I want Aurora to come to Mexico City. I want her to know my world."

Did he think I would be upset to know that he and Susana were having trouble? How dense could he be? If Susana was constantly fighting with him, my position improved. Though I tried to contain my fury, my voice shook when I spoke. "Susana is not Aurora's mother, and I am under no obligation to appease her."

"I'm sorry you feel that way, Amalia. I guess we'll just have to see what the law says."

We both hung up, angrier with each other than we'd been at any time during our twenty-two-year relationship. At this moment, I recognized that Toño's and my mother's repugnance for Alejandro was justified.

~

The new bond that my mother and I had begun to warily nurture would get a boost if she found out that Alejandro and I had fought. She and Papá would soon be coming to Merida for a visit—but not just to see us. Papá and his band had been invited to participate in a mega concert in Merida's main plaza. In fact, this weekend all manner of extravagant festivities were planned. Her Majesty Queen Elizabeth II of England would be in our city to inaugurate the new Sound & Light show at the nearby archaeological site of Uxmal.

For our governor, this seemed to be a big deal. Most did not imagine him to be a closet monarchist, but I thought he acted completely in character, considering his kingly attitude.

"He must have taken an etiquette course," Hortensia commented while we watched the television coverage of the governor greeting the Queen at the airport. "Look how he's bowing low, clicking his heels, and kissing the royal outstretched hand as though he's been doing so all his life." I wondered who'd gotten up the nerve to tell him that his sloppy *abrazos* and guffaws wouldn't be appropriate around the sovereign of England.

When Mamá and Papá's flight arrived, all of us went to meet them. Scooping up my daughter, Papá said, "*Ay-ay-ay,* you are the prettiest girl in all the land!" I smiled remembering how, when I was a little girl, he'd said those same words to me. Mamá hugged us and even acknowledged Paul.

By the newspapers' account, the official weekend activities went extremely well, except for the pouring rain during the inaugural Sound & Light show. Papá attended the event and he later told us, "Everyone scurried for shelter—everyone but the Queen. She remained stoically in her seat, protected under the black umbrella held by her ladies-in-waiting."

When we returned home from Papá's concert, my parents laid Aurora down for the night. She looked happy to have her Mexico City family here in Merida. After many good-night kisses for their granddaughter, Mamá and Papá joined Toño, Paul, Hortensia, and me for a light supper on my terrace. Papá expressed disappointment that Her Majesty had remained completely rigid during his performance at the plaza; she didn't even smile.

"Oh, Papá," I said, "protocol dictates her behavior. Your band plays with so much exuberance, she must have wanted to let go and join in the fun."

We all looked over at Hortensia pantomiming the English monarch dancing with abandon. She looked hilarious! Nana had aged the past few years, and it was a treat to see her playful side come out.

The recent rain left the air fresh and cool. The clouds had dissipated and the stars twinkled—the perfect setting for our family reunion. Mamá never drinks, but on this occasion she accepted two glasses of Burgundy and became more open than any of us had ever seen her. What a night of surprises.

"It's beautiful here. It truly is." My mother looked around and smiled. "But, Amalia, you should have called. We are always ready to help you."

Nothing she could have said would have shocked me more. In fact, all of us looked at one another with confused expressions. Finally, I asked her, "Mamá, what are you talking about? Called you about what?"

"You mean called you about *whom*. Your daughter, of course. It is obvious to me that you moved from La Capital so that Alejandro would be no threat to you. But he and that miserable wife of his have managed to get at her, haven't they?"

I felt as though I might faint. Absolutely nobody knew about this. Not even Hortensia. They all looked at me waiting for an explanation. I asked Mamá for confirmation. "You know about the custody claim?"

"Of course I do. It is a real threat, but one of my best clients is willing to help you. She is on the board of directors for the National Association for the Protection of Women. I donated two original evening gowns to their charity auction. At any rate, when Papá and I dropped off our donation, her husband approached us. He is the Chief Justice at Family Court. He told us about the custody petition. He also told me he would try to see that it didn't amount to anything major."

I wanted to ask how he would be able to manipulate such a thing, but Mamá cut me off.

"Don't ask too many questions, Amalia. You know that in Mexico *todo es possible*."

I knew better than to say more. "Thank you, Mamá. I am very grateful."

"No need for thanks, Amalia." Mamá looked tired. "I told you I would help you—that will always stand."

Toño grasped the situation immediately. "I suspected that once Amalia allowed Alejandro into Aurora's life, he wouldn't stop until he had taken her away. Thank you Mamá for foiling the plans of those Mexico City snakes." He pointedly put his arm around Paul's shoulder. "I don't know what we'd do without Aurora in our life."

Mamá looked at Papá for support. He took off his glasses and rubbed his eyes.

"Toño, we can see that you have a happy family here. We are glad that you are helping Amalia raise our grandchild. I can't pretend that I don't have great difficulty accepting your lifestyle. It is not what we would have chosen for you. But then, I've not been the father you had the right to expect. It's time to make our peace."

Toño looked on the verge of saying more. Papá's statements were not entirely conciliatory. But, I could tell by the way my brother blew air through his pursed lips that he wanted to come to terms with this situation. I guess he decided that our parents' grudging acceptance was better than none at all. He nodded and struggled to find the right response.

Paul spoke up. "*Bien.* Let's toast to new and more open communication—*¡Salud!*" We all raised our glasses and clinked—more with resolve than joy. I guess we needed time to digest what had been said. Mamá and Papá had lifted limp arms, as though the glasses were made of lead. Toño tried to get Paul to ease back; he knew this was *too much, too soon.*

Hortensia looked distressed but determined. She stood up and took a long, slow look around the assembled group. "I have been a part of this family for almost forty years. I don't know if you're the family I would have chosen, but you are what I have, and I love you. Since I left Santa Cecilia, I've never wanted to seek reconciliation with anyone there. I am not even sure if my parents are alive or dead. But seeing you make this night into one of healing has made me wonder if I should go back to my village and see if I can make peace, too."

Papá and Mamá reached out their hands to touch Hortensia, offering their silent support. Especially after that blow-up about

Maribel, I knew the rift between Nana and her family was painful to her.

I wanted to speak more to Mamá and Papá, but I knew I had to weigh my words. I closed my eyes. "I'm glad we've finally started talking about all that has been like rocks on our path for so many years. I'm grateful that Paul and Toño will now have the chance to visit comfortably with you, Papá and Mamá. I never imagined you knew about Susana's custody claim. If I'd thought there was a chance you'd help me and support me, I would have told you about it."

My mother wanted to know if Alejandro had come to see us again since Aurora's fourth birthday.

"Yes, he has," I told her, "but since the legal action, he's had no conversation with me."

I waited for Mamá's next probing question, but at that very moment, Paul, who had also drunk more than his usual wine ration, blurted out, "It's wonderful what can happen if people have their hearts in the right place."

He sat up straight to deliver his speech. "I know I speak for both Toño and me when I say you have made us very happy by deciding to finally accept us as part of this family. The past is now truly the past. I love your son. We love each other." He turned to Toño for acknowledgment, and my brother obliged with an awkward smile and a nod in my parents' direction.

Mamá and Papá winced a bit, but otherwise remained placid.

Paul's eyes brimmed with tears, and I just knew he wanted to go and hug my parents. Their furtive looks at each other, at me, and at Hortensia seemed to put a block in his path, which he —*gracias a Dios*—read correctly. He turned to Hortensia, not my mother, and gave her a delicate peck on the cheek. "Nana, thank you for a splendid meal. Toño, it's time we called it a night."

After the two of them left the table, Papá and Hortensia went to their rooms. I got up, too, anxious to lie down. But Mamá stopped me.

"Amalia, sit with me for a while, and I think I'll have a little more of that lovely wine."

I half-filled her glass and poured a full one for myself. I wondered what she had to say.

Mamá took a long sip then cleared her throat. "I am glad that you and Aurora are living in Merida," she began. "Alejandro continues to raise a ruckus—I see him on TV and he writes articles for the newspaper all the time. Because Susana's father is so connected, Alejandro's enemies cannot get at him, but I hate to think how Aurora's life—and yours too—could become the subject of too much public attention if Alejandro's enemies find out that he is her father."

I remembered that years ago Hortensia told me I would come to feel more sympathy for my mother once I became a mother myself . . . I took Mamá's hand and reassured her that since my daughter's birth, I felt like a lioness defending her cub. I'd never do anything to put Aurora in harm's way. Mamá nodded her white head, and for the first time in my life, I realized that she and I perfectly understood one another.

seventeen

"They aren't coming. I think we should leave," Héctor said as he shifted his weight onto his other leg.

We'd been standing in the university's courtyard for half an hour, waiting for Professor Espadas-Carrillo and Dr. Rosado. My legs and my back hurt. I had just opened my mouth to agree with my friend when I saw two men descending the long stairway. "There they are Héctor. At last!"

"They look deep into their conversation. Why don't we walk over to the bottom of the stairs so they won't miss seeing us," Héctor suggested.

"Good idea," I agreed and we placed ourselves at the foot of the stone steps.

"Ah, hello you two," our director said, placing his arm around Héctor's shoulder. "Shall we talk in Dr. Rosado's office?"

The venue seemed formal and our puzzled frowns prompted Professor Espadas-Carrillo to explain.

"We have not received the signed copy from the board of directors, but it looks like they are finally willing to grant us full standing as an incorporated School of Architecture."

Héctor had never looked happier. But our director's hands went up to signal that there was more we needed to hear. We fell silent and meekly walked behind him. Once we reached the president's private domain, he wasted no time in telling us about the catch. "In order for the governor to authorize our new school, your group will have to forfeit the two years you've put in and start from scratch.

On paper, these twenty-four months never happened."

No! Those two hard years with no services, the moves, the horrible facilities, and all the things I'd sacrificed—time with my daughter, the business. I wanted to cry.

Héctor crumpled.

Professor Espadas-Carrillo spoke for the first time since we had entered the president's Spartan quarters. "Try to be pragmatic. If we manage to get the school recognized, we'll have won what we want most."

"But erasing all the time we've already put in? What justification is there for that?" I asked.

"You'll receive the most thorough education of any group that will ever graduate, and graduate you will, but not for five more years."

I tried to maintain my composure while I fired questions at the two of them. "Must we take every course over, even if we know all the material? Could we perhaps be given a proficiency test?"

"Unfortunately, no," our professor said.

"Can we at least plead our case in front of the governor?"

"Absolutely not. That would probably make him change his mind again," said Dr. Rosado. "I understand your feelings, and don't forget, the faculty has invested the same amount of time as you have—with no pay, I might add. We've got to take this deal or shut down. The governor refuses to look like a fool in front of his constituency. And if he authorizes the college without extracting some blood, he would be seen as exactly that."

My throat felt choked with anger. I could barely speak. "We'll have to allow the governor to look as though he's the one who has brokered the agreement for the new college?"

"That's right," said Professor Espadas-Carrillo.

"You're talking bullshit!" Héctor screamed as he slammed his fist down hard on the desk. I could see a large vein throbbing in his neck.

Professor Espadas-Carrillo looked startled by the crude expletive. Héctor inhaled deeply and asked the same questions I had already asked.

Our director listened sympathetically, but eventually he said, "Look Héctor, what you want is what we all want, but this is how things are."

Dr. Rosado added, "Our cause has been championed by some high-level federal government agencies. The UAM in Mexico City has sent its curriculum for us to use. Private individuals have donated equipment and books for the library. Finally, our persistence is paying off."

"And the other new architectural colleges opening throughout the country?" I asked. "Are they in the same mess as we are?"

"Yes, they are, Amalia," the president confirmed. "The past few years have been like the dark ages. But you can't hide the sun by holding your thumb up in front of your eyes. The situation is starting to ease."

Héctor, who had been listening with a bowed head, quietly stated the obvious. "You want us to convince the others, don't you?"

"Well, that's our hope," said Espadas-Carrillo.

"Please, Héctor," said Dr. Rosado. "Fighting the governor will do no good. Our best bet is to swallow this like puppy dogs. Do you think the others can be persuaded?"

"Not if they're as angry as I am."

On the bus ride back to campus, Héctor asked, "How can the governor get away with this? Why does he have so much power?"

"The PRI is the longest-serving authoritarian party in the world. They get what they want by granting practical favors to their followers. But now that the party has gotten so big, they have to resort to putting pressure on the little people like us to keep their fat-cat cronies happy."

Héctor put his head in his hands and rubbed his eyes. "You make it sound as though we're being controlled by the Mafia."

"More or less. We're serving 'Governor Godfather.'"

~

Arriving in Itzimná, everyone in our group was excited to know what we had learned at the meeting with the university president and Professor Espadas-Carrillo . . . until the truth sunk in.

"We'll be selling out," Evangelina argued. Miguel issued threats in far worse language than Héctor's. We let them rant, and then I summed it all up in black and white.

"We learned from Professor Espadas-Carrillo and Dr. Rosado that there will be no compromise. This is the one option we have. No alternate path exists." Héctor and I understood what President Rosado had said about fighting the governor. We'd lose, and neither of us had forgotten El Charras' murder.

Grudgingly, most of our class accepted the administration's terms. But there were a few who refused to pay the high price and wanted to quit altogether. Héctor and I couldn't stop them, but if they left the program, our position would become still more precarious. Exhausted, I reminded them that "Mexico is not like other countries. Here you don't do what you want—you do what you can. Think before you make a decision you won't be able to take back."

Despite the negativity, our group went on taking measurements and mapping. By now we'd gotten good at surveying. The deep bond I had formed with Evangelina, Héctor, Jeanette, and Miguel during our nocturnal forays through the downtown core was not weakened by this upheaval in our program.

Under the cover of darkness we indulged in our resentment of government policies. Miguel felt the most troubled about accepting the terms under which our college had been incorporated into the University of Yucatan. He scratched his large head with his surprisingly delicate hands.

"Why is the government so opposed to educational opportunities that will make us productive citizens?" he asked.

"Miguel, they think they stand a better chance of keeping order if they limit the number of students. We are the ones tuned in enough to recognize how manipulative they are and that makes us their enemies. The PRI machine has not served the people since the pre-war days of President Cárdenas."

It surprised me that the others in my group considered me to be an authority on the history of political resistance in our country. I wondered what Alejandro would think of that.

In spite of the governor's best efforts, we knew that our training had produced results. Our professors praised the precision of our coordinates and the minutely detailed reports we submitted at the end of each week. Our work progressed well, yet one serious challenge remained. The cathedral's position in relation to the rest of the Main Plaza presented a particular danger. Héctor could climb like a mountain goat—he'd go up anything. But even he looked frightened at the prospect of hanging from atop the mammoth structure so we could take readings from clear across the esplanade. Clinging to a jutting cornice close to the top, our friend looked as small as the pigeons that strutted through the plaza. We hurried to finish, and once down again, he told me that he would not be climbing any more buildings. "That one did it for me!" he said.

Our survey confirmed how much major restructuring the city required. Existing streets needed to be leveled and sidewalks were in dire need of resurfacing and widening. Lighting had to be installed and a solution to the issue of flooding was imperative. Such renovations would require decades of sustained effort.

What a heavy price two extra years of school would be. Considering how hard it had been on all of us to accommodate my studies and our business, Toño said I should just quit, but Paul reminded us that if I didn't finish, our company would never be fully licensed, and the fees we could charge would not get the boost that my degree guaranteed. That cinched the decision for Toño.

It definitely helped that Alejandro's support checks arrived punctually, and twice a year, he continued to visit Aurora in Merida. But he and I had only minimal contact. While Toño and Paul made sacrifice after sacrifice for me, Alejandro offered no emotional support. This—and his attempt to take Aurora away—increased my resentment.

Nonetheless, I would have liked to discuss our difficulties at the university with him. He might even have ideas about how we could better defend ourselves. And, yes, I had to admit that even though I mistrusted him, I missed being in his bed.

After the governor's decree, our group dwindled to less than half the number of students we had started out with. And we learned that we'd have to move yet again.

Evangelina sipped from a thermos of coffee. "Another derelict place with poor ventilation, no services, and inadequate resources are once again to be our reality."

"But we're going to put up with everything," Miguel told her, "because there's a distinct difference in the legal status of this structure. This will be our permanent facility."

The reconstruction began as soon as the governor made the official announcement of our legal constitution. Tall glass panels

replaced many of the crumbling walls and light filled the dark, mil-
dewed rooms. Spaces were enlarged and arches connected the laby-
rinth of corridors. Hortensia helped out with advice for a botanical
garden. Finally, we had a school we could be proud of.

Our professors told us that a prime focus should be establishing a
profile for our institution. Héctor suggested we host a congress where
representatives from both established and new architectural schools
could exchange ideas. The class of 1980 all agreed. We invited forty
universities and received an overwhelming response. Three hundred
delegates would spend the first three days of March 1977 in our city.

We named the event Contemporary Urbanization of Colonial
Cities. We hoped to arrive at solutions that would affect needed
changes, but authentically preserve traditional ambiance and
unique architecture. Merida and other Mexican cities could boast
Spanish Colonial, French and Italian Baroque, Neoclassic, and even
vestiges of pre-Columbian temples right in their downtown cores.

Our group worked for five months, setting the agenda and book-
ing speakers for the professional conference. We arranged accommodations, transportation, the socials, the meals, and media coverage. The support we received from the community was phenomenal,
especially from the Hotel Panamericana. The manager agreed to host
the inaugural banquet and gave us an excellent rate on rooms.

When the weekend of the congress arrived, our careful planning paid off. After the round table sessions, I got to meet most of
the presenters at a special luncheon, and at the end of the first day,
feeling exhilarated by success, I had more fun at the after-party than
I'd allowed myself in a very long time. For most of the night, I sat
with a professor from Mexico City—Nico Beltrán.

As the activities wrapped up for the night, Nico lightly touched
my shoulder and said he'd look for me the next day. I blushed, infat-

uated as a school girl. Once he'd gone, my friends teased me terribly. "Whoa—what do you make of that guy?" Héctor asked everyone. They laughed as he strutted around the room with his eyes glued on me, exaggeratedly pantomiming how the attractive—make that extremely attractive—professor had behaved. I swatted at Héctor, laughing and trying to keep my composure.

On day two, after the sessions had finished, I led an informal tour through the city's historic center. I found myself walking back to the university with a collection of friends and three new acquaintances from Veracruz. Nico Beltrán halted right in front of our group, causing us to stop in our tracks. He spoke directly to me in an admiring voice that all took note of. "I have to say you did an excellent job as moderator of the panel discussion on the role of humidity control in the preservation of Colonial structures."

I'd been impressed by him too, but his long, sleek silver ponytail and day-old beard were quite a distraction. I thought he looked like the American actor Richard Gere. He didn't dress in a suit like the other profs—he wore tight black jeans, loafers with no socks, and a blue-gray button-down polo shirt under his slate-colored suede blazer. Yesterday I'd found myself wanting to get to know him better, and today it seemed he was looking for the same chance with me.

Such intense interest felt flattering, but hardly appropriate. I tried to ignore him, but he'd have none of that. He gently took my arm and steered me away from the others. "Last night, I couldn't stop thinking about you. Let's go have a glass of wine."

Oh, so tempting, but I had too many responsibilities. "It will have to be another time," I told him. "There's no way I can just up and leave with you. I have to get ready for tomorrow's outing to Chichen Itzá and the gala dinner in the evening."

"Ah, but remember—I'm one of the VIPs and if I need your

help, aren't you supposed to look after me?" I smiled at him, then moved back beside Héctor and Evangelina, who were watching the scene unfold. Like me, they wore badges: "Student Organizational Committee."

"Amalia, if the professor needs you to do something, we can manage here," said the ever-naïve Evangelina.

"*Hm-m-m-m,*" Héctor said under his breath. "I think I know what the good professor needs, and he looks your type, Amalia." His joking made me turn crimson just as it had last night.

"Shut up, he'll hear you!" I growled. Héctor grinned wider. I walked away, pretending to look for my files.

I saw the professor sidestep and wrap his arms conspiratorially around my friends' shoulders. They had known me, almost exclusively, as their ultra-serious, goal-oriented older classmate; they seemed astounded at Nico's flirting. I noticed their nodding heads, heard amused laughter, and soon, the intriguing stranger stood right beside me again. My friends made thumbs-up gestures and signaled for me to take off.

"Go on, Amalia, we'll handle whatever needs doing here."

"¿*Vamanos?*" Nico said.

I forced myself to make conversation. "What did you say to my friends?"

He leaned close. "I told them I'd make it worth their while to cover for you this afternoon. They were actually quite pleased that I'd come along to sweep you off your feet."

Why was I entranced by this man with such corny pick-up lines? He acted much too sure of himself, but his hand fit around mine like a soft leather glove. I was acting like a sixteen-year-old.

Our strolling took us to the Continental Patio, a restaurant-bar managed by Alberto Salum. He had been one of the guests at our first Christmas party and had become a good friend to Toño and Paul. I frequently took clients to his place, but this had to be the first time he'd ever seen me with anyone so—interesting. He winked and pressed his palm over his heart. "Amalia. Honey, where have you been hiding this magnificent man?"

I felt embarrassed, but my escort's eyes smiled at our host's outrageous behavior. He matched Alberto's effusion. "I've been lurking around the university's architectural conference just waiting to catch a comely co-ed."

Very indiscreetly swinging his hips, smiling slyly, and fluttering his eyelids, Alberto showed us to a round table on the tree-shaded patio.

"What can I bring you kids?"

"Something chilled and very alcoholic," said the professor.

I knew I should turn and run, but I couldn't. Even though I'd guessed what Nico had in mind for this afternoon, I lacked the will to protest. Such attention was a balm. I sat glued to my chair, totally enjoying the open flattery of this handsome man's words and the frank arousal in his eyes.

The table was not wide and he easily reached my hand.

"Amalia, we only met last night. I know that you're a student— but I need to know other things about you. Tell me, what makes you happy?"

"Professor Beltrán—you have no idea how grateful we are for the support your university has shown us. We use your curriculum and it's excellent."

"Please! Call me Nico. I'm glad you're using our material, but I don't want to talk about work. I want to share this afternoon with you—eating, drinking, and laughing."

Alberto's return with cocktails saved me from having to

respond. Pleased with himself and puckering his lips he said, "I have something very special just for the two of you. You've heard of the drink Sex on the Beach? I call this Love in the Afternoon. Enjoy."

"Terrific, Alberto. You and I have the same idea of what makes a great afternoon," Nico said.

Something that had been restlessly sleeping inside me suddenly came wide awake. I was so turned on by this sexy banter. I looked right into Nico's eyes and asked, "And how do you know it's the kind of afternoon I'm looking for?"

He dropped all guile. "If it's not at this moment, I'm hoping that a couple of cocktails and a luscious lunch will make it that way. I confess that I'm mesmerized by you. I want to see your passion, Amalia. What can I do to make your heart race as fast as mine?"

If I'd had the nerve, I'd have answered, "Keep on just as you are." I liked the way his eyes crinkled when he smiled. And I drank in his flattery like a marooned sailor. When his hand slipped out of sight and lightly touched my leg, I picked up my glass and fought the urge to gulp. I wanted to run my palm along his inner thigh—all the way to the point of no return.

Making menu decisions was a welcome distraction—we discovered a mutual taste for ethnic fare and decided to sample a selection of Middle-Eastern specialties—*kibi, tabule, tajine, kebabs.* Between savory mouthfuls, I told him about my years as a buyer and about the buildings I am helping to restore. I did not tell him I have a daughter—I couldn't talk about her in this setting. But I did mention that I live with Hortensia.

He laughed. "And does Nana expect her little girl to get home by midnight?"

I wondered what he'd think if he knew the full story. "With the congress on, she knows that my hours will be all mixed up—she won't be worried about me."

He leaned over and kissed me lightly but fully on the mouth. After four hours sitting with him, I felt like I was on fire, and he didn't look like he had plans to douse the flames. But Nico wouldn't insist. I knew the next move would be up to me.

Obscured by twilight, the canopy of trees came alive with the cawing of starlings settling in for the night. Like the birds, my inner voice sounded loud and clear: *Unless you're ready to follow through, you had better get yourself away from this situation.*

Our meal had long finished and the final cognac left me in a sweet swirl. The sexual tension between Nico and me was primed and set to explode. I shivered as I anticipated what kind of lover he'd be. When he asked if I wanted to leave the restaurant, I nodded, and he signaled for the check. I stood up and smiled at Nico—he steadied me with his outstretched hand—and I made my way to the rest room.

Looking in the mirror I recognized the longing that a blind man couldn't miss. My mind had conjured up all kinds of fantasies and I had no doubt that Nico wanted to fulfill every one of them. I inhaled deeply and when I let my breath go, the last of my good sense followed. It crossed my mind that skiers must feel like this when they are poised at the top of a steep run. They're aware of the danger ahead, but that doesn't stop them. They absolutely need the rush.

While contemplating the potential in store for Nico and me, I felt overwhelmed by an urge to remove my bra and panties, and no amount of self-censure could make me stop. As I meandered back to the table, completely naked under my skirt and blouse, I loved the way the warmth sneaked through the sheer fabric, tickling my erect nipples and blowing between my legs.

Nico seemed to be studying the difference in my walk. Intrigued, he helped me to sit back down and then slid his chair around until it touched mine. He'd obviously noticed the change in the drape of my blouse and liked what he saw.

The way we were wedged into the corner and shadowed by the cascading foliage, no one could see us clearly. He leaned over, and his hand cupped one of my breasts. He kissed me and I shuddered uncontrollably. My response encouraged him to more boldness. One of his arms encircled my waist and he stroked me through my gauzy skirt. He paused, lifted up the folds of fabric and his fingers explored further.

I unlatched my purse and showed him the beige lace nestled in with my wallet, keys, and lipstick. If he hadn't been sitting down, I think his knees would have buckled.

"Amalia. Let's leave right now!" he said.

The bill had been paid, and Alberto sent us off with his characteristic enthusiasm. "The night is young!"

Flaunting our passion was a thrill for me, and I felt way past caring what anyone would think. As I passed my friend, he kissed my cheek. Nico patted Alberto's shoulder with one outstretched hand, and seductively ran the other over my ass. I laughed, tossed my head, and followed the charming professor right to his hotel.

I felt as though I'd turned into another person. Before Aurora's birth, I had dated lots of men, but now I found myself with one who made them all look like choirboys.

As I knew would happen, my thoughts turned to Alejandro. I'd always thought that only he had such intense physical power over me, but obviously, I thought wrong. I hadn't been with Alejandro in more than two years, and Nico's long lean body had me so excited that the last-minute moral reservations of my muttering conscience could not hold me back.

We passed a darkened doorway and Nico steered me under the portico. He turned my face to his and his tongue unlocked my lips. As I kissed him, I felt one of his hands slip under my blouse while the other went straight down my waistband and deep into me. I moaned like a cat in heat.

Once through the door to his suite, Nico guided me to a quilted armchair in the corner of the room and gently sat me down. "Keep your eyes on me, Amalia." He undid the buttons of my blouse and smiled when he saw my ripe breasts. Giving a slow seductive caress to each, he moved his hands down, lowered my skirt, and parted my legs. My need made me feel like I'd go crazy.

"You look so incredibly sexy—stay just as you are." He didn't take his gaze off my body as he walked backwards to the bed, taking off an item of clothing with each step. I sat there, legs open wide, completely exposed—waiting for him.

Lying down on his back, he held out his arms and called, "Come over now, Amalia—slowly."

I stood and re-traced his steps. When I reached the edge of the bed, I lowered myself down close to him and whispered, "You are unbelievable."

In bed with Nico felt like a sumptuous feast—all parts of it: appetizer, main course, and dessert. Our lust that evening could be described in no other way. I didn't think about what he did to me, I just enjoyed the lush sensations that ran like a drug through my body.

He finally lay quiet, completely spent. Reality rose up into my pleasure-besotted mind. What had I done? I felt an emotional need for Nico that matched my craving for his body. But I could not fall in love with this man. I had too many responsibilities and commitments. I shook his shoulder and he turned over. The way he looked at me confirmed that he wanted to give of himself in more ways than I could deal with. After such intense lovemaking, my body throbbed with an exquisite ache and my heart sank at what it knew had to come next.

"Hortensia—she'll wonder where I am."

He kissed me and moved around to resume our intimacy. "Yes, Amalia, Nana will be worried, but I'm coming with you. I want to meet her. I want her to like me. We can stay at your place or you can collect a few things and come back here with me. I don't care where, but I need to spend the rest of tonight with you in my arms."

I couldn't see his expression because he had turned me face down. I felt his eyes watching the way my body opened up to him. Oh God! I forced myself to pull away, turned over, and touched his cheek.

"I have to go home. My life is complicated, Nico. I cannot have a love affair with you." I pulled out of his embrace and said, "I'm sorry, I shouldn't have let this happen."

His face fell and he looked at me with absolute astonishment. "Why are you acting like this, Amalia? What we've started is incredible."

"There's no easy explanation. I should not have gone to Alberto's with you." I made myself sit up and told him again, "I cannot get more involved with you."

"You can't mean that. Are you feeling embarrassed? I can tell you're new to some of this. If you now feel uncomfortable, I'm sorry but you have to believe me when I say that no woman has ever made me feel like you have. I can't get enough of you. Now you're tired and overstressed or are you married? Help me understand why you're suddenly rejecting me."

"The guilty, tired, and overstressed parts are true, but I can't explain any more. I don't understand it myself. But it's not because

I am married. I have no husband."

I got up from the bed and went into the bathroom. I dressed and when I had managed to recoup a small amount of self-control, I walked over to the corner chair where he sat. He had pulled the sheet from the bed and wrapped it around himself.

"Amalia, I've got pretty good instincts, and I sensed that you and I were at the beginning of something bigger than I've known before. I've never felt so much, so quickly. And you gave me every reason to believe you felt the same. Instead, you've turned me into a one-night stand. I don't understand what went wrong.

"Nico, this is not the right time," I said as I walked toward the door.

He didn't respond and he didn't try to stop me from leaving. Softly, I shut myself out of his life.

All I wanted was to get home. I should have run all the way; Hortensia would be worried. But I had to collect myself before facing her. I felt the pain of having ruined something that could have been worth keeping.

~

I took out my key, but Hortensia held the door ajar, a bemused expression on her face.

"You look as though you're in another world right now, *Mi'ja*. Do you want to look in on Aurora? She will help bring you back to here and now."

She said no more. Opening the door to my daughter's room, I saw her all curled up and scrunched into a corner. She always slept like that. Aurora's eyes stayed closed as I stroked her hair but she whispered, "*Hola Mamá . . .*"

During the stressful years I attended the University of Yucatan, Aurora held our fragile family together. My brother and Paul loved her and spent many hours with her. Sometimes I felt jealous when she would run into their arms before mine, and I hated the fact that Hortensia was usually the person who told me about my daughter's newest dance steps. But how could it be different? I adored my open-spirited child and I wanted to be around her more, but I often found myself saying, "When I finish my work today, it will be late so we'll do something special tomorrow, okay?"

It broke my heart the day she told me, "But it never gets to be tomorrow, does it Mommy?"

I cuddled her a few seconds, then she exhaled, went limp again, and I knew she'd fallen fully back to sleep. I pulled the covers close around her, kissed the top of her head, and left her to her dreams.

Hortensia had poured two cups of herbal tea. She laid her hand on mine. "I can see you're troubled."

My eyes rose to face her.

"Oh, I am not the right person for you to talk to about whatever happened today," she said quickly. "But don't think I disapprove, *Mi'ja*. Why don't you go to see Layla tomorrow?"

"I need to go to Chichen Itzá and then there will be the big closing ceremony in the evening. But I'll call her and try to see if we can get together on Monday."

Overseeing the final two events of the congress was a relief. I needed to put Nico out of my mind. But that turned out to be a hopeless challenge. I couldn't resist calling him to find out what he was thinking, how he was feeling, and telling him I missed seeing him on the tour of the Mayan ruins. So much conflict ran through me.

When he answered, I would use the pretext of needing to let him know when the airport shuttle would be by. I asked the hotel reception clerk to ring his room. She told me he had checked out in the morning and had taken a taxi to the airport.

eighteen

I phoned Layla the day after the conference ended and invited myself over. I knew she'd be sunning by the pool. I called out her name and she buzzed me in through the back gate.

Unlike many "transplants," Layla took to the humid climate like an iguana. Still, the sight of her full nudity came as a shock. "Don't you read about the dangers of overexposure?" I asked.

She sat up straight and shot back, "I don't have to worry about tan lines, do I? Overexposure? Don't be such a prude! You're just jealous because you aren't toasty brown like I am."

She ran her hands down the length of her body. Watching her, I had to admit that her dark golden skin set off her bright blue eyes. She looked just like the women she wrote about. Her books' successes were due in part to her ability to market her image and lifestyle. Every adventure-starved female wanted to look like her, live like her, and be loved like her.

"Come on, take off those clothes and join me. You'd look great with an all-over tan."

She did a double take when I actually wiggled out of my slacks, T-shirt, and underwear. I sat down quickly, trying not to flinch under her open stare. Although she wore dark shades, I knew she was sizing me up.

"Girl, something has happened since I last saw you."

"Layla, life can be unfair," I said, and told her all about Nico. Some of my other friends thought of Layla as flaky and superficial. What a mistake. She had the best perception and the wisest resolution of almost anyone, especially in matters of the heart—and related body parts.

"I can understand that you wanted to sail off the map with that gorgeous *chilango,* but as you say, the timing was way off, or do you think you could handle an affair with him while you're still hoping for Alejandro to come back into your life?"

I told her that I no longer wanted anything to do with my former lover, but she dismissed my protests with a flick of her wrist.

"Don't try to fool me, Amalia."

What I needed was her advice, not more questions. "I know Nico and I will see each other again—his university is sponsoring ours. He told me he'd probably return to Merida to help with course development. How can I make him *not* feel like a one-night stand? What kind of relationship could I—should I—establish with him?"

"Amalia, you can't undo what you did. If you contact him again, even if your next move is strictly professional, it will look like you want a second session in his suite. Or is that what you want?"

"I'm not sure. I never knew that I could be attracted like that to anyone besides Alejandro. Nico's smart and charming and sexy!"

"I can see why you'd want an encore. But after what you told him about your 'commitments and responsibilities,' he no doubt figures that you have a husband or live-in lover. However, I've yet to meet a man who isn't up for a little on the side."

I rolled over onto my stomach. I had to wonder at how foolish I was being. Here I had a chance for a relationship with a brilliant, fascinating man—one that would involve more than just sex and rehashing the past. But totally against all reason, Alejandro still held my emotions captive. It killed me that I had invested so much time in this man, and yet nothing I tried had tempted him away from Susana.

"You aren't the type to carry on with two men at the same time, are you?' Layla asked. "You want to see Nico again. Alejandro and you are not lovers right now, but you have a daughter together and that trumps all the lust and anything else you feel for Nico. Am I right, Amalia?"

"Damn it, Layla, you know you are. I want to be back in Alejandro's bed, and more than anything I wish that he, Aurora, and I could live as a full-time family—I admit it. But as I say, that's not possible right now. Nico is such a catch and it wouldn't take much for me to give in and have a fling with him. But that would be unfair because I am pretty sure he would fall in love with me. Doing the right thing is so hard."

Layla spread her arms out, palms up, making a resigned gesture. "The truth is, if you do the right thing, even when it isn't what you want, it will work out for you in the end," she whispered. Then, that said, she slapped me on the backside—not gently!

"Come on, girl . . . there's a great remedy for situations like this. It's called a three-martini lunch. Works every time."

And it did work that day. But I couldn't let myself indulge in that kind of lunch very often.

The years at the University of Yucatan moved along quickly for me, but not so for my partners. From time to time, Toño lost patience. One over-stressed Friday, he blew up.

"Amalia, you're exhausted. You're too thin. And I'm not the only one who thinks so—Hortensia agrees. I have to cover for you so much, and you know what? I'm tired, too."

Before I could respond, Paul shot back at Toño.

"Stop that now! We all agreed that Amalia's degree will make our business more profitable. Once she's credentialed we'll be saving a lot of money in the professional fees we'll no longer have to pay Benito."

"Maybe so," Toño grumbled, his jaw still clenched in anger, "but none of us expected the time frame would stretch into seven years. I'm afraid I'll be dead by the time she gets done."

Paul assured Toño that he could expect to live many more years and he reminded him of all the important concessions I'd made. My brother grudgingly apologized. "I'm sorry, Amalia, I know we're making money. We're doing extremely well, in fact. But it just seems like things have spun out of control. I have been feeling so frazzled lately." He slumped into a chair and laid his head on his folded arms.

I felt exhausted, too, and I needed my brother's understanding. I moved over beside him, placed a hand on his arm, and said, "I can see how overworked you are. We've got a lot on our plates—five homes on queue and we've been caught up with the place on Mejorada Plaza all spring. The time I spend at school is hard on you, but how do you think I feel? I have no life other than work, school, child, house, and responsibilities, responsibilities, responsibilities! I have nothing else in my life. But I can't give up now! I'm almost there and I need you to go the full distance with me."

Paul jumped in. "Enough. Let's stay focused on what we're accomplishing instead of what's grating on us. We could start with discussing the Mejorada place. It's been an enormous challenge, but I love how it is coming along."

Thank God for Paul. Toño and I were glad to be diverted from our grievances and get back to work. I wasn't sure the Mejorada property was the right subject to turn to since our plans required a huge concession from Toño. But we struck a deal. Toño would take a much-needed vacation once the project had been completed.

~~~

When we first went to see the house, the word *hopeless* came to mind. I thought the "title-holder" might have been set up by one of

Toño and Paul's friends who wanted to play a trick on us. The 1920s vintage two-bedroom house sat flush with the street. Several over-grown patios and gardens, all running into one another stretched back for at least sixty meters. The rear part looked so choked with vegetation that I couldn't imagine what might lurk back there under the dead trees and dilapidated sheds. Looped over a decades-ignored clothesline, I spied something that had once been beautiful and lacy. With a stick I found lying on the ground, I lifted it and spread it out. It was a semi-decayed satin wedding gown. Indeed . . . these old places had many secrets to tell.

I asked the owners, Ricardo and David, what their needs were.

"I am a sculptor and David is a writer," Ricardo started. "He must have an absolutely quiet room for his work, and I need lots of space where I can make all the noise I have to and not disturb him."

"Ricardo is minimizing what he calls noise," said David. "When he's working, it's like the Brooklyn Bridge is being dismantled!"

These weren't my first clients with very different requisites. But I liked these guys. I thought their quirky, creative personalities would make this project a lot of fun.

The house had a sound roof and thick walls. Once Benito and I began designing, the project came together nicely. We decided to add a second floor so there'd be plenty of room for a spacious master suite and David's office. We gutted one of the downstairs bedrooms that doubled the living-dining room area. The remaining bedroom became the guest room. It had doors on two sides and when they were left open, a crochet-covered four-poster bed would be visible from the living area, adding an intimate allure.

We enlarged the kitchen at the back of the house and attached a covered patio, perfect for dining or entertaining. A long, narrow pool, with lawn on either side, separated the back part of the house from the studio. To absorb still more sound, we planted fan palms along the high perimeter walls.

"I don't know why you're insisting on so much detailing on this place. The costs are eating into the profit margin at a rate we can't afford," Toño said. Obviously, he still felt ruffled and needed to make his point.

"Look, you and Paul know these two guys are artists. They recognize good design and superior workmanship when they see it. We can't go halfway with them. Besides, I bet they've got a ton of friends, and they'll recommend us." I waited for my brother's retort, but he looked at Paul and nodded his head slowly.

"You're right. You're right. Let's finish this house the way you see fit, Amalia. Let's get you graduated and then I can relax."

"Will we really go on a vacation?" asked Paul.

"You should!" I agreed. "Maybe to Europe? You can take loads of pictures and come back with great ideas for future projects."

"No way!" Paul told me. "If we go on a holiday, we won't even think about the business. We need to get away."

"It's a promise, Paul," Toño said "The week after Amalia's graduation, how about us heading for romantic Tuscany? What do you say?"

Paul's eyes glistened and Toño looked as though he'd completely forgotten that I was in the room.

"And a lady knows when it's time to take her leave," I said with a laugh.

～～

Like several others we had renovated, the Mejorada house was featured in a home décor magazine. It came as no surprise when clients' enquiry letters included the admission that they'd decided to call us because they liked the spread on a house covered in one of these publications. At first the flat package that arrived on a sunny

March morning in 1980 made no special impression, but when I saw it had come from Alejandro, I ripped it open to discover the mystery inside. After reading the first page of the letter, I called Hortensia to come and have a look.

> *Dear Amalia,*
>
> *I devoured the January issue of* Arquitectura Mexicana. *What magic you made with the Mejorada project. It is my hope that you'll help me with the plans I have for a hacienda I've purchased. Please have a look and tell me what you think.*
>
> *Always, Alejandro*

~~~

My nana definitely seemed intrigued as she and I sorted through the rest of the pages.

My eyes opened wide when I came to page five. "Nana! Take a look at this. Alejandro says that he wants his property to serve the community. As a first stage of the development, he hopes to build a center that will help a needy group—yours' might be a good choice, don't you think? For the time being, he will continue to live in Mexico City, but eventually, he plans to start a social justice NGO that would also be headquartered at the hacienda."

Hortensia's involvement with Opciones, the addicts' support group, had continued to grow more profound each year. Two men, Leo and Baltazar; and three women, Mayté, Sister Graciela, and Sister Belén; worked alongside her in the small storefront building where their old friend Sandra Hollis had started up a women's clinic years ago. Hortensia had mentioned that during her meditations each morning, Sandra often speaks to her and urges her to not only keep the project going, but to make it bigger. Opciones had become the cornerstone of my nana's life.

Most people brush off any talk of the paranormal as silly imagining, but I have lived with Hortensia my whole life and I believe what she says to be true.

She and the rest of her group work with whatever they can get their hands on. A few friends in the government's social assistance agencies have helped with funding. But there is no way around it, Opciones doesn't have enough room. They have to find a bigger place.

I'm sure my face looked as dumbfounded as Hortensia's looked serene.

"The ways of the spirit world are winding, wise, and wonderful," she said.

We leafed through several more pages: the land office's map of the premises, photographs of how the place looks now, conceptual notes, and a few rudimentary drawings of Alejandro's heartfelt hopes.

Finally we got to the page where the foundation's mission statement was written.

> *... Villa Aurora will offer a fresh start*
> *to all who cross the threshold. ...*

~

Villa Aurora. He had re-named the hacienda for our daughter.

"I wonder why he's doing this?" asked Hortensia. "When is his next visit?"

"In two weeks," I replied. "I think we need to call Toño and Paul and have a talk."

We set up a meeting for that afternoon. I got right to the point by showing them the package I had received from Alejandro. They both put their heads down and skimmed the contents. "Am I to assume that he will be coming to live here?" Toño asked.

He looked close to a heart attack, and I assured him that Alejandro moving to Merida was not part of the plan.

He and Paul had guessed that Alejandro and I were once again lovers. His visits had become more frequent and the weekly phone calls with Aurora also included time for just him and me.

No one could have been more leery of Alejandro than I had been. But three years ago, after a two-year dry spell, my resistance had finally broken down. He had come to see Aurora and I accepted his offer to join them for dinner and a movie on Friday night. I felt so happy with him on one arm and her on the other.

"Come with us to the beach tomorrow!" Aurora begged.

I could see that my usual excuse of needing to work would cause a huge fight.

"You have a new swim suit," Aurora said and Alejandro whispered that he'd like to see that.

Since my daughter's birth I'd been forced to focus—all the time. Much work and little sleep were the norm in my life. But that weekend broke my monastic routine and the night before he left, Alejandro and I made love all night long in his hotel room. In the morning, I once again found myself completely, hopelessly, totally infatuated with him.

My brief affair with Nico made me admit to myself that my love for Alejandro transcended everything else. And even though it seemed like our relationship would never be what I wanted, whenever he visited Aurora in Merida, I joined him at least once during his stay. I felt conflicted at first. But he looked at it differently.

"Amalia, you are the mother of my one child and you're the woman I love. I admire everything you've accomplished and, of course, you are the most desirable woman alive. Sex is a part of our love."

Indeed, this man had a powerful hold on me, as I knew I did on him. It baffled me that he couldn't or wouldn't get himself out of his "convenient" marriage. To hear him talk, Susana felt satisfied with her place in his life and with the "advantages" that their "partnership" brought to her. But maybe that was changing. A few things Alejandro had mentioned made me deduce that Susana had grown tired of his divided loyalty. I could see it in her writing; for years she had written political editorials for a Mexico City newspaper, but the ones I'd read lately were feminist oriented. I wondered when the showdown would come.

But whatever their real relationship was or was not, Alejandro continued begging me to allow Aurora to visit him and Susana in Mexico City, and according to the custody agreement, starting on her twelfth birthday, I would be obliged to do that.

Following Susana's unsuccessful attempt to gain custody of Aurora six years ago, she and Alejandro had let that issue alone. I confess to wondering if she had really been the one to initiate that battle. I suspected that Alejandro had convinced Susana to make the claim. I also wondered about the kind of fights that had broken out between the two of them over my daughter.

Aurora constantly pleaded with me to let her go, and that, combined with her father's insistence, broke me down just before the two-week Easter vacation last year—more than two years before the imposed date. However, I wanted Alejandro to come to get Aurora and bring her back. I couldn't agree to her going alone on the plane. He said this would be doable.

Aurora and I met Alejandro at the airport and the two of them boarded the same aircraft he'd only just arrived on. My daughter looked radiant holding the arm of her handsome father and I thought how perfect it would be if the tableau included me.

It seemed clear from their weekly phone talks that Aurora adored him, but what little girl doesn't love her daddy, especially if he is good looking and showers her with gifts and special outings?

He returned her two weeks later, and I could see the pain that the parting caused them both. I didn't ask Aurora for the details of her two-week holiday, and she didn't volunteer them. Summer vacations were coming soon and Aurora wanted to go back to Mexico City. I didn't know what I should do.

It upset Toño that Alejandro and I had reconnected, but he'd accepted it. He also knew that the purchase of the hacienda would deepen Alejandro's attachment to Merida. My brother feared that many established parameters would change still more to his disliking. I could see how he struggled to control himself and I turned the conversation back to the business at hand.

"I am almost finished with school, but one of the graduation prerequisites is to design a facility that could be used for community service. I've been wondering if the building Hortensia needs for her support group could be my project, and then I want to take things a step further: I want to actually build at Villa Aurora.

"Build a recovery center? Do you know how much that would cost?" Toño and Paul both looked at me as though I had suggested flying to the moon. It took a long time to explain what Alejandro wanted, why he wanted it, and that he would be the one paying for the renovation. I imagined writing the project introduction.

I was led to the idea for a recovery center by the spirit of my nana's dead friend, and then the father of my child, who is married to another woman, offered me a place to build and to pay for it . . .

I chuckled to myself. Such a prologue would be hilarious, but I wouldn't want the conservative university examining board to discount my project's viability before they even had a good look at it.

After his original negativity, Toño said he'd be willing to go along as long as he would not be shelling out any money.

"If Alejandro has the cash to renovate—and I'd have to see proof of that first—I guess his money is as good as the next guy's."

I felt ideas zooming around my brain and ricocheting off one another. Paul looked at me and shook his head.

"Right now you say this is still a proposal, but Amalia, I'm reminded of something that my daddy would have said—'Where that gal points her gun, you'll see smoke!'"

I laughed. "Obviously, what keeps me from getting one hundred percent excited about this property is that I can't quite figure out why Alejandro is offering this now, and I wonder what Susana thinks. But it's too good a chance to toss aside just because I am suspicious of the motivation behind it. And honestly, Toño, I have no idea how Alejandro can come up with that kind of money."

The Wednesday after receiving Alejandro's request to have us renovate his hacienda, I took the day off. Hortensia and I sat under the covered patio with Toño and Paul. Nana had outdone herself again with our lunch—*empanadas* stuffed with corn, cheese, and *poblanos*. Paul, Toño, and I needed strong coffee to keep from falling asleep. We had a lot to discuss.

"This morning I received a call from Alejandro," I began. "When he comes here in ten days, he said that he hopes we'll be able to talk about his ideas for the hacienda."

Toño did not want to deal with Alejandro or Susana. "If you want to go ahead with this project, I won't stop you, but I will only be minimally involved."

"What about the money? Even you said you didn't see how he could raise enough," said Paul. "Professors don't make that much."

Hortensia listened to their points of view. "I am anxious for this dream of Alejandro's—and mine—to become a reality, but I can understand that you have to talk facts, not dreams. I am going to leave the table so that you three can speak openly." Her future was at stake, but she calmly got up and walked to the house.

"If not for my concerns about the personal price I might have to pay, I'd be so positive about Alejandro's idea. I want Hortensia to have this," I told Toño and Paul.

"If we do build a facility at the hacienda, you know that she will want to live there," Paul reminded me. "Have you thought about that?"

My nana living elsewhere saddened me beyond words, but on the other hand, I felt thrilled for her. I realized it had been some time since I'd last seen her eyes glow. Full-time childcare had taken its toll on Hortensia. Since first learning of Alejandro's offer, she grinned when I looked at her and she seemed to have more energy than she'd shown for years.

"And there's something else bothering you, Amalia," said Paul, "Come on, tell us what it is."

I looked at his sympathetic eyes and decided to get my worry out in the open. "It's Aurora. Now that she has actually met Susana in Mexico City, she tells me how much she likes 'Daddy's wife.' And she says she wishes that I would let her visit more with Alejandro and Susana. I know if I carry on with my crusade, it's going to backfire. My daughter is too young to understand why there's such bad blood between Susana and me. And really, Aurora and I have enough con-flict without adding this continuing vendetta into the mix."

"What are you thinking?" Toño asked. "Do you want to allow Aurora to live with Alejandro and his wife? I understand that you want to keep the peace, Amalia, and I have finally come to see that Aurora should have the opportunity to spend time with her father, but his conniving wife is another story."

Paul seemed much more objective. "Aurora will soon be twelve. In a few more years she'll be of the age to make her own decisions. Amalia's right. This war between her and Susana has to end."

"I'm sorry I brought this up because we need to leave Aurora, and her wishes to go to Mexico City, out of the decision," I said.

Toño nodded in agreement.

"Absolutely, we need to do more follow-up on Alejandro's pro-posal. We owe this to Hortensia," said Paul.

"So we are decided?" I asked.

Paul gave Toño a meaningful look. "So we are decided," he confirmed.

nineteen

"I hope we're not butting in," Hortensia said as she and Aurora walked across the lawn. "Your daughter has been asking where you are."

"No, you're not interrupting us at all. Our meeting is over."

"Don't you ever stop having meetings?" Aurora asked as she leaned against the table with an *I-am-so-bored-with-all-this* look on her face.

Paul confronted her. "You should listen up, kid."

She hated being reminded of her age, but Paul had lost patience with her self-focused behavior. It seemed like a vindication to know I was not alone in my frustration with Aurora's insolence. I crossed my arms over my chest. I could easily lose my temper right now; Aurora had gotten so lippy.

I figured maybe she'd be less hostile if she were included in the discussion, so I asked, "Do you know that your dad has property here in Yucatan?"

"Yeah—a hacienda," she said, "Last time he came for a visit, he said we'd soon go see it."

"Well, what you don't know is that he wants to build a new treatment center on that property, and if the new facility is built, Nana will probably need to go live there."

She nodded and then a light seemed to turn on in her eyes.

"Daddy asked me if I thought it would be a good idea to build a place where sick people could get better. I didn't know he meant close by." But her expression quickly turned bleak, and she looked at Hortensia. "You're not going soon, are you?"

Aurora's earlier nastiness seemed forgotten; she inched over to me and sat down on my lap like she did when she was tiny. I saw she felt insecure and displaced, and I tried to reassure her.

"Hortensia has looked after us for many years and now she has the opportunity to do something she wants to do. It will be easier for her if she lives at the hacienda because she'll be closer to the people who need her. Yet she won't be far away. You'll be able to see her whenever you want."

"I understand that Mamá, but I wish all the people I love could live with me. Daddy is in Mexico City. The rest of my family, too. Now Nana is moving. I don't like it."

We stayed around the table talking about the center until late. I rubbed Aurora's back and after a while she got drowsy.

Toño lifted her up and together we took her to bed. "Sleep well, princess," he said as he tucked the covers around her.

She couldn't keep her eyes open and in just a few moments, she drifted off.

Through the following week, Hortensia and I huddled over my drawing board. I needed her to tell me what elements she required and then work them into the existing infrastructure—this way I could keep the project as cost efficient as possible. On the Thursday before Alejandro's visit, I finished drawing the plans for Opciones. I knew he would be pleased, and Hortensia said she felt as though the goddess had taken me by the hand. Nevertheless I knew Toño would object to some of the aesthetics. But this was Hortensia's dream; we couldn't go halfway. I'd have to work hard to win my partners completely over, and I figured that a hearty breakfast would help to get us through what would certainly be a long, polemic session.

The next morning, I set off at half-past six for the market, struck by the contrast between the first tentative bird song coming from the broad-leafed laurel trees and the fierce barking of the "watchdogs" that people leave on the roofs at night. How do the owners know if the mutts are sounding the alarm or merely terrifying passersby?

I rushed by them and continued my pursuit of pit-roasted *cochinita*; there's nothing better to set a person up for a good day than that flavorful pork inside a thick-crusted French loaf. As well, I picked up a few other things we needed. If Hortensia moved away, I'd best get used to doing the shopping. Actually, I couldn't wait until I finished school and would have the time to do simple domestic chores. It would be such a pleasure, especially if some of the time Alejandro would be with me.

Two groaning bags weighed me down all the way home. I loaded my purchases into three large wicker baskets that sit on the open shelves of my kitchen. Along the windowsill, I placed tall, multi-colored blown-glass vases and filled them with red gladioli that I had bought. Prisms of light reflected onto my white walls. Such a simple touch, but it looked beautiful.

At half-past seven, Toño and Paul came over. My brother stepped into the kitchen, took one whiff, and smiled.

"*¡Cochinita!*"

"What's up, Amalia?" he asked. "Being summoned to see you so early is not an everyday occurrence."

"Look at this, Toño," I said, holding out a roll of grid paper. He and Paul plunked down at my kitchen table and unrolled the plans for Opciones. Their eyes grew wide as they pored over the six drawings. Paul looked at me with frank surprise and said, "This is your conception of Hortensia's dream, isn't it?"

I nodded. "I got really inspired when I started thinking about Uxmal. The entrance to a section of the Mayan city is a soaring corbel arch. At Opciones we'll have the same kind of entryway. It will open on to a wide esplanade. I plan to convert the old machine room at the far end into an all-purpose treatment and activities center. Around the main structure, I want to build small *chozas*. Hortensia and I thought that the patients would like the less institutionalized quarters. There will be an apartment for Nana, separated from the others.

"On the eastern and western sides of the big room are a communal kitchen and a laundry facility. You can reach the manor house by curving around to the left of the former machine room. The treatment and recovery center will be quite independent from the rest of the hacienda."

"This design takes good advantage of the infrastructure already at the hacienda and incorporates traditional dwellings," said Toño, still mulling over the drawings. "It shouldn't be too expensive to build. A good thing because we don't want this to turn into a nightmare. Speaking of that, how is Alejandro going to pay the building costs? I can't imagine that his wife is very happy about this idea."

Aurora had joined us around the big table and she sprang to her father's defense. "If my daddy said he wants to build this, he will."

Toño grimaced. It still seemed as though he'd rather walk over hot coals than depend on Alejandro.

"Well, we'll know soon enough how he feels," I said. "He'll be coming to see Aurora tomorrow, and, for sure, the hacienda will be the main topic of discussion."

Later that afternoon Layla came over to see the plans.

"Aurora's got a hell of a role model in you—you do everything well. Can I interview you for a piece I'm doing on the changing roles of women?" she asked. I thanked her. I knew what a Layla byline would do for my career.

～

Usually, when Alejandro came to Merida to see Aurora, she and I would pick him up at the airport and then the two would do something on their own. This time, though, Aurora had been invited to a sleepover with her friend Tina and she didn't want to miss it. I told her I felt sure that her dad wouldn't mind. He would see her in the morning.

And I would have him to myself in the evening. We needed to talk about the hacienda.

Watching him bounce from the plane's gate and down the long corridor, I wished he would not be turning around and going back to Susana on Sunday night.

"Where's Aurora?" he asked.

"She's staying the night with a friend, actually. You'll see her tomorrow morning."

He smiled at me. "Okay then. I think you should go to a sleepover with your 'friend' too. At the hotel." He moved to embrace me, but I stepped away.

"I can't stay overnight with you this time," I told him. "But next visit, could you manage to arrive a day earlier? We just wouldn't tell anyone you're here and we could be together."

Alejandro looked at me with longing and said I could count on that plan.

A young couple from Guadalajara had moved to Merida and opened an intimate inn just around the corner from my house. When he came to town, Alejandro usually reserved one of their bungalows.

After I dropped him off to check in, I parked my car at home, and then set off on foot—back to the inn—carrying the roll of plans. I felt extremely nervous about showing them to him. I remembered the day when we were newly in love.

"Maybe one day you'll design a house for me?" he'd suggested. While I didn't hold the plans for his house in my hands, I had done this project for him. He reached to take me in his arms.

I pulled away. "Alejandro, we'll get to that," I purred, "but first I have something special to show you."

As he leaned over to take the roll from me, his ardor evaporated and he looked like a little boy ready for a birthday gift. Again I pulled back, keeping the plans from him. "A little patience, please. Before you look at this, I want you to level with me: Why are you and Susana so keen to help Hortensia?"

He stiffened and looked away from me: "Susana doesn't know about the hacienda."

I was stunned. "How have you gotten away with not telling her? Doesn't she wonder what you're doing with the money you've obviously spent?"

He told me that in 1970 he had invested a modest sum with friends who were buying land in an area that the federal government planned to develop for tourism. He'd never heard of the place, and he felt suspicious of the deal, but his buddies were so sure; they'd had a reliable tip that Cancún would turn into an international resort.

"Lucky for me, it has. A year ago my brother told me about the hacienda, and I sold a percentage of my Cancún shares to buy it. As the property is located so close to Merida and the subject of you and our daughter is a prickly one for Susana, I decided not to tell her."

"How can you manage to keep something like that from her?" I asked.

"It's easy. My brother pays the taxes and any maintenance fees from a joint account I opened with him at a Banamex branch in Merida. I've never used any of Susana's money on the hacienda, so she has never suspected a thing."

I couldn't imagine that a husband would withhold such important information from his wife. That marriage must be even shakier than I suspected. But I stuck to business. "Now that you are planning to develop it, how will the finances work?"

"I still have funds from when I sold my shares, and the money in the bank is paying a lot of interest, I have way more than I need."

What he said rang true. "But can you explain to me why you want to start the foundation with Hortensia's project and not your own?"

"I'm not ready, Amalia. I can't possibly leave the UNAM before 1988 or I'll forfeit a huge percentage of my retirement fund. As well, the kind of foundation I want to build is one that the country is not ready for. There is so much unfocused anger and I want this group to be a cornerstone for peace."

"Alejandro, we never talk about the night of Tlatelolco—not ever. I was one of those mindless citizens who thought politicians meant what they said when they told us that it's all for the common good. We were all betrayed. I can understand why people will have trouble embracing any peace-and-love idealism."

"For a long time I believed that resistance and a loud voice were the only ways to force the politicians to hear us," said Alejandro. "But after years of futile screaming, I've come to realize that this kind of thinking is unproductive. We need to move on. I want to build a place where ordinary people and our leaders will be able to meet as equals and create real change—like a think tank. I plan to call the foundation Paz Ahora—Peace Now."

How could the "hawk" I knew for so many years have transformed into the "dove" I saw before me tonight? "I think you have a great ideological concept," I said, "and you'll work out the practicalities as time goes by. When you're ready to start, it will be clearer in your mind. But what will happen to Hortensia when you move your foundation here?" I asked.

"Amalia, I believe in Hortensia's cause. I want to help her and even when I bring Paz Ahora to the hacienda, she will be as central to the operation as now. I want the complex to be multifaceted. I want other nonprofits to join us. They'll be able to share infrastructure and split the overhead costs. But if it will make you happier, I will draw up a contract that will give Hortensia's group *usufructo*— use and benefit—of the property for twenty years, fifty years—one hundred years, if that's what you want."

How could he have changed so much? Alejandro looked so determined and full of enthusiasm that in spite of my many lingering reservations, I felt eager to see how far he could run with this. What I'd learned from him over the past few minutes confirmed my feelings of late. He'd been a perpetual teenager, but it now seemed that his protest marches and posters had been replaced with lobbying and campaigning. Maybe his personal life would change as well and he would really move to Merida?

In any event, it was a great relief to know where the money was to come from. That information would certainly ease my brother's mind.

After our conversation I still had doubts, but I had decided that like Hortensia, I would trust fate. The time had come for the unveiling of my design. I felt my hands sweating as I laid out the six square, lined sheets. "Keep in mind these are just preliminary drawings," I told Alejandro. "I can make whatever modifications you need."

Alejandro didn't answer me. He looked completely absorbed in what I'd spread out before him.

After a full fifteen minutes, he took my hands and pulled me toward him. "These are much more than what I imagined. I can picture the center so clearly in my mind. I feel more anxious than ever to build. You are amazing. How could I have been so blind when I was young? Thank God we had Aurora. If we hadn't, I might never have found you again."

Our emotions lay totally exposed. I looked into Alejandro's eyes and saw sadness mixed with his elation. "Will we ever get it right?" I asked.

He buried his face into my shoulder and nuzzled me. "Soon," he answered. "This project will bring us that much closer to where we want to be. The pieces will fall into place—you'll see."

~~~

At midnight, I stretched and shook Alejandro's shoulder. "Come on, I have to go now."

"Amalia, I can't wait for the day when we can wake up together. I hate that one of us always has to go home."

I did, too, but for now we didn't have an alternative. Alejandro was married to Susana. I could not shy away from that reality. I felt this relationship was far better than none at all. And as of tonight, it would be easier. Although he had often said he "wished" he could end his marriage, I finally knew that he had begun to lay the foundation for a new life here—with me.

Arm in arm, we walked to my house. As I turned for a good-night kiss, I saw someone dressed in red ducking behind a car across the street. My stomach tightened. I knew that shape; it had to be Aurora.

"Come out from there!" I commanded. "What are you doing in the street at this time of night?"

She boldly showed herself and taunted me with the same question.

"Do not speak like that to your mother," said Alejandro. "Get inside!"

She did as he ordered—shocked to have heard him raise his voice to her. We filed into the living room, and each of us perched on the edge of a chair. Alejandro and I sat side by side; Aurora faced us.

Alejandro looked at his daughter. "Why were you outside so late?"

Aurora started to cry. "Tina and I had a fight and I went back to our house. Mamá wasn't there and I waited a long time—I didn't want to wake up Hortensia so I went looking for Mamá on my own. I saw you coming up the street. I didn't think you wanted me to see you, so I tried to hide until you'd gone inside, but Mamá caught me."

What could we say to her? I felt Aurora's confusion and her fear of getting in trouble. I felt very conflicted too. How much had Aurora figured out? I could not miss noticing her disappointment in me and her astonishment over the fact that her father had put her on the spot.

The two of us felt alarmed by Aurora's discovery, but then Alejandro's voice softened and he leaned toward her. "Aurora, why do you think your mother and I met at the inn?"

She had begun to recover her composure. "I don't know." She glared at me. I wanted to die—to lie—to tell her we were playing backgammon. Whatever! I relaxed a little when Alejandro said that I had been showing him the architectural drawings and we'd been talking about the center. But my reprieve was short-lived. He glanced my way, then he faced Aurora again.

"I am your father, Aurora. Your mother and I have loved one another forever, but for so many reasons, we can't be together. There isn't really anything else I can say."

She turned to me. "Why didn't you tell me?"

"Aurora, you never asked. But now that the feelings your father and I have for one another are no longer a secret, I'll tell you whatever you want to know."

"I don't want you to tell me anything. I only want to go to my room."

She didn't wait for our permission; she certainly didn't want a kiss and a hug—she ran from the room.

"What now?" Alejandro asked.

"I also want to go to my room. We'll have to discuss this tomorrow."

"She's only eleven years old. She doesn't understand much," he said. "I figure we should follow her cues—if she asks to talk about this further, we will. If she doesn't let us know she wants to, we won't. It's trickier for you because you live together. But I don't see what else we can do. We don't want to get her more confused by giving her a lot of details she's too young to deal with."

For the time being, I had to agree.

Aurora seemed to have forced last night out of her mind. She joined Hortensia and me for a trip with Alejandro to his hacienda. He looked anxious as we walked through the grounds. He could tell I was sizing up the buildings for soundness and feasibility.

"What do you think?" he asked.

"I'm willing to make this project a priority," I said. "How do you like it, Aurora?"

In spite of the fact that she was suppressing her full feelings from last night, I could see that my daughter was fascinated with Villa Aurora. "I love this place! Will you be moving here in the summer?"

Obviously she had been thinking about what Alejandro had

said, "Your mother and I have loved one another forever." She probably imagined that we'd finally be a family. I hoped that when that
day came, somehow she would decide that Susana wanted it too.
After all, she had grown close to her stepmother.

Her eyes shone with premature anticipation, and I had to
respect the way Alejandro gave her no illusions.

"*Cariño,* you have to understand one thing. Right now, I am
not contemplating a move here. This hacienda will be developed so
that Opciones can grow. Hortensia will live here and will manage
it. My work is in Mexico City."

As is common with not-quite twelve-year-olds, her budding
maturity deserted her. She turned her back and walked away from
us, but we could see her slim shoulders shuddering. Alejandro
wanted to run after her, but I urged him to wait. After a quarter of
an hour, she made her way back and tried to act as though nothing
had happened.

"It's hot," she said. "Let's go back to Merida."

～

What a roller-coaster weekend we'd been through, and I had much
to do if I expected to turn my project in on time. But when Aurora
came to see me in my office wanting to talk, I put my work aside
and we sat in the two chairs facing the window. I worried that my
daughter would ask me more about the relationship I had with her
father. Instead, she surprised me by bringing up an altogether different topic.

"I really want to spend this summer in Mexico City," said
Aurora. "Tía Manuela and I have spoken and she said that when she
comes here for your graduation, she could take me back with her."

I felt sure that if she didn't get the answer she wanted from
me, Aurora would bring up what happened on Friday night. My

emotional equilibrium felt as fragile as the air before a thunder storm. "I'll need to call your aunt. Can we talk about this again in a couple of days?"

My daughter looked at me with eyes too wise for an eleven-year-old.

twenty

I had lost count of how many times I'd casually set an assignment down on top of my director's desk and hoped for the best. But this time would be different. These were our final projects—they deserved some ceremony.

At eleven o'clock, when Professor Arcel Espadas-Carrillo walked into his classroom on our last official morning of class, he looked surprised to see Dr. Rosado and the other professors seated in the first row of desks.

"What is this all about?" he asked.

The university president rose, spread out his arms, and said he had no idea—his presence had been requested, so he came. He looked to me for an explanation, and I offered our stunned director a seat. Héctor turned out the lights and immediately a screen blinked on.

My classmates booed with mock disgust at the first takes that appeared on the screen—our original building. Next we murmured fond remembrances at the shots of classmates who didn't finish and of others who were in the room. Mercy and her children were shown distributing food and drink, and Héctor was there, waving from atop the cathedral. Our instructors joined in the pleasure of seeing pictures of our first congress and a host of other significant moments—more than three hundred slides. We had put together this presentation to document our seven years as students. The narrator was none other than Héctor, whose typical humor kept us all from breaking into torrents of tears. Nonetheless, at the end of the hour when the lights came back on, noses ran, and dewy eyes blinked.

My turn to speak had arrived. I began to recite the names of the Class of 1980. One by one we filed up and placed our last folders onto our director's desk. As the final student walked back to his place, we stood and clapped for our champion, Professor Arcel Espadas-Carrillo. Without him, none of this would have happened. Quite simply we would not be here—almost architects.

Our director and the professors sat staring at us, completely incapable of speech. The air felt pregnant, an odd word to use perhaps, but it seemed the only way to describe our feelings of imminent change and fulfillment.

"Let's go for lunch!" said Miguel. Every celebration in Mexico involves food and that day's fiesta at Alberto's Continental Patio is something I have never forgotten—one of my life's highest moments.

We festooned the restaurant with colorful cut-out paper flags. Balloons and canned music bounced through the room. "I believe in miracles . . . you sexy thing . . ." the tape recorder sang out as our director and Dr. Rosado came through the door.

Professor Arcel Espadas-Carrillo made a rare attempt at humor. He clapped the president on the back. "They're playing our song!" he said. We all groaned and then broke into hysterical laughter at the sight of the two of them dancing "the bump."

The whole place had been reserved for just our class and our mentors. As the empty beer bottles and the used plates piled up, Miguel and a couple of other guys brought out their guitars and the music took on a sweet melancholy. We sang all our old favorite drinking songs and watched two of the girls dancing in a swaying circle. By six, none of us could see straight and Alberto started calling cabs.

I waited until the last one came and piled in with Evangelina.

"Can I st-ay-ay o-ver at your place?" she asked me, leaning heavily onto my shoulder. "My m-other and f-ather ha-ve nev'r see-een me drunk-k an' they-ll bee-ee hor-ri-fi-ed."

I told her she could stay, but I also thought that on the verge of receiving her professional degree, she should stand up to them. She looked at me with crossed eyes and gave the cabbie her address, located in the most exclusive part of El Campestre, the city's elite housing area.

"Op-en up! I'm ho-ome!" she shouted as she stumbled out of the taxi. "Mo-th-errr!"

Clutching a religious medallion around her neck, Evangelina's mother rushed to the door. "Have you been drinking alcohol?"

"Yes-s-s . . . lo-t-s-s-s-s!" said my friend as she collapsed on the front steps.

"What are we going to do?" the distraught woman asked me.

"Bring a big bowl 'cause she'll be sick in a few minutes."

"Oh, Evangelina, this is awful," her mamá said.

I bit my tongue and passed my friend's purse to her mother. Stretched out on the welcome mat, Evangelina had begun snoring gently. The haughty matron stared after me as I resumed my homeward journey.

"See you at Commencement," I called back to her.

~~~

The final weeks prior to our graduation party flew by in a haze. We all felt too excited, and we fretted about final marks, next steps, and teary farewells. But I didn't have to wait for the grade on my final project. The university president himself called me into his office and, holding my folder out straight in front of him, he showed me the bold A+ written across the cover page. He suggested that I enter my design for Opciones to the National College of Architecture's contest for innovations being introduced by new architects across the country. Dr. Rosado told me, "The deadline for entries is tomorrow. You'll have to make your application in person at the Mexico City office."

Last-minute flight arrangements worked out, and when I arrived, I took a cab to the headquarters of the Architectural College, housed in a turn-of-the-eighteenth-century manor house. At Layla's suggestion, I'd dressed "memorably"—a tight-fitting navy blue pin-striped pant suit with a bright red turtleneck and very high platform heels. In an oversized suede purse I carried my drawings and the contest application forms. As Layla assured me would happen, I cornered lots of attention and felt certain that the male clerks would see to it that my submission got careful review. I'd learned that sometimes you do what you have to.

From there I went to see Mamá and Manuela; they both looked excited and happy with my surprise visit. We sat on the balcony, enjoying the warmth of the sun that burned through the typically gray afternoon sky of Mexico City.

This seemed like as good a time as any to tell them about all the developments with the hacienda and also about the evening when Aurora inadvertently discovered me leaving Alejandro's hotel. It impressed me that Mamá made no judgments. My sister asked if Aurora had been acting strained around me.

"Not more than the usual," I said and added that I hoped she didn't really know what we were doing.

A look passed between Mamá and Manuela, then my sister nodded. "Aurora called me from a long-distance phone booth. She is confused about her relationships. You know, Amalia, a separation would do you both a lot of good. She needs to have an opportunity to miss you and appreciate you."

"Your daughter loves our salon and says she wants to learn more about couture. I would like her to live with me. Here in La Capital she'll be exposed to so much—the kind of things she needs to learn," Mamá added with a hint of a smile on her lips. I guess I couldn't escape her digs entirely.

"Mamá, you sound just like Alejandro!"

Not giving our mother time for a retort, my sister cut in. "As Hortensia would say, 'the goddess brings us together when she knows the time is right.' This is obviously the right time."

"What do you mean by that?"

"Simply that you're slow to recognize help when it's offered. Amalia, we could ease the strain between you and Aurora."

My mother and sister looked at me and nodded encouragingly. "Nothing can change if you don't acknowledge what needs to change."

For once, I didn't get upset. "Mamá, maybe you and I are too much alike. I see myself making the same judgments you did. I want Aurora to be a certain way, but she's not. I want to spend more time with her, but *I* also need to work. She knows I feel conflicted and any chance she gets, she rubs the guilt in."

Mamá nodded. The tensions between us had been similar. We had irritated each other over the same things. "And you're not even mentioning the biggest complication—Alejandro. He was entirely to blame for the problems between you and me. Now he drives a wedge between you and your daughter. He's all wrong for you, Amalia. He made you turn away from me, and he's going to do the same to Aurora."

Manuela threw up her arms and challenged Mamá. "He's her father! You have tried to come between the boys and Angel Gustavo as well. Neither he nor Alejandro is perfect, but the bond between the child and the father has to be respected. I struggle with that every day, and I see Amalia does too."

Our mother looked shocked that Manuela had come to my defense. I probably did too, but it became clear that my sister had a compromise in mind.

"Amalia, I don't think that Aurora should move here, but why don't you let her come to Mexico City with us after the graduation? She could stay for the summer."

Mamá jumped on the idea. "Who knows how much longer Papá and I will be around. She's our only granddaughter and we hardly know her."

"I have no daughter, Amalia, and I would love to spend more time with Aurora. She is at the perfect age to explore Mexico City—and to learn some skills from Mamá and me," said Manuela.

"You're right, of course. It's a perfect time. But Alejandro will insist on seeing her too," I warned.

My sister moved over beside me and took my hand. "Maybe it is time for Aurora to know her father's world," she said.

I couldn't argue with her—and neither could Mamá. Aurora had already been to Mexico City, but I didn't tell my well-meaning sister about that. I let her and Mamá believe they had brought me to this decision. "I think what you're proposing might be best for all of us."

On the morning of my departure from La Capital, almost without thinking, I called Alejandro, and he invited me for lunch at the Hotel Del Prado on Avenida Reforma. I loved this landmark. In the lobby hung my favorite painting by Diego Rivera—*Un Domingo en la Alameda*. Many others share my preference. The work is whimsical, political, and shows the artist's fine talent.

We both wanted to order *Caldo Tlalpeño*—a rich chicken soup with rice, chipotle peppers, avocado, and melted string cheese. And we had *molletes*, too—crusty bread spread with a red bean paste and topped with more gooey cheese.

"Shall we have Champagne and toast your commencement?" Alejandro asked.

I said I'd never heard of drinking Champagne with the regional fare we'd be eating, but why not? It sounded like a grand idea.

"I love you," he said, "but I never thought you would turn out to be the person you are."

"What do you mean?"

"Lots of things I guess. But right now, I'm thinking about how I never believed you would finish your degree. It has been such a long, difficult haul. I deserve a big kick in the pants," he said.

So . . . I had proven myself to him, but why did he feel I had to? "A kick in the pants," he'd called my accomplishment. I wanted to give him a good stiff one right now! Why did he always look at what I did in terms of his opinion and how it impacted his own life? He had been so full of his own vision for so many years that he'd been blind to what I wanted and needed. I asked him to elaborate on his surprising statement.

When he saw my scowl, he started to explain away the "kick in the pants" comment. "I've always thought I was more committed than you, but it turns out, you are every bit as dedicated to your ideals as I am. I didn't see this until I got to know Aurora. She is so much like you."

He hadn't completely dug himself out, but that was how he'd always been. I smiled at him and he assumed he'd recouped my favor. I thought back to the afternoon when Aurora was an infant and Layla had just found out that Alejandro was her father. She had told me that he would one day realize that he'd underestimated me. How prophetic. I liked having Alejandro's approval, but I did not need it as I once had.

My whole body quickened when he rubbed my leg under the table. Maybe it was the bubbly. I would think about his lopsided compliments later on. Right now, I felt happy and I knew he'd suggest we get a room and—appropriate or not—I wanted that too.

"Come on, Amalia, let's tear up the sheets, and then I'll take you to the airport."

I guess some things never change. He would always be my wild card. I had no explanation for this or anything else related to the man. Maybe Alejandro and I were addicted to each other.

twenty-one

Not only did the entire clan accept my invitation to the graduation ceremony, but they wanted to attend the dinner-dance as well.

We would be hosting them for the whole weekend. "Mamá and Papá could stay at my house," I suggested to Toño and Paul. "Can you have Manuela and the boys?" Counting those from Merida and the out-of-towners, I'd have fifteen guests coming with me to the celebration.

Paul hugged himself in pleasurable anticipation. "I always wondered what it would be like to have your family stay with us . . . another blessing that has come into my life."

Toño laughed. "Let's see how you feel once they all start fighting."

On the phone, Mamá and Papá told me how much they looked forward to having their three children under one roof. This had not happened since 1940. Forty years ago! Maybe our family would, at long last, start acting like a normal one. Maybe the careless disregard we'd shown one another could be atoned for, and in the future we could look forward to closer ties? Six years earlier, when Mamá and Papá had visited Merida—at the same time as the Queen of England—we had made a start toward more acceptance of one another's differences. We had continued with what Paul called "detente" and I hoped this weekend would take us beyond polite approval and into the territory of actually enjoying one another's company.

As my parents stepped through the arrival gate at Merida's International Airport I felt sad to see how old they looked. Mamá in particular seemed hunched over and definitely favored her right side. Her bursitis must have flared up. Papá's ebony hair was completely gone and his shiny pate was pocked with age spots. They both peered uncertainly through the crowd and when they saw me, they beamed in relief.

"Mamá, Papá!" I called out. "I'm so glad you could come for my big day! Let's find your luggage and get you both home for a rest."

Wrong thing to say!

My mother looked at me with her characteristic combativeness and replied, "We may be slowing down, but that doesn't mean we have one foot in the grave. Before we go to your place, we want to go for drinks at La Prosperidad." This restaurant had always been popular at lunch time with locals and tourists. For the price of the beer, *botanas*—small servings of regional food—also arrived at the table. A band played and a local comedian named Cholo was the current headliner.

Papá perked up in this environment and grinned when the manager approached him. "Don Antonio Vásquez! I can't believe it. I'm your biggest fan. When I visited Mexico City last summer, I went to hear your band. Would you honor us by playing a little something?"

He finished a whole set. The house musicians gave it their all and the crowd got up and danced. Finally, Papá wiped his brow, put down the borrowed guitar, and returned to our table. Mamá looked at him with more admiration than I had ever seen on her face. This was going well.

But my mother wanted to see her son too. "Let's drive to Toño and Paul's place," she said. I put my arms around her, so pleased that she now fully included Toño's partner as part of the family.

In García Ginerés, we found Paul in his element. "What can I serve you, Doña Teresa? There's food and anything you want to drink."

My mother had the unique ability to change her opinion about anything or anyone—once she recognized this to be in her best interest. She saw now that Paul could become a great ally, and she had decided to win him over. "This is the best strawberry tart I've ever had," she said.

From Paul's experience with women like Mamá, he knew what it took to have her on his side. He made his eyes go wide and hugged her. "Do you really think so?"

Toño looked as though he'd burst with happiness.

I could see that my father needed a rest, yet Mamá insisted on staying until Manuela and the boys arrived. She'd only been separated from her eldest daughter since this morning, and she already missed her comforting presence. Toño urged Papá to lie down on a divan in the living room.

Manuela was the consummate confidante. As soon as she entered the house, it felt as though we were all drifting evenly on the Sea of Tranquility. Hortensia arrived shortly after—the second heaven-sent counterpoint to all the exhilaration this weekend held in store.

Hortensia greeted my parents with effusive hugs and enquiries about the trip. "How did you manage with the flight? Everyone travels by plane nowadays. Remember what travel used to be like?"

"Remember!" said my mother with horror. "I don't think my buttocks ever rounded out again after that dreadful voyage from Merida to Mexico City twenty-two years ago." My two mothers were wrapped in memories and I suspected they'd remain in the same state for much of the next two days.

Aurora behaved uncharacteristically quiet; she seemed to be soaking up the stories that she had waited so long to hear. I felt a moment's regret for not having given my daughter more occasions like this, and swore I would nurture this recuperated closeness.

The rest of the afternoon and evening played out smoothly. The twins barbecued steaks in the garden while Hortensia, Manuela, and I prepared the rest of the meal. Immediately after we ate, I drove Mamá and Papá home and they retired to their room. Very wise of them since tomorrow would be such a full day. I followed my parents' lead and turned in early. Once my head found a comfortable position on the pile of pillows, I slept soundly.

It seemed as though no time had elapsed, yet I saw light coming through under my door. Today was my birthday as well as my graduation day, and I could hear murmuring down by the pool. I threw on a caftan and hurried over.

"*¡Felicidades Amalia!*" My entire family had gathered. Paul had prepared a perfect Yucatecan birthday breakfast entrée: *huevos motuleños*—sunny-side-up eggs on a fried tortilla, topped with black bean paste, then heaped with diced ham, cheese, bright green peas, and a spicy tomato sauce. On the sideboard I saw a huge bowl of fresh tropical fruit, sweet rolls from the Panificadora Montejo, and a pile of presents waiting to be opened. While Aurora bustled about passing dishes and lavishing attention on every guest, Toño placed a mimosa in my hand, gave me a huge hug, and kissed my cheek.

"Aurora looks so proud of you, Amalia. It's been ages since I've seen her so happy."

I agreed. Seeing my daughter laughing and affectionate made me hope for more of the same from now on.

"Time to open the surprises! So many—they're all so pretty! I can't wait to see what's inside," said my daughter. "Open mine first, Mamá!"

The individually wrapped gifts each contained pieces of the

same custom-made Talavera dinner service for twenty. "I can see that I'll need to host Christmas dinner this year so that we can all enjoy these gorgeous dishes," I said.

Aurora slid a slim rectangular box over to my place. "This is from Daddy. He asked me to deliver it for him." I glanced around and saw how everyone shuffled in their seats. Inside the box I found a stunning string of antique baroque pearls with a note.

I hope you'll wear this necklace tonight . . . nothing sets off your beauty like pearls.

Aurora looked ready to argue with anyone who would question the appropriateness of such a public gesture. She came and put her hands on my shoulders. "Let me help you put on Daddy's pearls."

I blushed, embarrassed by my daughter's behavior.

Paul, who sat beside me, quickly and quietly counseled, "Don't you dare try to stop her—and after all—the necklace is very becoming."

So true, but each translucent bead felt like an exquisite drop of fire. Yet, why should I be embarrassed? It seemed that everyone knew about Alejandro and me. My parents and sister appeared nonchalant. Perhaps I had also earned a degree of acceptance?

In just eight hours the graduation party would begin at an outdoor banquet facility owned by the local bottling company. I felt relieved—there seemed to be no hint of rain. I elected to take a long, luxurious bath and spent the remaining hours primping for the party that night.

I heard the doorbell ring and my daughter's voice saying, "I'll get it. I bet it's Tía Layla."

"I've come to see you dress and help with your makeup and

hair. I need to be sure you're going to be the most gorgeous woman there."

Trust Layla to provide the diversion I needed. I had been feeling so emotional, but now it was time to party!

A week earlier, I had restored my curls to their original fiery glory with a little help from Miss Clairol. Layla approved and set to work on my makeup.

"You look good, girl!"

I emerged from my room wearing Mamá and Manuela's special creation. The snug fit and low neckline were accented by frilly Oaxacan lace—the ivory-colored gown looked both demure and daring. Layla piled my hair atop my head, and my eyes shone smoky after her makeup ministrations. I knew I looked as happy as I felt.

"You are the most beautiful graduate I've ever seen," said Toño. I wished he'd added a compliment about the pearls, but my brother wasn't quite ready for that.

At the gala, Evangelina was the first person who spoke to me.

"You look spectacular, Amalia. The rest of us are afraid that all the good-looking men will only have eyes for you."

I smiled at my friend, the brave young girl I'd met seven years ago. "We've come a long way, haven't we? I'll never forget the way you took charge on our first day of school and dragged me along to find a bathroom."

I didn't make any reference to last week's liquor-sodden celebration and her mother's bewilderment. The austere woman stood to one side, smiling at her daughter; I concluded that the whole episode had done them both a lot of good.

She laughed. "You remember our first friends, the neighbors who lived on the street behind that awful building? They have been invited to the graduation. I hope they'll come."

"They will, Evangelina. A few days ago, I ran into Doña Mercy and her eldest son at the market. She said that everyone who'd been invited would be there. They feel they are a part of our success and indeed they are." I led my guests to our place near the center of the room.

The director stopped by the table. "Amalia, congratulations!

"We wouldn't be here if it weren't for you," I replied.

He looked surprised when I gave him a giant hug and kiss. The rest of the professors and my classmates milled about laughing and drinking. And of course the president of the university and the politicians were puffed-up, taking one compliment after another, confident that our accomplishment was thanks to them—when in reality—it had occurred in spite of them.

But this was not a night for bitterness. We'd made it and that's what mattered most. Our group welcomed Mercy, her son, and Doña Landy. The two ladies had been to the beauty salon and had dressed up in finery that rivaled that of the governor's wife. They seemed so proud to be remembered.

At ten, the formal ceremony began. We listened politely to the congratulatory speeches and accolades the university leaders laid on themselves. It seemed unbelievably hard for me to keep myself contained as the sixteen names were read. One by one my friends took their places in the spotlight, among them—Miguel, Fernando, Jeanette, Evangelina, and Héctor. I felt such pleasure as I watched each of them accept their diploma.

I did not win the architectural contest; someone from Puebla received the 100,000-peso prize. But I couldn't have cared less. I actually froze when my name was called—the last on the list of the Class of 1980. I couldn't move, even though I saw Dr. Rosado waving at me, urging me to move up to the podium.

Toño gave me a gentle push. "Up you go, little sister."

"I'm really proud of you," said Aurora. She held me so tight I feared something was wrong.

"You all right? I asked.

"Yeah, I'm okay. I just wish that Daddy could have been here."

I kissed the top of her head—we'd talk about this later. When I finally moved forward, the evening enveloped me like a summer blanket.

Astonishment, gratitude, justification, satisfaction, and wonder all competed for the top spot in my consciousness. I looked forward to signing my name on all of our company's future projects—it seemed fitting that Opciones would be the first "Amalia Vásquez property."

twenty-two

With my daughter away in Mexico City, Hortensia and I had a chance to spend some time together—just the two of us.

To a bowl of greens and sweet mango chunks, Nana added toasted almonds and squeezed on lemon juice. We sat down at the round table in the kitchen and as we filled one another in on our respective comings and goings, we ate all the salad, plus a whole loaf of hot buttered *pan francés*. We also emptied most of a bottle of crisp white wine.

"I think I need to stretch out in one of the hammocks on your back porch," she said as she patted her lips with a napkin.

In no time, we both fell asleep, but I jolted awake when lightning jabbed through the leaden afternoon sky. Blackbirds shrieked as the first raindrops plopped down and sizzled on the hot patio. Hortensia and I saw the storm gusting through the tall avocado tree and we moved deeper under the awning.

Horizontal torrents of water pummeled my house; we heard the refrigerator shut down and the fans stop whirring. La Comisión always shuts the power off during weather like this. "No electricity for a while," I told Hortensia. "We may as well just stay out here on the patio." The stifling summer temperature had dropped at least ten degrees in a matter of minutes.

"It's going to be a long storm," said Hortensia, wrapping her shawl closer. We'd both been busy, especially since construction had started at the Opciones site, and it felt good to relax side by side with our feet up. Still, we couldn't avoid more talk about the center.

"I've never seen Don Luis' crew work so quickly," she said. "His group will continue their evening meetings in their neighborhood, but they know how useful it will be to have the center for their special events."

I smiled. "He told me that when he chose sobriety, he only had you and his wife to help him through the withdrawal. With caring people and a proper facility to help them through, more people will reclaim their lives—just as he did."

"How much longer do you think the construction will take?" Hortensia asked.

"I have hopes that we'll be able to inaugurate in a month's time, soon after Toño and Paul return from Europe," I replied.

"They've been having a wonderful time, haven't they? I'm so glad they got away. And what do you hear from Aurora?" my nana wanted to know.

"I think Manuela's idea to take her to Mexico City was brilliant. She loves my mother's *Salón* and spends most of her days in there. Mamá says she sews beautifully for a young girl." I felt a frown start to form. "And, of course, she had to add that I too could have been a fine seamstress."

At first Hortensia pretended not to notice my ever-present annoyance with Mamá's jibing. "I could see the artist in Aurora from the first time we put a crayon in her hand," she said. "I can also see that your mother isn't passing up a chance to needle you a bit. But don't be too hard on her, Amalia."

"I try not to be. I know that Mamá had to focus on her career—we would have starved if she hadn't. I can appreciate the parallels between her circumstances and mine."

~~~

Aurora arrived back in Merida just before classes were to resume.

She would be starting her first year of junior high come September. She seemed upset, but I decided to let a few days go by before making a big deal of her behavior,

"Susana wants me to stay with her and Daddy. I don't know why you hate her so much," my daughter said. I couldn't miss the defiant tone in her voice.

Aurora had never heard me say anything positive about her "stepmother." She didn't realize how challenging it was to hold my tongue when she spoke glowingly of Susana.

"You don't know the whole story," I told her. "One day I'll explain my feelings, but not now."

"That's what I mean. You treat me like a baby. Susana listens to me," Aurora said, resuming her insolent pout.

But she didn't choose now to bring up the late-night drama with Alejandro and me. I decided that the best course of action would be a diversion. "Do you want to go to the airport tonight? Your uncles are coming back from their trip."

"No, you go. I want to see Tina."

I let her have her way. She wanted to goad me; she wanted to provoke a big fight, but I figured that my earlier assessment had been right on. I had faith that she'd cool off in a few days.

Toño and Paul looked happy as they gathered their bags and waved at me through the plate glass window of the Customs and Immigration hall. Their luggage did not get inspected, so they came straight through. "It looks as though you had a great holiday!" I said, hugging them both.

"Oh, you have no idea!" said Paul, as he squeezed me back. "But I'm glad to be home."

Toño wanted to go to the house straight away. "Then we can give you your surprise," he said, looking as eager as a little boy.

As soon as we were through the door of the García Ginerés house, Paul pulled a velvet pouch from his carry-on and passed it to me. "Open it, Amalia!"

Inside I found an exquisite Murano necklace. "I can't make out the color," I said. Whatever I put the square-shaped glass beads up against, they reflected that shade. "They are fabulous. Will you put them around my neck?" I wore a green patterned dress and they picked up every hue.

"I think we must have looked at every necklace in Italy before Paul saw that one. We also bought a small choker for Aurora," Toño said. "How was her summer in Mexico City?"

"Good—*too* good. She doesn't want to be back here. Susana plays the *best girlfriend* role, while I get labeled as *mean old mom*—but I don't want to talk about that now."

"Okay, then tell me what's going on at work," said Toño.

"Hortensia and I have been waiting for you to get back so we can inaugurate Opciones. She figures the first day of autumn would be an auspicious date."

My brother and Paul looked excited. "This is great news to come home to," Toño said.

I enjoyed a welcome-home margarita on the patio around their pool, then made my way home. When I arrived at my house, I looked at the clock—just ten. I wanted to talk to Alejandro, but I worried that Susana might pick up the phone. I rang anyway and to my relief, I heard his deep voice on the other end of the line.

"We'll be inaugurating Opciones in just a few days. I want to know if you can be here."

He declined because he wanted to let Hortensia have her day without any extra stress. But he added that I should give her his best wishes. He then asked when we would have a chance to get together.

"Soon," I told him. I had missed him so much, and said I'd look for an excuse to travel to La Capital. But the goddess must have figured abstinence would help me become a better person at this time in my life because every time I tried to see Alejandro, something came up.

I should have been enjoying the best years of my life. Other men wanted to date me—but even though it seemed as though our relationship would never progress, my heart belonged to Alejandro.

The only real temptation was Nico. He called about once a month to discuss details of the courses we were developing for a new graduate program: "Restoration of Colonial Structures." I could tell that he hoped our conversations would reignite the passion that lay not-so-dormant.

The last time we spoke, just before hanging up, his voice lowered and he told me: "A colleague of mine went on vacation to Merida and at my recommendation he and his wife had dinner at Alberto's Continental. When he got back, he told me that the host sat them at a corner table surrounded by lush tropical foliage, and that Alberto winked and told them to enjoy, and then my colleague told me, 'Did we ever!'" Nico didn't have to say more—I felt hot and bothered for days.

~

Arriving at the center on September 21, Aurora and I could see Hortensia standing by the planter that stood to one side of the entrance. Her face shone brightly as she admired the *Pinoccios*—tiny multi-colored roses, *Adonis*—orange day lilies, and *Hortensias*—blue hydrangeas. "Did you bring in these plants?" she asked.

"No, I didn't, but I know who did." Don Luis, Don Chepo, and the rest of the building crew stood on the other side of the entrance—excitement all over their faces.

Hortensia hurried to them and said, "They are all my favorites! I don't know how to thank you."

"Flowers are nothing compared to what you gave me ten years ago—you gave me back my life," said Don Luis. After Hortensia convinced him to give up drinking, he helped his coworkers to do likewise and life had changed for them all. They owned their own homes, their children and wives were happy, and they felt prosperous.

The local newspapers, TV, and radio crews sent reporters. An up-and-coming young anchorwoman from Channel 3 waited to conduct the interview with Nana.

She shook our hands and asked, "Where can I sit for a few minutes and talk with Hortensia?"

Nana studied the woman's face carefully. "What's your name, dear?"

"I am Perla Suaste Martínez," she replied. "It is such a pleasure to meet you."

Hortensia flushed and reached out to take Perla's hand. "I met your parents once," she said. "Ask your mamá if she remembers seeing me in Dr. Montañez' office. Maybe you've heard the story of how I told them that you would have a brother and a sister."

Perla looked puzzled, but she promised that she would talk with her mother tonight when she finished work. Hortensia smiled.

The master of ceremonies, a self-important bureaucrat from the mayor's office, signaled to Nana. The time had arrived for the inauguration. She brought her coworkers to stand with her at the entrance where they could officially welcome the guests.

I suppose that the emcee thought Hortensia's friends were not attractive enough for the newspaper pictures, and he tried to place some pretty people front and center. Hortensia glared at him. Her friends were an unpretentious looking group—Leo, a bent-over elderly teacher; Baltazar, a former medic; two frail-looking nuns, Sisters Graciela and Belén; and the widow, Mayté. With a stubborn nod, Hortensia let it be known that her friends would be as prominently featured as she, and everyone reassembled the way she had originally requested.

Close to a hundred neighbors and acquaintances were on hand for the opening. Hortensia insisted that refreshments would not be necessary—money was tight, after all. But the crowd thought differently and arrived carrying soft drinks, tamales, flans, salads, and flaky *hojaldras*. Many brought guitars, tambourines, and flutes.

The mayor's official representative handed a pair of scissors to Hortensia. But before she cut the ribbon, everyone expected a few words from the woman who had dreamed Opciones into reality. She looked at the assembled group and bowed.

"Born poor in the small village of Santa Cecilia, I expected my life would be one of hard work and no frills. But one day, I got the opportunity to change all that, and I stepped out of the box that confined me. I began to learn the ways of the spirit, of the heart, and of the world. I learned to speak Spanish. I learned to read and write. I learned about the city. I learned to make use of whatever I had in front of me. Of course, I had help. The Vásquez family became my family. And that is what I hope this center will be for all of you. A big family home where we help one another."

No further words. Hortensia strode forward with the energy of a woman half her age and neatly sliced the red band. The two ends slithered to the earth like Chinese New Year dragons—dragons that would stand sentinel at the portal of Hortensia's dream.

twenty-three

Aurora and I had brokered a truce. She no longer pestered me to allow her to live in Mexico City, but she boarded a plane to go there from the first until the last day of every holiday period.

I walked into her room and ran my hand along her neatly made bed. How I missed sitting here with her—hearing about her day, her friends, her plans—she always had such grand ones. The affection she used to share with me, she now lavished on her father, my mother, and sister. It seemed ironic that I had uprooted my life, Hortensia's, Paul's, and Toño's so that Aurora could grow up in Merida. The four of us wanted her to live in a nurturing environment, far away from Alejandro and La Capital. And what seemed to be her preference? Exactly what we'd tried to save her from.

I thought back to an evening, years earlier when my neighbor Doña Fernanda and I had discussed the ups and downs of raising children. I'd told her that spending night after night nursing Aurora through frequent bouts of bronchitis made me feel so inadequate. I couldn't seem to do anything to relieve her suffering. I thought it would be easier as she got older. "These sleepless nights, watching her struggle to breathe have to be the worst," I said.

Doña Fernanda's children had already grown up and left home, so she could claim some authority on this topic. She straightened her back and warned me, "No, Amalia, when she's in her teens her respiratory system will be mature and she'll no longer get these awful infections, but it is during these years you will have the roughest moments with your daughter. When children are young, they step on your toes. As they get older, they step on your heart."

When life is moving along smoothly, time flies by. Weeks turn into months and before you realize it, the years pile up. And so it was with our business during the first half of the 1980s. Toño, Paul, and I developed a strong network. I courted the real estate agents—even the obnoxious Señor Jimenez. Trade writers and tourism types also received regular updates about our projects. And, of course, Layla did her bit to keep my name in the public eye. Competition had sprung up, but our reputation as trailblazers and continued presence in architectural magazines maintained our frontrunner position.

On the last afternoon of 1984, Toño, Paul, and I lazed around their pool. Hortensia had stayed at Opciones—the center had become her full-time focus. And yet she often seemed preoccupied. I wondered if dealing with such hard-core addicts had become too much for my gentle nana?

Aurora was in Mexico City for the holiday season—where else? I brought my forearm up over my eyes to shield them from the sun and soon I felt tears flowing. I enjoyed professional success—no doubt about that. But my personal life had about as much lushness as the Atacama Desert.

When Aurora was just eleven years old, Alejandro and I feared that she would discover us "sneaking around" again. His travel to Merida had ceased because she visited Mexico City so often. I made buying trips to La Capital as often as I could, but those romantic rendezvous didn't last long enough to keep our intimacy intact. We spoke on the phone several times a week, but he often sounded brooding and our conversation no longer flowed as easily as it used to.

Nico and I had not seen each other since 1976, but our calls had become cordial—we bantered with each other like old friends. Whenever we spoke, he never failed to mention that he hoped I'd allow him to visit me one day. I played along, but no way would I set myself up to such temptation again.

One spring the UADY invited Nico to Merida for to speak at a congress. I made sure to go out of town during the four-day event. I did not trust myself enough to risk seeing him. Self-preservation had become a high priority with me.

Our country followed its unsteady path, but for the most part, the wobbly truce between the politicians and the people stayed intact. The NAFTA free-trade agreement allowed international companies to establish themselves in Mexico. Shoppers thrilled at the variety of new products at Walmart, Costco, and the like. The old-fashioned local businesses could not keep pace and many were forced to close their doors. Inflation and the devaluation of the peso alarmed everyone, but for our business, it turned out to be a boon. Our clients' dollars bought much more in Mexico than they would have in the United States.

On a sweaty midsummer day, Toño came and sat on the edge of my desk. "I'm dying for some junk food. Let's go and pig out!"

Paul declined, but my brother and I had the same secret vice, and the idea of a fatty, juicy burger sounded like heaven. Into the pickup we piled. Leaning back against the scruffy seat, I laughed when Toño made the tires squeal.

We got onto the Paseo de Montejo and I could tell my brother had something important to say. "I've been seeing a counselor about my obsession with money," he finally revealed. "I want to celebrate my progress by taking you, Hortensia, and Paul to one of those really fancy resorts in Cancún."

"What great timing!" I said, "Nana has been out of sorts. This will be just what she needs."

I drove out to the center before going home; I wanted to tell

Hortensia about Toño's invitation. She seemed glad to see me, yet I still sensed the trepidation I frequently heard in her voice. When I told her why I'd come, she brightened.

"Oh, I'd love to go. And if you could manage, I want to ask a favor of all of you. I need to stop in Santa Cecilia. My mother is sick."

Her mother? This was the first time she had mentioned her in many years. In fact, I thought she had died. Maybe her mother's health was the cause of her anxiousness.

"I don't need to ask the guys, Hortensia—of course, we'll make a stop in Santa Cecilia. We'd all like to see where you came from."

A week later, without conscious thought, Toño, Paul, and I dressed much more somberly than we normally would have for a drive to Cancún. We'd be meeting Hortensia's mythical family.

~~~

Hortensia became increasingly agitated as we approached her village. When we arrived, the pueblo was exactly as she described it.

Visitors were still uncommon, and the children took long curious looks as we passed. I'd come prepared and brought out small bags of candy from my purse. I remembered that Hortensia told me La Madrina did this. Although a long time had passed, the kids reacted the same way. They scampered away to enjoy their treats.

My nana did not need directions; she paced calmly, but rigidly, to her old home. I stayed beside her until we reached a sprawling compound of seven *chozas*. "It looks just the same," she said as she entered through the gate, "except for the TV antennae."

"*Buenos días,*" she called. "*Soy yo, Hortensia.*"

A cheerful young woman wearing an immaculate *huipil* came out of the front dwelling. She told us to call her Pati.

"I look after my grandmother during the day while the others are away," she said.

"And how is my mother?" asked Hortensia

"Not good. I'm glad you came today," Pati replied.

"Where are the rest of your aunties and uncles?"

"Most of my aunts work at the plant a few kilometers away, and the men hang out down at the town hall."

I'd heard about this. Several months back, the *ejido*—the countryside cooperative system—had been dismantled. The agrarian reform of the 1930s had never met its expectations, but it took more than fifty years to break up the institutions and unions.

Two generations of men—in some families, three—had worked within the framework of this organization. They'd never had to do much. The government regulated all their activities, came to collect their crops, paid them, and nothing more was asked except when elections were held. Then everyone who lived in the village would be rounded up and taken in the backs of trucks to the mega political rallies. After the speeches, they'd be given a sandwich, a soft drink, and sometimes a souvenir—a T-shirt, cap, or flag—emblazoned with the politician's face.

Now that the *ejido* was gone, many of the men had sold their land for a fraction of its worth. These country farmers had no idea how to adapt. They spent their days doing a bit of work on land they still held and lots of time gossiping and reminiscing about their glory days. Many started drinking as soon as the cantina opened.

Meanwhile, the women had their children to feed, clothe, and educate. They let their husbands do as they pleased. But the mothers mobilized and took work in the foreign-owned factories that had recently opened. Because they now brought the money home, the women enjoyed much greater status.

Pati held her hand to her heart and asked us to wait while she went to tell her grandmother of our arrival. Hortensia grabbed my sleeve and looked pleadingly at Toño. She said she did not want to face her mother alone, so when her niece returned, my brother asked if we could all go inside. The young woman said that her *chichi*—Mayan for grandmother—would probably not even realize we were in her room. In a gentle voice she told us that the end was near. Hortensia's eyes regarded Pati closely. She seemed sympathetic and intuitive. I wondered if she had inherited some of her Aunt Hortensia's gifts. The energy between them made me feel pretty sure that she had.

"Will you come with us?" Hortensia asked and stood aside so that the younger woman could lead the way.

A serene smile settled on Pati's face. "Not just now, *Tia*—you are the one she needs to see."

Toño, Paul, and I filed in behind our nana. I still felt this must be daunting for the poor lady. After all, she didn't even know us. But Hortensia and Pati agreed; they doubted that the old woman would even notice we were there. Uncomfortable as we felt, we stayed because Hortensia had asked us to. She made it clear that she did not want to be alone at her mother's deathbed.

The form on the low-lying cot was not immediately distinguishable. She was emaciated and her voice was barely audible. Hortensia moved closer and spoke in Maya; the three of us understood only a little of what she said, but we could tell this was not a light conversation. Hortensia bent down and took the woman's head between her hands. She bowed her own and began to pray.

To give them privacy, we backed ourselves into the corner of the room. It became all too clear—we were witnessing a goodbye.

She finished her prayer and opened her handbag. She withdrew a package of herbs and some cocoa butter, then mixing the two ingredients, she spread the poultice on her mother's concave chest.

She made the sign of the cross through the air.

Again, reaching into her bag, she took out a candle, a stick of *copal,* and three holy cards. After lighting the candle and incense, she held her collection in front of her and carried it to the window, to the door frame, to the left side of her mother's house, and then to the right. Finally, she propped up the pocket-size images of Ixel, Tonánzin, and the Virgin of Guadalupe in the easternmost corner and set down the burning candle and *copal.* With circular movements, her arms that dispersed the smoke through the dwelling. I felt the air cool and go quiet. Hortensia remained absolutely still for a long time. Pati joined us, took Hortensia by the elbow, and I asked if we should move outside.

Hortensia nodded. Her face looked worn, as though she'd aged ten years. She didn't address her mother again. She walked unsteadily—I picked up her handbag—and Paul helped her into the car. As an afterthought, I gave Pati the cash I had in my wallet and scribbled our Merida home phone number on the back of a business card. "Use this for whatever you need," I told her. Pati knew what I meant.

After our visit with her mother, Hortensia sat down on the backseat and rested her head against the side window. The rest of us climbed in and Toño pointed the car east. With each kilometer, we felt the shroud lift. I wondered about Hortensia, though. "Would you rather not go to Cancún?" I asked.

Still slumped hard against the window, she shook her head.

"We're just a few kilometers from Valladolid. Let's stop there for a while," I suggested. I knew she'd be exhausted when she came out of this trance-like state.

The town came up even faster than expected, and Toño eased the Ford over a long procession of speed bumps. Once downtown, we found the restaurant El Meson del Marquéz.

"Hortensia, let's have some tea or whatever else you want."

She didn't seem strong enough to get herself into the restaurant, but she managed to convey that I shouldn't be concerned; she'd be fine soon enough.

I knew that Toño had prepaid a suite at the best beach resort in Cancún, but no way could Hortensia go there. Toño said he didn't mind forfeiting the money—he certainly had made progress in overcoming his issues. Paul brought water for Hortensia to sip. Toño leaned into the back and fanned her. I felt she would be better off with just me. I had seen her like this a few times before, but for the guys, it was a first. They both looked uneasy and our nana would pick up on that.

"You two go and enjoy yourselves. I'll find a little hotel and stay here with Hortensia. You can pick us up when you drive back to Merida on Sunday. She'll be her old self by then."

"Actually, the place where I bought the bottle of water has rooms. It's charming inside," Paul said. Done! One problem remained: I had given all my money to Pati. I had to ask my brother for some cash, which he gave me—without question.

The colossal size of the hotel's entrance way, the massive wooden doors, and the location—right on the main plaza—told me that the premises had been the residence of a governor during the Colonial period. I calculated the structure to be about three hundred years old. Graceful arches dripping with magenta bougainvillea and a graceful limestone fountain made this seem like the kind of place where my nana's spirit would be restored. "Come on, Hortensia, we're going to be fine here." I said.

Paul and Toño helped me get her into a ground-floor room. The owner addressed Hortensia in Maya and she answered with a short nod in place of words. Not even taking the time to remove her shawl, she burrowed into the soft bed and fell immediately asleep.

"Okay—off you go—I have the name and number of your hotel in Cancun, and you know I will call if there is a problem. I'll see you here for lunch at two on Sunday, then we'll all drive back to Merida."

A relaxed afternoon and evening, doing nothing more strenuous than paddling in the pool, felt as soothing as any pampering at the five-star Cancún resort. Hortensia snored softly and from time to time, moved or sighed; I didn't worry about her. The next morning she was ready to talk.

We sat together under a dark green garden umbrella, watching the Inca doves sip from puddles that had splashed from the fountain. I was pleased to see that she was revived by the hot coffee and eggs scrambled with *loganiza de Valladolid*—the region's famous spicy sausages.

"I am sorry your weekend has been spoiled," she said. "The situation in Santa Cecilia must have made you all very uncomfortable."

I tried my best to reassure her. "My weekend has not been 'spoiled,' it's been changed—that's all. This is an ideal place for both of us to relax and recoup."

"Amalia, you do realize that my mother passed over before we even left her room. I could sense the spirit leaving, and I felt the presence of those waiting for her. I did what I could to ease her way."

"I gathered that was your intention. But how did you know what you should do?" I asked.

"I don't know the *how*. I just do what my spirit guides tell me and really, once a purification ritual is done, I cannot fully remember all that happened. I do these ceremonies infrequently and, as you saw, they are exhausting."

"But she was your mother. Don't you feel badly?"

"Not at all. When I arrived, she wanted my forgiveness. I told her she had it. I thanked her for giving me life. We were not meant to spend a lot of time together and both of us understood that."

"But she banished you," I reminded Hortensia.

"She did, but that ended up being the biggest favor she could have done for me. How could I have lived as I have if I'd stayed in Santa Cecilia?"

"And what about Pati?" I asked. "Do you think she has your abilities?"

"You picked up on that—I wondered if you had." Hortensia looked peaceful and pensive. "Pati is under the tutelage of an important midwife in Santa Cecilia. The two will visit me at Opciones, I'm sure."

twenty-four

Alejandro and I had finished our weekly chat about Aurora.

"She seems to be in her element living at your mother's house," he said. "She's enjoying the sewing lessons and the people she's meeting. I'm glad you allowed her to come to Mexico City this summer."

He told me about an art exhibit he'd taken her to see, and then I noticed how his voice turned silky.

"Amalia, I won't see Aurora next week. She's going to Cuernavaca with your sister, and Susana will be at an artists' retreat in New Mexico. Really, I don't need to stay here all summer. Why don't I meet you in Merida and we'll go to Chiapas?"

A chance to be alone with each other! Except for the days after Tlatelolco, we'd never been on our own for more than an overnight. It was exciting to think that among people who don't know us we'd be able to openly show that we are in love.

"I can be ready as soon as you can get here," I said, already mentally packing my bag.

"Is tomorrow good?"

"Tomorrow's great," I replied, not thinking for even a moment about what a pushover I was.

Getting away from work proved to be easy. Earlier in the month, Toño and Paul had taken a ten-day diving trip; it seemed only fair that I should have a holiday too.

I didn't tell my brother that Alejandro would be coming along on my spur-of-the-moment trip to the mountains. I didn't want to deal with his disapproval. But I let Paul in on the secret. He took me to the airport and from there he drove Alejandro and me to the main bus terminal. The ADO motor coach to Palenque would depart at 10:10 a.m. We needed to hurry.

"Have a wonderful time!" Paul said.

"We will, and thanks for the ride," I called back. Alejandro squeezed my hand as we pushed through the glass doors of the terminal. I sighed with pleasure and anticipation for all we had ahead of us.

This would be a modest trip, but we didn't mind—spending a week on our own seemed luxury enough. While working for El Sol Imports, I had become seasoned to the springless seats of recycled school buses—riding the long distance in an air-conditioned coach would be a non-issue. And besides, my seatmate would not be some dusty farmer or a country woman nursing her baby.

"It has been too many years since I took this kind of a vacation," said Alejandro as he settled deeper into his seat.

I dozed with my head on his shoulder. The hot, humid air fogging the cool windows of our bus heralded the proximity of the rain forest and Palenque. I sat up straight again and gazed at the view.

"Many people say that Palenque is the most spectacular of southeastern Mexico's archaeological sites," I said, "and I can't wait to show it to you."

A small posada, located a block off Palenque's main plaza, would be our home for the next two nights. After the long trip, I wanted a shower and I left the bathroom door open. Through the steamy air, I watched Alejandro strip off his clothes. The sight of his naked body and the warm sudsy water trickling down my own was such a turn-on. I called his name.

Alejandro walked toward me. His eyes shone as he entered the small stall and he seductively rubbed against me while lathering his chest. I continued to wash the rest of his body. Rinsed off but still sopping wet, he held me by the waist and steered me toward the bed. Less than a minute later, we both lay panting on top of the covers.

"A teaser," he said, "to be continued later . . ."

We dressed and set off in search of a restaurant. I pointed to a building on the corner.

"There used to be a good place on the second floor," I said, and sure enough we found it, still doing a rousing trade. The dark eyes of the veteran waiter crinkled into a smile and he showed us to a table on the breezy balcony overlooking the street. We drank two cold Coronas and between us, we ate half a roast chicken with tortillas and tomato salsa. Once the sun had disappeared behind the mountains both of us were ready to call it a night.

We crawled eagerly into the double bed. "I don't have to get up and go home tonight," I whispered. He smiled and said he felt like a kid playing hooky. I laughed out loud. "You do? I never did anything like this when I skipped school!"

"Actually, you did Amalia. Don't tell me you've forgotten the time that we hid in the shrubbery behind the zoo at Chapultepec . . ."

My breath caught at the remembrance of that long-ago, daring tryst. He kissed me and we fell into the dance we knew so well.

We both woke up fully refreshed, long before the sun rose. Between kisses in the dark, I filled his head with stories of the wonders we'd see.

~~~

At the site by first light, we stood—humbled by Palenque—the City of Kings soaring up through the dense forest. Howler monkeys cried out and bright green parrots darted between the day's early sunbeams. All pervasive creepers twirled up and hung down from every tree trunk. Dewy moss coated the flat rock pathway into the site.

"Amalia, you look so at home—your skin glows, and I love how the humidity has your hair looking like wild jungle tendrils."

And that was true. I've always been a city girl, but something seemed to take over my urban self whenever I found myself in this magical corner of Mexico.

We climbed through the passageways where ancient rulers held court and later hiked among the trees until reaching a waterfall. The filtered light dancing on the cascade created shiny halos in the pool below.

"I think it's time for a swim," I said as I peeled off my blouse and sweat-stained shorts.

"You always have the best ideas," he replied as he removed his too.

After one more sensuous night in our third-floor nest, we hoofed it to the bus station and, not too much later, hunkered into seats fourteen and fifteen. Almost immediately, the bus began climbing.

Gazing out the dusty window, I wished I could pick the lanky canary-yellow flowers bending in the breeze. In the high altitude fields, bent-over farmers raked through the patchwork of plump, red coffee beans that they'd laid out to dry on hard-packed earth. Peering through the smoke of their cooking fires, shy Maya women watched our bus progress through their settlements. I wondered if they'd ever traveled more than twenty kilometers from where they'd been born.

We chose a popular San Cristóbal hotel close by the market. I told Alejandro I'd been there many times, yet he looked surprised when the owner recognized me.

"Come and sit in the patio so we can share the last warmth of the day," he said.

I knew that once the sun had set, the air would turn cold and the wind would feel like ice. We accepted his offer, and listened while the proud patriarch filled me in on the lives of his nine children. Fourteen grandchildren had been born in the decade I'd been away.

Declining a second glass of wine, we left our host and walked the steep streets of the old city. We reveled in the clear, high-altitude air, and after a sumptuous meal at a toasty bistro, we came out again into the brisk night air. Alejandro snuggled closer to me.

"These days, here with you, are the happiest I've ever spent. When I turn and see you beside me, I wish it could be like this all the time," Alejandro purred.

I didn't want to spoil the mood with a discussion about our separate lives. I put my head on his shoulder. "Me too," I said.

~~~

During our week in San Cristóbal de las Casas we took day trips to nearby villages. My old stomping ground—how many times had I been here—buying for El Sol Imports. The weavers recognized me, but would not approach because I had *un señor* with me. They were not allowed to speak with men who weren't family members. It troubled Alejandro to see so many children working hard—pushing heavy carts, selling bracelets, or caring for younger siblings—during what should have been school time.

"Parents are afraid that if their sons and daughters go to school, they'll get ideas about moving away," I explained. "Here, the whole family has to pull together if they want to eat."

"I know," he said, "but who protects these people? I spend so much of my time ensuring that my students receive the education they deserve, I can't believe that no one advocates for these forgotten souls."

He could speak so easily and convincingly about his students and about their rights. On the other hand, it was hard for me to articulate my own feelings about the inequality that plagues our country. Finding solutions seemed as challenging as plucking butterflies from the air.

"Amalia, you look so pensive," Alejandro said.

"The countryside—the heartland—touches something in me that gets lost in my day-to-day world. I feel grateful when I am in places like this where there are open spaces and a freedom that city dwellers never experience."

He shook his head. "But the people who live here are not free—they have no choices—and freedom means nothing if you have no opportunity to act on what you want," he said.

"That's true, when you are poor, what you are born to determines what you'll die as. Only people with incredible gifts and who have determination, like Hortensia, can change their fate."

Alejandro's eyes looked fiery. "From experience, I have come to realize that the elite in Mexico City don't care for anything but power, let alone about impoverished mountain people in places like this. They don't even seem to realize that they are the authentic Mexicans—the ones who create the unique crafts and sing the traditional songs. They are the ones who speak the languages of our ancestors and honor them in the *campo santo*."

Alejandro then reflected on something his father had impressed on him while he was a young man. "Poverty is a weapon of mass destruction. It kills hope and without hope the poor will remain poor. When Paz Ahora is up and running, I would like to sponsor an education project in Chiapas."

"Maybe I could help you? I have contacts here and I know their ways," I said.

"Yes, I can see that. All the faces in the market square lit up when they saw you. What I don't understand is how you can be so sensitive to the issues here, yet you never wanted to get involved with students' causes."

"Haven't you figured this out by now? Loud activism has always scared me off. Even before Tlatelolco, I felt that laying my life on the line would be a total waste—look how many have done that in vain. Nothing in the country has changed because of their deaths. And on a personal level too much was lost—the parents were robbed of the opportunity to become grandparents and their siblings would never be aunts or uncles. For sure our world lost future scientists and judges, musicians, dancers, and painters."

I could see Alejandro considering my words carefully. "Are you saying that activism can take many forms, that marching in the streets is not for everyone?" When I nodded my head, he slapped me on the back and gave me a thumbs up. I felt like I passed some kind of test, and that confused me. I'd not realized he still expected me to prove myself. I thought we had moved past all that.

Night would soon fall. We took a van back to San Cristóbal and dined at a quaint café where we devoured a savory lamb stew.

The meal satisfied my hunger but not my need for closeness. Alejandro seemed lost in his own thoughts and I suspected they did not concern me at all.

Once back in our room, I put my arms around his waist. This would be our final night together . . . but he pulled away and began packing his belongings.

"We have a long day ahead of us tomorrow," he said. When I protested, and tried again to tempt him toward the bed, he complied but his touch held none of the fire I expected. He acted as though our holiday had timed out.

Yet for me, no amount of time would have been enough. I wanted us to have a life together—dinners with friends, grocery shopping on Saturdays, walking hand-in-hand in the parks and plazas. I wondered if that would ever happen.

~

The bus ride back held none of the joy I felt on our way to the mountains. The scenery flashed by, and Alejandro snored beside me. By the time we rolled into Merida's main bus terminal, I could see that our holiday had become just a memory for him. He seemed preoccupied, and after a few half-hearted endearments and promises, he caught a cab directly to the airport. I headed home, on foot. I needed to walk out the kinks and cramps from my body, and also from my heart.

Separating so abruptly tore me up, but I didn't have much of a chance to feel sorry for myself. As I approached my front stoop, tacked up along the door frame, I found a note from my brother begging me to call him the second I returned.

But I needed to unpack and take a shower. I would call him after that. I had just started drying my hair when I heard the doorbell. Tying the belt of my dressing gown, I hurried to the front door and through the small side window I could see my brother standing there, with Paul right beside him. I opened up immediately.

Toño plunked down on a kitchen chair. "Mamá and Manuela have lost it—they have allowed Aurora to talk them into letting her stay in La Capital and go to high school there next year. I'm certain they'll call you today, and I knew you'd need some warning."

I felt my heart sink into my stomach. Toño must have more to tell me.

"What's going on? I need to know what I'm dealing with here."

Paul cut in. "Aurora called us. I guess because I'm a native

English speaker, she wants me to help her make an application to the Parsons School of Design in New York. She says that when she graduates that's where she wants to go."

Aurora seemed to be seeking out everyone but me. She must think I'm the same kind of roadblock I always thought my mother was. I longed for some reassurance from Paul and Toño.

"When Aurora was born I swore I'd be a perfect mother and I expected her to be a perfect daughter. She seems to trust everyone except me."

"You know that's not true. She's 15, and using the tricks a teenager uses to get her way," Paul said. "I think she wants to present you with a fully formed plan and an acceptance letter so that you'll be forced to go along with her."

"It looks like the main gist is to stay far away from me. I feel so bloody guilty—and resentful—and sick of this situation. I work so hard, but I never seem to be doing anything right."

Paul gave me a conspiring glance. "Amalia, you've always done what's right in your heart, so don't berate yourself and let guilt tear you up. You have a very headstrong daughter. But would we want her any other way?"

Dear Paul. He always helped me put things in perspective. But Toño looked as frustrated as I.

"'Headstrong' is one way to put it. You know, we have some claim on her as well. We've been here for her since she was born. Are you going to give in to her *Hermanita*?"

"I have to figure things out. I'm grateful that you have given me this news so that I have time to think. Gracias."

Both of them stood up, hugged me and made to leave. "Call us if you need anything," Paul said and then whispered, "I can't wait for you to tell me *all* about your holiday." No matter what, Paul could always make me smile.

~~~

Even though the phone started ringing soon after the guys left, I decided not to answer. I tried to relax and read my mail. Later in the afternoon, I went to see my nana. I knew she could help me clear my head before I spoke to my mother or to Aurora.

Although I could have seen Hortensia at my home, I wanted to feel the healing power that many claimed was all-encompassing at Opciones. The view from under the soaring archway, through to the central plaza, indeed felt soothing. I felt pride for Hortensia's incredible accomplishment, respect for Alejandro's generosity in funding the project, and gratitude for my opportunity to design it. Since the doors opened five years ago, it had become known as a model facility.

Before I could form a fist and knock on the door, I heard my nana's voice.

"Amalia! Come in. *Mi'ja,* I knew you would come today, and this is where you need to be. The spirits are powerful and we'll work through this."

I shouldn't have been surprised that she knew I'd stop by. I sat down at her table and she set a big mug of peppermint tea in front of me.

"I don't know where to start," I said, as I took a sip of the hot liquid. "But I know I have to do something or else Aurora will never come back to Merida."

Hortensia looked thoughtful. "I don't know if it is you who needs to do anything. Aurora doesn't know where she belongs and she needs to figure that out. Perhaps she has to be away from you so that she can recognize how important you are to her. Maybe your mamá and Manuela are the best influences for her right now.

They're doing a lot to help her discover who she is."

"I know. I'm not worried about them. It's Susana, and I must confess, Alejandro. They have a whole different agenda to mine."

"Of course, *Mi'ja*. Aurora adores Alejandro, but living in Merida, she is separated from him by distance. She feels the same love for you, but she has been with you all her life. She's always been assertive—'headstrong' is the nice word Paul uses, no? Actually, she reminds me of a quarter horse, always raring to charge ahead."

"You used to call me that," I reminded her.

"I have not forgotten, Amalia. Like mother, like daughter. As you did at 16, Aurora figures she can make her own decisions as to where and how she will live. Susana's lifestyle is alluring, but it's not Susana who's pulling your daughter in another direction—it's Aurora's own desire to shake off the harness. Everybody in Mexico City loves having her around and she's under much less restraint than she is here."

"Nana, I want to mean more to her than a 'restraint.' "

I got up and went to look out her window. On the basketball court, a game had started up, and the sight of those young men futilely chasing the ball seemed like a mirror image of my life—running, chasing, trying to catch up all the time—and then rejected by my daughter no matter what I tried.

I turned back to my nana. "I've been angry with Alejandro, jealous of Susana and possessive of Aurora for years and where has that gotten me? Nowhere! I tried to protect my daughter and yet she doesn't care about me. I feel defeated, tired, and shortchanged."

"Aurora will come back to you when she feels sure of who she is. But right now, she needs your mother, Manuela, Alejandro, and maybe even Susana to help her figure that out. And by the way, what does Alejandro say about Aurora wanting to live in the big city?"

"I haven't spoken to him about this latest development, but I know he'll be for it. If Aurora lives with Mamá, he will see her a lot. That's what he's always wanted."

"Alejandro has always been a good father, hasn't he? I know this situation is not what you want, but I think you should stop fighting yourself and everyone else. Trust Alejandro to be a positive influence. Respect Aurora's interest in fashion design. She'll get a leg up by living with your mother and being at the salón every day, so let that happen. Above all, don't make her feel guilty for wanting the moon."

Hortensia's reasoning sounded right on, but my daughter meant more to me than anything or anyone else. Why did all the changes she wanted have to be so difficult for me? Again, I recalled the long-ago words of my neighbor, "When children are little they step on your toes, when they're older they step on your heart."

I sat back down at the table. "I also want the moon, Nana. I want love, fulfilling motherhood, a career, friends, contentment, peace—lots of women seem to have all that—why not me?"

"You will have all that, Amalia, but your moon is not yet full and she needs to be sure you are ready for her."

Hortensia pulled me up and led me to the window. She pointed at the Earth's silver satellite rising in the east.

"Let go, Amalia. Trust that the spirits are watching out for you. Follow the flow and that moon will be yours—when the time is right."

twenty-five

September is the stuffiest month in Yucatan, and this morning was typical. With Aurora gone, I felt completely lethargic.

Last night, over the phone, she went on and on about the wonders of Mexico City, about all that Manuela and Alejandro were showing her, about how exciting her high school classes were, and about the newest designs my sister had created to the delight of her most affluent customers.

I said nothing about how her absence pained me. I had taken Hortensia's advice to heart: I was being "big" about this change. To prod myself into getting ready for work, I turned on the news program *Hoy Mismo.* I looked at my clock radio—7:20 a.m.—I wondered what to wear.

The volume on the TV rose. On the screen I saw the large lighting panel swaying back and forth above the newscasters' heads. María Victoria Llamas, Lourdes Guerrero, and Juan Dosal, the three news anchors, were looking up—I heard frightened screams in the background. This was happening in Mexico City—an earthquake! Right now! Aurora! My family! Alejandro! The terror I felt made my legs weak and I clung to the corner of the bed as though it were a life raft.

Standing there in my underwear I watched Maria Victoria Llamas similarly gripping the underside of the desk. I could see in her face that she hoped no one realized how scared she was.

Lourdes Guerrero improvised; she must have drawn on all her professional experience to appear serene and reassuring. "It seems that we are experiencing tremors, but please don't be frightened because we think this is just a small quake."

¡Ay-ay-ay! Alejandro lives close by that TV station. I took deep breaths. I needed to stay calm and figure out what to do. I prayed like never before.

I tried to phone Alejandro. He did not answer. I tried Mamá— same thing. Obviously, all phone service had been cut off. I had to know that my daughter had not been hurt. I called Toño, who had also heard the news.

"We'll drive to Mexico City if we have to Amalia—but hold on for a bit. Surely we'll get word soon. Come over and stay here with Paul and me today."

"I can't. I have to wait here by the phone in case someone manages to call," I told him.

Paul came on the line with a practical idea. "Do you know Ramón Briceño, the guy who owns the stationery store up the road? He has a ham radio. He would be able to send a message to another Mexico City operator who could in turn relay and receive a message from Alejandro or Mamá and Papá."

"Let's go see him now," I said as I stepped into a skirt and sandals. I pushed my arms into a T-shirt. "I'm ready!" I said. "You don't need to park. I'll be waiting outside."

When the three of us arrived at Señor Briceño's home, his befuddled wife offered coffee. "This is most unusual, having callers at this time of day."

We declined, with thanks; our nerves couldn't take another stimulant. A large group of aficionados—located throughout the country—had immediately begun to relay messages between Mexico City families and their loved ones living elsewhere. When we went to the door of his radio room, we found Señor Briceño monitoring calls. "Come in, come in. We're trying to find a Mexico City ham who can get through," he told us as he fiddled with a series of dials.

Twelve other frightened Merida residents had come here with the same idea as Paul. Finally we heard an echoing voice come on line: "CQ Merida, CQ Merida . . . this is MO7HH8 Mexico City . . . calling CQ Merida . . . CQ Merida."

"That's the operator we want!" Ramón grabbed the microphone. "This is MO9LB4 in Merida Yucatan—over!"

The operator took our messages and said his son would deliver them by bicycle. He couldn't say how long this would take. I waited all day, and at 9:20 p.m., we finally received word back from Alejandro.

> *Señorita Aurora Méndez Vásquez, Señor Alejandro Méndez, Sra. Susana Lara and the Vásquez-O'Horan family are all safe. They will call as soon as telephone service is re-established.*

¡Madre purisima! I swore I would never complain about anything ever again. Aurora was safe! Everyone else too! I thanked Señor Briceño over and over again. I later learned that after the quake some of the radio hams worked as long as thirty-six hours with headsets on, relaying news. Now I had to think about how I could get to Mexico City to be with Aurora.

~~~

Two hours after being forced off the air, Lourdes Guerrero began broadcasting live from the studios of XEW-TV. She told the world that the quake measured 8.1 on the Richter scale, and that the earlier Televisa transmission ended because a nearby ten-story building had collapsed on top of their studio. She made no mention of casualties.

As happened during every crisis, the government ordered a news blackout. Confuse, confound, and conquer the community was the only strategy they knew. But because of the magnitude of the disaster, most of the media, including TV journalists like the now-famous Lourdes Guerrero, disobeyed. She appeared nonstop on Channel 2, a reassuring, comforting, consoling presence. The president did not address the situation at all until thirty-nine hours after the event.

Confined to four of the city's neighborhoods, eighty percent of the earthquake damage and nearly all the buildings that collapsed were located in a zone that included Tlatelolco. Once again, a tragedy of unfathomable magnitude had hit the largest housing complex of the city.

"There will be a call for volunteers," said Toño. "I'm going to the Red Cross and see what I can do. You should come along, too, Amalia. You need to get your mind off your worries."

What I really wanted was to get on a plane, but all the seats had been booked; I would have to wait ten days. I could not concentrate on anything. When would I hear Aurora's voice again?

At the Red Cross warehouse, Toño, Paul, and I got to work keeping inventory and packing crates with relief supplies. I had never seen so many bags of rice, sugar, beans, bottles of oil, and cans of tuna. The Yucatecan citizens pitched in to do all they could to relieve the suffering of the thousands of displaced Mexico City residents.

After eight days, I believe I "willed" the telephone's silent receiver to life. On a barely audible line, Alejandro reassured me that they were all safe, but the situation had become desperate.

"The homeless are sleeping in tents everywhere. It is so cold at night that cases of hyperthermia are becoming common."

"I need to see all of you. I have a ticket for Thursday. Is there any way for you to pick me up at the airport?"

"Sorry, I can't. There is a shortage of fuel and many roads are still choked with rubble. But if you take public transit to your mother's house, I'll come to see you. Shall we say at six in the evening?"

I looked at my watch. That would be three days and six hours from now.

~~~

The sun had set by the time I arrived at Mamá's home. Aurora ran to me calling, "Mamá, I love you so much!" I'd not had spontaneous affection from my daughter for so long; her endearments took all my tiredness and worry away. Alejandro had been there for the past hour, and he told me how comforted he felt just knowing I was in the same city. I could see how he longed to hold me—I gave up all pretenses and threw my arms around him.

"Thank you for taking care of our daughter!"

No one flinched when we hugged and kissed one another. I dared a look at Mamá and saw no hostility. Did she finally realize that the situation could not be changed?

"Alejandro has been a wonderful help this past week," she told me. "He has brought us food and other goods that are in short supply."

As well as demolishing buildings, it looked like the earthquake had toppled a lot of old resentments. In the middle of the tragedy around me, I couldn't help feeling hopeful.

I too had brought food. I got it out of my luggage: canned hams, butter, cheese, powdered milk. I had aspirin and other over-the-counter remedies. Hortensia and Paul sent homemade baked goods. My family's eyes went big. In a very short period of time, the shortages had made life difficult for everyone.

~

The following day I went alone to Tlatelolco. I wanted to volunteer with the reconstruction. Soon after walking onto the wide esplanade, I met a group of professors and students from the UAM— Nico's university! I knew I'd see him, and I worried about how we'd both react. But I was determined to get over any discomfort; much bigger concerns were at stake here.

Many teams from all over the country had joined forces with the hope of getting the buildings habitable as soon as possible. The groups included architects, engineers, urban planners, and builders.

I asked about Nico, and a young woman who seemed to be serving as a one-person clearing house for all questions, told me that Nico was the director of their group.

"Do you know Professor Beltrán?" she asked.

"Yes, my name is Amalia Vásquez. Your professor and I met a few years ago at an architectural conference in Merida."

She looked up and smiled at me. "I'm Monica Simón. You're from Yucatan? I have always liked the idea of living there. It's like another country. And now after this, I am even more interested. Do you know about the job market? I will be receiving my degree soon, and I'm anxious to work in a city like Merida where architectural history has been preserved and respected."

I told Monica we should talk about this again after I'd had a chance to get some information. I decided I'd keep an eye on her. Actually, our firm wanted to hire another intern and having someone from Mexico City would add a new dimension to our design team.

I ran into Nico that afternoon. When he and I spoke across the wire, we felt comfortable with one another, but this face-to-face contact caused a physical jolt. Even in his stained, rumpled work clothes, he looked better than I remembered.

He took off his dark glasses and propped them atop his head. "Amalia, what are you doing here?" he asked. His eyes openly scanned the full length of me until I felt as though they had burned right through my clothing.

I coughed to distract him. It had been a mistake to think that our attraction had run its course. Looking at his handsome face and tanned torso made me think of the "encore" Layla had once suggested.

But we had to douse all that; the situation at Tlatelolco already seemed stressed to the point of bursting. I felt helpless seeing the terrible conditions that the Mexico City citizens faced. I told Nico I could stay as long as needed.

"¡*Excelente!* Amalia, we can really use another architect with your restoration experience. Some of your colleagues from the University of Yucatan are here and actually form part of the group that I did orientation with this morning. Would you like to work with them or with people from another school?"

"I want to go where I'll be most useful. You know about the work I do. Much of it should be transferable to this situation."

"That's just what I need—flexibility. Thank you, Amalia." He quickly summed up the issues we faced. "There are no services. Whatever water the residents need must be trucked in. They are cooking on gas burners and coal braziers, and they only have lanterns at night. All the buildings have been damaged—some worse than others. Assessing the repairs is what we need to focus on now. Once we identify what has to be done, construction crews can carry out the plan. They are already lined up.

I admired Nico's professional skill and the way he gave people the truth. Three days later he asked me to go with him to a meeting where he spoke compassionately, but practically with a group of two hundred homeless. "I want to be honest with you," he said. "The damage is extensive. It will be more than a year until we're able to get you back into your homes. Please call your relatives and friends who live elsewhere in the country and ask for a place to stay. We'll help you find their phone numbers, their addresses. We have counselors. We'll give you the money to travel to where they live. Hang in there!"

When one of the most desperate victims demanded a more speedy resolution, Nico held him by the shoulders. "We can't move any faster. There are too many buildings, and we're working day and night. I'm sorry, we can't do more."

Seeing him again confused me, to say the least. I called Alejandro later that night, and when he realized he had me on the line, his voice turned sharp.

"Amalia, don't call me unless you have an emergency. Susana and her folks are here right now. I can't talk." Barely giving me time to ring off, he hung up. If I had been befuddled before calling him, I was doubly so now. I never knew how he'd react.

The quake took victims from every strata of society—street vendors, sewing factory workers, and even close family members of the world-famous tenor Plácido Domingo. The tragedy brought the citizens of Mexico City solidly together—grief fell citywide. Groups of young people organized work parties. Plácido Domingo himself helped to sift through the debris and also staged benefit concerts.

Every day wealthy matrons, who the press called *las Palomas de Polanco*—the Doves from Polanco—rolled up their silk sleeves, prepared vats of nutritious food, and delivered them to the downtown rescue workers. Caravans arrived with relief supplies from Canada, the US, Central America, and from every state in Mexico.

There always seemed to be someone in acute crisis, like Teresita, a young woman from Oaxaca. She had nothing, except her four half-dressed little children—twin infants and two toddlers. She refused to return to her home state. From the fear in her eyes, I knew she'd left an abusive situation back there. An indigenous Triki, she could not read or write, spoke only a little Spanish, and had no skills but those of a domestic. What to do with someone like her? It took me two hours to find temporary lodging for Teresita and her babies.

Some of the volunteers had no clue as to where they should start. "Right where you're standing," I told them. "All the buildings need to be assessed, so dig in!" I kept one eye on Nico as he walked back and forth supervising his students—and he knew I was watching.

At the end of our fourth day working together he said, "Amalia, I think we need to talk."

Although I dreaded having a conversation about "us," I knew that's what he had in mind.

"Yes we should, Nico, I want an opportunity to explain a few things."

"Perfect. I'll meet you here at seven and then we'll have dinner together."

I tried to act light-hearted, but in truth—I felt terrified by the feelings I had for him.

twenty-six

Good God! I had to get a grip!

"Why don't we go to my place?" he suggested.

"Nico, I know a family-style cafe near my parents' home. I think it's a more appropriate choice."

"Yes, I guess you're right," he conceded. "Whatever you think is best."

Compared to what I had become used to seeing at Tlatelolco, the plain bistro was cozy and charming—with clean tablecloths and a cheerful staff. Being with Nico soothed my frazzled nerves. Conversation came easily. He ordered tacos and beer. I wanted a glass of red wine with *queso fundido*—melted cheese wrapped in tortillas. Before our orders arrived, he took my hands in his.

"Amalia, I can't believe you're here. Maybe you're worried we'll open ourselves up to gossip? But I think we can behave professionally in public, irrespective of what's going on between us."

I laughed—perhaps a little too nervously. "I thought that's what you wanted to talk about. Tell me what you think will happen 'between us.'"

"Amalia, you know what I want. I'm sure you can see it every time I look at you. But I don't want to press you. I realize now that's the mistake I made ten years ago in Merida. I was too insistent, too sure of myself. I tried to push you into doing what you weren't ready for. What happens now is up to you."

A man who tried to shift the blame onto himself? This was novel for me, but I needed to take my share of responsibility as well.

"It's a mess, Nico," I said and launched directly into the whole story—about Aurora's conception on the night of violence at Tlatelolco—how her father was married at the time and is, in fact, still with his wife. I gave him an abridged story about Alejandro's current involvement in my life and Aurora's. Finally, I told him that I could not give up my hope for a life with Alejandro—like a family.

Nico looked crushed. He saw that with Alejandro, Aurora, Susana, and my parents living here in La Capital, we couldn't contemplate anything romantic between the two of us.

"Amalia, now it makes sense to me—I can see why you acted as you did in Merida. I should have guessed there was something complicated that I didn't know about." He reached out to take my hands.

I pulled them back from him. "Nico, what I feel for you is so different from the chaos Alejandro brings into my life. But I can't deal with pressure from you to take our relationship further. I don't know what will happen in my life, and I don't want to be unfair to you—again."

"I see," he said. "You spend time with me, but I can't expect anything more from you than friendship?" He pushed the uneaten tacos away and used his napkin to mop his brow. Looking at the table rather than at me, he murmured softly, "I love you, Amalia, and I want you to love me. But it looks like you need to sort out your feelings before we can go any further together."

When I nodded, he put the napkin down, rose to his feet, and said, "It's getting late. I'll take you back to your parents' now."

~~~

The urgent situation at Tlatelolco kept us from dwelling on our awkward dinner. Every day brought new emergencies to light. Heavy-duty recovery machinery hadn't been used until five days after the earthquake because of fears that the bulldozers and trucks would cause cave-ins and bury survivors. An unexpected number were rescued, but once a week had elapsed, mostly corpses came out from under the debris. The engineering team worked as quickly as possible to get the rubble removed so that the rebuilding could begin.

Mexico City's residents had a reputation for not getting involved with one another. But following the disaster, there were countless acts of heroism, like those of *los Topos*—the Moles—a group of young people who spontaneously grouped together and risked their lives by crawling into collapsed buildings to look for survivors. The Moles had no equipment, training, or knowledge of rescue tactics, but they were instrumental in saving countless people, including the babies from Hospital Juárez—the most heart-wrenching, heart-warming story to come after the earthquake.

Nearly all the neonates in the nursery at the time of the earthquake survived without nourishment, water, warmth, or human contact for seven days. Interviewed by the press, one of the Topos explained, "We had been walking silently through the hospital wreckage when someone heard a faint whimper. Immediately we all began digging—some of us with our bare hands."

No one present or the millions across the country who watched the coverage of the rescue on TV will ever forget the sight of the narrow-hipped teenagers pulling baby after baby from the rubble. They became known as the "Miracle Babies of Hospital Juárez." And the Topos became national heroes. Unfortunately, not many of the post-quake stories had silver linings like the story of the Topos. The Hotel Del Prado collapsed moments after the quake began. A gas leak started a fire and made it impossible to rescue anyone. The hotel had been 70 percent occupied and no survivors were found.

~

On September 30, as I worked at Tlatelolco with the displaced families, I raised my head and saw Nico approaching, shoulders drooped. Even from a distance I could tell he carried terrible news. "Amalia, sit down."

I let myself drop in the dust and got ready to receive what I knew would be something very, very bad.

"This morning, Susana Lara joined an art rescue team digging through the rubble at the Amaya Gallery. Because it was sunny, natural light illuminated a shaft, allowing access to the chamber. Apparently, she wedged in with two coworkers and they commenced relaying the valuable pieces out to others on their team. No one knows why, but after only a few minutes of work, the fragile tunnel collapsed. One of them died instantly, the other and Susana survived, but her condition is critical."

My brain could barely grasp what he'd said. Susana Lara— Alejandro's wife. If I hadn't already been on the ground, I would have collapsed like the tunnel.

"My truck is over there. If you have the address, I'll take you to see Alejandro," said Nico. "I figure you have to go."

I wondered if our arrival would help or make the situation more difficult, but Nico was right—I had to go see Alejandro. I thanked Nico and climbed up into his truck. All the way, he talked about the out-of-control rescue and restoration practices. How could the authorities have allowed Susana and her colleagues to go into the unstable tunnel?

I mentioned that nothing of this magnitude had ever happened before—it was somewhat understandable that the efforts were uncoordinated and desperate.

"No, Amalia. There has been ample warning that such a disaster would occur one day—there should have been a proper plan. Buildings aren't built to code. If they were, the damage and loss of life would have been greatly reduced."

I counted at least sixty people gathered at the apartment. I had difficulty moving through them, but I resolutely made my way toward Alejandro sitting slumped on a living room sofa. He looked as though he'd lost his best friend. Everyone there saw Susana as precisely that. I wondered what she really meant to him—because the heartfelt grief I was looking at did not jibe with what he'd been telling me all these years.

Maybe I had it all wrong, or at least partly wrong. Perhaps Susana didn't really have it in for me. She knew about her husband's on-going affair with me in Merida and she had tolerated the infidelity. Suddenly, it seemed all too clear—I had never looked at our complicated relationship through her eyes—and I should have.

Alejandro seemed surprised to see me. "Amalia, I didn't expect you would come." He grasped my arm and whispered hoarsely, "I need Aurora to be here with me."

Of course, it would be Aurora he needed rather than me. But under such circumstances, how could I argue or refuse?

He didn't move or say more. I stood to one side for several minutes and listened to the commentary swirling through the room. Obviously Susana had her fans. "What will he do without her?" . . . "She' s the brains behind their success." . . . "She does everything for him." . . . "Poor Alejandro!"

No one at the apartment, except for Alejandro and Nico, knew who I was. My anonymous face caused no warning lights to flash. Seeing Nico leaning against a living room wall, I moved over to stand beside him. For a while we remained there, watching the crowd negotiate their way toward Alejandro. His command that I immediately fetch Aurora contrasted starkly with the stoic gratitude he showed to everyone offering condolences. Each visitor's almost reverent approach made the Alejandro in this Mexico City apartment look like an icon; he certainly had cultivated a following. No wonder he hesitated to leave the life he had built with Susana.

I thought we should say a few words to him before I went to get Aurora and bring her back here. I took Nico's arm and crossed through the throng once again. I found a tearful girl, draped across the chair next to Alejandro. I figured her to be a student trying to gain his favor—and maybe even entry into his bed—in his "time of need." It probably was mean-spirited to think of her like that, but her eyes couldn't hide her not-so-secret thoughts.

"Would you give me a few moments, please?" I asked—she sullenly moved out of the way. "Alejandro, this is Nico Beltrán from the UAM. He and I are working together at Tlatelolco. He's the one who told me about what happened to Susana and brought me here."

Alejandro nodded, and then he raised his eyes and took a good look at Nico, who returned the intent inspection like a man sizing up his rival. I felt embarrassed by the fact that both these men had been my lovers. I wanted to run, but my feet felt bolted to the floor.

Nico realized my discomfort and hurried to say goodbye to Alejandro. "I'm sorry we've had to meet under such unfortunate circumstances. I'm impressed by your political efforts, and I'd be interested to talk with you about them. But Amalia and I need to get back to the Tlatelolco site. We have a lot to do."

Nico shook hands with Alejandro, whose face betrayed a skeptical smirk. I told him I'd return soon with Aurora. Then Nico placed his hand under my elbow and steered me through the crowded apartment. I could feel Alejandro's eyes keeping careful watch on just where Nico's hands might roam.

It took Nico more than an hour to drive through the dreadful traffic to my parents' house. We talked about the accident and how so many of the people at Alejandro's elegant flat seemed to have no business being there.

"I felt as though they were holding a wake—but Susana is still alive," I said.

He nodded and agreed with me. "Mexico City academics are like that, Amalia. That scene was all about seeing and being seen."

I thought about how hard it must have been for Nico to meet Alejandro—for the first time—and under these circumstances. I knew that he put himself through the prickly experience for my sake. I felt grateful for that. When he left me at my mother's Colonia Narvarte home, I found myself wishing he would stay. But I'd already asked too much of him.

~~~

Aurora had gone to bed early, and she looked dazed when I shook her awake. "We're going to your daddy's place. I want you to pack up enough of your things for a week or so."

She had no idea what a huge drama this had become for me. At Alejandro's this afternoon, I'd overheard someone say that Susana's convalescence could last six months. I knew that I would be needed at Tlatelolco for at least that long, and I wanted to support Alejandro and Aurora all that I could. I had Hortensia's old room at my parent's house, and while I certainly couldn't call the arrangements ideal, I knew I could manage. After all, I hardly spent any time there.

A cabbie drove us to Alejandro's. The traffic had thinned out so the ride didn't last long. But it took enough time for me to tell my daughter all I knew about the accident.

"*Ay Mamá,* I know you don't like Susana, but I do—and no matter what you think, she's good to Daddy. What's happened is so unfair."

She and Alejandro could better discuss Susana without me, so as soon as we got to his place, I retreated to the kitchen and let her grieve with her father. Aurora clung to him as they cried together.

I found a well-stocked fridge and took out eggs, ham, onion, olives, and tomatoes. A spicy omelet with buttered toast and *café con leche* would go far toward restoring everyone's spirits. When I heard them speaking in calmer tones, I suggested they come to the table.

"Superb, Amalia!" Alejandro said, looking tenderly at Aurora rather than at me. "It's good to have you two here. I'll show you where your room is. Let me take your suitcases."

"I didn't bring one. My parents' house is so much closer to my work site, it will be best for me to go back there as soon as Aurora is settled."

"You're not staying with Daddy and me?" Aurora asked.

I couldn't tell if she was excited for the first chance to have her father all to herself or a bit frightened. But maybe this would develop into one of those opportunities Hortensia spoke of, the chance to discover her potential, and to miss me. Both she and Alejandro tried to change my mind, but I had already compromised myself so much over the years, and I sincerely felt that I needed to respect Susana's home. I could not stay here.

"I'll call or see you every day, *Mi'ja*. This will work out best for all of us."

Aurora finally accepted my solution as a logical compromise, and in the days that followed, she settled into a routine, keeping up with her lessons, and helping Alejandro. When I visited, I'd watch her with her father, bent over chemistry formulas and resolving algebra problems. But I could see what he enjoyed most were the fiery debates they had over philosophical and political theories. Alejandro seemed to thrive on the opportunity to shape his daughter into the committed young woman I had never become. I envied his easy rapport with her. I came to see a nurturing, caring side of Alejandro's personality, and I wished more than ever that we could live as a family.

He took a leave of absence from UNAM and divided his time between Aurora and visiting Susana at the hospital. His only meaningful interchange with me was to inquire about how the restoration work was going. Since our physical intimacy had stopped, he acted distant—I accepted his disconnection as a temporary necessity.

And I had to admit that Nico's admiration for my work, his compliments on my clothing or my hair, and the way he always acted like such a gentleman, had begun to turn my head. I admired his strong body as he'd lift and heave along with the workmen. And then he'd turn around and tenderly cradle an infant while the mother dressed her toddler. He carried a pocket full of candy and coins. I wondered what Layla would think if she could see me right now. I suspected she'd call me a fool for letting such a man slip through my fingers.

I had much to consider, though, and I couldn't allow myself to fall into a situation I'd regret later. But being around Nico, while shut off from Alejandro's touch, had become difficult—especially on one particular evening when we finished work late. The bus to Mamá's house had stopped running for the day and I couldn't get a cab.

"I'll drive you home," Nico offered. He leaned from the driver's side of his pickup to open the passenger door, and then watched intently as I climbed in. The big step up made my skirt ride high over my thigh. Even without looking up, I could feel the desire in Nico's eyes. Layla had guessed correctly when she said I was not the kind of woman who could carry on with two men at the same time. But Alejandro and I had no physical relationship right then, and Nico was indeed a very sexy man.

Nico tried to make a joke. "Amalia, I don't care if you are not free to love me, I'll settle for just sex!"

~~~

It's a wonder Susana didn't die. Crushed by a ton of rubble, she had been trapped for more than two agonizing hours. Fortunately, a medic had been able to connect an IV line and sedatives were pumped into her during the rescue efforts. Without that, she would have succumbed to the terrible pain before the jaws-of-life finally lifted her out. No one could tell what her permanent limitations would be. Alejandro told Susana that Aurora had come to stay with him, but spared her the knowledge that I was still in the city.

Work took up nearly all my energy. As part of a team of architects and structural engineers from several different universities, I supervised an entire squadron of exceptionally dedicated laborers. My first job had been to come up with restoration plans for the largest housing units. I determined the minimal repair that the buildings needed and suggested more extensive follow-up. Some structures were so compromised they should have been torn down. The engineers did their stress tests, and the crew worked as fast as possible to strengthen the weakened walls and foundations. Lifting sunken floors and filling cracks with a pressure-injected mixture of cement and adhesives was the standard procedure. Once the repairs had been completed, we could reconnect the water and electricity.

The thousands of people still living in tents caused constant anxiety.

"Couldn't the families go back to their apartments and live there while the repairs are being done?" asked the government housing board representative. "It freezes nearly every night. Many of the kids and old folks have respiratory infections."

In some instances, we let their arguments sway us. "What could be worse?" our team members asked one another; we had no precedent to follow. We could only speculate about how long the work would take—an intolerable answer for the displaced families. If we didn't carry out the repairs properly and the precarious buildings had to face a quake even half as strong, the fissures would crack open and the structures would crumble immediately.

I reached the limit just after Christmas. I'd gone to inspect a complex that I would start to work on the next week and found several groups of people in their flats. They had no right to be there. Only after I became insistent, they finally showed me their *permisos*—the authorization slips for which they had paid 1,000 pesos each. They confessed that the local superintendent was selling them "*como pan caliente*"—like hotcakes.

The relocation issue had turned political. With corruption firmly established, my usefulness had been reduced to a minimum. I spent most of my time negotiating public safety with government types who wanted to win future votes by getting the survivors back in their homes.

In the meantime, Alejandro and Aurora had established a routine; she felt helpful and well occupied. She wanted to stay with her father instead of going back to Mamá's house. I knew I'd have a *revolución* on my hands if I tried to separate the two, and so—as I seemed to do a lot—I gave in.

~~~

Three days before my return to Merida, I dropped by Alejandro's apartment with the hope that Aurora would be able to go with me for an early dinner. We'd done this several times over the past months, but that afternoon, she needed to go to the stationery store and then work on a school project in the evening.

She hugged me. "Can you stay here and talk with Daddy? We can visit for a while when I get back."

The minute she closed the door, Alejandro rushed over to me. It was the first time we'd been alone since I had arrived in the city.

"Amalia," he began, "I didn't realize things could be so awkward between us. I haven't been near you since we took our holiday in Chiapas five months ago, but don't think I haven't wanted to."

I turned away and sat down on a chair across the room. "Of course it's awkward," I replied. "This is Susana's home and I told you how I feel about that, especially with Aurora here. What's the matter? Haven't you and Susana grown closer since the accident?" Yes, I was fishing, but I needed to know how he felt about his wife.

Alejandro's head slumped into his hands. "No, Amalia, we have not grown closer. In fact, the opposite is true. She grows more resentful toward me every day."

The time for us to define the direction of our relationship was long overdue. This limbo we had lived in for seventeen years had exhausted my patience. As well, a nagging voice inside my head had grown louder and louder. It dared me to consider that maybe sex held a much higher priority for Alejandro than a committed, equal relationship.

I sat up straight in my chair. "Alejandro, I've had enough sneaking around. We need to be open and honest. And that will only happen when you and Susana make up your minds about what you want to do with your marriage."

Alejandro turned evasive, which should not have surprised me. He always did when I tried to bring up our future. Lifting his eyes cautiously upward, he ventured a long, hard look at my face, my clothes, and my body.

"You look strange, what's wrong?" I asked.

"I can't help but wonder if there's something going on with you and that Nico."

Now who was fishing? "I'm not even going to answer that," I told him. "I work with Nico and, yes, he is my friend. He's been nicer to me during my time here than you ever have. I've waited for you and hoped for more commitment for way too long."

"Amalia, I am in an extremely difficult position. . . ."

"You always have an excuse. Now you are adding accusations. You expect me to be available to you whenever you want me, and you figure I should blend into the scenery when you don't."

He looked cornered. "You are the one who has been so busy. You are the one who has refused to make love ever since you got here."

"I have been working hard. Yes, I have told you that there can be nothing physical between us under this roof, and my reasons are valid. But being in bed together is all you think about. Didn't it ever occur to you that perhaps I would have liked to join you and Aurora at the theater one night? Or go out for dinner with the two of you? Or even for a walk through the park? The whole time I've been in La Capital you have not included me once . . . unless it's been me doing the cooking."

All my pent-up frustration rushed out. "I've been working twelve-hour days, trying to buoy my parents' spirits, and worrying about how Paul and Toño are overworked with our business responsibilities in Merida. We've all rearranged our lives to help you get through this terrible time. But obviously that hasn't been enough."

I had to wonder if Susana felt the same way. I could now see how she had lived—married to "Mr. Manipulative." I clenched my teeth so that I wouldn't burst into tears.

Alejandro tried to take back his accusations, but I felt too angry and confused.

"We'll have to talk another day," I said.

Aurora returned to find her father and me sitting in armchairs drinking tea. It must have looked all too obvious that we'd been fighting. Without a word, she retreated to her room. Had she stepped out in order to give us time alone? And did she understand how unfruitful her consideration had been?

When my departure day arrived, I told my daughter and her father that I'd prefer to stay at an airport hotel for my final night. "Traffic is so congested around the reconstruction sites and near the refugee camps, I don't want a rushed, tense farewell in the morning."

"Alejandro, Aurora—look after one another," I said as I stepped into the taxi.

"We will," Aurora replied. Leaning into the cab, she hugged me tight and buried her nose into my neck. I hoped that the renewed trust and openness we now shared would last. Up until now, neither of these virtues had been our strong suits. I turned my cheek toward Alejandro for a farewell air kiss, acting as though this was all I wanted or expected—I felt exhausted by his games.

He said he loved me, yet in public we pretended to be "just friends." I guess a few acquaintances considered us "co-parents." He'd never told me how he explained Aurora's existence to his friends and colleagues. I felt resentful of my supporting role in his drama—I wanted to be the leading lady. But this seemed impossible with Susana's continuing health issues. Rightfully, his attention needed to go to her.

I'd held back my tears, but when the taxi turned the corner,

I let them flow so freely that the driver kept looking at me in the rearview mirror.

"Don't worry, I'll be fine," I told him. And I would be fine—I had made up my mind to be fine.

I checked into the airport hotel, stored my bags, and stretched out on the wonderfully soft king-size bed. It felt like total luxury after the narrow cot I'd slept on at Mamá's house. She had done her best to keep me as comfortable as possible, never grumbling that I spent so little time with her and Papá. She understood the pressure on me. Yet the moments we did have were a gift. During those five months I felt as though we overcame our lingering differences.

Lost in my reverie, I startled when the phone rang. On the other end, Nico asked, "Are you really determined to leave, Amalia? Can I come by your hotel? We could have a farewell drink at the bar. I really need to see you before you go."

I agreed to meet him in an hour. I disliked feeling used by Alejandro, but hadn't I done the same thing to Nico?

As soon as I entered the lounge, he hurried over and escorted me to the corner alcove he'd already occupied. I noticed how other women followed us with their eyes, and I realized that many of them would have taken my place in a heartbeat. In his buttoned-down plaid shirt with khaki pants—and tanned from working in the sun every day—Nico looked good. He held out my chair and we sat down. The waitress immediately placed a small glass bowl of salted nuts on the table and gave us cocktail menus. Tonga Lily, Sex on the Beach, daiquiris and the like, reminded us of our long-ago, alcohol-drenched afternoon in Merida. In fact, much about tonight made me feel like I did during that unforgettable lunch.

Nico eased his shoulders and craned his neck from side to side as though trying to ease a cramped muscle. "I'm going to have an extra-dry gin martini. What about you?

I said I'd have the same, and once we'd ordered from the pretty waitress in the short-short skirt, he sat back and his eyes took in every inch of me.

"I know your partners will be glad to have you back, Amalia, but I am going to miss you more than you can imagine." When I made no reply, he added, "Our team could not have accomplished all we did without you."

I wondered why I didn't stop running after Alejandro and give Nico a fair chance. I could have a good life with him. But we had to get off this topic. "I remember that you told me you'd be making a trip to Europe this coming summer. What places will you visit?"

"Italy!" he practically shouted. "I have been there many times, but I never get tired of it." Then he chuckled, "I tell people that I'll stop going when I get a bad meal. Amalia, why don't you come along? I could show you all my favorite places."

I smiled. "That's a tempting offer, but we both know that me going with you to Europe is not possible right now. I'm so behind with my work in Merida. Paul and Toño are worn out, and I have to pick up where I left off."

I looked at his handsome face; I knew he wanted to come up to my room. My body begged my mind to say yes. But if I did, leaving Mexico City would be impossible. I should not have accepted this invitation for drinks. I drained the last of the martini, gathered up my purse, room key, and shawl.

"Wait, Amalia, before you walk out of here I need to ask you—if Alejandro was not in the picture, would you love me?"

"Oh, Nico, don't make me answer you, especially now, because I'm feeling as incapable of resisting you as I did that afternoon in Merida!"

He moved closer. "Why fight it, Amalia? How can you keep denying that we're perfect together? I think about being with you all the time. Don't leave just yet. Let's talk some more—why is going with me to Italy such a long shot?"

"Truly, Nico? Simply because the idea is so enticing and I'm not free to sail away with you right now."

"Not free 'right now' you say? *Hmmmm*—I'll hang onto the hope that you soon will be. What a time we could have. I don't know why you don't just dump Alejandro. What I saw the night we went to his apartment did not impress me at all. It seems clear to me that he doesn't appreciate you. Maybe once you're back in Merida and not so confused by having both of us around, you'll realize that you deserve so much more."

twenty-seven

"We must look like a couple of red tomatoes by now," said Layla. She's the one who taught me to love the sensation of getting warmed all through and then plunging into the cool water.

I called her as soon as I got home. We arranged ourselves pool side and soaked up the sun while I gave her an abridged story of the past six months—from Chiapas to the earthquake, Susana's accident, and my final decision to turn Nico down on my last night in Mexico City. I told her about the reconstruction work at Tlatelolco and how my frustration with the bureaucracy had caused me to leave before I'd planned. Finally, I detailed my improved understanding of Alejandro's relationship with Susana and my truce with Aurora.

Layla peered over her sunglasses at me. "Are you saying the tension between you and Aurora is over? I don't think she's ever going to let you dictate the terms, but it sounds like she's more civil than you used to be with your mother. I'd say it's time you relaxed. She's doing just fine."

Without interrupting her assessment of my situation, Layla turned over to brown her back. "Now, about Alejandro and Nico— there's no doubt that Nico's in love with you. Thank God you didn't lose your mind on your last night because in my book that's called, *wham bam thank you man*. Amalia, you know the minute Alejandro crooks his little finger—and he will do that—you're going to run back to him. If you insist on being with Alejandro, you've got to put that dazzling Nico out of your mind. Dangling another man on a string just isn't fair."

"Layla! You go too far! Now that Susana has been injured, I can't see that Alejandro will ever 'crook his little finger.'"

"You've heard the expression: 'Be careful what you wish for, you might just get it?'" asked Layla. "Alejandro is totally spoiled. You've let him get away with too much and you still l-o-v-e him. He knows that all too well. Girl, you need to stand up for yourself—and stand up to him."

I felt my face redden. "I do stand up for myself. I made myself very clear during the five months in Mexico City."

"Okay, give me one more example when you really did that. In Mexico City you had few chances to be alone, so that barely counts. You've pined away for decades and ruined your chances to marry other, better men, like Nico. Look at how blithely you went running off to Chiapas with Alejandro on a half-day's notice. You gave in to him and allowed Aurora to go and live at his house. All this and he's still married to Susana!"

"I've told you all the reasons why things need to be like this for a while longer."

"A 'while longer?' And when do you think Susana is going to let him go, Amalia? Furthermore, from how you described Alejandro's grief after Susana's accident, are you sure he really wants to leave her? If Hortensia was here, she'd be saying that the goddesses are trying to tell you something, sweetie. From the sound of things, Nico would walk over hot coals for you. What am I missing here?"

"A few things, Layla. What about Aurora? Alejandro is her father. What would she think if I dumped him for Nico?"

"Aurora is almost grown, Amalia. She doesn't consult you when she makes decisions."

Her confrontation came as a shock. What happened to my best

buddy Layla? Without another word she stood up and slipped a cover-up over her head. She walked toward me, put her face right up to mine, and muttered, "I need to get something from the house—wait here."

I didn't have any idea what she had in mind, but I followed her lead and put on my caftan. I moved out of the sun and sat at the umbrella-shaded table.

She came back quickly carrying a tray. On it I could see two full bottles of tequila, some lemon wedges, a little dish of salt, two double shot glasses, and a deck of cards. "We are going to play Truth or Dare. You take a card and then I take one. The high card wins and the other person has to tell a truth or accept the dare. And, the one with the low card also has to take a shot from the bottle. Got it?"

I did, and when she passed me the deck, I cut it and turned up the king of spades. She got a three of diamonds. "Truth or dare?" I asked her. "Dare," replied my friend. She lifted up the bottle next to her and poured herself a full glass.

I narrowed my eyes. "I dare you to tell me why we are playing this game."

Layla laughed. "I am going to get you so drunk that you'll let all the tension and secrets out of your uptight little self."

Having a few drinks sounded like a fine idea. I lost next. I poured from my bottle and belted back the fiery liquid. Actually, I did have a "truth" that I was dying to tell. "I almost slept with Nico on my last night in Mexico City."

I held my hand in front of Layla and pressed my thumb and index finger tightly together. "I was *this* close."

"You've got to say more than that. I want details."

"Layla, you disappoint me. You missed the clue. I told you that I nearly slept with Nico 'on my last night in Mexico City.' I didn't say anything about the other nights."

"Spill it. Right now," Layla hissed at me.

I told her about the evening when my skirt rode way up my legs as I climbed into Nico's truck, and how he'd laughed and said, "Amalia, I'll settle for sex!" The way his slate-gray eyes traveled up and down my body completely did me in. How I felt so tired of saying *no*.

"We'd been working hard and we felt we needed—that we deserved—a reprieve from denial."

"Amalia, you don't have to justify anything—just tell me what you did."

"Hold on," I said, "I'm getting to that. He started the engine and drove for a short distance. We had stopped at a red light and he caught me looking over at him—what I wanted was all too clear. Before I had a chance to get my mind back on track, he pulled over and parked on a dark street. He looked all around and when he saw there was nobody anywhere near us, he lifted me out of the truck and wedged me into the small space between his parked pickup and another one.

"I was on fire, but the night air felt cold when he unbuttoned my blouse, opened the clasp of my bra, and pulled both breasts free. I tried to cover myself, but he pushed the fabric away. 'No, Amalia, let me see,' he said. Then he lifted my skirt, grabbed hold of my panties and tugged them down. I turned to jelly as he undressed me in the street, and I clung on to him like plastic wrap.

"'Amalia? I'm going to drive us to my place,' he said, but I had lost all control. 'No Nico—now—right here,' And it finished for both of us in an explosive gasp.

"Wordlessly, we pulled our clothes back on, slipped back into the truck and he took me to Mamá's."

Layla's eyes went wide and she clapped her hands. "Well, well, well. A fuck behind a truck has a certain earthy appeal."

I didn't know how to respond. She obviously relished hearing about this turn of events, and when she saw how flustered I got, she slapped me on the back. "Oh, come on—you've heard the word before! Maybe your obsession isn't as profound as I thought. Now finish the story!"

I threw back my head and ran my fingers through my hair. I felt like Layla was playing with me, but I had no one else I could talk to. The memory of those weeks with Nico was driving me crazy. "The first couple of times, he and I didn't talk about having a future together. I felt guilty, but not guilty enough to stop. And after a week, I couldn't deny that I wanted more from him than just the sex."

"*Uh-huh*. So what came next?" Layla would not stop the questions.

"We had planned to meet in his office at lunch time. I'd just arrived and he walked through the door—half-carrying someone. 'I found her down by the church. She's bleeding,' he explained.

"We knew that the hospitals and clinics were filled to capacity. I asked him for cloths, hot water, soap, and rubbing alcohol and cleared a place on the floor for a blanket."

Layla looked absorbed in my story.

"I did the best I could, but the woman needed more help than I could offer. I left Nico in the office—giving her tiny sips of water—while I went to find a midwife I knew.

"Doña Mechita took one look, confirmed a miscarriage, and told us the girl needed to be in a hospital. Nico said that there was nowhere to take her. The medical centers were bursting with the critically injured. 'Then she'll have to stay with me,' the midwife said.

"Nico carried the girl for ten blocks and gave Mechita money for her care. When we checked on her the next day, she had stabilized."

Layla had stopped her edgy teasing; my compassionate friend had come back. She held my face between her two hands and looked right into my confused eyes. "I have to ask. Amalia, are you in love with Nico?"

"I don't know. I honestly don't. What is love anyway? I've always thought I loved Alejandro, but I know you're right when you say he doesn't act like he loves me. I've asked myself if he's just a habit I can't break," I said. "And Nico? He says he loves me and yet I'm so unfair to him. I just don't know what to do. I've been with Alejandro for so many years." Again, I pressed my thumb and index finger tightly together. "And now we're *this* close to a committed relationship. Can I just throw all that away?"

By six o'clock, Layla's bottle had been long emptied and she started on mine. She looked surprisingly alert. I won the next cut. "I dare-re you-ou-ou to tell me why-y-y I'm shit-faced and you-ou-ou are s-s-still okay."

She took another pour from the remaining tequila in my bottle and holding the glass out in my direction said, "A brilliant—and very eloquent—observation, Miss Vásquez. I'm mostly sober because my bottle had water in it. It's you who needed loosening up. I've only had three shots of the real thing."

I'd had many more than three. The garden swirled all around, but I managed to ask, "Layla, what do you-ou-ou think I should do?"

"What do you want to do, Amalia? From what I've learned sitting here, I think you know, but you can't face the truth."

"I wish I could be like you," I told my best friend. "You're b-beautiful, you have your independent life and your books—you don't care what people think."

"But I do care, Amalia, I care very much. I have to cultivate my image and looks. It's hard work."

My head felt all muddled. I needed food. Layla brought me roast chicken and potato salad that she'd bought at the supermarket take-out. Thanks to the little bit I got down into my sour stomach, I managed to keep from being sick. Layla drove me home and I went straight to bed.

I felt almost sorry when my hangover started to lift around noon the next day because with it went my excuse for self-indulgence. Even though she couldn't help me come to a decision, it had been good for me to tell Layla about my dilemma: Alejandro or Nico? I had to get my head together and concentrate on other pressing issues in my life—like our business.

In the wake of the earthquake, many families and individuals were moving out of La Capital. We'd hired Monica, the architectural student that I met during the restoration work at Tlatelolco. She got along well with our company's other three interns, and already she'd shown Toño, Paul, and me what a good addition she was to our team. Monica's hip business persona and her big-city attitude brought an edge into the office. She thought in terms of "majestic" when she approached the aesthetic parts of her designs, yet she never excluded practical concerns, such as traffic flow.

At an in-house seminar, she strutted back and forth in front of us, her stiletto heels clicking. "Merida doesn't have excessive numbers of cars on the road," she said, "but it soon will."

Persuaded by her prediction, Toño, Paul, and I bought two commercial properties with multiple access routes that we knew would be good investments.

And Teresita, the young mother from Oaxaca, also found a home with us. When I told Hortensia about her, my nana's eyes watered and she urged me to locate her.

"I feel as though we're meant to bring Teresita here. If you can track her down, I'll find somewhere for her and the children to live, and I'll find work for her."

My contacts located Teresita, but I don't think she quite understood what the offer from Merida entailed. Nonetheless, she gathered her few possessions and her four babies. "When does the next bus leave?" she asked.

I can imagine that the panorama of Yucatan's flat landscape and sparse, dried-out vegetation must have looked so foreign to this woman who had lived her whole life in the high country. After a twenty-four hour trip, the bewildered family pulled into the Merida terminal.

Hortensia watched Teresita climb down from the bus with two infants in her arms and two toddlers clinging to her skirt. Nana moved more quickly than she had in a long time, and reached for the twins. The babies snuggled into her, and I watched Hortensia instantly commit herself to their care.

"Teresita and the children will live with me at Opciones," she announced.

Malnourished, but agile, and used to hard work, Teresita stoically cared for even the most critical patients. In the early morning hours, she'd be hanging up freshly washed clothes on the lines, and at night she liked to do the mending. She could produce a hearty meal using whatever we had on hand. Although at first the food tasted blander than we liked, Hortensia showed her around the center's kitchen and soon delectable entrees and desserts became regular fare at Opciones.

Teresita and Hortensia had challenging language differences—Hortensia's native tongue had been *Maya-Yucateco* and Teresita's only fluent one was *Triki*. But from just a look, Teresita knew what Hortensia needed, which proved to be providential now that Nana felt her age. She often seemed tired and achy. She had not lost her wit, though. As she hobbled into my house one morning, I felt so concerned about her obviously painful hips. "Nana, we need to take you to the doctor," I said.

Giving me one of her enigmatic smiles, she said, "At my age, *Mi'ja*, if nothing hurts in the morning, it's because you're dead!"

For Nana, the arrival of this family meant that she would never be lonely—Teresita and the children called her *"Mamita."* At first hearing that, I had a twinge of jealousy. She was my "Nana"—not their *"Mamita."* But I quickly stomped down that selfish thought. I needed to follow Hortensia's generous example and I wanted to.

During Aurora's childhood and the years of building up our business, common goals kept our unconventional family united. Now we were all moving in different directions. "Change is the way of the world," Hortensia reminded me.

I finished the sentence for her. "And the ways of the spirit are winding, wise, and wonderful."

twenty-eight

On the first day of spring, I called Aurora in Mexico City. The sun had just set and I began our conversation by describing Merida's night sky.

Like everyone who has ever lived in Yucatan, she longed to feel immersed in the sultry nocturnal humidity. She told me how much she missed the pungent aroma of the night-blooming vines. The temperature drops significantly after dark, and it's easy to forgive the scorching daytime heat when the world is bathed in *luz de luna*—moon sparkle.

After reveling in the sensations, my daughter heaved a sigh and changed topic. It seemed that Susana and Alejandro were having problems and she felt uncomfortable with their fighting.

"You can come back to Merida," I quickly suggested, "or go to your grandmother, if you prefer."

"No," she said, "I'll be okay here. I've almost finished school, and I want to support Papá. Susana no longer seems to want him around, and he visits her less and less. Still she needs the benefits she gets through his university's medical plan. It has been eight months since the cave-in and she can't yet walk unassisted. He feels responsible for her."

"Maybe because he's so busy with you, she's feeling a little left out." I offered.

"I don't think it's that. Last Tuesday when I went to the hospital to drop off this month's issue of *Vanidades* for her, a stranger passed me in the hallway. I knew he had come from Susana's room. When

I knocked, Susana called out a man's name—Rodrigo. 'So you've decided to stay with me after all?' she said in a low voice. I walked through the door and she looked flustered. She stuttered and said she'd been talking to herself. We both felt embarrassed, so I left the magazine and went home."

I wished Aurora would give me more details, but she had no more information to share. "Do you want to talk to Daddy now?" she asked. "I'll go get him."

While waiting for Alejandro to come on the line, I realized that I did not enjoy talking with him like I used to. Our conversations felt artificial. If I wanted to straighten out the difficulties in our relationship, I felt that we needed to see each other in person.

"Our daughter will turn eighteen in July. Can you come to Mexico City so we can celebrate together? Better yet, maybe you could come early and help plan the party?" he suggested.

Our daughter. Yes, she did have two devoted parents.

"I think that we need to speak now rather than in three months," I said. "Why don't you take Aurora to my parents for a weekend and come to see me? Her birthday isn't all we have to talk about."

"Will I stay at your place or should I make a hotel reservation?" he asked.

I felt confused, and obviously Alejandro did not feel as secure about me as he once did. A lot had happened over the past year. But I wanted to give our reunion in Merida every chance for success. "I want you to stay with me," I replied. I needed resolution. I wanted a life partner—not an impossible love.

Three Fridays later, Alejandro's cab arrived. At the sight of him, my heart leapt and lodged in my throat. I opened the door, and the light in his eyes showed how glad he was to be in Merida.

"You're going to have a hard time getting rid of me," he said.

Kissing me deeply, he wanted us to get reacquainted before plunging into all we had to discuss. He suggested that we move out to his favorite spot—by the pool. I nodded and arm-in-arm we walked through the garden. He looked around and said the starry night sky reminded him of a van Gogh painting.

"I'm sore from the flight. Let me take a swim," he suggested with a wink. Obviously, he wanted to move things right along. Conversation could wait. He knew my body so well—no arguing that.

But tonight I couldn't allow passion to absorb the tension. I needed to broach the subject that made this reunion so important to me. "We need to hold off," I said.

He grunted—whether in agreement or annoyance, I wasn't sure. It confused me how quickly Alejandro turned off the charm and switched over to all-business.

"Okay then, first of all, we need to talk about Susana," he said. "You aren't clear about her situation, are you?"

I shook my head. My stomach was now tossing up and down like a rowboat on a choppy sea.

"The crux of it is that she's having an extremely hard time and is taking it out on me. Since the accident she has hardened her heart completely and has come to some very strange conclusions. You won't like it when I tell you what she's thinking."

"I don't care, Alejandro. Just give me the truth," I said.

"Amalia, Susana blames me—and you—for the accident."

What? I had no idea where he could be heading with such a startling disclosure. My stomach tightened even more.

"When you arrived in Mexico City to help with the restoration efforts, and I acted so proud of your brave spirit, she says she felt forced to prove herself."

I couldn't follow. Why would anything I did or didn't do be important?

"I think she wanted to prove to me that she was still the person who could make or break my position at the university," he replied. "The jealousy she feels toward you completely overtook her. She had her doubts that the gallery entrance was secure, but she went in anyway."

I felt a slow burning. It sounded as though he wanted to make me feel guilty for Susana's injury, and he had not yet finished.

"She claims that if I hadn't been so besotted with you and if you had not tried to upstage her, she would not be in the situation she now finds herself."

Did he expect me to accept the blame? Had he conveniently forgotten that he'd been the one to set up the initial competition between Susana and me nearly thirty years ago? Unwilling to remain the scapegoat of his nonsensical rambling, I asked him, "But why should she still be trying to compete with me? You've said she doesn't feel the same way for you as she once did. If you're trying to tell me that you can't leave Susana because you feel guilty about her accident, then spit it out. Otherwise, stop trying to heap this guilt trip on me."

"I'm not trying to make you feel that you're solely to blame, Amalia. It's just that this is yet another complication." Alejandro got up and moved to the bar. He had his back turned to me, stalling for time as he chose something to drink.

I figured that I could use one too. "Pour me a Cinzano while you're there," I said. He brusquely passed me a glass and sat back down. I read anger in his body language.

"A week ago, Susana told me that Rodrigo Dominguez, one of my UNAM colleagues, has been her lover for two years. She says he's been more supportive of her during the convalescence than I have, and she wants me to leave the apartment so that they can live there—together—that's her way to get back at me. She's turning me out."

Alejandro's fury that his estranged wife had a boyfriend went beyond normal jealousy, and though no supporter of hers, I couldn't help registering how ironic and misdirected his temper was. I wondered how many years it had taken Susana to become fed up with his double standard and macho attitudes.

He seemed unaware of my ambivalent sympathies and kept on as if I were there to help him make a comfortable arrangement for himself.

"I don't know what to think. Susana says she wants to leave the convalescent home at the end of June. Aurora will have finished high school by then."

I cut in. "She will hopefully come home for the summer and then she'll be leaving for Parsons."

Alejandro practically growled at the reminder. I wondered about the real reason he was so reluctant to allow her to study in the United States. I took one of his hands and traced my finger along his palm, trying to coax an explanation out of him. "At first, I also felt dead set against her plans. But I've learned I cannot dictate what she does with her life. She needs to be free to make her own decisions. Are you concerned about what people will say—the daughter of one of Mexico's most outspoken social critics going to *Gringolandia* to pursue such a *frivolous* career?"

To my surprise he did not deny this. "In just a year and a half, we'll mark the twentieth anniversary of the Tlatelolco massacre. My team at UNAM has already begun planning a commemoration of the tragedy. I had hoped Aurora would be a part of that, but if she's not even in the country—it's not going to happen."

At least he didn't seem to be blaming me for giving her the non-socially involved part of her character. But he looked at me even more intently.

"Amalia, I want to come to Merida when Aurora finishes school, but I don't know how I'll be able to manage that so soon. I need to find out about my pension, and with the anniversary coming up, my students can't manage such a huge event without me. If I let Susana have the apartment, I will have to find somewhere else to live."

Did I really expect anything more from Alejandro than this? He had more reasons than a judge for putting me off yet again. What he really wanted from me became clear when he asked me about my apartment in Mexico City.

But this time I refused to let myself cave in like I usually did. "I still own the apartment," I responded evenly, "but I have rented it out with a five-year lease. I wish I could offer it to you, but I can't."

Alejandro shook his head when he heard that and I caught the annoyance in his eyes. I'd bet anything that he had been expecting me to hand over the keys. But I needed to get back to the main subject. "Alejandro, I'm glad you told me about how things stand between you and Susana, but what about the two of us?"

He looked me straight in the eye. I'd seen that *righteous face* before and knew I was in for more blame-casting.

"Yes," he said solemnly, "what about the two of us? I had so many hopes, Amalia, but the last time we talked like this, you got overly defensive when I mentioned Nico. Is there something between you two that I should know about?"

When I hesitated before replying, his mouth tightened and he insisted, "Don't I have a right to know what's going on?"

"You do have that right, Alejandro," I said, stalling a little longer—I didn't quite know where I wanted to take this conversation. I'd dreamed of having Alejandro for my own for so long. He talked as though he wanted to come to Merida and live here with me, but as always, there was caveat. Why didn't this upset me the way it would have even a month ago? I couldn't deny that Nico had further complicated a situation that had never been straightforward. What was wrong with me that I couldn't sort out my feelings?

Alejandro looked at me, waiting for me to divulge something, but instead, I dished up a bold-faced lie. "There's nothing to tell. I've waited so long for you to make a commitment to me and I'm overwhelmed right now. I still don't fully understand what you plan to do. I thought this would be the night you'd clarify everything, but obviously you're not ready to do that. I'll come to Mexico City for Aurora's birthday. We can discuss this again. For right now, let's just enjoy the time that we're together." I moved toward him and sat on his lap.

He did not need much convincing—he loathed confrontation. We were back on the same footing as always. He continued to fill my head with half promises, and I went along with them. Really, I wasn't sure I could give up the fairy tale. I had spent so many years working toward *happy ever after*, did I want to throw all that away? I had lost my nerve at the last minute—again. So much for my determination to resolve our relationship.

~

The next day we visited Hortensia at Opciones. As he strolled around the grounds, Alejandro looked justifiably proud of his contribution toward setting up the center.

"These have been seven fat years," Hortensia told him. "So much good has come about because of this place." As she introduced him to the volunteers, the staff, and the clients, many shook his hand or kissed his cheek. I could see his genuine concern and goodness. This was the Alejandro I loved.

The following Monday morning, as I watched him saunter down the airport corridor toward the plane that would take him back to Mexico City, I heaved a sigh of relief. I didn't like saying goodbye knowing that I'd not been truthful with him, but how many times had he done this to me?

I'd been so tightly wound up for the entire three days he was with me, I needed to be on my own to recoup and reflect. Layla's words, "Be careful what you wish for, you might just get it," had run through my brain all weekend. It seemed clear to me that if Alejandro and I were going to be together, he would need to make major compromises—like giving up some of those "obligations" preventing his moving to Merida. Could he do that?

~~~

Toño's low opinion of the man who'd been my lifelong obsession hadn't budged. He couldn't forgive Alejandro for using me time and time again. I worried that he'd be upset to know that Alejandro had been in Merida, but when I told him, he shrugged his shoulders.

"Amalia, I have stopped trying to talk even a little sense into your hard head. So let's just change the topic, okay?" He then added, " Besides, I have been looking for the opportunity to sound you out about something important."

I did not like the sound of his voice. This would be the second heavy conversation I'd had in as many days. I sat down in the closest chair and waited to learn what he had to say.

"There's no easy way to say this, so I'm just going to lay it right out on the table, Amalia. Paul wants to go back to Austin, and I can't say I'm against the idea."

I jumped up. "What are you talking about?" I asked, more than a little alarmed. "You've come to this decision so suddenly! Why the rush? Are you sure this is what you really want?"

Toño looked sympathetic, but he stayed firm. "Paul and I have indeed thought this out carefully. Do you realize that we have fully renovated seventy-four residences and made significant improvements to double that number in the span of eighteen years? We are tired and feel we have two choices. One, slow down, or two, sell. The timing is way off for option one, but for the second, it couldn't be better. Not only are international people moving to Merida, but a good number of Mexico City residents who lost their homes in the earthquake, or fear they'll do so in the next one, have opted to move to Yucatan. No earthquakes here. Our company would be a solid investment for the right buyer."

~~~

The day after Toño told me that he and Paul wanted to leave Merida, I went again to Opciones. Seeing Hortensia in the element she was born for made me so proud. I felt that my hand in this had partially paid her back for the lifetime of selfless love she'd given me. We still saw each other a lot, but her "new family" and Opciones had changed our relationship. A little distance had been created, but we both knew it had to be so.

After settling ourselves down among the flowers on her porch, I told Hortensia about what my brother wanted. She didn't look at all surprised, though she did look thoughtful. "The winds of change are blowing through your house, Amalia. I know you feel the shift, but you're resisting; it will be much easier for you if you allow things to work out as they are meant to."

I fidgeted with the gold chain around my neck. "If Toño and Paul leave Merida, we'll have to sell the business. I can't keep it going on my own," I said.

"But, Amalia, I suspect that's what you want—am I right? I can see you are ready for something new."

"Layla says the same thing, but I feel so conflicted. We built that company up from nothing. Not having it anymore will make me feel as though I've lost a huge part of who I am."

Hortensia got up from her chair and moved closer. She looped her arms around my neck and massaged a pulsating nerve. When she let go, the tremor had abated and she sat back down.

"*Mi'ja*, why did you three start the business in the first place?" she asked.

"We needed an income. You remember that."

"I certainly do. That was a worrisome time and the three of you worked as hard as I've ever seen. But your gamble paid off and you made more than an income. You've made a lot of money. Now it's time to let the business go to someone else."

Maybe that needed to happen, but I didn't want it to, and my nana could sense that.

"Will selling the company really be so difficult, Amalia?" she asked me. "Can't you think of other places where your many talents and experience could be utilized?"

"If we sell, I'll miss the excitement of entering into new projects. I never seem to run out of ideas for the designs. I have always liked to begin by going into the house on my own. I walk through the rooms and look out the windows. I let the house talk to me. Each property has its own voice and offers something unique." Yes, that was the part I loved about our work. But the tedium of the actual rebuilding process had worn on me too. Constant negotiations with the clients, suppliers, workers, and the bureaucracy had lost their allure.

~~~

On the first Saturday in May, Paul and I planned on spending the whole day relaxing by the pool. We had just settled on our lawn chairs when we heard the whistle of the mailman.

"Please, God, let there be nothing more demanding than a supermarket flier. I can't stand the idea of looking at photographs of one more crumbling Colonial ruin," Paul said.

That cinched it for me. I knew there would be no turning back; we'd soon be selling. "Perhaps we should take the offer we received from Héctor, Evangelina, and Fernando?" I asked. My three best friends from the architectural college were part of a consortium that wanted to buy us out. I knew the business we'd built up from just an idea would continue to flourish in their hands."

Hearing my words, Paul's face held equal amounts of sorrow and relief. "Yes, Toño and I want that too. But before we decide on anything, we need to see that you're okay. After we leave, there won't be a day we don't miss you."

There seemed to be no sense in making this harder on ourselves. We closed at the end of the month and came away with more money than we imagined. Paul and Toño agreed to stay in Merida to give the new owners a three-month orientation, and I planned to see them as often as I could during the grace period. I hoped that their final season in Merida would be full of good times. I wanted them to leave feeling that the city was still a fine place to live.

My brother and I went to my house after the signing, but Paul wanted to go to the García Ginerés office to look for some old photographs that he needed—he had thousands. Paul and I needed to decide which images we'd use in the album we were putting together. We would no longer have our company, but we wanted a tangible record of the years we'd poured our all into it. "I never would have guessed that Paul wanted to return to the US," I told Toño. "He's always cheerful and positive."

"He chooses to be. He's the best partner in that respect and in so many others. Above all, he's been successful at keeping you and me on good terms. I bless him for that because I love you, *Hermanita*, and I fear if Paul hadn't cooled my temper on many occasions, I would have damaged our relationship past the point of repair."

"I've also done things that you never liked. I know my affair with Alejandro has been very hard on you, hasn't it?"

"You have no idea . . . but I don't want to stir up all that just now."

"Well, why don't you call Paul and ask him to hurry up? I have something that you two will be interested to know." He tried to worm the secret out of me, but I insisted on holding out until my dearest friend arrived.

When I asked Toño if he and Paul knew what they'd be doing in the States, he sounded full of plans for their re-entry into Austin's social whirl. Paul joined us just as Toño wrapped up his story about the huge party they'd hold for the Fourth of July. "Now, you have to tell us your news," Toño said. "We've been patient long enough."

Toño and Paul knew nothing about Nico, and even though Toño might be thrilled that I was considering another man besides Alejandro, I also knew he wouldn't approve of the fact that I had been "unfaithful."

I had to tell them this evening and suggested we move to the covered porch. I served Kahlúas and we settled into the rockers. I drank mine in one swallow and they looked at me with surprise.

"What brought that on? Are you okay?" Toño asked. He looked at Paul, then back at me. "We're here for you, Amalia, unless you tell me you're pregnant again." Paul looked horrified, but I saw my brother's sly smile and burst out laughing.

"No, no, no . . . I'm long past that." I patted his hand and accepted the second Kahlúa that Paul poured.

I resisted belting back that one as well, and then blurted out, "I have met another man. He is very different from Alejandro."

Toño threw both arms over his head. "*¡Gracias a Dios!* My prayers have been answered!" Then he turned serious. "Amalia, I'm shocked but not unhappy. You know how I feel about Alejandro. Now tell us more."

"Nico is an architect like me. I met him in 1975 during the first congress at the university. Aurora was small and I was fixated on Alejandro, so I didn't allow myself to carry on any further with Nico. But during the reconstruction at Tlatelolco, we became— reacquainted."

Paul offered me a third Kahlúa, but I turned it down. "Do you love him?" he asked.

"I wish I knew. I have loved Alejandro for such a long time. Is it possible to love two men at once?"

"You need to be truthful with him, Amalia. Go see him in Mexico City and talk honestly with Alejandro as well. I bet that your decision will resolve itself," said Paul.

"Actually, Hortensia and I plan to go to Mexico City for Aurora's birthday. Why don't you guys come with us?"

"Amalia—the timing for a trip to La Capital is perfect for us right now. But I wonder if you should plan your *tête-à-tête* with Nico around another occasion—a drama on your daughter's eighteenth birthday would not be right."

"Oh no, don't worry," I said reassuringly. "Nothing will happen until after Aurora's big day."

twenty-nine

Not since 1968 had Toño, Paul, Hortensia, and I been together in Mexico City. Aurora's eighteenth birthday was the happy reason for the trip and, as well, we needed to visit Mamá and Papá. Both of them were unwell.

On the day of our planned visit, when we arrived at their home in Colonia Narvarte, Manuela answered the door with a sorry look on her face. "They are both sound asleep," she said. "They laid down for a nap so they'd be well rested when you arrived and they haven't woken up."

Taking advantage of the respite from her duties, my parents' nurse sat reading on the sun-splashed balcony off the spacious bedroom. She waved at us and made to rouse our parents, but Manuela signaled her to stay as she was. We would leave them to their rest.

"I thought just Mamá was sick. What's wrong with Papá?"

"They've been together for so long, and for the last fifteen years they have been inseparable," said Manuela.

"It's odd how they changed. When we were kids they fought all the time," Toño observed.

"You know that's because Mamá resented his freeloading. She had to work hard to provide us with all we needed while he hung out with his buddies. When he put together the band and started to contribute financially, she relaxed and they grew close. Their doctor said a very unconventional thing the other day. 'Watching her suffer is taking him, too. He's dying of a broken heart.'"

Hortensia shook her head. "I don't think that sounds strange at all," she said. "I've seen many such cases. When the emotions and sentiments are completely attuned between two people, their physical bodies become likewise."

When we realized that my parents would not be waking up that afternoon, we left them in the nurse's care. Manuela wanted a luscious lunch and suggested Rosita's, a popular Argentine restaurant. Afterwards we felt as stuffed as the *empanadas* we had gorged on.

I watched how naturally Manuela and Aurora shared bits of food and much intimate laughter. A year ago, I'd have bristled with jealousy, but now, I felt nothing of the sort. Aurora had bonded with her Mexico City family and I concluded that when she finished up at Parsons, she would probably make La Capital her permanent home.

To please Susana, Aurora and Alejandro had vacated the big apartment on Avenida Reforma, and he had rented a small, two-bedroom place three blocks away. Really, there was not enough space for him and Aurora, but once she was gone, I knew it would be perfect for him.

The next morning, when my hotel phone rang, I thought it might be Nico. We had talked the night before, and if plans worked out, we'd be seeing each other today. But the call was from my sister. "Today's a good day," she said. "Mamá and Papá are both alert and we're having chicken at lunchtime." Although Paul and Toño had planned on attending a noontime performance of the *Ballet Folklorico* at Bellas Artes, they canceled their plans and we all hurried over to our parents' house.

Papá had pushed Mamá in her wheelchair all the way to the front door, and they waited there ready to greet us. Mamá gave Aurora a special smile. "What are you wearing today?" she asked.

My daughter had on one of her own creations, a short, coral-colored semi-circular skirt with a cropped blouse that she had crocheted out of strips of the same fabric. A lapis lazuli choker and earrings accessorized the ensemble. As Aurora pirouetted for her, Mamá beamed. "You are definitely your grandmother's girl!"

We spent three hours in the bright living room, talking about all the good times we'd had as children. Paul and Aurora had not been there, of course, but they'd heard the anecdotes so often, they felt part of our stories. Mamá still had the passion that had made her wildly successful in her career and the adamant opinions that I too frequently rejected when I was younger. I wished I could ask her about Nico and Alejandro. Would she be delighted that I'd found someone other than the man she had disapproved of for much of her life?

～～

To celebrate her birthday, Aurora wanted to have dinner at Café Tacuba. Dressed in a creamy yellow dress that she had sewn herself, she looked so much more self-assured than the other girls her age. A rhinestone-studded headband held the unruly dark curls off her face and reflected her chocolate eyes.

I felt so proud listening to her talk about her plans for New York. But by his uncharacteristic silence and slumped posture, I could tell that her father remained less than enthusiastic. We hadn't talked to each other at all during dinner—we were seated too far apart. I wondered if it was only Aurora's imminent departure that had him in a funk.

Following the family celebration, our daughter would be meeting friends and going to a club. At ten we all got up from the table and she said her good-byes. As she headed for the main door, she licked some bits of birthday cake icing off her fingers. Most of the male eyes in the large dining room tracked her progress through the crowded restaurant. But before she disappeared into the night, she held up her arms and extended her hands. Lowering them again, she put the tips to her lips and made a throwing motion toward us—*besos volados*—flying kisses for all.

Alejandro watched her leave and shoved his hands into his pockets. He told me that he felt a lot of concern about the men who would pursue his daughter.

"Every father feels that way," I said. "You have to trust her. Are you going to miss her terribly? I know I already do."

"It's more than that. She's so bright and inquisitive. Studying fashion design will be a waste of her intellect," he said. "And, besides, I worry about how she'll manage alone in New York."

"Don't obsess over this, Alejandro. She'll settle into the city and her studies at Parsons as smoothly as she sews seams. She's making her own choices and starting a career she loves. And Toño and Paul will be just a short plane ride away from her."

I could tell he had stopped listening and had something else on his mind—he wanted to spend the night at my hotel.

"You can't," I told him. "Hortensia is sharing a room with me. Toño and Paul are staying at the same hotel, and Aurora is with you at the apartment." I tried to joke with him, and poked him in the ribs. "This is a *family* celebration. Remember?"

Alejandro did not look appeased. His pouting made me realize once more that the time had come for me to choose between the two men in my life. Surprisingly, the prospect of doing this soon filled me with peace.

~~~

I told Hortensia, Toño, and Paul that I'd see them in a couple of days. My daughter and her father weren't aware that I didn't get on the plane to Merida as planned. With a firm agenda in mind, I booked a suite at the Hotel Maria Cristina in Colonia Juárez—just a half hour's walk from the heart of downtown Mexico City. The vintage 1920s property, with its winding central staircase and lush gardens, had always appealed to me, and the fact that I'd never stayed there before made it a good choice. I didn't want to glimpse any memories lurking in hidden corners.

I phoned Nico early. I could picture him picking up the call in his modern two-bedroom flat. Maybe he'd be looking out through the bank of widows at the leafy street below. Perhaps he'd be admiring the wall that features his collection of pre-Columbian Maya, Zapotec, and Mixtec ceremonial masks. Or would he still be lying in that antique four-poster that I'd had the pleasure to know?

"I didn't realize you were staying this long," he said.

"I extended my return, hoping that we could see each other," I replied.

He suggested that he visit me at the hotel in a couple of hours.

"That's exactly what I want," I said. "It's a perfect Mexico City morning."

A long rain had soaked the city the night before, clearing the air and allowing the flowers planted along the main boulevards to release their unique high-altitude aromas. I unpacked my small suitcase and by eleven-thirty I sat in the hotel lobby waiting for him to walk through the entrance way. When he did, I had to stop myself from jumping up and running into his arms.

"Amalia, you look wonderful, but a bit flushed. Why don't we take a walk? It is such a gorgeous day."

He got our conversation moving along in mostly professional veins. He told me that my alma mater had approached him about taking on the directorship of the faculty. I spent more time than necessary telling him what I knew about the internal politics of UADY. We talked about the weather. We touched on the national presidential election that would be held soon.

Finally, I said that I wanted to talk about "us." His eyes crinkled and he urged me to continue.

"Nico, I care so much for you, but you know there is also Alejandro. I have always believed myself to be in love with him, but since re-connecting with you, I don't feel so sure. I want to see you more, but I don't see how I can cut the father of my child completely out of my life."

Nico looked perturbed and insisted that I could sever my ties if I wanted to. "Other people have done it, Amalia. Half the couples who are divorced don't interact with each other on anything but a minimal basis." Without rancor or bitterness, he told me, "Changing your attitudes is up to you."

I couldn't help but compare his maturity and reasoning with that of the man I had clung to so tenaciously—at least until recently.

Nico offered me a full life, and I knew he truly loved me. Aurora would be living in the US, and the business was no longer my concern. Hortensia now saw herself as *Mamita* to another family that would keep her happy and well-occupied. Nico was absolutely right—I could change whatever I put my mind to changing.

"Nico, we have so much in common."

We had walked an hour and without looking, I sat down on the sidewalk bench. It had not completely dried after last night's shower and the water soaked through my skirt. I jumped up, but the wet fabric stuck to my legs, showing everything underneath.

Nico laughed. He held my elbow, turned me around, and I could tell he was admiring my outlined backside.

"Your panties are wet. Maybe you should take them off and tuck them into your purse."

I nearly choked from embarrassment at his reminder of my Merida indiscretion so many years ago. But I lightened up when I saw the humor in his eyes.

"Don't be embarrassed! In my whole life, I'd never been so turned on. You are smart and sophisticated. You look so in control. But when you give in to your passion, you excite me like I can't describe! Once you asked me why I have never married, but I think you know the answer. After meeting you, I knew I'd never want to be with anyone else, and I will always feel that way."

I wished I was free to just throw my arms around him and tell him I felt the same way, but I held back. Wise as it was, Nico's advice about how to deal with Alejandro just felt too uncomfortable, too final, too contrary to the dreams I had nurtured for so long. I knew I had to talk with Alejandro. I made an excuse to Nico about feeling overstressed—as well as wet. I promised I would meet him again tomorrow and have an answer for him then.

"No, Amalia, with too much time your decision will be calculated rather than true. We need to see one another tonight—at nine. Your heart will tell you what to do. If you choose me, we can decide together whether we will live here in Mexico City or in Merida, where I could take the job at UADY."

He gave me his sweater to wrap around my waist and walked me back to the hotel. I agreed to be in the lobby at nine. He nodded, kissed my cheek, and didn't look back.

In my room, I untied Nico's sweater and buried my face in the soft gray wool. It smelled of his strong body, and I felt my eyes brim with emotions I couldn't name. My tears would ruin the sweater, so I hung it over a chair. I changed into dry clothes and called Alejandro. More urgently than ever, we needed to talk.

"Amalia, you're still here? Why didn't you say you'd be staying?"

I ignored the question. "I want to meet you at the entrance to Chapultepec Zoo at four. Can you come?" I asked.

"Of course I can," he answered and we rang off.

Hearing the anticipation in his voice made my eyes water again. Nico had been right to insist on an answer today. This situation had carried on for too long.

The afternoon felt humid, and I regretted taking the muggy Metro all the way to Chapultepec. Relieved to emerge into the refreshing air in the park, I made my way through the large grove of trees—El Bosque—to the zoo area. When I got there, I saw Alejandro by the gate, just where I'd asked him to be. He wore a light-weight blue shirt and his faded Levi's. His bare toes peeked out of leather *huaraches*. I looked down at my own faded jeans and pale blue T-shirt. How coincidental that I had put on an almost identical outfit this afternoon.

He saw me and hurried right over. Holding me tightly, I could feel the emotion—and yes—the worry running through him. "Is something wrong, Amalia? What is it?"

"Let's go sit on the grass behind the fruit stands," I suggested. "It's cool and shady there." We settled down on a mossy patch and I wondered how many times we had done this very same thing. The place allowed privacy enough for conversation, yet people milled all around, offering the safety and the restraint of a public area.

Alejandro looked confused and nervous. "Amalia, I'm happy that you decided to stay longer. Because of Aurora's birthday celebrations, we hardly spent any time with each other over the weekend."

"Yes, once again some other occasion, or situation, or event kept us from expressing our true feelings. We've coasted along—never fully committing to each other for nineteen years—and Alejandro—I can't take it anymore."

"But we are committed to each other, Amalia. It's just that—you know—we need some more time for things to get sorted out."

"What 'things,' Alejandro? This is just what I mean. We're always waiting for 'things' to get sorted out. Now that Susana has filed for divorce, I want to know why you haven't signed the papers yet. Your financial affairs have been resolved and you're eligible for retirement in one more year. You say you have no contact with Susana and that Rodrigo has taken your place. Still, you and I are no closer to resolving the question of when and how we will be together."

He tried to give me more of the same old excuses, but I didn't want to hear them. I shook my head. "When you came to see me in Merida, I did not completely level with you. Someone else has come into the picture," I said.

Alejandro turned white, and then his face flushed red with rage. He jumped up and looked ready to storm off. His hands clenched to form fists. "It's that Nico, isn't it? You were never 'working' at Tlatelolco! You spent all your time with him, didn't you? ¡Chingale!"

"Stop saying things you're going to regret!" I shot out at him.

"And why can't I ask? Why are you doing this? We have such a history together and I don't understand how you can just throw it away!"

"Yes, we do have a history together and you are repeating a particularly painful part of it with your actions and your words. If you run off, that will be it. We'll be completely over," I said. This was an ultimatum.

He looked like he did two decades ago in the café when I had told him about Aurora. He was ready to bolt.

"I don't want any more secrets. I am going to tell you about Nico and me and then we need to talk about whether or not we can get past this."

"I knew that guy would be trouble as soon as I saw him," said

Alejandro. "Why have you done this?"

I spent an hour answering his many questions. I told him how Nico and I met in Merida at the first architectural conference. "That happened shortly after you and Susana contested custody of Aurora. I felt so betrayed by you, and there was Nico—gallant, handsome, and sexy. What do you think I should have done—gone to you and asked permission to date another man?"

Finally, he could take no more. He said he could understand the fling while I was at the university, but he could not forgive me for taking up with Nico again after the earthquake.

"But Alejandro, you virtually ignored me when I told you I would not share a bed with you under Susana's roof. Did you take me for dinner even once? Did you include me in your life with Aurora? Not once. Nico and I were working together and there came a point when I couldn't resist him any longer. He is a solid guy. He loves me and I have to say I need a good reason not to take the happiness he can offer me."

My words seemed too much for Alejandro. "I can't digest this right now. I can't make promises to you other than what I've already made. I want to move to Merida, but there are still complications here that I can't leave hanging—Susana, my students, the twentieth anniversary of Tlatelolco, my retirement portfolio. It's impossible to do what you ask of me."

Same old—same old. I thought about all the years—the good and the bad times. I remembered his love and how well he cared for our daughter. It seemed strange to even contemplate living without the electricity he brought to my life.

The big clock above the snack stand read 6:24. If I wanted to be ready for dinner at nine, I needed to go back to the hotel and shower. Should I meet Nico? Alejandro looked like maybe he would recant and beg me to come home with him. I waited to hear the words, then I took his hands in mine and begged him, "*Por favor* Alejandro, tell me what you really feel." His mouth had frozen into a hard line; he pulled his hands away and they fell limp at his sides.

Although I knew I'd sound totally corny, I told him, "Love is like a garden—you have to take care of it." Alejandro looked as sad as anyone I'd ever seen. He silently took my arm and walked me to the Metro station. Would that old cliché be the final thing I'd ever say to him?

"Amalia, I love you. But I don't know if I can be the man you need. We'll have to talk about this some other time."

And so we left one another—our issues unresolved—as always.

~~~

Battling the Metro rush-hour crowds kept me from falling apart. And as soon as I made it into my room, I turned on the bath. Hot water steamed up the mirror, and I thought how that seemed such a fitting metaphor for my state of mind.

I dressed with much care and when I came down the stairs and into the lobby, I breathed in the scent of white roses. They hadn't been there when I went up to my room two hours ago, but now they overflowed every vase in the lobby. Nico stood in the middle of the room, holding one perfect bloom out toward me.

"*Buenas noches,* Amalia," he said

He was such an uncomplicated, straightforward man. No woman in her right mind would say "no" to him. But was I in my right mind?

thirty

Aurora now lived in the United States. I missed my daughter and yet I felt excited about all that would be coming into her life this year.

Her first year in New York, her first home of her own, a new language, new friends, new learning. All this would mature and shape her. I didn't worry. Hortensia assured me that the spirit guides would be watching over her. Layla said I should not blithely believe all the "woo-woo stuff," but Nana had been right so many times that I trusted her instincts.

Aurora and I had spent the summer together. She'd been away from Merida for most of last year, and I saw how much she had missed her childhood home. One morning I found her sloshing water from the pool onto the patio until it formed a puddle. "What are you doing?" I had asked.

"*Sh-sh-sh*, Mamá. You'll see." We sat quietly and watched the jays swoop in for their morning bath. After they had flown off, we checked each of the fruit trees and picked the ripest oranges, mangos, and mandarins to share at breakfast.

Looking out at the garden, she swept her arm through the air. "I'll miss all this when I'm in the cold North," she'd said. Even though she didn't tell me so, I knew she meant that she'd miss me too.

At least twice a week, we visited Hortensia at Opciones. Aurora enjoyed Teresita, and we both marveled at how her children had adapted to their new surroundings. Quite often they'd come with us to the beach and spent hours running along the edge of the shore picking up shells. Teresita had never seen the ocean before her arrival in Yucatan and looking out at the immensity of the Gulf of Mexico, she felt too nervous to let her little ones go into the water any deeper than their ankles. But by the end of August, she allowed the oldest to go out as far as her waist.

"Maybe the kids could take swimming lessons," Aurora suggested, and I told her I'd look into that.

I gave her a few basic cooking classes, and she designed and sewed an embroidered red caftan for me.

But my favorite times with my daughter were the long afternoons in our hammocks, swinging back and forth under the slow swirling ceiling fan. We talked a lot, but I held back telling her about my life changes. When I finally did, she bolted out of her hammock and stormed to her room. The slamming door sounded like a gun going off, and the final five days of her time in Merida felt as tense as when she'd been a young teen. I went along with what she wanted; I wished she'd accept my choices.

I took her to the airport on the day she left Merida and it took a Herculean effort to keep myself composed. But I had to trust that time would mellow her critical opinion. I also felt comforted knowing that Toño and Paul would be meeting Aurora in Houston. They'd be flying with her to New York because my brother insisted on helping her get settled into her apartment. I had no doubt that he'd also put in a good word for me.

That must have happened, because three days after leaving home, she called. I listened as she talked—all out of breath—about a fuzzy pink sofa bed that Paul insisted on buying for her. She laughed and I sensed that the ice had already begun to crack. I would wait patiently for a full thaw.

"Uncle Paul told me that every girl needs a campy couch," Aurora said. "I agreed with him, but when he came back to my apartment the next day with zebra-print cushions and a high-gloss, black-framed photograph of flamingos that perfectly matched the sofa bed and the striped cushions, I told him that I couldn't possibly accept one more gift. He seemed to take the hint."

Her uncles had returned to Austin feeling gratified to have assisted their niece.

"She's as happy in New York as catfish swimming in a muddy lagoon," Paul told me.

～～

The thermometer hit forty-two celsius on the first day of fall, and no matter how much I watered, my lawn would not be restored to green. Even the potted palms around the perimeter of the pool looked droopy and thirsty. The humid air felt like a cloying curtain. At five, the breeze from the coast blew in cool relief, and quite unexpectedly, the sky split open. In minutes, big bloated raindrops banished the burnt tinge on the trees.

When the deluge stopped, I took a long swim, then showered and rubbed body lotion into every pore. I ran my fingers through my hair to lift it up off the nape of my neck and reached around to spray a little lemon scent down my spine.

Slipping on Aurora's sheer scarlet creation, I moved outside to sit in my garden and enjoy the loamy smell of the rain-soaked red earth. It seemed as good a place as any to wait.

The anticipation of tonight's reunion had me feeling hungry and excited. I seriously considered a double shot of tequila to calm myself down. But as I turned to go into the house for it, my ears picked up the hum of an idling vehicle out on the street. At last!

I opened the garage door wide and made hand signals to the man behind the wheel. I wanted the truck to occupy the place I had cleared. There would be plenty of room for it beside my blue Topaz.

He backed up a little, and then slid in easily.

I saw him gathering up his wallet, a map, a pair of sunglasses, and a camera. He said he couldn't wait to tell me about the long road trip from Mexico City. He added that the hundreds of kilometers he'd traveled had closed up a long chapter of his life.

"And once I undo this seat belt, I'll begin a new one with you, here in Merida," he said.

~~~

Merida's harvest moon shone down on the water of the swimming pool—it was not hiding behind smoke and sadness like the night when Aurora was conceived. Violence had been the catalyst for what would happen over the next two decades—to me and to so many others. But now, I wanted to put all that behind me. This would be a new start.

The motor wound down. The door on the driver's side opened and one khaki-clad leg emerged—then a second. Nico stood there.

I smiled my welcome, and when he moved to close the small gap between us, I threw my head back and stretched my whole body up toward the silvery sphere in the sky.

Nico slid behind me, gently blew his warm breath on my back, and laced his strong arms around my waist.

"It looks as though you're holding the moon," he said.

I lowered my arms and pivoted so I could loop them around his neck. We kissed, and the breeze made my frothy crimson caftan dance around the two of us.

"You know what Nico—I've always wanted the moon."

He pushed a fold of the red chiffon out of his eyes. "And?" he asked. "Do you have it now?"

"Oh yes—I'd say I do—all wrapped up in a billowy red bow."

Book club discussion points

The Woman Who Wanted the Moon is a perfect choice
for book clubs. Find a list of topics to discuss at
http://hamacapress.com/bookclub

Learn more about me and read my blog at
http://writingfrommerida.com

Contact me at **writingfrommerida@gmail.com**

—*JvdGdeR*

Suggested reading

These books, all written in English, give more in-depth
information on some of the novel's themes.

TRUE TALES FROM ANOTHER MEXICO: Quiñones, Sam
Socio-political relationship between the US and Mexico

MASSACRE IN MEXICO: Ponitowska, Elena
The Tlatelolco student massacre

GODS, GACHUPINES AND GRINGOS: Grabman, Richard
History of Mexico

MEXICO: A TRAVELER'S LITERARY COMPANION: Mayo, C.M. (editor)
Collection of translated short stories by Mexican writers depicts
customs, values, and attitudes

TIME AMONG THE MAYA: Wright, Ronald
Anthropological/travel memoir

LIKE WATER FOR CHOCOLATE: Esquivel, Laura
Novel portrays close relationships between female relatives, friends

A YUCATECAN KITCHEN: Scott-Miller, Loretta
Definitive Yucatecan recipe collection

ART AND ARCHITECTURE IN MEXICO: Oles, James
Mexican ambiance and style

GUADALUPE: Zabreska, Carla
Spirituality in Mexico

ACKNOWLEDGEMENTS

"Write what you know," say the successful authors, and I have followed that advice. Amalia, her allies, antagonists, family, and friends are fictitious characters, but I created their personalities and their life stories from my own experience and yarns that have been shared with me here in Mexico. The cultural and political content of the novel is historically authentic, and I hope that when my readers have finished with this book, they will have gained a better understanding of the multi-faceted people and places that make up this country.

It has taken me five years to write *The Woman Who Wanted the Moon* and without the support of present and past members of the Merida Writers' Group, I know I would never have been able to keep trying—again and again—to get it right (especially the first page). Thank you to all: Rainie, Marianne, Cherie, Marietta, Lorna-Gail, Theresa, Bob, K, and Gwen.

Other friends critiqued bits and pieces, and encouraged me to continue. You all know who you are and be sure you have my profound gratitude.

I have published other works, but this is my first novel. I must extend many thanks to the freelance editor and educator, Ruth Wood, who led me step by step along the fiction writers' path.

Ruth and I met at the fifth annual San Miguel Writers' Conference. My appreciation to Susan Page and her team for organizing this event that brings Mexico's bilingual writing community together, and allows us to meet wonderful mentors such as Elena Poniatowska, Sandra Cisneros, Luis Urrea, Michael Schussler, Araceli Ardon, and C.M. Mayo.

Hamaca Press' publisher, Lee Steele, and editor Eileen Fischer were generous and helpful from the start of the publishing process. Without their professional skill, *The Woman Who Wanted the Moon* would have remained *The Novel That Never Left the Nest*.

Over time, many of my blog followers have also cheered me along and I feel blessed to have such a supportive following.

Yet no one deserves more gratitude than my family, especially my husband Jorge, who supports me in large and small ways—every single day.

Joanna van der Gracht de Rosado
Merida, Yucatan, Mexico
Autumn 2013